THE
FOUL MOUTH
— AND THE —
FANGED LADY
THE KING HENRY TAPES

RICHARD RALEY

NOVELS BY RICHARD RALEY

List of Mancy Types

Ultra Class 2009

Student's Name (Mancy Type)

King Henry Price (Geomancer)
Heinrich Welf (Necromancer)
Valentine "Boomworm" Ward (Pyromancer)
Asa Kayode (Hydromancer)
Miranda Daniels (Aeromancer)
Estefan Ramirez (Electromancer)
Debra Diaz (Electromancer)
Curt Chambers (Spectromancer)
Malaya Mabanaagan (Spectromancer)
Quinn Walden (Spectromancer)
Ronaldo Silva (Cryomancer)
Raj Malik (Cryomancer)
Hope Hunting (Cryomancer)
Miles Hun Pak (Sciomancer)
Eva Reti (Sciomancer)
Naomi Gullick (Floromancer)
Preston "Pocket" Landry (Floromancer)
Tamiko Lewis (Floromancer)
Nicholas Hanson (Floromancer)
Sandra Kemp (Floromancer)
Patrick "Rick" Brown (Faunamancer)
Jesus Valencia (Faunamancer)
Jessica Edwards (Faunamancer)
Robin White (Faunamancer)
Athir Al-Qasimi (Mentimancer)
Isabel Soto (Corpusmancer)
Samuel Bird (Corpusmancer)
Yvette Reynolds (Corpusmancer)
Jason Jackson (Corpusmancer)
Nizhoni Sherman (Corpusmancer)

Session 1

I SUPPOSE IT'S CONSIDERED RUDE to start one of these things with a question. Too abrasive—like a first kiss that includes some tongue. Well . . . screw it, I guess. I'm an abrasive kind of guy, a tongue on the first kiss kind of guy too. A question is how I want to start this bitch; best way to put your mind into the receptive place I want it. To get you thinking outside your cozy little life.

That question is: have you ever heard of Necromancy?

Quite a question, ain't it? Bit dangerous, bit insane. It's a question that should never be asked. Might as well ask you: do you believe in flying pigs? Simple to answer—*you think*—but you're wondering if there's strings attached.

That's good.

Always look for the strings in life and always have yourself a good pair of scissors. It's not a simple question, nothing's simple.

The answer is: they make TV shows about it. So sure you have, everyone has. Raising the dead, zombie armies, skeleton warriors. All that bullshit. Of course you've heard of Necromancy, because necromancers are douchebag showoffs—and a few more of my favorite words on the side—

who think too much of themselves. I've never met a necromancer I ever liked.

That's a string right there. I'll point it out to you beginners. A big one— need some industrial sheet-metal shears to cut it. Would it surprise you to find out that necromancers ain't the only mancers around? Well, it probably wouldn't since that pretty string just confirmed necromancers themselves exist and your mind's open to possibilities like I want it, but forget that shit for a moment.

Focus on the story.

That's what this tape is supposed to be about—my story for your benefit. So you see the strings I didn't. So you don't make the mistakes I made. So you go in knowing there *is* a game and *you* are playing it.

More mancers than necromancers and what is your mind going towards? Pyromancers? That's right, they exist too. Give yourself a pat on the back, or a cookie with some chocolate chips, you play too many video games and read too much. Pyromancers . . . showoff douchebags too. Throwing around fireballs like they're in some summer movie with special effects teams to back them up.

That's okay though, I like pyromancers. They got style.

Here's another string, kiddo: these powers have been around for thousands of years. They have made myth and legend, and go beyond necro and pyro. The oldest of the bastards who taught it to me call it *Elementalistic Harnessing of the Anima Natures of Mankind*, but to anyone born after the Culture Clash of the 70s, it's the Mancy and if you use it, on whatever you use it on, you're a mancer.

There's a lot more kinds of mancers than you'd think, lots more mancers than you'd think too. They even got a school for gifted youngsters; some real Charles Xavier meets Hogwarts kind of shit. It's even called an institute of some sort or another, all official like. Like I ever paid attention to official titles like the *Institution of Elements, Learning Academy and Nature Camp* or the *Elemental Learning Council* or all the rest of that turn-of-the-last-century, still-speaking-Latin bullshit, to me it's just the Asylum.

THE FANGED LADY

The Asylum keeping us all locked away . . .

Every day of my first couple years enrolled I cursed my mother as a selfish bitch for sending me to the place, instead of keeping stupid-young-me from signing his contract, but hell, not like I never called her worse for less.

What?

You thought someone with this filthy mouth had a good upbringing? Up until fourteen when I was—expunged—my best parent was my father . . . and he whipped me every other month.

If you don't want to hear about it, don't want to hear the bad words that might burn those ears of yours—then turn off the tape. One click, story ends. I'm only doing this because the woman who owns my soul forced me to, what do I give a crap if you listen?

Take the string, don't take the string.

Stick around though, you might learn a lesson or two, especially if it's like I expect and this is being used for new students. It might rob you of your expectations of greatness. Get you all good and ready for the disappointment we all experience.

So fourteen.

Four-*teen*.

I was screwed up beyond all repair by then. Only reason I hadn't been to Juvie was that I had an extra something the other delinquents didn't have, not that I realized it at the time of my crimes. All I knew was that I was *lucky*. Yeah, cursed more like it. But back then, it sure was nice to be sitting in the ShopsMart contemplating stealing some magazines or candy bars or Chinese-assembled electronics when a display magically fell apart to be the distraction I desperately needed.

Cigarettes and electronics had been my steals of choice right before I was co-opted into another life and if it wasn't for the Asylum, I'd be well on my way to lung cancer by now, or dead twenty times over. Not from hard stuff like you're thinking—worse I can admit to is bumming some weed when I could—but from fighting. I loved to get into a fight.

Still do.

RICHARD RALEY

Here I am, twenty-one years old and I'm lucky to hit five-foot-eight on some very generous tape-measures. Back then, middle school and elementary shitholes with babysitting teachers and cruel lunch-ladies, it was even worse. Some district counselor got all doctor on me and diagnosed it as a Napoleon Complex; that I was trying to prove I was tough despite my size. But it wasn't that.

I liked to fight.

And a little shit like me? Draws bullies just like girls with daddy issues draw bad boys with motorcycles. And I should know—I'm a bad boy with a motorcycle.

One word: *magnet.*

High-schoolers do nature well, with the hormones flaring they ain't doing any actual thinking, and picking on the runt to improve the genetic pool by killing it off—that's as natural as you get. Genetics was the other half of what started the fights, usually when some bigger shit would say I fought so much I had some Mexican in me.

Racist shit to get pissed over, but I was big on knowing I was pure white trash, something to hold onto back then I guess, as if being an arky-okie hybrid cast-off whose family tree was almost wiped out by a dustbowl is something to be proud of. But back then, I grabbed at anything I could. Even strings.

Really, playing the racist white boy in a city that is as America is affectionately called, a '*Melting Pot*,' and unaffectionately called a '*Shit Hole*'— where whites ain't majority so much as morejority—that just gave me more opportunity to fight, more Mexicans and Asians and Blacks who want to try the little cusser. And that's what I wanted, and it was the best part of my week to thrown down back then, and it was *every week*, if not *every few days*.

Me fighting someone after school damn near became a school sponsored sporting event by that last year. I can't say I never lost, but I won a lot too. Hands like steel—more than you know assholes . . . *more than you know.*

More than I knew.

THE FANGED LADY

So fighting and stealing and cussing, limping by on 'Ds' and the occasional 'C,' since the California school system didn't and still doesn't give a crap as long as you're drawing them funds for sitting in your seat. Fucking too. Fourteen and I was well on the way to getting my also white trash girlfriend pregnant by thinking pulling out before the big bang was the best trick ever invented.

One of those 'Ds' was in Sex Ed.

Probably would have stolen some condoms with the cigarettes if I'd known better.

Guess you could say I was *saved*, born again in the blood of the Mancy—by the Asylum, by the Institution of Elements, Learning Academy and Nature Camp. Guess I was. I might be screwed up to this day, I might have never got any of the cussing and cursing out of my system, and only some of the fighting, but they did a good job putting in some education and drawing out that racism, stealing, and all the rest.

I'm probably better off than the other me, twenty-one with lung cancer and a kid or two of his own to beat just like Dad did me. You're falling . . . strong enough string will save your life.

Of course I'm better off; I'm a fucking geomancer, a fucking Artificer. But at the time, fourteen-year-old-me thought he shit gold. Like I've said, I was a little screw-up.

[CLICK]

September 2009

It was a hot September day in Visalia, California when I first heard of the Institution of Elements. I'd just gotten home from school, which meant 6PM after I'd finished an hour of detention for cussing in class, followed by some time with the girlfriend if her mom was working, time with the friends if she wasn't. Friends . . . dickheads-I-hung-with more like, just to keep boredom away. Another bit of nature is safety in numbers, even if you can't stand the people who make up your numbers.

Three digits still that year, an extra hot year in an extra hot town and our little shitty house had to make due with a swamp cooler that only worked half the time and probably spewed more mildew than cold air when it did.

I'd stolen a portable fan from Wal-Mart that I treated like it was gold-plated. I had it chained to my bed with a bike lock to keep my sisters from taking it. Especially JoJo. Or at least . . . that was the reason at the time, they were both moved out by then, one the day she turned eighteen and the other didn't even wait for then.

But the fan . . . the fan never got free.

Just me and my folks, miserable all three of us. Mom was continually drunked out on the couch, but at least she wasn't a mean drunk, just dead to the world and one time when an older friend came over—frisky. Dad *was* a mean drunk, but he only drank on the weekends. During the week, he'd come home after his long day plus four in overtime and smoke a joint in the backyard to help numb out the physical pain, maybe the mental pain too. He'd cook dinner also, which is probably the only reason I ever came home during the week. I'd learned not to come home at all during those weekends when the booze started flowing between Mom and Dad.

I was a bit surprised to see an unknown car in the gravel driveway. It wasn't expensive, but it was *new*, which was out of the class of anything Dad or Mom could manage. As far as ours went, we had a truck and a SUV, both over ten-years-old and one of them always worked, though which one had a habit of changing every few months.

So . . . new car and I know something's up. None of my dad's friends from the warehouse had new cars either. You're probably feeling bad for how poor we were, but don't. Lots more worse off, Dad always said, and he's right about that. We had insurance at least, and when I got my arm broken in a fight during fourth grade taking on a sixth grader just a bit too big for me, I got it fixed no problem. Plus checkups. Plus dental.

Take your pity somewhere else, assholes. Turn off the tape and go read "*The Note Book*" or some other weepy crap.

THE FANGED LADY

Mom and Dad were waiting for me in the kitchen, which on accounts of Dad being the cook made it the cleanest room in the house. Couldn't do anything about the heat though. Fucking Central Valley summers, never ended when they were supposed to and always tried to sneak their way into Halloween.

Mom was having a 'Good Day.' Doctor got his doctor on and said she's Bi-Polar, an extreme case of it, which means good as in *up* or *hyper and happy*. 'Good Days' always freaked me out way more than bad ones.

There was a woman I didn't know sitting at the table with them— probably just past thirty I guessed, the kind of just-past-thirty you only see in movies or in those celebrity magazines my girlfriend loved to read so much that I stole them for her.

Wasn't I romantic?

This woman would have fit right in. Well, her face and blond hair at least. She was too thick for Hollywood, not enough bone showing, though normal people would call her thin. Her blue eyes were sharp as she took me in, all of five-foot nothing, ratty shirt with some MMA fighter on the back and jeans that probably needed replacing. She had a sharp smile too, so sharp it cut.

"King Henry Price, this lady wants to speak with you," Mom said—she only took the lead on 'Good Days.' Mom smiled too. Pissed me off at the time . . . what woman deserves to smile when she named her kid *King Henry*? And no, I am not joking about that crap. King Henry Price. Like the height didn't start enough fights already.

"I don't know her," I eloquently back-talked, resisting the urge to call the lady '*bitch*' while pulling out a can of generic soda from the fridge.

A whole three seconds of heaven wrapped itself up in that burst of cold air. Popping the can, I took a sip. If the words I spoke and the cigs I smoked didn't rot my teeth, I wanted the high fructose corn syrup to do the job for me.

"Son," Dad told me, "best be respectful this time." Dad hunched over a metal chair, his frame settled so heavy on it that if gravity magically turned off it still wouldn't have floated away.

"I didn't do anything," I said to the lady. Huge lie. I'd always done something.

Her smile cut at me again, amused by me. Annoyed I could do in spades, but amused was new. And, funny enough, I found it annoying. It actually threw me off enough to forget about respect. "What you laughing at, bitch?"

Dad moved to cuff me across the table—and who can blame the guy?—but the lady waved him off quick enough to stop the blow.

"My name is Ceinwyn Dale," she said, "and I am a recruiter for a very special school." Like I told you, some real Charles Xavier shit. "Would you prefer to be called *King* or *Henry*?"

"Both."

"*King Henry* . . . and what do you rule, King Henry? England, Ireland, and France?" Ceinwyn Dale asked, again with that smile. Snip, snip.

I wanted to haul a right hook into her and scream, '*Your face!*' but, for once in my young life, prudence won over anger. "I rule the kingdom of *me*. It's small, but big enough where it counts, ya know?"

"What if I told you that you rule nothing? That you're completely powerless before outside influences? That fate will kill you one day and there is nothing you can do to stop it?"

It's like she was asking for it. I didn't know it at the time, but Ceinwyn Dale's an aeromancer with more besides and could have shot my little ass out of the window like I was a cannonball.

"I'm trying to be nice, lady," I told her.

"You like to fight, don't you?" Ceinwyn Dale observed.

Mom tried to wave that off, seeing the chance to get rid of me dying before it was born, but the lady stopped the waving with a look. There is something about Ceinwyn Dale that makes you shut up and listen when she commands your attention that has nothing to do with the Mancy.

"You like to fight, King Henry, like to punch and take a punch especially, I'd guess."

"So? The shirt of the guy beating the crap out of the other guy give it away?"

THE FANGED LADY

"It's the only time you can feel above," Ceinwyn Dale kept up, talking around her smile. "The bones, that's what you like. Bone hitting bone in one perfect punch. Their bones cracking and your bones holding up. Instant gratification."

"You want gratification? Got other ways to give it . . ." Dad *did* cuff me then. "Hey, man!"

"Watch it or I'll *give* another!"

I turned angrily back to Ceinwyn Dale. She watched me like she might eat me one day, like I was some lamb going *bye bye* come harvest day. "Enough games, you crazy smiling lady, what do you *want*? Who gives a crap if I like fighting? What kind of fucked up school are you a part of? And why should I bother to care?"

"You're going to be so fun to break, King Henry." She reset her smile. Going from annoying me to freaking me out. Current educated me always thought of the Cheshire Cat. Old white trash me saw reruns of Jack Nicholson playing the Joker from Saturday afternoons when there was nothing worth watching on the TV.

"Fuck you," I told her. Real snappy wordplay at the time.

"You're special. One in ten-thousand at least. One in a quarter million perhaps," she explained. "Does this make you feel above? Does it make you tingle and give you goose-bumps?"

Damned if it didn't.

Damned if it didn't piss me off that she called me on the feeling, belittling it into nothing. Typical Asylum maneuver—making me seem like some pathetic little emo wimp.

I popped up from the kitchen table, pointing a finger at my parents, ready to spread my favorite word around. "Fuck you two for talking to her," and pointed at Ceinwyn Dale, "and double fuck you with something rusty!"

I ran into my little room, locking the door. Know I did. Still remember the lock turning, like amber frozen in time. All the good memories from before Mom got sick have faded away, but that one stuck . . . me turning a lock. Something small—something *huge*.

Lying out on my unmade mattress of a bed, I clicked on my aforementioned gold-plated fan. The bike chain rattled as the tiny motor kicked full speed, clanging the bars of my headboard. A prisoner's cup making noise to make noise and pass the time. Fitting sound for a fitting room.

Running away from your problems and hiding in your room when you don't understand what's going on is a long-standing teenage tactic. In my house, with its thin doors and even thinner walls, it didn't work too well. You could still hear everything. But at least I didn't have to see Ceinwyn Dale's smile any longer.

I lit up a cigarette to calm down. Smoking was forbidden in the house . . . actually it was forbidden at all . . . but doubly forbidden in the house—I wasn't giving much a crap at the moment.

My fan rattling and wafting exhaled smoke, I heard the aftermath. "Sorry about that, Mrs. Dale," Dad said in his gruff voice which only got kind when he talked to my mother.

"It's Miss still . . . and don't worry yourself over him, I've seen worse. The Institution of Elements is very capable at handling young men with his type of problems."

"Then you'll still take him?" Mom asked. Her voice was happy, almost relieved.

"Of course we will . . . he's a special boy, deep down. I wanted a reaction and I got one, my job is to see how applicants react to situations they don't understand. As I said, I've seen much worse. He has hidden potential."

"Let's not get hasty. He don't want to go, he ain't going," Dad reminded the women who were deciding my future for me—getting enough strings together to make me a baby bootie.

"He'll want to," Mom complained. "Once he calms down and hears Miss Dale out."

Like hell I will, I told myself.

Pathetic little shit, I was. I popped on a stolen iPod, picked up a stack of stolen comics—told you I had a habit of getting lucky with accidents—and completely tuned them out, on the idea I was going nowhere. Special. One in a quarter *mil*. *Fuck her*. My life could suck, but it's *mine*. I wasn't leaving what I knew for some reject school that probably stole more money from the government on some crackpot scheme to *improve* troubled kids than I ever had.

Guess who my favorite comic book character was? Wolverine. Got to love a fighter. He's short too. Got hurt, but could take all the pain—that's better than being invincible. Got all the women he wanted without having to deal with relationships like that poor sap Cyclops with his girlfriend who died fifty times. A teenage boy's wet dream. Comics, cigs, girlfriend, fighting: my life.

My life, assholes, take your strings and shove them.

A couple comics finished and lots of heavy metal songs later, I realized I wasn't alone anymore. Over the rim of my comic book I saw the smile.

How you doing, Alice?

My next look went to the door, which was still locked. And it wasn't one of those shitty locks you could pop with a hairpin, but a nice deadbolt I'd stolen from Home Depot. Yeah, I stole a lock, bite me and go find your own irony.

The music still beat from my earbuds as they dropped away. I screeched a little from the shock. "*Who the fuck are you, lady?!?*"

"Ceinwyn Dale, a recruiter for a special school for special people." I checked my window, still shut. She noticed, but commented on something else, "You like comics?"

"Yeah." The '*bitches*' and '*fucks*' were largely killed dead in the face of the impossible.

"And music? Metal? That's fitting . . ."

I sat up on the bed and put out what was left of my cig.

"You can check the door if you'd like," she told me, matter-of-fact about my astonishment. I checked again. The nasty-ass *clothes* I'd kicked in front of the door hadn't even moved.

"I ain't going to your school, lady."

"Why not?" She was genuinely curious. Ceinwyn Dale, always the interested observer.

"I'm not a freak. I get by. I got a life. So I fight, who gives a rat's ass?"

She picked up my iPod and browsed through the playlist. She had beautiful hands. Not a body part most guys notice, and Ceinwyn Dale had some others that were pretty noticeable, but her delicate fingers and sapphire fingernails drew the eye when she used them in front of you. Nimble manipulation, just like the rest of her, turning those fleshy stubs into the finest tool, skinny and elegant. "Is this the entirety of your reasons?"

"I got a girl."

"And you *love* her?" The smile quirked extra.

"Sure. I guess." Love wasn't a big emotion in the Price household. We had trouble managing *giving a shit*.

"Or do you just like what you get to do with her?"

"That too."

One part about Ceinwyn Dale I started figuring out during that first conversation is she mocks *everyone*, but she treats her kids the same as she does adults. Which I wasn't seeing much of back then. It was inclusive and part of the reason she's such a good Recruiter.

"You'll have to give her up."

"One more reason to not go to your stupid school."

She tapped the iPod screen with a sapphire nail. "Did you steal this?"

I calculated an answer in my head. My usual answer was to deny, deny, deny. But . . . who wants a thief at her school? So . . . logic train . . . "Yup, I steal all the time."

"An iPod, comic books, and your girlfriend's virginity, what a thief!" Ceinwyn Dale mocked me.

"Again, *fuck you*." The whole door-being-locked thing had to wear off, though I still couldn't figure it out. But another very teenage skill is to never let the facts get in the way of some hating.

"Say your favorite word again, King Henry. I dare you."

THE FANGED LADY

And just as I moved my mouth to oblige the lady, a ball of compressed air lodged itself between my jaws. Yup, shit got real. I started choking. Panic came right on its heels. Eyes went wide, pulse went high, arms grasped, trying to grab onto Ceinwyn Dale to either make her stop or get her help.

She watched it all with her smile. "How long will it take? I do wonder . . ."

"Please!" I tried to say, but it came out as a ragged hiss. Another round of grabbing followed, which she batted away. All my fighting and I felt like a baby as I drifted down to the floor, eyes going foggy.

[CLICK]

When I came to, my jaw was still locked open. I was on the floor with my dirty clothes, stained with blood, spit, smoke, and teenage lovemaking. That day is almost eight years ago and I want to take a shower just *thinking* about the floor. Ceinwyn Dale reclined on my bed, looking down at me from her side, a comic book draped over one hand.

"I do wonder . . ." she repeated. "How long will it take you to realize you have a nose, King Henry?"

"Guu Ou, Baa!" I told her.

"Yes, yes. *Fuck you, bitch*, I know. That mouth is going to get you killed one day, King Henry. You're thinking, *what do I care?* But that's only from the assumption on your part that the world is as safe as you *assume* it is. Safe to steal, safe to have a girlfriend giving you those mighty three minute grunting and humping sessions, safe to get into fights with whomever, whenever.

"A world where all you have to worry about is a mother that wants free from her psychosis and a father that has never been able to control you. What the world really is . . . is a dangerous world most never bother to see, a one in ten-thousand world, a one in a quarter million world. A world where a woman can vaporize herself past a door and five minutes later stick a ball of air into your mouth to . . . Shut. You. Up. For. Once."

Douchebag showoff aeromancers.

Fourteen-year-old-me stayed silent—not by choice—and considered what she'd said. Strings be multiplying.

Ceinwyn Dale flipped a page of the comic with a nimble finger. "The Institution of Elements is a neutral faction *within* that world, King Henry. It seeks to find the special few and train them *for* the world as a whole. This includes a normal education and a one in ten-thousand education. It is not an easy ride, but if you survive it, you'll survive quite a lot. You'll be able to make something of yourself and . . . you'll be able to escape your parents' fate. Stuck in a small life with little money and shackled by children you hate just as much as you love."

The ball of air in my mouth dissolved in a puff of smoke. "What's it like?" I asked, finally interested.

Maybe if I'd been older, I'd have questioned her more about '*magic*' existing, but after the demonstration I took it at face value. There is something in the Mancy that calls us to it. I could escape a crappy life, but I couldn't escape it. The Mancy is the biggest string of all.

"It will change you." Ceinwyn Dale smiled. Least reassuring smile I'd ever seen up to that point. It's still Top Ten. "You won't like all of it, but certain lessons will open you up like a butterfly, something new and beautiful and true to itself."

I got up on the bed and sat next to her. Butterfly . . . not exactly the best metaphor to use on me, but I got the image. "So it's like Hogwarts kind of?" Between three minute grunting and humping sessions as Ceinwyn Dale called them—though to my credit they were actually *five* minute grunting and humping sessions—the girlfriend liked to read books aloud to me, usually as I smoked a post-sex cigarette out her window.

For the first time I heard Ceinwyn Dale laugh, a short and quick '*ha!*' That's all I ever hear from her. A quick '*ha!*' A bark, you could call it. Never real laughter you can't control.

"I'm not some friendly giant, King Henry. The Institution of Elements isn't a fairy castle. There will not be magical duels or trips to town to try steaming candy or Christmas vacations. You may write your family, that's all.

Other than that, you'll be stuck. Seven days a week without a way to escape us for four years if you're a one in ten-thousand kind of person, seven years if you're a quarter million kind. We'll break you . . . we'll forge you . . . we'll make you a mancer."

"A mancer?" I already liked the name. Like she'd said, it made you feel special. Every kid wants to feel special. Every grown-up too. Of course, I was already imagining many things about the Mancy which didn't happen. Spell after spell, throwing around fire and lighting.

Bullshit.

It takes about a minute to focus enough anima into a '*conjuration of magnetism*' on yourself, more for something outward, usually much more. As a weapon in a straight up fight, the Mancy is often useless. Preparation is its weakness, but over the years stories get spread and imagination goes bonkers. For example: over 1500 years ago in Britain you might have some Irish and Welsh facing off in a battle line, shouting and drinking and waving ass and peckers at each other trying to work up the courage to charge, all the while druids on either side are gibbering and screeching and acting like a bunch of fucktards.

But one guy doesn't. One guy is calm and focused and after about five minutes of staring down his enemies, he raises his arm and sends down one bolt of lightning. *One* bolt of lightning. In five minutes, with lots of set up. That's what the Mancy will get you. Let's name the guy who shot the lightning Merlin. Merlin would cause my expectations to soar and eventually they'd crash to the ground. Sooner rather than later. In the end, a mancer is a fucktard just like everyone else and Ceinwyn Dale is *weird*.

She looked at me as if judging my ripeness. *Is it harvest day yet, little lamb?* "Let's get back to your parents and finish the paper work."

RICHARD RALEY

Session 105

I'VE LOOKED AT THIS RECORDER quite a few times over the last twenty years and thought about doing what I'm about to do. At first I was just too busy; running a shop, falling in and out of love, trying not to get myself killed. Then . . . then the regrets and the lies began to pile up like cast off spare change and even though I never picked it up, the idea of the recorder felt heavy in my mind, a growing mound of metals. It gained a density beyond its size. A nickel here, a penny there.

It's fitting, I suppose, that once again I feel forced into doing it. This time you have my daughter to thank or to blame, depending on your view of my distinctive place in mancer history. I don't know how exactly she found them. They'd been locked away in one of my oldest storage cabinets for years, dragged from the old shop to the new shop and then yet again to my home office, but she found my old tapes—little SD cards, most computers don't even have slots for them nowadays, but she found one that did.

My own inventive genes slapping me in the face.

King Henry Price as a disgruntled young man thinking about being a broken angry teenager. That's bad enough, the idea of your teenage daughter learning about your antics in that way. Listening to her father curse and curse and curse some more just for the fun of it, because he likes the sound and the feel of those violent words on his lips . . . coming up the back of his throat and out of his mouth—back before I'd even started to get creative with the cursing as a way to win myself a smile or laugh in dangerous

23

situations, back when it was only to put a person off and repetition after repetition to blast the senses, to create a wall. Listening about her mother as an object of sexual desire, and about the women besides her mother. Listening about her favorite uncles getting into fights and breaking rules that you've told her not to break a dozen times.

It's bad enough she listened to them.

It's rather amazing she treasured every moment . . .

But then she made copies.

And then she handed them out to her new friends during the first month of her schooling at the Institution.

And then I got a phone call from the Dean.

If it wasn't my kid responsible, I'd be laughing about the woman getting caught in her own webs. How funny the whole mess would have been *then*. Instead, I drove to the Institution stern faced and disappointed in my little girl, just a bit angry that she'd stolen from me, and just a bit more ashamed about what she'd heard from me, and just a bit fearful that Dad's curse '*you have one just like you*' came true. It was the same drive that takes place in the first tape, or near enough to it. I even stopped to have lunch at the same place. I found it nostalgic.

Once I finally arrived and had my meeting with the Dean about the damage that had been done, my anger and shame and my fear only grew. The tapes were copied into a million forms of information and no matter how many times the teachers confiscated a copy, more seemed to show up, spreading at the speed of rabbits breeding. The kids loved me. I'd already been a legend for my deeds and misdeeds, now I'm a folk hero from my own telling of it all. A twenty-year-old graduate student asked me for my autograph . . .

My little girl had the guts to give me what I call her why-am-I-in-trouble-daddy-don't-you-love-me? face. And the damn thing worked . . . I was ready to ground her, to banish her to stay alone at the Institution for the summer off-month like I had to experience seven times, to put my foot down, lay down the law, and suddenly I felt like I was the one being unfair, that I'm the one really at fault for not destroying the tapes in the first place . . .

I think it's the flattery that really did it. *'I just loved them, Daddy! So did everyone else!'*

How does one combat it? No wonder my old man always tried to give my sisters whatever they wanted while I got hand-me-downs. I was outclassed! Outgunned! Fears or not, I was never so cute!

Instead of yelling at each other in the typical teenager versus parent deathmatch, we talked about the tapes like adults. I explained I was a lot angrier with the world back then, that it was before her mom and I got things together and before I became a father, especially before I worked some facts out in my head about my own childhood. And she understood all of it.

'If anything they make me love you more.' Well . . . again . . . how does a father fight back against it?

To my surprise, she wanted to know what happened next. There were rumors at the Institution among the students, passed down whispers from parents to oldest brother to youngest sister. No one knew what the truth of the story was, but it sounded even better than the first tapes had been. Like the tapes were some television show and she wanted the next season to come out already.

I gave in, big wimp that I am, and started to tell her about my old shop right then. Only she shushed me.

'No, Daddy, I want more tapes just like these! Other people want to know too!'

'That was a long time ago,' I told her. *'They won't be the same. I'm not the same person.'*

'Couldn't you try to remember?'

And here I am. Telling you this little intro as I try to remember. The twenty-one-year-old man, just graduated from the Institution . . . the Asylum I suppose he would call it, was much closer to the school boy than I am to him. Seven years fresh in the mind versus twenty years which seem so long ago. So small and innocent.

I've changed.

More than you can ever imagine.

You'll notice I haven't said '*fuck*' once so far. Having kids will teach you to watch your mouth a lot quicker than even Ceinwyn's papercuts. I'm different now. I've traded anger for silence. Hunches and guesses for certainty before I act. I faked being a respectable man for so long, I eventually stopped faking and just *became*.

He had yet to have three children, a wife, even a pair of dogs. He hadn't started wars and ended many more of them. He hadn't saved the world and then broken it yet again in the same week.

He knew nothing about what the Mancy could *really* do. He had no idea of the terrors waiting for us all, of death and loss and of even worse. He was a little foul-mouthed fool and he had it easy. Even talking about my upbringing with my parents is child's play compared to what will come in these new tapes.

But I do have some advantages. I've had kids. I've learned how to narrate a bedtime story. Welcome to the most fucked up bedtime story you're ever going to hear.

[CLICK]

January 2018

If September in Fresno is a hellhole, then January is just depressing.

Fresno is always depressing, a mass of consumerism, a growing tumor in the middle of a fertile crescent that can out-produce all the other fertile crescents that have come before. The land around it feeds millions with its rich earth—there's colors, of fruits and vegetables and cotton and nuts, so much green you see it in your dreams—but inside the asphalt and concrete maze there's nothing but shades of gray, the splash of tan to occasionally spice it up. Tract-homes, shopping malls, sidewalks and street lamps. Nothing to do, no way to escape it. Just living the same schedule, day after day, and trying to make yourself forget you're trapped in your little cage you pay to be trapped in and pay to improve, got yourself a refinanced loan to redo the kitchen on. You might not own it, but hey, bitch is pretty with those granite countertops.

That's Fresno.

In January the highs hit low fifties if you're especially lucky, mostly it's forties day in and out, but it's not the temperature that's depressing. Not the people covered up head-to-toe, not the dead trees and yellow grasses. It's that there is more gray than ever before. Gray clouds hold from horizon to horizon and they don't even care enough about you to piss some rain on top of your drooping head. They just linger, blotting out the sun and stars. Most days you judge the time by which cloud looks a little brighter than the others. That's your best bet for where the sun is at.

And the Fog. Capitalize the word. The Fog. I'm convinced it's a living god. People in the other parts of the United States think they know fog, but they don't. They know mist. They know haze. They know the Fog's little brothers. Fresno fog is so thick some days you're lucky to see the house next to yours when you wake up in the morning. It lingers just like the clouds, holding from what passes for dusk till well towards noon. Hours and hours, blinded, a whole city living and functioning on sounds, eyes trying to pierce into the gray wall. A city of half-a-million people cut off from each other, alone. Exposed. Easy prey . . . just like the hunters like it.

In one part of Fresno, a commercial district among many commercial districts, there was a store pretending to be something it wasn't. That particular district was known for its small shops, its artsy clientele, and for a burger joint that had been open for over sixty years and was good enough to fight off fast-food chains. The shop fit right in . . . unless you knew better.

Sometimes to know a secret, you need to know a secret exists in the first place.

King Henry's Hidden Treasures. It was on the sign, a sign personally painted by the owner using toxic lead-based paints, but not painted with a brush. Another way is quicker.

To the many old ladies and middle-aged mothers who wandered in, it was an antique store. It was run by a nice young man who owned the place, just him, six days a week, ten to five, don't go around lunch, he takes an hour off. He tries his best to help you, but he really doesn't understand anything about antiques, so be sure you know what you're buying and research it ahead of time. No impulse buys, girls!

His language was coarse, even vulgar, and he had to stop himself from uttering a curse word every sentence when the old ladies brought their grandchildren with them. He was good with the children however, better than most expected when they first got a look at him. He had a rack of comics and candy machines at the front of the store, and would often slip in a free comic—just for them—into grandma's bags when she wasn't looking, with an accompanying conspiratorial wink.

He wasn't tall, short actually, with close-cut brown hair and common brown eyes. Not handsome, but men don't need to be handsome to be attractive. His arms were well-muscled, his shoulders and chest stocky for as short as he was. There were scars on his face and hands, especially around his knuckles. He wore odd clothes, jeans and tennis-shoes, but over a white shirt he wore a brown coat of thick fabric, even in the summer when the temperature was over one-hundred and his AC ran full blast. He never took the brown coat off; it hung, unbuttoned, *always*.

There was a leashed quality about him, like he held back a great many parts of himself. Smiles were tight, eyes were hooded. What he showed was the edge of anger, and many women wondered how much more was buried beneath and what had created it and—if these women were young and hadn't learned better—maybe if they could fix it.

His name was King Henry Price and he'd flashed his driver's license more than a few times to prove it to his customers.

His shop was a normal antique store. It had old books and records, old furniture, clocks and gadgets, glassware and utensils. His biggest section was his teapots. Women loved teapots. It wasn't a busy store, one or two customers at a time and the customers preferred to be left alone. King Henry spent all his time at his register, doodling and drawing, running figures and making strange diagrams the ladies couldn't understand. It was a normal antique store.

But then . . . that's all bullshit.

First of all: *fuck teapots*.

Second of all: I give the kids a free comic because what kind of horrible grandma takes their poor kid into an antique store? They deserve something for the psychological damage that's being done. A free comic is the least I can do.

Third: it was an Artificer shop. The only free-owned Artificer shop, unconnected with the Guild of Artificers, in the entire United States. The price I paid to get freedom was to give it up. Ceinwyn Dale owned my soul since I was fourteen, now she owns my future as well.

My future was worth about a million dollars, that's what I owed her for paying the upfront of building and stocking the place. I told myself I'd actually pay her off one day. That I wasn't just kidding myself with this experiment outside the Guild structure. That I'd show those cocksuckers they were wrong.

I'd been graduated from the Asylum for about a year and a half, the shop had been running for a full year, and I still bled cash every month. The antiques selling like deep-fried crap didn't help, but they weren't my big problem.

The problem is: anima is expensive.

The Asylum pumped out hundreds of mancers a year, but anima's still worth its weight in gold. Anima, vials to hold the anima, materials for the artifacts, designing the artifacts, experimentations to make sure the artifacts did what they were supposed to do—it all costs a ton in cash.

And then when I finally had myself something to sell . . . either for cash or a straight-up anima trade, I had to find a mancer willing to cross the Guild. The Guild agreed to let me do my own thing when I told them to back off shortly after graduating, but they didn't agree they wouldn't bury me in shit. Even in the normal world, people don't like crossing a union picket line; now imagine that the picket line is set up by another corporation and the other corporation is the only game in town. You going to bet on little ol' King Henry Price all alone or on Wal-Mart's huge stores with a billion Chinese kids behind them pumping out product?

A year in and I had eight loyal customers, all of them under thirty save for Ceinwyn. I went to school with four of them. That left three I'd actually won over.

Only because the Guild wouldn't make them what they wanted. That's the thing with the Guild. It ain't flexible. It makes what it makes and it has always made it for hundreds of years. And it's going to cost. Well . . . at least until I try to sell something similar, then there's a blowout sale. Guild cocksuckers know the game, let me tell you.

Only they have a weakness.

That's my one out. My one advantage. I could experiment. I could make something new. It's the reason why I was doing it. The status quo's going to blow a hole in the world's gut, so someone has to change the way things work. That's me. No, sir, I'm not vain or nothing . . . no delusions of grandeur on my part. I just know the Price that's coming due. Someone better start trying to pay the bitch back early before we go bankrupt, so why not me?

[CLICK]

It was your usual gray day in January when the so-called exploits of King Henry Price began. I met with my most loyal customer over an experimentation we had conceived between the pair of us. A lot of hard work looking like it might finally pay off some. It was later in the afternoon, the Fog held at bay by pieces of sun escaping from the layer of cloud. Even that wasn't a relief. The light was so weak it was just sad, like a retarded kid raising his hand to answer a question. You knew the happy wasn't going to last long.

Two old ladies were in the shop—one at my clock wall and another trying to break a ninety-year-old school-desk by swinging the hatch up and down, *up and down*, the non-lubricated metal squeaking in protest. Getting louder

30

and louder each swing. No means *no*, lady. If I fiddled with a woman screaming like that, I'd be in jail.

When my real customer came in, the old ladies marked the door opening and closing—a different noise than the desk, something more like a *swoosh*. Their eyes went wide at the sight of him, their hands reflexively finding their purses to make sure they were zipped shut. Racist little old ladies I'll tell ya, probably still used the word '*colored*,' if not worse.

My customer is black, about six-foot-four and weighed three-hundred pounds. Not muscle . . . you don't get much muscle sitting on a couch playing video games and they were T-Bone's primary pastime. T-Bone. Guy hated when I called him that shit, but how could I not tease him with it? It's so opposite from his actual makeup. He was so middle class he couldn't even *pretend* to be gangster. His parents wouldn't even let him watch those movies growing up.

Tyson Bonnie . . . as he told the story . . . was born to a teenage unwed mother and placed under adoption to a pair of mid-30s professionals who had tried plenty but couldn't have kids themselves. This is how he ended up with a white mother who's a registered nurse and an Asian father who's an accountant . . . and not even a mob accountant, not even a scumbag corporate accountant, a *family* accountant. Before the Asylum got their claws in Tyson Bonnie, he was spoiled upper-middle class—real middle class, not the fake, on paper kind the politicians made up to cook the stats—going to the best school a shithole like Fresno could offer. At fourteen, a smiling woman came for him and Tyson Bonnie's old life ended.

Now he's the only other Ultra in Fresno besides me. When the pool of your peers is so small, you don't have any choice but to be friends. Sure, there were other mancers; Intras doing their thing, but it's not the same.

We were at the Asylum together, but our paths never crossed that I noticed. He's four years older than me, which means he was well into his graduate work by the time I became particularly infamous. An electromancer, a Stormcaller. Electro-anima and someone who knows a thing or two about currents and batteries . . .

Which led us to the box I pulled up from under my register and put on the countertop. "T-Bone," I greeted.

"King Henry, how many times do I have to tell you to stop?" he asked from far above me. Just once I'd like to be friends with someone who's shorter than me.

The old ladies left without buying anything, while I honorably distracted the big black guy that so didn't care about them. "How many times I got to ask you to come by after hours when I'm actually doing Mancy stuff?"

He glanced around the empty store, raised too middle class to realize he caused it. "Yup, you're real busy. Want me to come back in an hour when things quiet down?"

I flipped the box lid open. I hadn't made the box. Bought it at a dollar-store for cheap. Thousands of dollars worth of anima construction protected by a dollar box. I liked that.

Inside was a place for two rings, among cheap fabric stapled to the wood. One ring was already missing—it sat on my right ring finger.

It felt heavier than a normal ring and wasn't a perfect loop. I'd thought about silver, but went with copper, which is cheaper and less likely to be stolen. The copper was coated with an insulation rubber beside the skin to protect against feedback current. The face of the ring was a large circle, a line of copper carefully manipulated into my initials. KHP. T-Bone's was simply TB. Guess that made him unhealthy.

He picked his up, looking at it, studying the initials, then weighing it in his palm. Damn thing looked small against so much palm. "It works?"

"Just like you came up with and I designed."

"Not off anima?"

"The Mancy is just the containment. Think of it as a reactor."

"But just electricity? Not electro-anima?"

"Shit, T-Bone, you're talking about step number one-hundred and five, we're on *two*."

"I know . . . I just . . . get into this stuff. It's the coolest part of my week talking theory with someone who understands it." He put on the ring, flashing his hand into a fist that didn't look like it had a lot of practice being in the shape. "And stop calling me that."

"Yeah, yeah." I put the box back under the counter. "Takes about two hours to full charge using static electricity, quicker if you find a piece of carpet and start rubbing your arm against it. Theoretically you could attach it to a power-pad, but I wouldn't recommend it—too much power too quick might blow the containment field."

"Wow, King Henry," T-Bone said, his face all lit up as he swung a lazy punch across his chest that was far too much arm and not enough body torque. "This is awesome. It's just how I imagined it."

"Speaking of that, satisfy some curiosity on this . . . how *did* you imagine it?"

A brief bit of embarrassment crossed his lit up face, his forehead wrinkling. "Stole it from a fantasy novel."

"*Shit . . .*"

"I know, you hate the them."

I shook my head. Hated them? Nope, I was jealous that the douchebags had it so easy with their 'magic.' The Mancy's a long way from some homoerotic wand flipping and twirling. "Next, you'll want me to make you a lightsaber."

His eyes got bright with crazy dreams. "Could you?"

"Get the fuck out of my store," I told him. If I ever did make something even resembling a laser sword, Tyson Bonnie was the last person I was trusting with it. He's mean with a Wii U remote, but he'd cut his arm off in five seconds with anything real.

"Okay," T-Bone agreed, "no more sci-fi stuff, we stick to real theory. But it did work this time."

"It did," I said, wondering privately what robe-wearing-fruit out there in bookland had a magic punching ring. "Worked wonders."

"What's the power level on it?" he asked.

"Bit more than a Taser. It will put a man down good, as for a Were or something else? Not like I can test it."

I'd worked for weeks on the damn thing figuring it out. Burned through enough anima to wear both T-Bone and myself ragged. But in the end I created something that hadn't existed before. Every time I did it, I felt a little relief from my worries. The cocksucking Guild of Artificers didn't have a damn thing like these rings. Let them try to make them. They'd probably start with a pure electro-anima version before they even realized what I'd done. Then they'd be stumped for months.

"Feedback is minimal, mostly a tingle of static in your fingers, nothing serious. I'd take it off before you play with your computers and game systems though."

"Oh . . . sounds like a good warning." T-Bone worked as a computer consultant for about twenty different companies around the Valley, called in to help them with their security setups. In the oldest days, Stormcallers were left doing lightning rod duty before Benjamin Franklin came along to invent the more permanent version of a metal shaft, then it was work for power companies and Edison regulating flows. Now that the world runs off the 1's and 0's of binary code, the question ain't 'what can Stormcallers do?' it is 'what *can't* Stormcallers do?'

"And the activation?" he asked.

"Anima burst, no matter the discipline."

His face went frown. "Isn't that dangerous? Accidents happen."

"It was the biggest problem after I figured out the how of it," I explained to alleviate any fears of an accidental discharge frying your poodle. "Hair trigger and you're zapping yourself every time some heavy emotion makes you bleed anima, too tough and you're left with the same problem we all face: got to sit around on your ass building anima up while bad shit is happening to you."

"So what did you settle on?"

"Five seconds," I said.

"Better than five minutes."

"Sixty times better, last I checked."

THE FANGED LADY

He put his hand out to shake. The hand with the ring on it, despite the fact it was the left one and T-Bone's a righty.

I flipped him off.

It made T-Bone smile, his teeth a flash of white against his dark lips. Guy had a big smile. "I had to try, old electric finger gag."

"It's not a toy," I reminded him.

Problem with growing up middle class is you don't realize the world will smack you in the face. You think it's okay to play around. T-Bone is a good guy. He just needs a smack. Usually the Asylum provides a few, but for T-Bone, he went through in a year known for its easy-going kids who got along. He didn't have a Welf. Or even a Soto. A whole class of Maliks . . . how boring . . .

"I know, I know," he said, but I could tell he was going to zap someone with it like it was a practical joke. Well . . . as long as it wasn't me, why should I give a crap? That's some King Henry wisdom right there.

He pulled out his wallet with a raised eyebrow. "Cash?"

Cash.

I remembered what cash looked like. Sometimes the old ladies gave me some of it. I'd yet to get paid money for my Artificer work. All trades. Creation for anima. Copies for myself. Anima vials to build other stuff. Imagine trying to build a table that takes thirteen different types of wood and all you have in your own backyard is a tree of one type. That's what it's like being an Artificer free from the Guild. I needed anima worse than I needed cash. Ceinwyn owned my future already. What's another million?

When I pulled out an anima containment vial from under the register, T-Bone gave me a big grin. He put out his thumb and stuck it to the metal top of the vial. I felt the flash of anima drain from him and into it, trapped by the Artificer's gift. "I know you so well I was saving up."

I shrugged. "I need to make more rings, means I need more anima. It's the way it works."

"Yeah, I know." Turning his eyes away from mine, he stayed silent for a bit, before he seemed to come to a conclusion about the quality of my product. "If you give me like . . . twenty-five percent of the profit? I can donate to you about once a week. Maybe twice if it's light at work."

Hell . . . every once in a while even King Henry Price sees the sun through the gray. How about that?

"Sounds great, T-Bone."

"Don't call me that, King Henry."

"Want to shake on it?"

He studied my static ring. "How long has it been on your finger charging up?"

I smirked. Only thing to do when you get caught. "Since I opened the store."

"Right . . . think I'm going to take off then and do without the ambulance."

"New video game?" I asked.

I can't be sure since this is all by memory, but if I had to guess it was likely a Tuesday. T-Bone would always come into my shop and then go get his newest video games that just came out. Sometimes I'd even go back to his place with him and play some myself, try to forget about anima and artificing for a few hours, but that was in the future. That particular day he just nodded. "Always," he told me.

Then we shook hands.

The ones without the rings.

Session 2

CEINWYN DALE GAVE MY *EXCITED* little ass a whole day to '*settle my affairs.*' She just *might* have been mocking me and the girlfriend with that word usage.

What amazes me most looking back is how quickly my *jaded* little ass took up the idea of the Institution of Elements as being a great place to go to. I suppose it's similar to the amazement you see on the faces of kids, no matter how abused or screwed up they may be, when they get to go to the zoo for the first time. Something about the wonder in newness, the joy of the unexplainable, as if the Mancy or watching a lion can fix all that's wrong with the world. Hope . . . they call that word. Or I suppose I might not be as much of a badass as I thought I was. Whatever the reason, for the first time in my messed up life I was interested in something other than stealing, smoking, fighting, or fucking, and I threw myself into not screwing it up.

After Ceinwyn Dale left with her paperwork—and my soul tied up in a nice set of strings—Dad made dinner. Some kind of stir-fry with bright veggies and big pieces of fat marbled beef. Peppery enough to burn your lips. I've always had a thing for pepper. Mom made margaritas. Dad had one in place of his usual nightly joint. Not enough to get him drunk or mean, luckily for me.

We talked.

About how it was a good chance for me. About how I had to behave myself and watch my mouth, about how if I was good, Ceinwyn Dale said they'd let me come home in the summer and Dad would come pick me up.

My parents might as well have asked me to shit gold-foil origami cranes, but after all the talk Ceinwyn Dale had fed them, how the Asylum was a remedial school with hard-nosed but caring outlooks, complete with enough bullshit statistics to make my brain hurt like I'd gulped a gallon of slushie, it was expected to get some parenting for once. Mom ended the forced lovefest with, "time for bed, King Henry Price," already tipsy and eyeing my father's wide shoulders like she had a habit of doing when particular thoughts were circulating inside her head.

And I went to bed. Smoked a last cig for the day. Probably whacked one out too. Gross, horny teenagers and their nasty impulses. Disgusting, eh? Was probably thinking about Ceinwyn Dale when I did it too. What, you were expecting a glass of water and a bed time story?

[CLICK]

Mom woke me up the next day to get ready for school. To which I responded, most of my goodwill already gone from the night before, "Why the fuck I want to go to school when I'm not going there no more?"

"You don't want to say goodbye to your friends?" Mom asked. Another 'Good Day.' Two in a row.

I thought about my *friends*. Yeah. Guys-that-bet-on-me-to-score-cash is a better term. "Not really. They won't give a shit."

"No little ladies to break hearts with goodbyes?" I hadn't told her about the girlfriend. But then, she occasionally was the one who washed the clothes, so she might have figured out something was going on when she smelled the sex and cheap-teenage-girl perfume on them.

"Nope, not really," I lied.

Mom pouted at me. Big curvy lips worked wonders for her and she always liked to pout to get her way. Even though she was closing in on forty.

THE FANGED LADY

Especially since she was closing in on forty. "I still have to sign you out of the school, King Henry Price."

Well . . . shit. She had me there.

I dressed. Jeans. T-shirt with a pro-wrestler on it this time. It might have been *'fake'* but there was blood and big-breasted women, and that made it okay in my book. Wallet with twenty bucks in it I'd stolen from my math teacher's purse earlier in the week. House keys I wouldn't need after that day. A mouth freshener spray-can. And that was it. No knife. Like Ceinwyn Dale noticed, I got off on the impact of a punch. Also no cell-phone—not enough money made at Shithole Price to waste it on text messaging.

Mom dressed too. Dress, makeup, her dark hair done up real nice. It really sucks having a hot mom.

An example of this being when we got into the principal's office and he flirted with her the whole time she signed *more* papers to get me off the school rolls, all while Mr. Brett hoped to get Mom out of her dress.

"Really, Mrs. Price, it's no problem at all."

"I'd hoped not."

"A very simple process."

"I've always found it easy too . . ."

While he was distracted by my mother's hips, tits, and lips, I launched a preemptive attack by stealing Mr. Brett's car keys and his flash drive hanging half out of his pocket. What was he going to do, expel me? I doubted Ceinwyn Dale would care. I wasn't stupid—uneducated sure, but I could put two and two together and her little tricks and my lucky accidents were linked.

When Mr. Brett finished drooling at my mom, we left, King Henry Price officially off the rolls of Redwood High. Free at last! Free at last! Strings be cut! Strings be cut!

But not quite.

"Now we go home, right?"

"I'm thinking about doing some shopping."

"Like . . . what kind of shopping?"

Mom's smile told me she wasn't done with me yet.

Ceinwyn Dale assured my parents that the Institution of Elements would take care of my clothing needs, since everyone wore uniforms—real Commie Kim Jung Il shit—but Mom felt the need to spend some of my father's hard earned money at the Visalia Mall trying to get me a suitcase, grooming kit, shavers, stuff like that. We actually had a pretty good time, considering.

The biggest problem with Mom's 'Good Days' is that she's happy during them. That might seem ass-backwards, but imagine someone being a total crank to you probably three-hundred days a year, *at best* they could be zombiefied and care less if you existed—but for the other sixty-five days, at random, they love you. Completely. With no reservation. And they don't understand why you don't love them back, or why you're mad, since for some reason they can't remember being a cranky zombie.

That's a 'Good Day.'

It gets real hard to forget all the crap and be nice after awhile. Mom had been having 'Good Days' for over half my life, so it was extra hard to forget by then, but since it's the last time I'd have to do it for awhile, I gave it a shot and had some fun shopping with my mom, even when she tried to embarrass me in *Victoria's Secret*.

"What 'bout this one?"

"This is child endangerment or something."

"How dare I treat you like a grown-up . . ."

"Mom, I could be fifty and I wouldn't want to hear about your lingerie."

"How 'bout this one?"

Mostly, I tried to make accidents happen. I thought at the time that Ceinwyn Dale's hinting screwed my luck up . . . that actually knowing what was going on, about the Mancy, completely shut me down. One of those *'only invisible when no one is looking'* things. In reality, fourteen-year-old-me pushed around anima like a pyromancer would and the geomancer juices got all blocked up worse than a week's constipation.

Ignition versus solidity.

THE FANGED LADY

After I had my travel goods—complete with a few new comics that had actually been bought for my car trip—and Mom had some new skimpy things I tried not to think about, we stopped by the food court and gorged some sodas and burgers.

"So are you excited, honey?" Mom asked.

"I guess . . ."

"New place, new friends . . . new girls . . ." she teased me.

"I don't think that's what this Institution of Elements place is about, Mom."

"It's a school, honey; schools always have girls and friends. Provided you don't beat them up and get kicked out." Hmm. This was a serious realization for little shit me. No fighting. *No fighting.* And if I did get in a fight we'd both probably be mancers. I got so excited at the thought I think I popped a boner—and one of those just-woke-up-from-sleeping-can-cut-metal boners too. Either that or it was me watching the lemonade girl with a tight shirt pushing up and down on her wooden masher stick.

Hard call.

"I'll try to be good, Mom."

"I know you will, honey."

We ate in silence for a bit before Mom opened up. "I know it hasn't been easy on you. Your sisters leaving . . . your father working more hours and me getting . . . well . . . it's been hard on you. Lots of kids would have turned out much worse from less, and . . . I'm proud of you, King Henry."

I tried so damn hard to be tough and not start crying. I couldn't keep it all in. My eyes leaked like broken faucets . . . drip, drip, drip. These tiny tears that just collected up on my cheeks and wouldn't fall. Part of it was being happy that maybe deep down Mom actually knew what it's like to live with her, part of it was pure burning anger that she fucking *dared* to give me a speech after all those years of crap.

The emotion shifted some anima around in a purely stone-hard, rock-solid, geomancer kind of way and a fat guy sitting down on the other side of the food court with a pair of cheeseburgers got a nasty surprise when his metal stuck-to-the-table chair broke clean away from the table half of the equation.

Mom mistook the look of shock on my face for something having to do with her and stepped over to give me a hug. "I'm going to miss my little man, honey."

The fat guy got up with soda all over him, throwing a pudgy kick at the broken chair like it was at fault. *Amazing.* "Yeah, Mom, I'll miss you too."

Fifty-fifty on if that was a lie or not. I guess I don't know how I felt, or how I feel even today. Hard things emotions. We keep them so bottled up, they mix and combine like alchemic elixirs and become feelings we don't even have words for. Yearning for something else. But I didn't have a name for it.

"You promise to write me?"

I nodded my head. Now *that* was a lie.

[CLICK]

I'd had about as much Mom Time as I could handle, so when we got home I locked myself in my room, packing. Packing was pretty much taking all the new stuff I had and throwing it in the equally new suitcase. I added some extra comics just in case the car ride to the Institution of Elements place was really long, change of clothes too . . . just to be sure I didn't arrive naked.

Hell if I knew how to pack.

I'd only been on one overnight trip in my life—to my grandma's when I was five, and only to Fresno. Hour ride, whoop-tee-do. We didn't even know anything was wrong with Mom then . . . Dad had just called her '*fiery.*'

Mom sat at the couch, being *fiery* with a rum and coke when I finally left my room. 3PM. Late start for Mom. "You all packed, honey?"

"Yeah," I mumbled while pouring myself a coke sans rum.

"Miss Dale called." Mom was watching a soap opera. I wonder how many women have been turned into alcoholics by soap operas over the years? Maybe they should have a warning sign like cigarettes.

THE FANGED LADY

"What she say?" There's something inherently scary behind the thought that Ceinwyn Dale had my phone number.

"Just wanted to make sure you were being good and not running away. Nice woman."

"Still here . . ."

"I see that, honey."

"Actually, Mom, I think you were right, I'm going to go ride and say goodbye to my friends."

"Just *friends*?"

"Mom!"

"A mother can hope, can't she?"

I pulled my bike out of the garage and headed for the girlfriend's. My bike had come via hand-me-down from my middle sister—Jordan Josephine Price, Mom sure could name them—and it was a girly bike. Pink. At first I'd planned to repaint it with spiders and snakes and guy stuff, but after awhile I saw the upside. Pink bike? More reason for fights! Besides, with all the mud caked on it you could hardly tell.

The girlfriend greeted me at her door after I'd checked to see if her mom was working. The girlfriend is named Sally. She was taller than me by about five inches, had black hair she always kept in a ponytail, and had big tits. Which is what fourteen-year-old-me really liked about her. I was deep back then. To be fair, I also liked that her house was in a better part of town and was clean.

She and her mom lived without a man around, prison followed by abandonment, but the United States government stepped in to help out and it was a very nice little house. Complete with air conditioning. Glorious, glorious AC. We had vents at school, but being in a stuffy class ain't the same as sitting in front of a pouring stream of cold air during the summer time.

Tell you the truth, fourteen-year-old-me could never figure out what Sally saw in him. She got decent grades, had friends she didn't beat up every other time she saw them and I wasn't much of a catch looks wise. I'm not an ugly guy outside of a broken nose, but I'm not handsome either, and fuck, man, I was just around the upside of five feet tall.

Besides her big tits I liked that she liked me. That was the crux of what I liked about Sally. Big tits, nice house with AC, and liked me for some unknown reason. Fucking deep.

Twenty-one-year-old me could fill fourteen-year-old-me in on some info, like how Sally became a stripper working for some bad people, and that she had some serious daddy insecurity issues that left her seeking out the baddest, toughest guy she could find to shack up with, and at the time . . . hello, King Henry Price, you pugnacious little shit. But since twenty-one-year-old me doesn't have a time machine, fourteen-year-old-me was screwed and left in a cave of wonder regarding Sally.

She hugged me at the door, but then turned colder than her AC. She'd heard from a friend that worked in the principal's office about me leaving the school. And, of course, was mad I hadn't told her.

"I didn't know until yesterday. It was all last minute, baby." Baby. If a guy ever calls you *baby* then kick him in the balls. He's an asshole.

"And you're just *leaving*?" Sally crossed her arms under her tits when she was mad. It's distracting. Way worse than hot dog girl.

"My parents are making me," I focused.

"This is because you get into fights, I know it!"

"You *like* that I get in fights."

"Well . . . not anymore. Not if you have to leave. Can't you promise not to fight and stay?"

Not fighting, not learning the Mancy, all to stay with the girlfriend. Why didn't she just ask me to sacrifice my left nut like Lance Armstrong? "They already signed the paperwork, baby."

She huffed. She had *a lot* to huff.

"Well . . . how long do you have to go to this place?"

"Like four years." *At least* . . . I left out.

"Four years!"

THE FANGED LADY

"I know . . . it totally sucks." We should be clear if you haven't figured it out: at this point fourteen-year-old-me knew he was going to forget Sally existed the next day and was just looking for a way to end the relationship without kicking and screaming . . . okay, maybe a little screaming.

"Kingy!" I know, fucking '*Kingy.*' And Ceinwyn wonders why I didn't have stamina at that point in my life. You try going at it with a girl that's screaming, "Yes, Kingy, yes!" Of course I didn't last. I was trying too hard not to laugh.

"I know, baby. I just . . . came over to tell you goodbye, and that I love you, and that I'm going to miss you a lot." One out of three ain't bad.

"Oh, Kingy!" And another hug.

Followed by kissing.

Followed by undressing.

Followed by a super-duper, amazing, never before accomplished in my life, *ten* minute grunting and humping session. Take *that* Ceinwyn Dale! Hell, I think the girlfriend might have even felt something that time. She sure was yelling '*Kingy*' enough.

While Sally was cleaning up our amazing contraception practices, I used the break from her to get some clothes back on and borrow her laptop. Mr. Brett's flash drive wasn't even protected. I rummaged through it. Memos. Short stories from college when he thought he could become a sci-fi writer like all the other loser geeks out there. Divorce documents. Couple of movie files of some pornstar tied to a bed.

Promising.

Second set of divorce documents. Pictures of his house. Pictures at the school. Pictures of his poodle—Mr. Tibbs. Pictures of Mr. Brett in glow-in-the-dark latex with his ass cheeks hanging out, getting spanked by my algebra teacher Mrs. Allison.

Win.

Massive win.

Sent to the entire Redwood High directory. Oh yes. Bridges be burning down.

Picking up her cell-phone, I did another bad thing and snuck a picture of Sally, still naked and cleaning up in the bathroom, totally unaware of my actions.

I sent it to her mother's phone with a suggestion to buy her daughter birth control. Maybe *bad* is too harsh on fourteen-year-old-me. Sally never got pregnant in high school at least. That's got to be a good deed . . . even though she didn't get pregnant during all of freshman year because she got grounded . . .

My relationship decidedly over and my humanitarian work done, I dressed the rest of the way and gave Sally one last kiss before leaving. She wanted me to stay for a while longer, but I didn't want to be around when she picked up the return phone call from her mother.

I wouldn't talk to Sally again until after I graduated as an Artificer. I was a much different person by then.

I used a condom.

. . . What?

[CLICK]

I got home just after Dad did again. He was out smoking in the backyard, watering with a spray hose. Cooler than the day before, maybe ninety something, but that's still hot. Dad didn't seem to mind. Joint in one hand, hose in the other, he twisted himself around in a circle with his shirt off, chest covered with graying hair.

The water made the backyard shimmer. Made it cooler too. Almost bearable. Central Valley summers. Fuck, I hated them. Fuck, I wasn't going to miss them. Fuck, why did I move back when I graduated?

"Where you been, boy?" Dad asked, taking a draw afterward.

I figured, what the hell, eh? "Gave the girlfriend a goodbye present."

Dad's hose sprayed erratically for a second before he got it under control. "Oh?"

"Yeah."

"You safe, boy?"

THE FANGED LADY

"Yeah." I thought I was.

"Huh." Dad focused on our only tree. A big willow that made great shade. "Since you're opening up for once, what girl?"

"Sally Hendrickson." I smiled at her name.

"Not bad, boy."

"Thanks."

"Too good for you."

"Yeah . . . true, true."

"Your mother was too good for me."

"Dad . . ."

"She was . . . she *is*, I mean. Don't hate your mom for being sick, she can't help it. Remember what she was like before all this."

Not knowing what to say to that, I filled in with, "We shopped and had lunch today."

Dad looked me in the eye. He always looked you in the eye. "You sure you want to go with this Kind-Wind Dale woman?" *Kind-Wind*, that's exactly how he said it. Maybe he thought she was part Indian or something. "Got me, got your mom, got your girlfriend . . . we can still say no. You could do good in school here just as easily, if you put your mind to it instead of your fists."

It wasn't a lot, but it was *something*. I was tempted to call it off but for one thing. *I made a chair crack in two.* "I gotta go, Dad."

Dad nodded, matter decided. "Just know, boy, that you can't run away from your head. Thoughts, feelings, that's all going to go with you. All that stuff is tied around you too tight to get away from it by running. People think they can . . . can't do it."

"Ain't about that no more, Dad. Ceinwyn Dale . . . she told me some things about me that made sense. I got to find out the rest, ya know?"

"Kind-Wind Dale . . . that woman sure is . . . *different* . . . but your mother trusts her."

"Really?"

"Yup. How about that, eh?" Dad finished the joint and turned the hose off. "Your mother don't trust any woman, boy, not even your grandmother, but she trusts Dale to keep you safe. How about that?"

"Guess I'll try to trust her too." As far as I could spit on her.

Dad gave me a hug of his own, much more like a wrestling hold than a hug. "Why don't you get in the kitchen and start chopping up onions and peppers while I take my shower? I'm thinking for my King's Going Away he's have his favorite mole enchiladas for dinner."

"Yeah?"

"Sure thing, boy, sure thing."

THE FANGED LADY

Session 106

THE FOG WAS THICK AS sewer water by the time my shop neared closing. T-Bone had left after busting my balls over my display of particularly delicate glasswork, some in shapes of animals, others like mythological creatures. Good thing he didn't know I made them myself. Back off me, I learned it for a girl . . .

One old lady came in, bought a couple of shot glasses that were probably worth more than she paid, then left. Everyone was gone. Just me. All alone. Nice and quiet—good lighting and plenty of space on the counter for me to spread out my papers outlining my next bit of Artificer experimentation.

I'd been praying for silence ever since I was three, the very day I started to realize what sisters were and how loud and annoying and bossy they could be. In my shop, I finally got it from time to time.

Is it wrong that I actually like it when the customers stay away?

Guess that means I like losing money. Electricity costs. Water costs. Retail space costs. It all adds up. It all weighs you down. If the static rings didn't become a seller to more than my already established customer base I was going to be in deep shit. I was burning money at a rate of higher five-digits a month. Eventually, Ceinwyn was going to tell me to get lost, call me a failure, and probably kick me right in the balls—no matter how much she claimed she didn't care about the money.

Maybe it's from being born without anything. Anything I couldn't steal, at least. I didn't like spending money if I could help it. At the Asylum, everything's provided for you—food, clothes, school supplies, even entertainment—if you needed something black market, you either traded or you scrounged or you stole without getting caught. Even for anima. There was no cash. No debt. Especially not at the levels I was dealing with for my shop.

I burned through more a month on anima alone than my father had made in a year. After two years of operation, I will have accumulated more debt than my father ever made in his life.

The fuck!

The! Fuck!

When I allowed myself to think about it, the situation staggered me silent. Even the glory that is *fuck* can't come to describe how screwed I was. Just like the problem I was trying to fix, my shop couldn't keep going at the same pace, something was going to break one way or the other.

My fingers found my temples and started rubbing circles as I eyed over my papers for the third pass. I don't know what's worse: my ledger or going over anima conversion formulas. At least the ledger's simple. Got to give it that. The answer's the answer. A bad answer, but it was easy to come to. My formulas . . .

Thirteen different anima types acting thirteen different ways, plus if I got the formulas wrong bad shit would happen. Like explosions. Like pure, unadulterated anima burns. As Plutarch used to say, *'you only get one anima burn in your life, if you make it to two you'll be dead before you leave this school.'* It hurts—a lot. Imagine being burnt by the very essence of earth. Yeah . . . it hurts. That meant double and triple checking every formula I wrote, especially the parts interacting with each other. The last thing I needed to add to my ledger is hospital bills.

My fingers pressed in on my skull, pushing, trying to relieve my headache. "Maybe I should take up drinking . . ." I muttered to myself. "Couldn't make it much worse . . . runs in the family . . ."

THE FANGED LADY

That's when the door opened.

Tangle, tangle.

Door had a bell.

Tangle, tangle.

That's broken.

It took gall to be a million dollars in debt and be cheap enough to not fix a doorbell, let me tell you.

I glanced up from my formulas to take in a woman as she stepped clear of my door. I grunted, headache forgotten. Old ladies, mothers, the occasional college girl who's young-cute but not actual-cute hunting accessories, but none like this one walking into my shop.

This woman was the kind I went to school with. The kind who knew she could burn your eyes out or smother your balls in ice if you gave her too much trouble. It's in the walk, in the shoulders, in the tilt of the head. It's not about actual attractiveness, it's about a mindset.

For this woman there was no submission to the truth that I'd been born male and she'd been born female. No submission that as a male I was supposed to be the stronger, the hunter. This woman didn't believe in clubs over the head, in being *claimed* or *sold*. Not on the basis of modern feminism, but on the basis that it would never have been applicable to her during any period in history.

I've always said that every man only sees two features on any woman. For Ceinwyn, her smile and hands. Cutting you—one after the other. For my first girlfriend Sally it was . . . well, it was her tits really, and only her tits . . . always her tits, but let's add in her lips too for the few times I was staring at her face. I was fourteen, give me a break. Don't jump on me for only talking physical either, this rule is only for physical—mind and personality, those are more complicated—don't all men know it . . .

For the physical, it's only two features. For this woman it was her neck and eyes.

Neck?

I know, not something you notice usually. But for this one, she wanted you to notice it. It was a long neck, with a great swath of smooth skin that had every man thinking about touching instantly, like they were one of the five-year-olds who ran through my shop breaking merchandise. At her neck's middle point she had a choker about an inch and a half in width that wrapped around in a complete circle. Real metal through and through, not cheap modern shit that's fake on the inside. It was made of silver, worked with dark gems in a crossing pattern. At its center was an unmistakable large golden 'B,' with teardrop pearls dangling underneath. It drew you to the neck and then the skin and those long lines did the rest for her.

The eyes were brown so dark to be black, seductive velvet pools. At the Asylum, Valentine Ward's were similar, but there they were fire—threatening to ignite and burn. Here was darkness, a slow dance of her irises to fall into and be gobbled up, bare hint that the iris is there until you're looking for the touch of color against her pupil.

Darkness is more dangerous than fire; don't let anyone tell you differently. The cavemen in ancient history knew the score. Fire—you respect, you're always aware of it—you treat it well and it's your friend. The thing about darkness is that you start to enjoy it, start to sit down and rest, start to think you're all alone . . . until it's too late.

The rest of her was class, clad in three-digit jeans and a hand-woven black sweater that stopped halfway down her forearm. No coat, which should have been the first warning, but I'd forgotten what warnings were in my year and a half away from the Asylum. I'd gotten complacent. Rings on her fingers, bracelets at her wrists, thick hoop earrings. Dark hair, long. Dark eyebrows. Everything about her was dark escaping from soft white skin, except the pieces added by her hand to give a glitter—but those were just camouflage.

"You're not closed yet, are you?" she asked in a voice that could make clothes unbutton themselves.

"Almost," I murmured, just looking at her.

"Good," she said, advancing towards my register with a sure, unquestioning stride. "This won't take long."

My hands shuffled my formula papers to have something to do, while my eyes kept on staring like a love-struck freshman. Give me a break, okay? I'd been busy working on the rings, it'd been awhile since the stupid part of my brain had gotten to come out and play. You're lucky I wasn't drooling.

"Can I help you with anything?" I asked in an attempt to hang onto some professional dignity.

"Yes," she said. She let the word sink in. Then she smiled. Knowing Ceinwyn Dale, I know smiles. This one was damn good. She could bend her lips without really moving them. Something like that can make a man groan just looking at the woman who does it. Makes a crude man like me wonder what else the lips can do. "You own this store, yes?"

"Last I checked." My hands put my formula papers away. She might have been hot-stuff, but for all I knew she was from the Guild trying some corporate espionage on me. Takes a lot more than a pretty face to catch me completely off guard. Give me some credit. Survival instincts like the ones I learned as a kid were baseline. They worked with either my smart or stupid parts leading the way.

"*You* are King Henry Price?"

Price. My eyes went over her again, searching for clues as to who this magnificent creature was. She knew my name. Interesting. Not here for teapots then. The antique people don't know about Price. Made the smart part wake up a bit. "I am . . . and who are you?"

"I'm Anne," she told me.

Anne. Simple name. Never trust the ones with simple names.

My gaze went to the large golden '**B**' at her throat. Anne B. A name comes to mind straight out of history, but I didn't say it. With my name being *King Henry*, I couldn't say it. If I said it, then I'd know without a doubt that the Mancy was playing a practical joke on me.

"Bonnie?" I guessed.

Could have been T-Bone's mommy, right? Named after a pirate chick by parents as screwed up as mine. Sure . . . nurses totally look like this . . . in romance novels and porn movies at least.

"Not quite," she said. She was middling height for a woman, so not that much shorter than me. With her heels, we were about even as she got right against the register to study my face. "I expected you to be handsome," she complained. "I suppose it doesn't matter . . . but spending time with a handsome face is so much easier, don't you think? Handsome never ceases to remind me to enjoy my lot in life."

An insult. Nothing quicker to get my smart brain back in the driver's seat. My shoulders set tight. Muscles bunched. I forced myself to keep my hands where they were on the counter, flat against the top. They strained against it, wanting to curl into fists. Eight years from that little boy and I still wasn't over wanting to smash a person's face in over teasing. "Does the '**B**' stand for *bitch*, then?" I asked. "Anne Bitch? Or Anne Bitchly maybe?"

She laughed it off with a placating little smile that was still all lips. "You're King Henry, I'm Anne . . . what could it *possibly* stand for? Did you study English royalty at your school or have they nixed those classes for creationism?"

I ignored the obvious again. That would just be too weird. The Mancy couldn't be so cruel. "My luck with women is still holding," I muttered to myself. "You'd have to be a total whackjob to come in here and be as hot as you are."

Anne's head tilted from one side of her shoulders to the other, long neck bending with it. Like she's trying to see if the view changed my appearance. The '**B**' on her neck shined with a flash, a damned beacon trying to get through to me.

"King Henry Price?" she asked again.

"I already answered you."

"I'm sorry." She shrugged, hands on her hips, rings rubbing against rough denim. "You're just so ugly, aren't you? Broken nose . . . so many scars. There's nothing perfect about you. I thought with all the rumors

54

about you being a hound that you'd be better looking. I supposed I shouldn't be surprised, since we live in a time where every woman will stick a toaster in herself if it vibrates quickly enough.

"Women have no standards at all anymore. They don't want to work for the complete experience. Seduction takes too much time, better to make a blog post about wanting to *get to know people* I think the phrase is."

"Rumors . . ." I said.

I locked on the word, ignored the rest. Yup, she wasn't here for the teapots. Good to know. Asylum toady? Guild spy? Another mancer testing me before she bought a commission? Could have worked for the government . . . but then maybe not with the clothes she wore. She might have been related to Welf too. All possibilities, none the correct answer.

"Look at his little brain go *click*," Anne said. "So cute."

I glanced at the 'B' one more time. "If I'm King Henry and you are really Annie B, then doesn't that mean I get to cut your head off?" I asked, lips pulling back along my teeth.

Something shifted in her. The second gear that Asylum women have when they're about to put you in place. "You're going to close down your shop and then you're going to come with me for a few days," Annie B told me in plain terms suffering no argument. "I need someone with the skill-set for an Artificer kind of problem, one that isn't prisoner to the Guild bylaws, and you've been volunteered for it. If you try to cut my head off, I'll kick your little ass. Understand, King Henry?"

Volunteered? Who would volunteer me? Who *could* volunteer me? Short list. Plutarch, Ceinwyn, or the Lady. "I don't hire out or build or design without a contract and unless I say so and last I checked—you didn't offer me payment." My hands couldn't take it anymore—they curled into fists. Plutarch, Ceinwyn, or the Lady. Which one would get a kick out of volunteering me without mentioning it to me? *All of them.* That didn't help . . .

"Get out of my store before I build up the anima to smash you across the street, you pushy psycho bitch."

That's when she punched me in the face so hard I tumbled backwards five feet and slammed into my shelf filled with glassware.

A few thousand dollars worth of antiques cracked behind me as my body splayed out from the impact. My feet slipped under me. You get hit in the right spot on the chin and your legs will go out, no matter how hard the punch. Has to do with the torque on your neck. Nerves don't meet up with the rest of your body and until the electrical impulses sync up with the brain again you're out of it. Those impulses take a few seconds to get back together, so my butt hit the floor.

I did three things in those seconds.

First, I pooled anima like only an Ultra can. I was going to need it.

Second, I realized I hadn't felt anima being drawn before she punched me. You might not *see*, but you always get a feeling something is going down, like an added sense. For aeromancers it's like a breeze at the back of their necks. Pyromancers, a heated forehead. Cryomancers, their dicks shrivel up or something. For me and other geomancers it's a slight rumble under our feet. Like a big truck going down the street kind of rumble. It didn't matter what anima type was being pooled. It all registered the same. A rumble. More anima, bigger rumble.

This time . . . no rumble.

Third, I realized the hand that had punched my face wasn't pumping blood at ninety-eight-point-six. It had more in common with a summer day than the foggy night outside my doors. Right . . . My eyes went to her choker immediately. Not to the 'B.' To the side of her neck, that place where you can check for a pulse under a person's chin.

Anne's pulse was so strong *I saw it*. A shiver. A heart over-processed like some computer chip in a cold chamber. A heartbeat hitting four maybe five-hundred beats a minute. Crap . . .

I'm in trouble.

The darkness said *hello.*

"Fucking vampire?" I said aloud as my legs joined the party and popped me back up on my feet. "A *real* fucking vampire?"

THE FANGED LADY

Her hand flourished to draw attention to her lips. "I'd show my fangs, but we don't actually have them. It's actually one of the more disgusting myths you humans have created about us, I've always thought."

"Fucking vampire . . ." I said again.

Damned if I'd ever thought I'd really see one. Ceinwyn told me to leave them alone, so I left them alone. Weres too. *'Leave politics to the professionals, King Henry,'* that's what she'd said. They were around somewhere . . . just like homeless people or gangs or drug dealers are around somewhere, but I didn't want to have to deal with Vamps and Weres just like normal people don't want to have to deal with the other problems. My shop was enough worry. I figured I'd leave the supernatural treaties to the Asylum's ESLED— Elementalist Security and Law Enforcement Department.

"Are you properly scared now, little mancer? Will you come without any more complaining?" Anne grinned a mouthful of normal white teeth just to further prove her point about the lack of fangs. "I promise I won't bite unless you ask for it. Deal?"

I resorted to my most tried and true reaction, straight from my childhood. "Fuck. You. Bitch." I even pointed with each word.

She shrugged, unconcerned with my puffed up bravado. "I don't want to beat you senseless, but I will. You don't exactly scare me . . . perhaps you're not a crusty old man like most Artificers, but . . . come now. You run a shop, don't you? Straight out of school, don't know how the world really works. Just living inside their lies, thinking you're in on the secrets. Do you think you stand any chance against me, scared little boy?"

"That's right . . ." I agreed with her first comment, fists coming up to a normal stance. It'd been awhile . . . still felt *good* . . . always felt *good*. Fighter's stance with my fists up . . . no anima conversion formulas here. No debt or ledgers either. Just me and her. Easy problem to solve. Right that moment, instantaneous gratification, not some day in the unknown future. "I'm not a crusty old Artificer working for the cocksucking Guild. I run a shop and you damaged my property. So let's dance our little dance, Annie B. I won't even use the Mancy to throw you out the door. Nothing but my hands."

Some kind of freaky groan escaped her, her eyelashes flickering and her tongue arching out to touch her top lip. "Well, well . . . now I know why you get the girls. So very *tough* . . . do you vibrate too?"

My jab at her face caught only air.

Newsflash: she was fast.

We had a lesson on Vamps, but you think I could remember it in the moment? Just like all schooling: it deserts you the moment you don't need it for a test. Why should *History of Elementalism* be any different? I grasped at the knowledge I knew was in there somewhere . . . but it was no good. Everything went out of my head. Smart part, stupid part, all gone. It was all instinct. It's a *fight* and I'm King Henry Price.

It's what I *did*.

What . . . I *did* . . . after my jab missed, was catch a kick to my hip that threw me sideways and eventually returned me back down to my ass. Could have been worse. At least I missed crashing into another shelf. Not that there wasn't a therapeutic aspect to smashing the crap, but I couldn't afford to keep it up. Shrinks cost less than broken antiques.

Rolling over on my shoulder, I let out a hurt gasp I couldn't control. It was a strong kick . . . I got up feeling it over most of my body.

Annie B hadn't even moved from her spot by the register. I'd been flying around the store like a dumbass nerd trying to fight a linebacker, but there she was, feet in the same place, not a scratch on her, clothes still neat and tidy.

"I've been doing this for longer than you," she told me with another twist of her lips. "But don't worry—I'm sure I'll feel something if you keep on poking at me. You'll get the rhythm down eventually . . . it's all in the hips . . ."

Right.

I kept saying that to myself with every bit of information.

My biggest problem in life was I always went for smashing through the wall as my first instinct. It's not until I'm stopped short that I begin to look for a creative way towards my goal. The Asylum taught me to control my mind and go for the creative right off the bat, but it hadn't taught me the trick with my body yet.

My body wanted to smash. It needed to get creative. No time to learn like the present.

She was faster, she hit harder. My advantage was the Mancy. I had just enough pool built up to do something internal—to myself. She'd been doing this a longer time, she said. Which meant she knew what my average anima pool was going to look like too. She knew how to fight mancers and I had no clue how to fight a vampire.

I stared across at Annie B and saw it in her posture as she finally moved, shifting from facing the register to towards me, where I stood thinking. It wasn't a full stance—her arms were at her side, carefree—but her legs looked ready to kick, wide-set.

"Going to try harder this time?" Annie B teased me. "I so like it *hard* . . ."

Yeah, she knew mancers alright.

Look at me in the corner.

I didn't say anything witty. I was never witty before a fight, rarely during too. I was all business. Showboaters pissed me off. Solid fighters who got the job done, that's what I'd always tried to emulate as a kid. *But she doesn't know that,* I thought.

Right.

She knew *mancers*. Not *me*.

I smiled on the inside as I roared toward her with an out-of-control punch aimed at her face. I missed again . . . by like a foot . . . but that was fine. That's the way I'd planned it. Annie B didn't know that either. She thought I'd blown my anima charge on the punch. Good old *iron fist* which had stopped so many of my fights back in elementary school.

Annie B thought wrong.

She dodged with a slide backwards then her foot came up just as expected, straight in front of her to land what's called a push-kick. Push-kick ain't really about a lot of damage; it's about making space, keeping the other guy back away from you. Push them away with a stiff foot to their chest.

Only she's a vamp with her muscles as tight as a virgin's asshole and what's considered her blood is flowing at three times the speed of the human maximum. Means she can throw a push-kick that can end fights. At the very least—a push-kick capable of breaking ribs. Anyone that thinks a broken rib is an easy injury has never had one. It will finish you, your breath gone, your chest a mass of pain with every movement of your lungs. Reminder: lungs got to move for you to breathe.

It will finish you . . . unless you're a geomancer who's holding back on your anima pool for *defense*. Good ol' solid earth burst in my chest, taking the brunt of the push-kick, keeping me right in place. Her eyes flickered in recognition, but it was too late. One thing any good fighter knows is that if you have the balls and the jaw to take a punch, you can lay into your opponent. This wasn't boxing. No clumsy gloves, no referee to save the day. No bell after three minutes. And if you got to three minutes you were going to be a bleeding mound of flesh, from orifices you didn't know you had.

I shifted my weight from my right to my left with a step of my foot, moving into her space. *Get in close*—any short guy's creed.

My left arm came up, not to punch, but to hook around her leg pushed firmly against my chest, sliding it to the crook of my arm, holding her where she was. One foot in my grip, one foot on the floor in three-inch-heels . . . vampire or not, most of Annie B's concentration instinctually went to keeping herself standing. Instead of covering up, her hands moved to balance the both of us, out at her sides like she was on some balance beam going for the gymnastic gold.

Which left my right hand free to do whatever it wanted.

My right hand wanted to beat in some vamp face.

The first punch caught her in the throat, stunning her, trapping air. It wasn't *iron fist*, my anima was burned, my pool was less than a puddle. It was starting to build back up, drip by drip, minutes from being useful. Second punch smashed just above her stomach into her diaphragm, pushing what air was still there out. Third punch clipped her head. All that I'd done to her and Annie B was still fast enough to make it nothing more than a glance.

A reflexive turn of her neck kept me from delivering the full force of the punch. It still snapped her head back, and, so close to her, I saw those velvet eyes lock on me.

In them, I heard that beast in the darkness give a content little gurgle at what she'd found. A part of me, in that split second, remembered my *Elementalism as a Weapon* teacher, Fines Samson, telling me how above all things vampires are collectors always seeking the best shells.

The way Annie B looked at me . . . like she was thinking I'd make a nice vacation home. It stopped my fourth punch.

Nope, it wasn't one of those frozen moments of pure prey-like fear. Have some faith in King Henry. I kept moving . . . *I just went bigger*.

I threw an elbow instead.

A nice tight elbow won't knock a guy out as easy as a punch, believe it or not. One less fulcrum of strength, less muscles, all that physics crap. An elbow is all in the shoulder. Big muscles, compact motion.

Won't knock you out as easy.

But what an elbow *will* do is cut you up quicker than an exacto-knife. Sharp bone ground itself against Annie B's pale face, right across her cheek. The skin caught on it, twisted, bone on bone in a clean part.

She screeched at me, hands finally stopping their attempt to hold us up. I had a moment to realize I was about to get my ass kicked.

It wasn't a good moment.

Annie B grabbed at my coat and flipped backwards, legs flinging out as I twisted into the air, the judo throw to end all judo throws. There was no hope for me to roll. I was in the air. Not a place I like to be. Especially when my feet are closer to the ceiling than my head is. It's just not natural. My shoulders, back, and ass took the impact in a wave as I tumbled over my head and back down. Then I slid a couple more yards just for fun.

I got to my feet slower this time.

But I didn't gasp.

In fact . . . I was kind of enjoying it.

Annie B's hand found the gash on her face. Blood dripped. But not human blood. A thick string of the deepest red you could ever imagine spurted from the wound, like a container too full had ripped a seam. It hung, crimson goo, until Anne's hand rose to it, touched it, pulled it out to stretch over her fingers, and out until she could study it with her eye.

The . . . *blood* . . . moved.

It curled itself around a finger, finding its way like some snail out of its shell. It twisted on itself, Annie B's hand guiding it back to her cheek. Damned if it didn't go worm its way right back into the hole and disappear, the only hint of its existence the trail of what looked like red slime more than blood left on Annie B's hand.

Her eyes wandered back to me. I wasn't alone in the darkness any longer. "I haven't been forcibly damaged by a human in years," she whispered, both amazed and excited.

"Maybe you need practice at it." I couldn't help myself. Nerve was about the only thing holding me up. My back ached. My fist was sore. Punching her is like punching concrete with a layer of padding, not a human. My anima was built up again, ready for something small, but nothing small was going to save my ass from whatever she wanted to do to it. I needed to buy time.

My thumb touched my static ring. Yeah, that would help. So would some of my other artifacts maybe. Of course . . . they were in my shop behind the front, not out here with me.

All I had out there with me and the vampire were antiques. Antiques . . . I stood next to my teapot display. They had to weigh . . . what? Five pounds each? Made of ceramic? Round enough to cup them in a hand . . .

Better than nothing.

"We can stop, King Henry," Annie B tried. "Just come with me. Two days for your services, that's all I ask."

"If you'd asked, maybe I'd have said *yes*," I decided. My hand found a teapot behind my back and grabbed onto it. A sadistic part of me hoped it was pink with flowers. "But you ordered . . . and I don't like ordering. Don't like people that order, either. Don't like people who *bully*. If you are even *people*. I saw the look, Annie B. Saw the look like you wanted to wear me like a fur coat. Don't think I'm going to just walk off with you after that one. This fur coat goes down with a fight."

Her neck bent from side to side as she moved her tongue to touch her lips once more. As a gesture, it was more animal than human. "And I saw the look in your face, King Henry," she accused me, her expression all hunger.

I frowned. "What look?"

"The look at the counter . . ." she moaned, throaty, dark tendrils of sound pulling me into her. "Like you wanted to rip my pants off, turn me around, and *wear me* like a sleeve."

Vampire or not, she had a fair point with that one. "Didn't last long . . ." I apologized. "It's been awhile . . ."

"Neither did mine . . ." she returned. "We all have our urges, human or . . . *other*. Perhaps if we have a moment of peace and quiet, we can . . . share them with each other."

My dick dropped out of my pants and ran for the back door. "Come near me and I'll beat your ass again."

"Promises . . ." she whispered, feet advancing towards me.

I backed up pace for pace, teapot hidden behind the bulk of my geomancer's coat. Over my shoulder, the door from the antique store into my shop got closer. "No more playing, Annie B! You come at me and I'll mess you up, you hear?"

"Bluffing little boy," she snarled at me, hips, arms, her whole body swaying in a way that got a man's blood pumping. "Doesn't have enough of a charge to do anything about the nasty predator stalking him, but is showing his feathers to try to buy himself time."

Shit.

Annie B leapt the rest of the way to me without any forewarning. One moment it was a slow step by step and then she sprang like some type of

Olympic athlete, ten feet through the air, arm whooshing towards my head. If it hit, it would have knocked me out. There's this kind of jumping punch in MMA called the superman-punch. This thing made all those punches look like the superboy-punch. Would have ended my night early. No time for dessert. Straight to bed, little boy.

Except for my teapot.

You can bet I've never ever wanted to have to utter those words.

Except for my teapot.

I chucked the teapot at her the same time she jumped. I'd meant to take her in the head, but because of her leap it nailed her in the chest, five pounds of pain. It didn't break apart. Nice. Once upon a time they made products to last. The teapot stopped Annie B cold, her punch left swinging wildly in the air as she crashed to the ground.

My feet sped up, running me towards my back room.

FYI . . . teapot was red with a yellow chicken on it.

Old ladies will buy anything . . .

[CLICK]

I figured I had time to make a grab for one artifact before she followed me through the door into my shop. I didn't even think about which one until I stood over them. It's not like there were tons. Geo-anima, cryo-anima, aero-anima, floro-anima, and fauna-anima were the types I had steady supplies for. Everything else I had to buy and everything else I was out of.

It's not practical to make artifacts if they cost me too much. Supply/demand, all that stuff you slept through during your *Economics* class. I used most of the bought anima for experimentation, but so far, other than the static ring, my experiments weren't going anywhere unless they exploded first.

The static ring. I had it, full charge. I had enough anima built up in my body to do something with the Mancy. I had my artifacts. Only one of which was going to be of use in a fight. The first one I ever made . . . I grabbed it.

THE FANGED LADY

They were metal cuffs, lined with a glowing white light to let you know there was something going on inside. Cold Cuffs, I'd called them back at the Asylum. Slap them on and watch cryo-anima cool down the person's body temperature until they can barely move, too busy fighting off hypothermia. With a charge long enough for one hour of use before they ran out, that's more than enough time to figure out what to do with the vampire. Or at least call Ceinwyn and have her figure out what to do with the vampire.

Ceinwyn . . .

Volunteered . . .

She wouldn't . . .

Annie B burst through the door with enough impact to crack one of the hinges. She blinked, taking in the room to line up where I was at. There was a nasty look on her face. It was the only warning I had before she threw my teapot back at me with so much speed it would have killed me.

Only she missed.

Not by accident. She'd meant to miss.

Hitting my wall at Mach 3, the teapot finally broke. The shards of ceramic clattered all over the floor, a dust of red mist spraying over the room. *Poor chicken . . .*

She wanted me alive to use the Mancy for her. Couldn't be good, vampires being vampires. It was never supposed to be good with the Vampire Embassies. Infighting and personal feuds going back thousands of years. Bad mojo to be a part of. Especially for the food. But whatever she wanted from me, no matter how bad it was, it meant she couldn't kill me.

I can win this shit.

"It's cute you're fighting back, King Henry," Annie B told me, "but you're making this much harder on yourself than it needs to be. I'm not making you into a slave . . . more like an indentured servant. Two days, your opinion, maybe a bit of Mancy, that's all. Am I really so scary?"

"You want to fuck me and then eat me," I growled at her from across the room, my worktable the only obstacle between us. "Of course you're scary."

"Now, now," she whispered as she strode forward. "No reason we can't do both at the same time, is there?"

"Leave, Annie B, last time I'm telling you." The Cold Cuffs clicked in my left hand, the ring sat ready on my right hand, and anima bubbled in my chest. "I ain't your normal mancer."

"No . . . you're far more fun." Her hand flicked at her face where the cut had been and now very much wasn't. "Have you ever had a woman *inside you*, King Henry? Slipping in, running through your veins, tasting every part of you as her body rides on top of you? It only takes two small cuts on our hands . . . I promise it won't even leave a scar . . ."

My dick hollered from where it had run away to hide, "*I ain't ever coming back, I hope you know that!*"

For once, I was speechless.

Annie B started circling the table. I circled it with her, the opposite way. "No answer?"

"Leave me alone."

"Final answer?"

"You come at me again and I'll do everything in my power as an Ultra to destroy you, Annie B," I told her, feet still circling.

With another lick of her lips, she made the mistake I'd been waiting for. She hopped up on the table to try to get to me. She'd kind of done a sloppy free-running move to get over it. Hands down, butt sliding forward, legs out in front to make sure I didn't rush her. Only I didn't need to rush her.

The table was metal.

Yeah, motherfucker. *Metal*. My favorite. Better than soil, better than stone, better than glass. Wonderful meee-ee-e-e-eetal. Oopsie daisy, Annie-bo-fanny.

Anima burst from me, ten full minutes of build up. A lot more than a little trick. More than we were ever allowed to hold at the Asylum actually. Ten minutes. Would have been something . . .

Anima poured into the table, manipulating the metal. Some types of mancers can actually create with their anima, Firestarters as the ultimate example, but not Artificers. We have to use what's there. But . . . boy, could we use it. I could have made a spike of steel flash straight up into her head. Probably should have. But I went the other route. Which was to make the metal flex and form around her hands and thighs, becoming fluid, molding like liquid water, then returning to a solid state in a second. Nice and easy. One trapped vamp.

She could have been modern art.

Annie B glared down at the table with a grunt. She pulled at it, but it didn't give. "Kinky, King Henry."

I let out a sigh of relief. "Just shut up."

"Perhaps not the best position," she decided. Her arms were deep into the steel, holding up her chest, while her legs splayed out in the middle of her slide, twisting her frame so she couldn't lie down or sit up all the way. Had to be hell on her back. "And you'll have to rip my pants to get at all the really good parts."

"I told you to shut up," I repeated, leaning in closer than I ever would have if she was unbound.

She didn't shut up. "A wonderful show of anima manipulation, however. Which only confirms that I need your skills to help with my not-so-little problem . . ." She pulled at the metal one more time.

"Has to be thick enough to take any accidental explosions," I explained, banging the table with my knuckle. "You'll never break it. Even you, fanged lady."

"I told you . . . *we don't have fangs*."

"But you still bite," I said seriously.

"Only for foreplay," she teased, tongue riding the line of her teeth. "Would you like to see a trick?"

"I'll pass."

I heard her thumb break itself a split second before her hand was free of the metal and wrapped around my throat. "I've had fun teasing you," she panted as she choked me, "But this game is at an end, I think . . ."

Thank the Mancy I hadn't set down my Cold Cuffs. They clicked around her wrist with a nice finality. A yank of my arm and her hand was off my throat, another yank and the other half of the cuffs locked in place around her second wrist. The cuffs flashed white, then the anima inside them released.

Cold flooded into Annie B. Cold like an iced-over lake. Cold like a snow-bath. Cold enough to make a human being cover up, more worried about getting warm than trying to hurt a person. The kind of cold that makes you shiver and shut up.

Of course, Annie B wasn't human. She was a creature living inside a human body. That wasn't warm-blooded but *mega*-blooded, that lived in environments never reaching over seventy degrees. They liked the cold.

They really like the cold.

A moan escaped from Annie B, the first sign she wasn't reacting the way I'd planned. Her body twisted against the cuffs, against the metal still holding her thighs. Hands free, she flopped over backward on the table, back arching. Her black sweater rode up her body, revealing a stomach that even hours of crunches would have envied. She moaned again, hips pushing. Her eyes were wide, flashing toward my face.

"My God . . ." she whispered. *"You do vibrate . . ."*

The white light on the cuffs faded, anima drained. She'd burned up enough cryo-anima to put down a human for an hour in about thirty seconds.

"Son of a bitch . . ." I growled. "Did you just . . . *did you?*"

Her thumbs broke in a crunch, Cold Cuffs flopping to the floor. Annie B didn't rise from where she was laid out, like she'd been worn out by hours and hours of good ol' grunting and humping. "Please tell me . . . are they for sale?" she asked.

King Henry Price. I either created the first vampire sex toy or what was essentially vamp-nip. I don't know which is grosser.

Okay, I do . . . definitely vampire sex toy . . . but I was trying not to think about it . . .

THE FANGED LADY

I smiled down at her. Two strikes, one to go.

My right hand reached out, touched her face. Annie B sighed, nuzzling it. It might not have knocked her out, but in the process of whatever else it had done to her, the Cold Cuffs had caused lethargy to sweep her body. She pulled her head back, exposing her throat and offering a chance for me to sweep my hand down it. Her choker glinted once more. If there's a greater sign that she didn't fear me, I don't know what it is.

Don't fear me at your peril.

I kept smiling as I activated my static ring and electrocuted the bitch.

Moans turned into screams. Her back arched in pain, not pleasure. Her hips fought against their holds. Her arms flopped useless as the current raced through them. Her head clanged against the metal. Lethargy was replaced with a stunned body.

Cold. Crossed out. Electricity. Check mark, motherfucker. "That's more like it!" I yelled at her.

Her velvet eyes hadn't left mine. "You asshole . . ."

"I know. I'm an asshole," I said. "But who's sparkling now, bitch?"

If only I had remembered about keeping my mouth shut . . .

That's when the crimson string of blood flew from where her cut cheek had not quite as disappeared as I thought. Only it wasn't as weak as it had been before. The blood was thick, pulsing, and powerful as it lunged up my arm, snake-like in the time it took me to blink. It wrapped itself around my throat and squeezed—a constrictor.

My air disappeared. My strength as I tried to pull it off got me nowhere, and only got weaker as seconds ticked by without oxygen. My feet went out on me again. I leaned against the table, face close to Annie B's.

She pouted her lips, rope of blood hanging from her cheek. "Go to sleep, King Henry. We have a long drive and no more time for games."

The blood gave a final squeeze and I dropped to the ground.

I'd learned my first lesson of fighting a vampire. The blood . . . that was Annie B. The body . . . that was only where she lived.

Don't forget it.

RICHARD RALEY

Session 3

CEINWYN DALE AND HER NEW car showed up the next morning, early enough that she waited in the kitchen—hanging onto an *I Love Mom* mug some teacher forced me to make in Elementary School—while I took a shower. In case you're wondering, Elementary and Elementalism school don't have a whole lot in common.

Morning in the summer is about the only time you felt cool in that house, by 11AM some days the temperature would already have passed ninety, which means there ain't a whole lot of relief. Even the people with AC complained—for us it was torture. Hot in the summer, cold in the winter, so much pollen in the air during the spring and autumn a normal person's nose stops working. All of it locked in a box with a pair of drunks and unable to escape. No relief—that was my life. Trading stained strings for silk ones.

And the minute I got my relief, Ceinwyn Dale sitting out there like the fairy giant she wasn't, I was scared to death. Cutting off a gangrene foot can be considered relief if you see what I mean. But you still miss the foot.

I think I spent an hour in the shower trying to convince myself it was just a normal Saturday. Get out of the shower, put some clothes on, and run off to find Sally or some of my bet-on-me-buddies. That's all I had to do . . . right . . .

Mom decided on a 'Bad Day' and was comatose on her bed, eyes blinking along to some psychedelic forced-happy morning show, but Dad sure yelled at me to hurry up every other minute. He was some kind of manager at the warehouse and usually worked a couple extra Saturdays a month, but he'd given up the hours so he could have the day to see me off.

Eventually, I faced up to reality and got out of the shower, dried myself to the sounds of Al Roker giving the weather like the fairy giant he was, and dressed myself in some of my new clothes—shirt with a heavy metal band on the back. Probably the first new set of complete clothes I'd had in three years.

When I walked out, Mom was lying there. Only shower in the house was in the parents' room, no way around seeing her. 'Bad Day' alright.

"Bye Mom," I told her, with a little half-hearted wave.

Wasn't expecting a reaction and didn't get one. Might have been an extra blink or two. It hurt, fuck it hurt, but I was used to it, so I refrained from having my last words to her in probably four years be my usual favorites. Instead, I manned up with, "I love you, I'll write." Both lies I thought.

The suitcase was already in the car, I guess. It was just me and my empty room. Hadn't bothered to clean it. Guess Dad did eventually. Of course, my sisters' room still had their stuff in it too, so who knows if he ever got around to it or they just walled the door up.

"Bye, you piece-of-shit squeaky bed . . . you too, clangy fan." The clothes didn't even deserve comment, raggy corpses of those that were getting left behind on the battlefield, victims of all the tears and cuts we'd taken together in our fist fights. Pocketing my iPod and grabbing a stack of comics, I left the room, then my house.

Bye, piece-of-shit house.

Ceinwyn Dale and Dad had moved outside. I remember my fourteen-year-old thought, *Holy crap, this is actually going to happen.* Ceinwyn Dale smiled at me, but when didn't she?

Dad . . . he was a bit more communicative than Mom, the bed, or the fan. "You be good, boy."

Who did he think I was? A queer-ass Jonas brother? "I'll try."

"Miss Dale reminded me that if you're good you might get to come home in the summer for a month, maybe even Christmas. Try not to mess it up."

THE FANGED LADY

One thing about my dad, he always thought I was capable of being better than I ever actually managed growing up. Maybe that's why he got mad and whipped me with the belt. Mancy knows I disappointed him enough times to earn it. Not coming home would just be one more time. Not like I wanted to go back anyway, even if I got a promise it would be a whole month of 'Good Days.'

"I'll try," I repeated.

"No fights, no stealing. Fresh start."

I nodded and got in the car before either of us started crying. I knew I couldn't take that emotional shit after being raised on repression. That was my goodbye. I was in Ceinwyn Dale's hands just like that. And if you don't think my parents are screwed up enough already, might I point out they had the judgment to sign me over to Ceinwyn-fucking-Dale and her freaky ass smile.

[CLICK]

Inside of the car, sitting on the nice leather seat and enjoying full blown AC, I continued the well-practiced teenage art of pretending the world doesn't exist, with a bit of no-one-can-understand-what-I'm-going-through for fun.

My weapon of choice was my iPod and an *Iron Man* comic. Despite what my present twenty-one-year-old self would call an odd correlation of profession, fourteen-year-old-me hated Iron Man. Billionaire whose parents died. It was like my dream and all the jerk-off did is brood about things and treat his friends and girlfriends like crap. *Give me that life*, I thought more than once, *won't see me whine at all.*

I don't know how normal, caring parents go about getting a child's attention when they're plugged into earbuds. If I guessed, I'd say loud yelling or hand gestures, maybe a tap on the shoulder. Heck, I could even get slapping the back of the kid's head. I went to school with teenagers. They were little assholes just like fourteen-year-old-me, they could probably use a slap on the back of the head.

Ceinwyn Dale would never win a contest for either normal or caring. I'm pretty sure she views other people as disturbances to be studied as they get in the way of her precious air flows.

My music blared, head nodding along in a little trance for over half an hour before it stopped with a sudden silence—that alert silence where you hear everything and I heard nothing. Picking up the iPod, I tapped the screen trying to figure out what was wrong. It worked fine. But no sound.

Ceinwyn Dale smiled like she had a private bet to see how long it would take me to figure it out. Anyone who had five minutes won. When I pulled my headphones off, I noticed they weren't connected to each other or the main cord snapped to my shirt. She had used a slice of air or air friction or something else I haven't thought of—I'm not an aeromancer, I don't do flows, I don't do tools that are here and gone again—to sever the wiring.

How cruel is that shit?

Still smiling, she watched me cradle the worthless plastic earbuds in my hands just as much as she watched the road. Expensive, modern machinery made worthless by a ten dollar piece breaking . . . and like I had an extra pair.

Stop ignoring me, King Henry.

I wanted to ask her why she's so mean. Wanted to ask her how she did it too. How I did what I did, what was it all about?

Forget that, it was *war.*

My finger found the window controls. Child-locked. Insulting. A solid piece deep inside me tumbled and whatever part of the car that controlled the child-lock, specifically the metal pieces of it, went *crack.* The window rolled downward.

The iPod and the cut up headphones went out the window. Bastards would probably take them from me anyway. Better to wreck them myself. We were moving too fast down the highway for me to watch them break apart on the road, but I hope it was spectacular. Promise I didn't blow up my toys as a kid, but that one time . . . sometimes you get pushed too far, you got to wreck something.

THE FANGED LADY

If I ever had any doubt that the Central Valley is a shithole, the next half hour of my life cured me of the affliction. Rundown farm equipment, outlet malls, pavement and asphalt, yellow farms that had more weeds than vines in the summer, and cows, lots of cows—with the window down and my face turned away from Ceinwyn Dale I smelled every one of them.

There's something oddly pleasant about the smell of that much cow shit being together. Go figure . . .

We eventually made our way to Fresno, which was low on the cows and heavy on the pavement and asphalt. Ceinwyn Dale pulled the car off the road and into a parking lot.

"Time for breakfast," Ceinwyn Dale announced. I didn't look at her, but she was probably smiling.

Even that defense deserted me once we were sitting at the table in the diner. Nowhere else to look but across that small gap at her face. Smiling lips, smiling eyes. She just ate up the whole situation. She was going to win, but *how* was she going to win? The question of it excited her. She had all the answers to my many questions and we both knew it.

The *how* excited her; the *why* pissed me off. Why Ceinwyn Dale? Why the Institution of Elements? Why me? Why did the *how* excite me too? How did I break that table or that lock? How did Ceinwyn Dale cut my headphones? *How did she get through the door?*

The waitress brought me a kiddy menu on account of my height. I'd never been in a sit down restaurant before. The best I ever managed was sixth grade when my oldest sister—Susanna Belle Price, Mom again—would take me to a bakery before school for pastries and doughnuts, by seventh grade Susan moved away and it was back to cereal because Dad went to work early and Mom was usually passed out on the bed or on the couch. But I still knew it was an insult.

Kiddy menu. Cruel shit.

Ceinwyn Dale started playing with the crayons they'd left for me.

She ordered some raspberry thin pancake woman-watching-her-weight French crap while I engaged the waitress enough to order the most expensive omelet they had, with chopped steak and melted cheese and even sautéed mushrooms piled higher than I could ever eat. My stomach was the biggest part of fourteen-year-old-me. Okay, second biggest part after Prince Henry.

What? Stop sniggering.

This was a Mom-and-Pop kind of diner—they did still exist back then—so the food was long in coming. Fourteen-year-old-me watched the other diners instead of talking to Ceinwyn Dale. Like I said, it was Saturday, which meant quite a few travelers. People driving to Los Angeles. People driving to San Francisco. No one drove to Fresno—it's an in-between place. Some surfers heading to the beach or like Dad, blue collar truckers who never got a day off.

The larcenous spirit deep inside me started eyeing a girl's i*Something* hanging half out of her pocket. Couldn't blame it. Small pocket—fat ass.

"Try stealing anything and I'll give you a papercut on every single finger, you won't be able to touch anything for days." Ceinwyn Dale didn't even glance up. She concentrated on her crayons and the paper in front of her.

"What would you do if I started screaming about how you were trying to kidnap me?" I asked to get back at her.

She wasn't even drawing. No idea *what* she was doing. Using a butter knife, she shaved little piles of crayon onto the paper. Voodoo for all I knew.

"I'm used to sulking and fear and occasionally friendly obedience, defiance is such a nice change of pace, King Henry." Blue crayon changed to yellow. "I'd leave you here."

"You spent three days in Visalia just to leave me? Don't believe it."

"That's it." Yellow to black. "You can walk back to your charming little childhood home and never attend the Institution of Elements." Black back to blue. "Do you think your mother would even notice you came back?" Blue to gray, like she hadn't just ripped my heart out. "And just like her you'd be fine until you neared thirty, then the lack of control and anima saturation would start to drive you insane."

Fat ass girl was totally forgotten. "Mom's a . . . like me?"

THE FANGED LADY

"I'd guess corpusmancer, body manipulation, judging from how little she's fallen into middle age despite the drinking, not to mention such a beautiful body shape despite how much time she spends lounging. Not an Ultra or she'd already be in a mental ward." Gray to green. "But still talented—one of the strongest Intras I've seen. It's regrettable we missed her. For the both of you."

The food came and I was glad for it. It let me ignore what Ceinwyn Dale said and concentrate on my plate. Maybe that's how fat ass girl got a fat ass.

Go insane like Mom . . .

How do you throw that at a fourteen-year-old boy with all the problems I had? I can *barely* handle it now. I *still* get urges to put a fist through a wall, back then she's lucky I didn't break fat ass girl's seat and cause an earthquake from all the jiggle hitting the floor.

When I couldn't eat any more of my omelet, I finally broke from all the ignoring and what I thought was a don't-give-a-shit attitude. "Is this when you turn out to be an evil werewolf that wants to eat me or something? 'Cuz that's some mean shit."

Out of one mind-fuck and into another. "Werewolves are rather pathetic actually. There's very few of them and what do exist are scattered across Wyoming and Montana. Hardly a threat . . ." She smiled at me as she put a delicate piece of crepe into her mouth. *I have the answers, be good and ask the questions instead of getting confrontational.* "Any type of Were isn't much of a threat when alone; it's when their Nation gets large that they become troublesome for mancers in the area. The Coyotes are the largest in the United States, but luckily for us we have a treaty of mutually ignoring each other."

"Coyotes?" Who would want to turn into a piece of crap, cat-stealing coyote? "There's more than one kind?"

Ceinwyn Dale nodded, pulling me into my new world, down the rabbit hole, through the looking glass, second star on the left, strings tight enough to turn me into a wooden puppet boy. "Grizzles in Alaska and Canada. Otters along the Pacific Coast. Jaguars in Mexico. Nothing on the East

Coast worth speaking of, the wild life's been too decimated of large animals, but you do find the occasional sorority that thinks it's cute to dabble in horses or some backwoods people that like badgers or raccoons."

Horses . . . "So . . . what else is there?"

"Vampires," Ceinwyn Dale's eyebrows shot up.

"You're just fucking with me now . . ."

"Such fantasies for such a *little* boy."

"Hey . . ."

"Unlike Weres, they're dangerous . . . if you actually manage to graduate as a four year without getting expelled, then stay away from them. If you're a seven year . . . be extra careful."

Part of me thought she was full of very stinky shit. A part of me bigger than my stomach or Prince Henry combined. "What about fairies?" I tested. Fairies real, yeah right. Tinkerbell this, asshole.

"Corporeal Anima Concentrations. Most last weeks, a few special cases have been around since Elementalism was Codified in 490 B.C. Maybe longer." Mind be blown.

It became a competition to come up with something that was really fake. "What about dwarves, elves, that hobbit shit?"

"All extinct. Dragons as well."

Dragons. Fuck me. *Dragons?* How do you just throw that out in the conversation and go on eating your breakfast? "Centaurs?" I wearily asked.

"Corpusmancer and faunamancer co-experimentation along with minotaurs, griffins, hippocampus, and chimeras. Outlawed in the 27 B.C. Augustus Reforms. You'll learn all about it in your *History of Elementalism* class."

"Aliens?"

"Now you're just being silly, King Henry."

Fairies, dragons, vampires, Were . . . coyotes? *Wereotters. Werehorse sororities!* That put a whole new spin on reverse cowgirl.

The ideas were so big, so outrageous, that my mind kept jumping from one to the other, unable to lock on and digest anything. It made being able to break a table seem small. And it is small. For most of us, even Ultras, the Mancy is about planning ahead, small tricks and little wonders. Breaking a lock, cutting a wire, bending a lamppost. Not going to war on the frontlines. Fourteen-year-old-me would take years to accept that. There were lots of disappointments coming for him, poor little shit.

But then, sitting across from Ceinwyn Dale, maybe reading comics had damaged my poor little brain. Stomach big. Prince Henry big. Brain small. "I broke a table in half the other day. I think I broke the child-lock on your car too."

Ceinwyn Dale finished her breakfast and sipped at some latte coffee drink—ever mancer has their kinks; Ceinwyn Dale is fond of light or whipped food. "Interesting."

My heart—another big body part—thumped heavily in my chest. "Is that . . . good?"

Her eyes smiled again, blue flashes. "It's interesting you asked about the Mancy. Most students from non-elemental families are scared of it and would never admit they used it for mischief. Their first question is usually about the Institution of Elements. The classes, how many children, what the teachers are like, what there is to do on off day, sports, clubs, that sort of thing."

"That's bullshit."

"Is it? Consider that most students also don't have the lifestyle which forces usage like your fighting did. Or that the Mancy is elemental into thirteen disciplines."

"So many . . ."

"I'm an aeromancer," Ceinwyn Dale told me, as if I hadn't figured it out. Okay, maybe not the name, but I knew what she could do. "You're more than likely a geomancer. Earth and metal to stop the question before you ask it. You broke a table . . . a girl in your class you'll meet tomorrow is a pyromancer, a very strong one. Do you know how she found out about the Mancy? A neighbor's dog was barking while she tried to study for a test.

She told it to shut up, only it didn't, and the second time she got mad at it the dog burst into flames. More traumatizing than breaking a table."

"So . . . I feel bad about the dog, but being selfish . . . if I annoy her, she can't make me burst into flames, can she?"

Ceinwyn Dale gave a sharp '*ha!*' for that one. But she didn't bother to answer me. The conversation was over. Back to the road and moving towards the Institution of Elements, wherever it was. Maybe I *should* have started asking questions about the place first.

"Don't forget your picture, King Henry."

Ceinwyn Dale handed me the piece of paper with the crayons. Only the haphazard crayon piles were gone. Fourteen-year-old-me had no clue how she did it, but I know now. The piles were placed, charged with anima to puff out in a dust at the same time. On top of that, a sheet of air is pushed down so the dust coats the paper about as well as any laser printer and with a more aesthetic sheen. Ceinwyn Dale, impressive as always. I've seen other aeromancers do it, my classmate Miranda Daniels among them, but Ceinwyn Dale . . .

The picture had Mom and Dad at the kitchen table; how they'd looked the night they'd spent talking with Ceinwyn Dale about my schooling. Dad looked tired. Mom looked happy. I still have it today. It's in a nice wooden frame that Pocket made for me.

"*Elementalism as Art*, Bi's take it during second year," Ceinwyn Dale told me as I cradled the paper more carefully than I had my broken earbuds. "Your teacher is scheduled to be Rainbow Greenbrier. Very good spectromancer . . . bit of a flower child, though."

[CLICK]

North of Fresno is just as boring as south of Fresno. More cows, less asphalt.

Question and answer session seemed to be over. Typical Ceinwyn Dale: make me fight for something and then refuse to give it up. Testing, always testing and calculating, weighing and measuring. I'm graduated, a grown man, and she's still doing it by having me make this stupid tape.

It's not her fault; it's just the Asylum way. Especially with Ultras. We might be rarer than diamonds, but if one of us is going to snap and let off a suicide tsunami on the Pacific Ocean, then the Asylum needs to know, needs to be prepared. Part Gandalf—part Freud.

Back in that car, fourteen-year-old-me wasn't as forgiving. Ceinwyn Dale had taken me out of my shithole, but she was treating me like seven-day-old dog crap, even if she was treating me like *adult* seven-day-old dog crap.

"So where is this place?" I asked to try to ride the current.

We drove past some more cows. How many hamburgers does America need anyway? "Lake Tahoe, near enough."

One of those 'Ds' was also in geography. "Where's that?"

"California."

"So very fucking helpful."

"Do you want another mouthful of air or your first papercut? Your choice."

"So very helpful, *Miss Dale*. You're the best teacher ever." I probably glared a little bit too. Might have considered flipping her off as well.

"In the mountains, close to Nevada," she explained. "Nevada is the state to the east of California."

"I know that." Got a 'C' on that test. Helena, Montana. Montpelier, Vermont. "How long's it going to take?"

"Few hours."

"Like five hours or like three hours?"

"As many as it takes."

I went back to my collection of comics I'd brought with me. Spider-man and Captain America and the rest of the Marvel Universe lasted me until we got to Sacramento. Big city. No idea if it has more people than Fresno or not, but Fresno is wide and spread out. From the highway, Sacramento has some big buildings. Bigger than any I'd ever seen up until then. It was still in the Valley, so they were probably shithole big buildings, but they were impressive in that big, phallic kind of way men and boys enjoy. Enough that I gave up on the comics. Didn't want to reread them anyway.

"What's the school like?"

Ceinwyn Dale gave me a smiling glance. "Why ask now?"

"You said most kids do, so I figured I should at least know what they know." Even back then, when I wanted to know about something I devoured it. I was only bad at school because it was boring compared to fighting and stealing and five minute grunting and humping sessions. I probably read more than half the kids my age, it just wasn't school books or literary rich-people-with-marriage-problems shit, it was comics and magazines.

"Interesting," she said yet again but didn't answer me.

Rolling down the window to remind her about the child-lock, I threw out the comics to flap behind us as we sped along. I figured by then—and I was right on the money—that the Institution of Elements people were going to take them from me. Maybe the way I did it, some poor homeless guy could burn them for warmth or something. Besides, I liked doing things on my terms. Might not have been broken like the iPod, but it's the same in the end.

"Do you think if I try hard enough that I can break the axle on the car?"

"I know you could. When you're trained, at least."

"Badass."

"The Institution of Elements has sixteen-hundred four-year students at any given time. Plus staff, seven-year Ultra graduates, and teachers, we'll call it an even three-thousand people . . . but it varies, usually much higher." She paused to get my thoughts.

"That's more than I figured."

"There are more Mancers given population numbers, but that's the extent of how many we can handle. Those we can't include eventually go mad. This particular problem is getting worse . . ."

It cut me. "Like Mom."

"Yes. It's hard to lose them, but we can only take the best of what we find and even then we don't find them all. Your mother isn't even in the Institution records as an identified mancer, which means she was missed completely. It happens, even with Ultras . . . which is harder still."

"You keep saying that word."

"I do," she agreed.

Okay . . . "Why keep track of mancers you don't train? You could get them help, I guess . . ."

"Think, King Henry."

"What?"

"About your own situation."

"Oh . . . so you check to see if they have kids who are mancers."

"Correct. See, you *can* use reason."

"Especially these Ultra assholes."

She finally answered me. "An Ultra is a special mancer. *Ultra vires.* Beyond the powers. Rarer. They have abilities and affinities that a normal mancer can never hope to have."

"Badass again . . . Am I one?"

"We'll see."

I was one.

"One in a quart, that's what you meant, that's how rare Ultras are." I *could* use reason.

"Class is in session from September until the last day of July. There is a winter break around Christmas; your mother, however, signed an agreement to see you stay with us all year around." I must have scowled. "Don't blame her; she wants you to get away, to get the training she never did—so she made a sacrifice for the both of you."

"She knows? What she is?"

Ceinwyn Dale frowned for once, the smile dropping off her face. "Let's say she suspects you're special like she is. She doesn't know the rest."

I wiped at my face, turning my head away and changing the subject. "All year . . . for four years at least."

"You aren't the only one. Many exchange students stay. As well as those from poor families. Those that leave for August are usually four-year students from families you'll probably hate anyway."

"But some kids have parents that went to the school, right? They know all this stuff going in."

"Old families exist and, yes, you'll have a number in your class. It isn't genetic, but the Mancy likes to find itself."

"No promises on me not beating them up."

Pretty sure she ignored me. "A school week is Monday to Saturday—"

"Six days!" I yelled.

"—from six in the morning until six at night," Ceinwyn Dale finished with a special smile just for that cruel little fact.

Twelve hours. Fourteen-year-old-me almost threw *himself* out the window.

Yes, twelve hours, five morning classes, three afternoon classes. So much work and pressure. It's named the Asylum for a reason and the teachers and faculty are masters at learning just how far to push us before giving a break. It's difficult . . . but at the same time I occasionally find myself missing the place—and comparing it against a normal high school experience . . . a little crazy is good, ain't it? It better be . . . every mancer is . . . some more than others.

If Ceinwyn Dale really uses this tape for new recruits and that's who you are listening to me . . . don't worry, if I survived, you'll survive. God damn it . . . Why the fuck am I doing this? Fucking Plutarch . . .

[CLICK]

We didn't stop our trip until we were up in the mountains. I didn't know it at the time, but Ceinwyn Dale took a roundabout way to the Asylum. Who knows why? Perhaps she liked the view or, looking back on it, she could have decided I needed the extra day with her to accept the changes I was about to go through.

We took the long way and I passed the mountains that would become my home for seven years. Ceinwyn Dale might not have wanted fourteen-year-old-me to get ahead of himself, but I'm as Ultra as you get. And what better place to teach a geomancer than surrounded by all that good soil and granite, hills and peaks flowing with minerals?

We had a late lunch at one of the most beautiful places I've ever seen. Picking up burgers and fries from another Mom-and-Pop shack by the road we'd used as a restroom stop, Ceinwyn Dale held back until we found a lake, where we parked and ate right near the miniature, wind-borne waves. Silver Lake, a little hidden treasure that reflects blue sky and is surrounded by green fields. It's quiet, peaceful. It was so enchanting I barely even tasted the burger. There's not even much traffic, just the occasional car when you forget the road exists a few yards away from you.

I grew up in a city. Noise is what I'm used to. Silence was different.

"Badass," I whispered.

Ceinwyn Dale smiled a bit more than usual. "Sometimes a water *fairy* forms at the bottom of it."

"Really?"

She nodded, crumpling her wrapper and tucking it away in a plastic bag she'd brought along. "Most lakes form one from time to time. Tahoe has a number that jockey for the favored spots . . . some live for years. A great deal of anima has collected there . . . time and nature will do that."

"Anima? You've said that before too."

She took my wrappers away from me and added them to the bag. With my hands free, I dug through my pocket, found my packet, and I lit up a cigarette. Blessed relief.

Ceinwyn Dale looked out over the lake, ignoring my puffing. "Think of anima as a power source with thirteen colors. Both in nature and inside of humans. When you use the Mancy, it's from you focusing anima within you and then letting it out on the world. Legend says that the *elves*—before they died—tapped into the natural world . . . but we can't. Only what's inside of humanity. We can store it in items called artifacts for specific uses, but we can't pull it from other places. As you train, you'll learn to feel it inside of you and to control it and then use it with meaning instead of on instinct."

"So, the Force meets some crazy Japanese Anime?"

"Something like that . . . just remember: it's easier to imagine something happening than to actually do it."

A flock of ducks circled the lake. First time I'd ever seen a duck in the wild. I remember watching them skim the water and go back up, only to do it again. They weren't fishing, hell if I knew what they were doing though. Maybe it was futile avoidance of a predator that's not there. I like futility.

I took a long drag, a bit full of myself. "I broke the child-lock just fine. Didn't seem that hard."

"Wasn't it?"

"I did it the moment I knew you had me locked up like a kid," I muttered around the cigarette, the smoldering end swaying.

"Did you?"

"Are you trying to piss me off again? I stopped the *'fuck you, bitch'* stuff, but I can go back to it if you want."

"Think about it, King Henry. When did you first want to break something?"

I thought about it. "Oh . . ."

"Yes." Ceinwyn Dale wasn't watching the ducks, but the clouds. Winddancer, that's what aeromancer Ultras are called. I've never found out if they can actually fly or not. But Ceinwyn Dale's expression said she thought about trying it over the lake that day. "Not as easy now, is it?"

The ducks landed, flapping water all over themselves with their wings and making little quacks. Even animals only have so much room for futility. "I got mad when the music stopped."

"Yes," she repeated.

"But that was like five minutes before I broke the child-lock."

"Correct." Ceinwyn Dale reached out to touch my shoulder, forgetting the clouds. "What we do isn't easy. It might get easier, but it will always take effort. Five minutes for one little tiny child-lock. You have to fight for it."

"For what?"

"That . . . is the wisest question you've asked."

THE FANGED LADY

Her phone rang. Damn good reception, I must say. Wonder what plan she was on . . . She answered it and I listened in, since I'm pretty nosy to begin with and every word Ceinwyn Dale spoke was gospel at that point in my life.

"Dale . . . Yes, I have him . . . yes, like I expected . . . I'd put money on it." A '*ha!*' "Tomorrow . . . he's rough but smart . . . Any problems? He's a Welf, it's expected . . . did the Mabanaagan girl arrive yet? Good . . . and Reti? Very good. You're doing fine, Russell, stop hyperventilating . . . she's a Firestarter, deal with it . . . well, keep her calm, once she learns control in a few months you can put away the extinguisher . . . I know you're busy. I know four-hundred new students. I owe you one . . . I need to go, tell the Lady she can come for breakfast tomorrow and meet him. Yes, Russell . . ."

He was still talking when she hung up.

"My girlfriend would never shut up either," I said.

Ceinwyn Dale's smile got a bit frosty. "That was Russell Quilt; he'll be testing you for placement tomorrow."

"So you think I'm smart, huh?" I teased her.

"I couldn't say you are a thief, vulgar, barely look like you're twelve, have a problem with authority, and represent the worst aspects of the Scots-Irish borderman American after I spent this time finding you, could I?"

"Ouch . . . well, at least I'm a smart thief . . ."

"Get in the car, King Henry."

I did.

Heading deeper into the mountains for a swing around Carson City, Nevada and towards the Institution of Elements, it would take us a few more hours to get there. Ceinwyn Dale and I didn't talk much for the next hour.

I was pretty shocked when she up and stabbed me in the neck with a giant needle.

"You fucking bitch!" Yeah, probably predictable.

"Sorry, King Henry. It's a policy to keep you from finding the school until you're graduated. Most come inside of buses where they can't see outside," Ceinwyn Dale explained, acting like it wasn't a big deal.

"You fucking bitch! You just stabbed me with a giant needle!"

"Go to sleep, King Henry."

I did. I didn't have much choice. Can't blame her though. I keep telling you, fourteen-year-old-me was a little shit. But he was a *smart* little shit. Ceinwyn Dale said so.

THE FANGED LADY

Session 107

IT'S A DAMN SHAME THAT I've made it to twenty-two and still haven't broken a car axle. And the sad fact is: I wasn't going to that night either.

I woke up in a trunk. Which ain't exactly the place you want to be when you're enduring a car crash. Car companies don't design around protecting grocery bags, they design around protecting the driver. If I'd broken the axle, King Henry Price would have been smashed into King Henry Pulp.

These thoughts came long after I realized where I was. At first . . . it was pathetic. I went from unconscious to conscious with a whimper, a slow rise from the dark of sleep into a different dark. My eyes opened to nothing. Sight was no use to me. Car companies also don't care if your grocery bags can see.

Feel worked best to reorient me. First my body. The pains where Annie B had punched and kicked and thrown me. My back ached down the entire length of my spine. I was on my side, thrown in like a test dummy, no care taken for how I was lying or what would happen to my muscles if I stayed in a cramped position until I woke.

I let out a breath, eyes adjusting some more but revealing only more dark. Underneath me, I felt the soft vibration of highway driving—that straight ahead, no stoplight speed. My hands reached up to run along the unforgiving metal of a trunk top and my feet banged against the sides. Being short worked to my advantage, keeping me from being cramped into a vice.

I could just barely move if I pulled my body in tight. Shift to one side, shift to the other side. Feeling my prison.

My neck and throat hurt the worst of anything. I'd been choked out by super-condensed blood formed into a noose. That took a special kind of idiot. My own Cold Cuffs had probably even helped her do it.

Cold Cuffs, I thought with a sudden spike of realization.

My hands went from pushing against the metal of my prison to feeling my person. Jeans, shirt, and my geomancer coat were still on me. Static ring—gone . . . *shit*. The cuffs too. *Double shit . . .*

I felt my pockets, found my wallet with the same contents I always had: about forty dollars in cash, my California ID, my mancer ID, and the key to my motorcycle . . . which was probably getting stolen outside of my shop right about now.

My other jean pocket was empty, like it always was. But in my coat pocket I found the anima vial T-Bone donated earlier in the day. Pulling it out, I ran my hands over it. *Triple shit.*

Oh, I could use it as a weapon. Not like an electromancer could, shaping the bolt into something lethal, but I could break the seal and unleash pure anima into the bitch, which would be the anima burn to end all anima burns. Wouldn't kill her, but it might buy me the time to escape. Only . . . the vial was worth about five-thousand dollars. I had a hard time convincing myself my life is worth five-thousand dollars. The poor kid with the hand-me-downs didn't like it.

In the darkness, I had time to let my brain work. I had time to let the lateral thinking come out. In the near-silence, I outlined my plan of attack. Inside my body, I built anima. Best of all, I had time to remember what my teachers taught me about vampires.

[CLICK]

Hello, a bit of out-of-character here with some information from the old and experienced King Henry, not the idiot in the trunk who's been kidnapped.

THE FANGED LADY

Just about when I entered into the Asylum in late 2009 there was a vampire fad hitting the United States at full tilt. Vampires were everywhere and in everything. Movies, comics, literature, television shows. Everyone wanted stories about vampires and every kind of vampire too. You got your regular, everyday vampire myths thrown into this whirlwind: fangs, silver, garlic, daylight—all the classic bits of weaknesses and strengths. But the most popular of the fad was vampires who could go out in the day . . . that *sparkled* in the sun.

Good vampires.

The first thing Fines Samson told my class when we started studying them was to throw all the bullshit we thought we knew in the garbage, that's essentially what our concept of a vampire was worth. My first fight with Anne proves this to be true. I knew better, I'd been told they weren't the boogeyman I expected, and I still got beat up.

To get his point across, the first book Samson had us read on vampires didn't have a thing to do with them. It was Marco Polo, the famous explorer, and his account of his travels. He also told us the story of the Kingdom of Prester John. Samson got his point across fast: people love to make stories up. I'd also add that even more people love to believe in the make-believe. Fangs, silver, garlic, and daylight . . . it's all made up to enchant us with its exotic flare. Only two of these myths even have a basis in reality. As far as the sparkly *good vampires* . . . did Anne seem very sparkly to you?

What a vampire really is . . . is a creature of blood living inside a human body. Think of them as a hermit crab with a shell. It's the best analogy I have for you. The body is just the shell, the actual vampire, the actual creature, is the blood inside the shell, flowing all throughout the human circulatory system. Their strength is that they can control the body to levels humans can't. They can heal wounds, they can speed up the heart, they can rebuild bones so their fibers are stronger than some metals. You realize the advantage? A vampire is a lethal creature.

Since they're nothing but blood, they like the cold. Which is where the partial myth of sunlight comes into play. They don't mind sunlight, what they don't like is *heat*. They're like supercomputers running on human hearts. The hotter it gets, the slower the beat. They like the cold. Which is why Fresno during the winter is such a big hunting ground for them. Nice and cool but not too cold. After all, blood needs to be fluid to flow. There's a small range of temperature where a vampire can function at one-hundred percent efficiency. This makes them move around a lot chasing temperatures.

The other myth which has some truth to it is silver. Not that silver hurts the vampire—notice Anne's choker is silver and her neck ain't being burnt in half—but that vampires will often keep silver knives on their person when they feed. Vamps don't really have fangs, so what they'll do is a slice job on themselves and then a slice job on their victim and there is the opening they need to slide into.

This is about to get even grosser than it already was. They don't drink the blood with their mouths. To use another sea example, like a starfish, they extend themselves out of their shell and enter into your body to digest your blood there.

It gets grosser. People threw up during this class, trust me. Big tough Jason Jackson was spewing all over the place when the slideshow started. Fines Samson wanted to get his point across. Sea examples continue to be what works best for them, since they're really nothing but a blood amoeba. Besides exiting their shell to feed, as they get older they learn to multiply, and the way they do this is to drain a victim of the majority of their blood, causing death, then they spread themselves between the two shells and split in two. Just like a simple cell.

The original half goes back into the old shell, same memories as it had before. The new half crawls into its new body and races up into the brain, digesting memories in some way I've never had an accurate explanation given, but apparently it happens. Thus awakens a new vampire, with the memories and thoughts of the human prey, even the name of the human prey, with all those defenses built in and prepared in seconds. For a time, they struggle with not being human, but they ain't, trust me. They're vampires. The body is just a shell to live in, don't be fooled otherwise. They don't sparkle. But they will kill you and then wear what you leave behind, so nice and comfy.

How do you kill one? Stake it through the heart, then burn the body. The only myth that's right on the money. Stop the heart and then the majority of vampires can't function for long. They're trapped, unable to mount any defense as you find the kerosene to toast their shell. The older ones start to do like Anne did. They learn to exist outside their shell. But with the heart down, most are finished.

You have to stab them through the heart . . . it's the only sure way.

Back to the idiot in the car trunk.

[CLICK]

I drowsed in the trunk for probably an hour . . . time is strange in the dark. It can be longer or shorter than you think. You're left with guessing. With nothing but yourself for your reckoning and as we all know: humans are shit at dealing with their own reckonings. Maybe meditate is a word for what I did, but I'm not very Buddha. What I did is pool anima to levels I'd never even bothered to try before.

At the Asylum, they teach you to look ahead, pool what you're going to need, and then use it. Don't hold on, *especially* don't try to see how big you can go. They never said why. Just looks and '*it's dangerous.*' Which, maybe it is. Anima saturation is what drove my mother mad. It's driven more than her mad and killed a great many people too. Maybe pooling big speeds it all up, starts to affect a normal mancer too.

The Asylum is more concerned about control than power. Ultras know they can pool faster and longer and probably more than an Intra, but we never get the chance. We were trained in one-minute and five-minute pools, nothing more. We were trained in the number of five-minute pools we could make in a row: pooling, using the anima on a conjuration, and then pooling

93

again. The amount of consecutive pools varied per person and we took it as our *power* levels. More than once, I wondered if it wasn't one big scam to sidetrack us from the real game. But I never looked into it.

Not until my life was on the line.

Not until that car trunk.

I pooled for an hour straight.

Forget the axle. I could have cracked the car in half.

That much anima is euphoric. A beast of its own making, like some kind of hurricane that's gotten so big it builds on itself. I didn't want to move. I wanted to sit in the warm water and get bigger. I didn't want to open my eyes more than slits, despite that they saw nothing. Seeing nothing was too much for me.

This is some of what Mom felt, I remember thinking. *This is what it feels like to be saturated with anima.* To be a walking, talking anima vial.

One hour and I could have held more, but I stopped myself. An iron will of restraint, believe me. Stopping in the middle of sex. Putting a candy bar down halfway through. Just one chip. Smelling coffee, but not drinking it. Not clicking a link on Wikipedia.

One hour of anima . . . I had trouble conceptualizing the amount. Sixty minutes divided by five . . . okay, twelve five-minute pools. All lumped together.

Fuck me. I was going to cause an earthquake.

No wonder the Asylum staff didn't want us trying this. I'd always wondered if the bastards weren't downplaying what we could do, always wondered about how easy it seemed for Ceinwyn or the Lady to do some of the things they did. Trick after trick after trick. Now I got it. A five-minute pool compared to what I was holding ain't nothing. It made a five-minute pool seem smaller than it had ever felt before.

And I could have pooled more.

It's a damned secret, I thought in the darkness. Another damned secret just like all of them before it. A secret any Ultra can do, they just have to be in on the game. There's nothing over the mountains, kiddies. Yes there was . .

. the world was over the mountains. Only if an Ultra had a normal life with a normal job, or at least a *normal-ish* job, why would they ever need to pool more than five minutes? They wouldn't. So the Asylum teachers didn't train us beyond that amount. They pretended like doing it would hurt you. Maybe it would eventually. But it wasn't a straight up *cross the line and blow yourself up* kind of deal. Maybe if I kept pooling like this I'd turn into Mom. Maybe not. A secret . . . a secret well-hidden out in the open. I didn't have a normal life or a normal job and it *still* took a vamp kidnapping me to get to this point.

"Fuck me sideways," I said just to feel the magnitude of it.

My eyes opened in surprise. *What else could I do?*

"Fuck me sideways with a shovel-wielding pelican."

The car slowed down, turned off the highway, drove and stopped, drove and stopped, turned, drove and stopped, turned again and stopped. I didn't have anything else to study our movement, so I paid a great deal of attention to those simple changes.

The car's engine shut off.

Showtime.

A door opened and shut.

Steps walking off.

Nothing for awhile.

Off in the distance, I heard a road. I thought about shattering the trunk door and escaping, but decided against it. I had an hour of anima and I wanted to smash Annie B's face with it after she'd strangled me *with her blood*.

Escape wasn't good enough. I needed to figure out what this was about. How did she find out about me? What did the person get out of telling her? Did anyone else plan on using me? Was dealing with Vamps going to keep happening or was it a one-time deal? The kind of questions most job applicants figure out over coffee, for me would be done only if she was tied up and I had a gun to her head. A gun might not even be enough . . .

The footsteps eventually came back, stopping by the trunk of the car where I eagerly awaited with my can of whoop-ass.

"Are you awake, King Henry?" Annie B asked the trunk.

I thought about it. *Why not?* "No . . ."

"This is going to go two ways," she said with a tone so sure of itself I just wanted to punch her . . . again, "Either I'll open the trunk and you'll attack me, probably using the anima you have stored up. Only that one conjuration won't do enough to kill me, it will only hurt me, and then I'll be *mad*. I'll take it out on you by beating you unconscious yet again. Once you're unconscious, I'll drag you into the motel room I've just purchased and have myself a snack . . . and I don't mean something out of the mini-bar . . . I mean something out of your mini-body."

"No liking that one," I yelled.

"In the other possible outcome: I still open the trunk . . . but you don't attack me. You get out and we walk over to the motel room and we *negotiate* an exchange of services."

I'd never met a woman who could make me turn down sexual advances so easily. "Why do I get the feeling these services involve me getting cut by a silver knife?"

"It doesn't hurt, King Henry."

If anyone ever tells you something doesn't hurt—tighten your asshole. "Guess you open the trunk and we see what we see, Annie B."

Click.

It was automatic. Slow rising. Just this graceful movement as the trunk rose up free of any hand. God damned technology. I'd hoped she'd open it by hand and be right there for me to kick in the face.

The street lights outside burned my eyes, reflecting over the gray of the fog. We weren't in Fresno, so it wasn't the Fog, but we were still in the Central Valley, and the whole Valley could be covered as well some nights, though not to the extremes I'd learned to live with. Fog and the lights made the world a hazy reflection of silver.

There was a building—the motel. Annie B was nocturnal, all vampires were. Sunlight didn't boil them, but it doesn't mean they liked it compared against the chilled darkness of night. I had trouble convincing myself she'd stopped so I could get a nap in. Bitch was hungry and I'm handy. Negotiating . . . like I'd let her just slip into my body and suck on me for a piece of ass, even a quality piece of ass like her own.

I rolled out of the trunk, found my feet. They were shaky. I took a breath to settle myself, then glanced around to find her leaning against the driver-side door. Her body and head were against the metal, like a reptile sunning on a rock, only in this case she enjoyed the cold, especially the drops of dew from where the fog had left behind moisture.

"I was always able to seduce you, my dear king," she whispered to me. The look on her face had a fair chance of bringing me to climax without her even touching me.

Why did this chick have to be a vampire? And a crazy vampire? Just my luck. Beautiful chick . . . fucking crazy. Story of my life. "Cut the crap, lady," I told her, "You ain't Anne Boleyn. I ain't buying it."

Her tongue reached out to lick a particular large drop of water. I've changed my two features theory just for Annie B. Neck, eyes, and tongue. That tongue has to be included in the party . . . "I suppose I'm not," she said.

"What's the B stand for then?" I asked.

My legs were starting to feel stronger. Any minute now.

She didn't answer right away. Her velvet eyes just kept looking at me, daring me to jump into them for a swim, to reach and see how deep they went.

"I'm sorry I have to do this," she finally said. "We don't have time for me to find another."

Yup, bitch was going to eat me alright. "Find your inner anorexic and go without."

"I've been too busy to eat the last few days." She rolled over, pulling her shirt up just enough so her back pressed against the metal. "When we get hungry, it gets harder to stay cool. Like an engine without oil. I should have made it back to San Francisco for a donor, but you were more trouble than I expected." She rolled over to her stomach. "It took too much out of me.

I'm old enough to manipulate my blood, but not old enough to do it without wearing myself out. Sorry . . . it has to be you . . ."

"Well . . ." I said. "I guess I'm sorry too then. You're okay for a crazy lady, but I have a rule that only I get to put foreign objects into my own body."

An hour worth of anima snapped out of me in a torrent. A dam burst. There was no stopper to it. No way to let some out and then more later. One go. So much I could only control a piece, not even a half of it. The rest escaped, filled the air, found the ground and sunk. The wall behind us cracked. A street sign across the parking lot bent like rubber. A car's window broke.

Annie B took them all in. "That was a waste, wasn't it?"

Only I had more than enough left for myself. To do what I wanted. Anything I wanted. Only requirement was to be earth or metal or glass and was limited to what my imagination could come up with. The way she leaned against the car . . .

The idea formed.

Oh, baby.

I flipped the car over and smashed her ass flat like she was a Wicked Witch of the East and I'm Dorothy with some pretty little red shoes.

It wasn't the car itself I moved. I'm not Magneto. A geomancer can't make metal float, it can only manipulate its form. What I manipulated was the ground around Annie B. A huge circle of it. Some scientist watching over a seismograph noticed a very local, very large seismic shift. One strong enough to twist the ground. To sink the car's right tires and pop the car's left tires on over—center of mass doing the rest of the work. So much force that the car got air, turned and slammed roof first into the ground, flattening the vampire who happened to be rubbing against it like it might . . . *vibrate.*

All I could see from where I stood was her hand, poking from under the caved in roof. Her fingers twitched. I remember the glass from the windshield scattered all around it, the asphalt ground tilted. What was strangest was the silence. After that one crunching boom, there was nothing else. Just the sound of the highway not too far away.

The parking lot was deserted. The front office of a motel renting rooms by the hour is paid to look the other way. The louder it got, the farther their neck turned. All that noise for just me . . . and Annie B locked up all nice under a ton of metal.

She's lucky I wasn't in any position to start pooling again. I could have crunched the whole thing flat. The much talked about Hammer of God entering reality. *Could have*, because I couldn't. I was drained. It was like I'd run a mile for the first time in my life and was then asked by some personal trainer to do jumping jacks. *Could have*, because I couldn't even do one measly jumping jack.

I was a gutted mancer. I'd gone anima slut. Who knew when I would tighten back up?

Good thing Annie B wasn't going anywhere.

"Much like your piece-of-shit foreign car," I said, noting it was Japanese, "It seems the tables have turned. Or one might say . . . *flipped*." Got to give it to Annie B. Her hand flipped me the bird. That was cute. Woman knows how to work from the bottom. "How about we start with you telling me what city we're in?"

"And what will you do if I don't, King Henry?" Her voice sounded unsurprisingly like she was having trouble getting air into her lungs. They came fast and weak. Not in pain though. Cool vampire fact: they can turn off pain receptors.

"I have a vial of electro-anima you didn't notice in my coat pocket." I took out said vial and tossed it end-over-end in my palm. "Figured I'll open it into your hand and see what happens."

"We're in Los Banos," she answered quickly.

"That's more like it." Los Banos is a shithole of epic proportions between Fresno and San Francisco. I've yet to figure out why anyone not running a fast-food shop or hotel would want to live there. "Now . . . why did you kidnap me?"

"It's a long story . . ." Annie B whispered.

The car shifted. For a moment I thought she might try to lift it, but it settled back down. Her hand hadn't moved. "You ain't trying to escape, are you? If you ain't escaping, it looks like we have some time to ruminate." Learned that one at the Asylum. Always liked it. *Ruminate*. Good word.

Her voice came from somewhere under the car, from lips I hoped were pressed against concrete, each word scratching them raw. Being kidnapped had brought a surprisingly sadistic streak out in my usual abrasive personality. "An artifact placed in our keep has been stolen. I need you to confirm the artifact's ability based on the anima it left in its safe."

"It's leaking anima?" I asked, unable to help myself.

"Yes."

"Enough to saturate the area and not burn off?"

"Yes," this time weaker.

I thought about it. That's something I wanted to see. "It's not going corporeal is it?"

"We don't believe so. Sorry about the lack of details, but the geomancer I used first wasn't worth his weight in blood."

She should have told me this crap before she tried to kidnap me. Would have saved us a lot of time. I said as much. "Why the hell didn't you tell me this before?"

"I was asked not to . . . Can you get this car off me?"

"No . . . I can't pool for nothing right now." Which was probably stupid to say. "I'll call a tow-truck and then you can get loose and he'll be your snack, what you say?"

No answer.

"Annie B?" My foot touched her hand. It slapped at me. *Okay*. "Who told you I was available for this?"

"An old friend," the barest whisper.

I had a sinking suspicion. Plutarch, Ceinwyn, or the Lady. Who would screw with me first and foremost just to see what would happen? "Fucking Ceinwyn do this to me?"

THE FANGED LADY

No answer.

I touched the hand yet again with my foot. It touched back. "You okay?" I asked again.

"I'm fine, King Henry."

This didn't come from the car.

This came right behind me.

Like a dumbass, I turned around. Give me a break. I was in shock or something. Annie B was standing there, her right arm missing from the elbow down. It wasn't like seeing an amputee with folded over skin. The cut was open. Muscle, bone, all easy to *see*, a clean cut, only all covered with a layer a gooey vampire blood. Like I told you: starfish, amoeba, a sea-creature, nothing human.

Her punch into my stunned face hit me so hard my legs went out from underneath me for the third time that night. My plump booty hit asphalt too.

Annie B looked down on me with an expression that said, '*bad food.*' "Ceinwyn says hello, King Henry," she told me. Then she smashed her foot into my balls so hard I blacked out.

Stay away from the vampires, King Henry. Don't cause problems, King Henry. No fighting, King Henry.

Always bullshit with that woman.

[CLICK]

I woke up lightheaded. There was water running. I was in a bed. I knew from the sound of the springs as I moved my head back and forth to check out the room. The only light came from a table-lamp that had seen better days. Actually . . . the things the table-lamp had seen are probably what made it look so haggard.

I stayed there in my haze. Bitch had eaten me. I could feel it in the lost blood, the kind of woozy dreamlike state where you're barely aware the world exists. Weirdest part was . . . my hand felt numb. I pulled it up with my other, since it didn't feel like working very well either, and was unsurprised to find a Band-Aid slapped over a cut, blood crusting around my palm.

Bitch had eaten me.

And then used a *Carebears* Band-Aid.

That's some cruel and unusual punishment right there . . .

The shower went off. A hiss to a drizzle to nothing.

Barely awake, I couldn't help but feel betrayed over Ceinwyn apparently hiring me out to this crazy bitch. I mean, I owed her money, and never let anyone tell you Ceinwyn Dale ain't a hardass, but this was a step too far even for her. Why did I deserve getting eaten? Or getting knocked out? Why give *my* name?

Unless it was because she trusted me to do something . . .

Unless it was because she didn't trust anyone else with this item . . .

Unless she was trying to teach me some kind of lesson which only getting surprised by a vamp could bring . . .

And here I thought my school time was over.

Annie B stepped out of the bathroom, still mostly undressed. All she had on was a pair of black underwear that showed more than they covered. Any other woman stepping out of a bathroom and I'd have been ogling her body. Hips that knew the word '*hourglass*,' a stomach so tight it defied anatomy, and a pair of tits at just the right size before too-large, that didn't know the word '*gravity*' and had never experienced it. And shoulder-bones and a hint of collar bone, and a neck that went on and on, and lips twisting in enjoyment as I studied her, and eyes that whispered what I could have had but had turned down.

I didn't ogle at all this amazing physicality that naturally defeated any plastic surgeon alive because my eyes couldn't leave her right arm, back where it *hadn't* been earlier. It wasn't even bruised.

"Is it the same one, or do you grow a new one like a lizard?" I asked.

Annie B laughed. With a shake of her head, she ran her hands through her hair. Water dripped from it to the floor. Without the help of a towel, it dried in seconds. She kept at it, bending over to arch her back towards me, showing me the other side of the moon. She looked better from that angle . . . I think . . . it's hard to decide . . . I'm a big fan of both . . .

"It's the same one," she finally answered about the arm.

"Huh," was my expert opinion.

Her hair dry, she stood straight and finally got about clothing herself. New clothes. A pair of shorts and one of those airy looking half-dress, half-shirt things most girls wear during the summer with another top beneath it. I don't know the name for it. I remember it was violet though. January and she was dressing for July. A slutty no-bra, no-undershirt July too. It looked cold. Douchebag showoff vampires.

"Do you go naked in the summer then?"

It was too easy for her. With a straightforward look-you-in-the-eyes glance on her face, she told me, "I go naked whenever I possibly can, King Henry."

"Huh," was my continued expert opinion.

Give me a break, guys. She could have stripped naked and dry humped me, it wouldn't have mattered. I didn't have the blood in me to walk without feeling woozy, Prince Henry popping a stiffy would have knocked my ass back out quicker than an eighty-year-old geezer downing handfuls of Viagra.

Annie B continued with the freaky, putting her hands through her hair and styling it like she had globs of styling junk. Only there was nothing. The hair knew what she wanted and stayed exactly where she put it. Retaining the exact amount of fluid to keep the position. Douchebag showoff vampires. A press of finger at her lips and cheeks rushed in blood, completing the look without a single bit of makeup.

When she moved to put her heels on, I decided it was time to talk. My head was starting to feel better and I knew I didn't want to leave that room without an understanding between us of what's cool and what's *not cool*. "Why didn't you just tell me Ceinwyn sent you?"

Her heels looked sharp. I reminded myself I didn't want to get kicked again that night. "Ceinwyn didn't send me. I informed Ceinwyn about my problem and then she mentioned you might be helpful. She seemed to think you could handle yourself, but I decided I'd test you out."

"I'm going to guess I passed since I'm alive."

"Yes, you passed." Annie B walked over to me and sat on the bed. "You passed after the first fight. I was going to bring you here and we were going to play a bit and then I was going to tell you everything I needed from you. From your reputation and a joke of Ceinwyn's I never thought you would turn down a little tumble. The second fight was very naughty, King Henry."

"So you thought that since you have the best ass I've ever seen," I figured, "you'd just wiggle it and I'd do whatever you wanted?"

She licked her lips again. "Something like that."

"Did you tell this idea to Ceinwyn?" I asked.

"Yes . . . she seemed to think there was a chance it could work."

I started laughing. Ceinwyn Dale. Still testing me. Still seeing which way I jumped. And not just me either. "You got taken, Annie B."

Her tongue disappeared. Her lips went straight. "She knew you well?"

"Yeah, she knows me as well as anyone does."

"She used us to test each other," she thought aloud.

"Yeah, like that."

I'd seen the look that came over Annie B's face before. Usually I was the one wearing it when Ceinwyn screwed with me. "I'm almost five-hundred years old and she treats me like a toy," she said in a hiss.

"Only twenty-two, but yeah . . . feeling ya."

She studied me. "Will you still help me?"

There's an interesting question. As I ruminated, already knowing the answer, I couldn't help but feel the irony that it wouldn't be my dick getting me into trouble with this gorgeous creature, but my brain. "It's really leaking anima?" I asked.

"We believe so. We, however, only have a simple geomancer in our service."

I ruminated about it some more. My brain's going to get me killed one day. "And you're paying me?"

"Of course."

"And you won't eat me again?"

For the first time since she'd come into my shop and my life, Annie B seemed embarrassed. "I'm sorry our misunderstanding led to your blood being required," she mouthed out, like it was a great difficulty. I suppose it was. Not like I told pigs sorry before I ate bacon. If I told bacon anything it was, *'you're so yummy! Yes, you are!'*

"Well . . . I guess dropping a car on you was a bit much . . ."

"A bit shocking, yes," she agreed. "So was the ring."

"I want it back," I told her.

"Of course."

"And my vial of anima."

"It as well."

"And the Cold Cuffs."

With a perfectly innocent face she said, "I don't know what you're talking about."

RICHARD RALEY

THE FANGED LADY

Session 4

I WOKE UP IN EASILY the most comfortable bed I had slept in at that point in my fourteen-year-old life. You know what . . . check that, the bed is still the most comfortable I've ever slept in. It was missing the embrace of a beautiful and hopefully naked woman, plus the musk of ten hours of raging grunting and humping sessions, but we won't hold it against the bed. That's not the bed's fault. So most comfortable ever, created by expense and a lack of use most likely. Ceinwyn Dale's guestroom bed.

Yeah, that's where I was. Took me awhile to realize it.

First, I had to remember the day before ending with the giant needle into my neck. That wasn't very damned pleasurable. Here's free advice, children: bring up the blindfold before the needle comes into play, because once the needle comes into play the bastard is entering your body and it's not going in the fun places people generally like to get poked.

I sat myself up to have a look-see. Some say you can take a look at what a person's home has in it and say what they're like. I don't know if that's true. Probably bullshit like all the rest. If a person's poor, they're going to have poor shit. If a person's rich, they're going to have rich shit. What the fuck does that have to do with personality?

Ceinwyn Dale's guestroom is clean, wood floors and soft rugs. Blues and whites . . . very—airy, as it were. There were pictures too. Made the same way she had made my little one of Mom and Dad. Mountains and villages, town houses, shanties by the sea. Tons of tiny little pictures taking up the walls. Small looking large by being all together.

Ceinwyn Dale is the Head of Recruiting for the Asylum, she's flown throughout the world and back again. *How many late arrivals have woken up in the bed just like I did?* I ask myself, looking back on it.

Most kids, it's easy. Parents are mancers or someone in the family is—there are whole computers dedicated to family trees somewhere in the administration offices, in the vain attempt to figure out *why* one family member is a mancer and another ain't. Others . . . mancers keep an eye out around their neighbors. Little Val caught the dog on fire. Cousin Heinrich talks to his dead grandfather. That kind of thing.

Another common way is for countries friendly to the United States, without schools of their own, to offer up an exchange student for cash. Sure, Europe has had a school of their own for almost as long as the Asylum has been around, so do the old USSR countries and China. Ottoman Empire used to have one, the Papacy too. India had built one, and Brazil was working on it by the time I got recruited—think they just finished it actually. But if you're from shithole Nigeria or equally shithole Mexico like two of my classmates were? Ceinwyn Dale is going to be the one to bring you to the Asylum.

Sometimes it ain't even shithole countries, it's just population problems. Ratio breeds true as they say—they got computers for it too. Do the math. You got seven million people in your country . . . this means you got twenty-seven Ultras, one born every three years we'll assume. You got yourself a fourteen-year-old sciomancer from Israel and no sciomancer to train her; you can either ship her to one of the schools or let her go insane. What do you do? A sciomancer . . . especially a Shadeshifter, that's a valuable tool to let rust. For Eva Reti, you have a meeting with a smiling blond lady and your family magically gains a Unites States visa for seven years.

Immigration, Ceinwyn Dale's biggest weapon.

As for how I was found . . . let's just say I made a lot of noise. When hasn't that been true of my life?

THE FANGED LADY

I woke up pissed that day. I'd been drugged and hadn't been drugged enough. No cigarettes by the bedside. No cigarettes in the room. I'd had one smoke the day before, below my average as it was, and no more were in sight for the new day dawned. None of my stuff was in sight. So I woke up pissed off. More than usual.

Not a good thing for me or anyone I was going to meet that day—especially Heinrich Welf, but we'll get to that Nazi asshole later.

The pictures followed me into the hallway. Kids. Tons of them. One after another, smiling or glaring, it didn't matter—black, yellow, red, one punk girl with green hair, every color under the sun and some so white it looked like they went without it, all of them watching the hesitant, exploring steps I took.

My feet were bare on the wood. Someone had changed my clothes, which I tried to pretend was a purely magical transformation and not Ceinwyn Dale stripping me naked. Gone were jeans and t-shirt. Instead I was in some kind of uniform. I knew it was coming, but I still hated it, even though it was probably more comfortable than a uniform has a right to be.

Long legs, some undershirt, and a coat. Fucking coat in the summer. Even in the mountains, that's an unusually cruel. We were always hot during the summers at the Asylum, save for the cryomancers. You know, all these years wondering about it and I think I finally just figured out what Welf saw in Hope Hunting. Must have cooled him off like a popsicle.

Popping the coat buttons open and pulling the shirt loose from its tuck into my pants was the first gesture of rebellion I took directly against the Asylum and not against Ceinwyn Dale. Rebel without a cause, my next feat was finding a bathroom to scowl into a mirror. She'd given me a haircut too. Okie-long hair was gone and in its place I had a conformist-trimmed cut. It made me look ten. Like I should be holding my mommy's hand.

As for the uniform, it was a deep brown job. Think fertile soil, not dog crap. Get that mind out the gutter, that's my fucking job. All deep brown, a rich lush fabric. Probably the most expensive thing I'd ever worn up to that point. Lot of records set that day.

There were tags sewn on the front breast. White. One was my name: King Henry Price. Second one was my year: Single. In case you're wondering, years go Single, Bi, Tri, Quad, Pent, Hex, and Hep with a corresponding visual aid. For fourteen-year-old-me it was a lonesome little dot. The third was my class number, blank at the moment. The forth was my Mancy, Ceinwyn Dale had already jumped the gun and added '*Geomancer.*'

Okay, maybe with the coat unbuttoned and the shirt out, the uniform wasn't too bad. Kind of rakish outsider going for it. But the hair, that's bullshit. I'd been growing that piece-of-shit, bangy mullet for years, man! It was redneck cool.

I found her in the kitchen.

Ceinwyn Dale leaned back in a chair, at ease with the world, slim-fingers grasping the stem of a cup probably holding more latte. Robed in some kind of slinky fabric, a long leg was exposed on its way to the floor, but the rest of her stayed hidden. The leg distracted fourteen-year-old-me and I temporarily forgot I was supposed to be mad at her for a good twenty seconds. I didn't know they made those things that long . . .

Sitting down the cup, a flick of Ceinwyn Dale's wrist engulfed the leg back inside her robe, where it hid with the rest of her. Her other hand hadn't left her newspaper—we still had those back then—while her always present smile twitched.

Without looking my way, she commented on my near drooling, "Enjoying a show, King Henry?"

I remembered I was pissed at her. Being made fun of often has a crystallizing effect on my anger, no matter how much I've learned to control it . . . and the amount of that is a truthful not very much even today as a wise and learned graduate of the Asylum. *Wise and learned.* It's on the diploma. "Not as much as you enjoyed the show last night, bitch."

"Are we really back to that, King Henry?"

"You drugged me!"

"School policy."

"With a giant needle!"

THE FANGED LADY

"Would you rather I used a rag dipped in chloroform?"

"You shaved my head down to nothing too."

"You really should thank me if you ever want to find yourself a girlfriend in the next four years." A sip of latte broke up the scold. "We don't allow much at the Institution, but we do allow love to bloom . . . not that much would bloom with the ill-layered mop you called hair. But now . . . maybe a little. Just like the rest of you."

"Whatever, I'm over it. Where are my cigarettes at then?"

"Ah . . . we come to the root of the problem." Her eyes twinkling, she motioned for me to sit at the table with her. I did . . . reluctantly. "Love blooming and maybe even turning our gaze the other way when it comes to love making. However, there's no smoking at this school, even for teachers."

I was already starting to get a headache, my fingers reaching for my pocket where I had always kept my pack. "You've got to be shitting me. I've smoked for like over a year . . ."

"You'll survive, King Henry."

She got up, got me a glass of water, and sat it down in front of me.

"I quit," I said. "I'll walk if I have to."

"Too late. You're enrolled. Four years at least. Testing later today, then you'll meet your classmates. It should be exciting for you. No fighting though, we don't allow it either."

Behind me on the wall, a piece of new-aged metal artwork shattered into a thousand pieces, clanging down onto the floorboards in a waterfall of steel. Musical notes piled on top of one another in an imitation of a high school garage band, though the falling metal probably had more talent.

There was shocked silence from the both of us in the aftermath. I lowered my head. "Sorry . . ."

"You're as bad as a pyromancer, you know that?" Ceinwyn Dale accused.

"I said *sorry*. Maybe if I had a cigarette I wouldn't be so irritable," I tried to reason with her. Also a first for me. "I got a 'D' in Drug Ed, but I'm guessing it's a side effect, me being so understanding and lovable usually."

Ceinwyn Dale actually *tutted* me. "The nicotine will be out of your system in a few days. You haven't had the habit for long . . . you'll survive, King Henry," she repeated, adding, "We've had children addicted to far worse make it."

"Oh?"

"None of your business."

She returned to her paper.

I sipped my water for a bit, looking out the back door at a wooded yard. There was some kind of red bird picking at the bark. Nature Science, also a 'D.' Be lucky I know what a bird is. "Where are we?"

"The Institution of Elements, Learning Academy and Nature Camp."

"Looks like the suburbs out there . . . with trees."

"Each of the staff has a house for themselves and their family. Though, size depends on your position in the rank hierarchy." Ceinwyn Dale's expression was bored. With me, with the paper, even with the Asylum. I suppose after the ten-billionth time, the explanations get old. Plus, Ceinwyn Dale ain't exactly the type of person who sits drinking coffee at the table with a newspaper every morning. For my stay at the place, she was away from the Asylum more than she was there.

At the table of boredom, her paper turned a page in her hand. She's one of those people who folds the pages and destroys the paper by reading it. Just selfish.

I drank more water, watching the red bird get all horny with his bark picking. "Don't suppose you have a TV?"

"No, I don't."

"Everyone has a TV."

"I'm not here enough to bother."

"Ah . . . so I'm not living here with you? There's a relief." False bravado. Ceinwyn Dale and I fought, but I didn't mind it and, bereft of my parents, I gladly would have latched onto her house as a home, especially a home with a busy parental figure.

"Once you're tested, you'll be assigned a room with your classmates—they're communal," she droned.

My headache flared. Communal. I didn't know what the word meant back then, but it sounded both hippie and communist at the same time and that had to be a bad thing. "Good, you couldn't contain yourself for long after what you saw last night."

The smile twitched. "I don't recall seeing anything worth remembering."

"That's just mean . . ."

"Of course, memory is a funny creature," she continued running over my pride. "As an example, if one was dosed up with a certain drug, they might not remember changing into new clothes or taking a shower or even whining through a haircut."

Oh crap.

I thought about it. Damn if it wasn't a perfect mind fuck. Still don't know one way or the other to this day. Suppose I could make a joke about the birthmark on my ass when she ain't expecting it and see if Ceinwyn has a reaction or not.

"You're full of it."

"You'll never know." Might as well have cursed me. Not that the Mancy can curse . . . but to use the expression in the common vernacular. The education again. Gone way past *communal*.

She switched to the business section, ruining more dead tree and stinking ink.

"You live in this big house all alone?" I asked.

"Yes."

"Must be high ranking."

"Yes."

"Don't think you could handle me, so I'm not offering, but you should get a guy. You'd make a swell mom with all the threats and stuff. *Do the dishes or I'll papercut you! Take out the garbage or it's a ball of air!*"

Her paper finally lowered. "I did . . . have a guy once . . . he died."

One of the few times I've ever seen Ceinwyn Dale get emotional enough to be near tears. Fourteen-year-old-me went awkward. "Sorry about that, Miss Dale. Bet he liked your legs."

"If I give you the sports section will you shut up?"

"No promises."

[CLICK]

After awhile, Ceinwyn Dale headed to the shower with the promise that if I even went near the bathroom door, she'd know and would react accordingly, which I took to mean papercuts, a mouthful of air, and probably some horrible affliction I hadn't thought of yet that involved my asshole.

The unknown is often more terrifying than the known . . . more beautiful too. Us humans love and fear the uncharted map. Once you get the game down, game gets boring. We don't have any uncharted left, which is probably why we're so screwed up now.

Fourteen-year-old-me stayed away from the door. Instead, I went about making me some eggs—no bacon or sausages in Ceinwyn Dale's cupboards—so I had to settle for cheese, pepper, and a couple herbs sprinkled in and scrambled. Helping Dad in the kitchen again. First time that day I thought of him . . . followed by thinking of Mom.

Probably a mistake.

Mom.

A mancer like me.

Dad always said she was a special woman. I tried not to think about it, but it was hard not to. Ceinwyn Dale said the Mancy drove you insane if you didn't use it right—one of the few things Ceinwyn Dale told the total truth about—and suddenly my screwed up life wasn't the blame of one cowardly screw-up parent, but partly the product of fate or chance or an asshole universe that likes to play with people and God and dice and strings and crap.

THE FANGED LADY

Some mancers start thinking of the Mancy as the enemy, you can see why. Me—never. It's my ticket out of my shithole. But I felt bad about Mom for the first time in years. I felt bad about Mom, about her being crazy, about me being away from her for at least four years, for not being able to help her.

I was smart—Ceinwyn Dale said so—putting those eggs on a plate, I'd already figured it out. Ceinwyn Dale telling Mom the truth, Mom trying to save me from the same fate. Mom knowing she's doomed to die crazy one day.

Let's just say that the eggs, despite the skills Dad had belted into me, tasted not-so-hot. It wasn't the eggs fault either. Or my cooking. Just my attitude.

The doorbell ringing distracted me. Not just the noise but the fact that there *was* a doorbell. Doorbell, suburb housing, uniforms—damned Asylum.

The mundanity of it all—taking magic, fucking *magic* and making it not so special at all. Looking back on it, I'm pretty sure the effect is intended. These people wanted four-hundred usable tools graduating each year, not heroes trying to save the world. Ultras get a bit more about the whole story, but not much. I learn so every day. You will too, kiddies.

Mundane . . . take the door for example, I got ready to open it expecting any number of possible badass people. What I got was an old lady. Wrinkly, little chunky, veins showing and skin patching like a farm during summer, probably had saggy tits somewhere under her burgundy sweater too. She looked about as excited with me as I was with her.

"Yeah?" I asked.

"I see . . . our late recruitment. Aren't you a cute little boy in your uniform?"

A great beginning to a legendary relationship. Well . . . infamous relationship at the least. But I never got caught, that's what counts. "Can I help you?"

She had one of those old lady metal-canes with the four rubber prongs on the end, which she used to prod me out of the way.

"Where's Ceinwyn?"

"Shower, I guess." I frowned at her as she walked into the kitchen like she owned the place. *Technically* she didn't own it, but then . . . no one was going to claim she didn't either, so what's the point quibbling over the fine points of possession? "Are you like a friend or something?"

"Something more than friend if I had to classify the relationship," the old lady mumbled, starting to eat what I hadn't finished of my eggs, which on account of my brooding over my mom had been quite a lot of the plate. "My . . . these are very good. Touch of rosemary?"

"Yeah . . . I was kind of eating them."

"Really? Oh well . . . you could use the protein it looks like . . . I must say, I don't know if I'm more surprised that a little thing like you knows how to cook or that Ceinwyn has *food* in her house. I wonder, how does it get here? I really should know . . ."

She went on eating the eggs. "Good, but needs a sauce . . ."

I started trying to make her cane crack in half. Yeah, I know, I'm a troublemaker. Sue me. Not like I got any success on that front anyway.

"I see Ceinwyn has already put you in your badges and your colors. Always showing initiative that girl. One of the brightest students we've ever had."

"I hadn't noticed."

"Oh yes, first of her class—90' or 91' I can't remember which. Used to annoy Obadiah Paine to no end, I remember *that*. He was a geomancer like you. You are geomancer, yes?" the old lady asked, pouring herself a glass of water. "Had a bit of an accident on the trip in to let Ceinwyn know what you are, did you?"

I got distracted from answering . . . I got distracted a lot back then. Mancy, legs, boobs, Valentine Ward making books explode, it was horrible. This particular time, was because instead of using the faucet, the old lady poured a thin stream of water directly from a finger. "Ain't that a waste of animal or whatever the hell it's called?"

"*Anima*, that's what it is called . . . and anima . . . anima gets easier as you get on with age, one of the few parts of life that does. I have got on with a

116

great deal of age, so anima is a great deal of easy." A flick removed the stray remaining bead of water. "Ceinwyn must have found you difficult to begin an introduction class; usually she ignores recruits the moment the papers are signed."

If I hadn't seen the hallway wall with the pictures, maybe I could have agreed and sized Ceinwyn Dale up as a professional, but it didn't really fit. She'd annoyed me, she'd pushed me, but I figured she cared somewhere in her hollow aeromancer heart. As long as I kept being interesting, at least.

"I broke the child-lock on her car," I said proudly. What a little badass I was. Broke a child-lock. Watch out world.

"Isn't that something." The old lady took a sip of the water. Which I think may be considered cannibalism. Cannibalism or a very odd form of recycling. "Did you break anything else perchance?"

Like they were going to throw me out . . . why not? If they did, I'd get to find a cigarette. "Bunch of shelves, a table, and some kind of wall art thing, you can still see it—what's left of it. Been trying to break your cane since you poked me with it, but no luck."

All I got was a shake of the head, not even a batting eye. "Indeed . . . so much effort to harm someone."

"It doesn't work when I try, seems like . . ."

She laughed. Unlike Ceinwyn Dale, she had a real laugh. But old like the rest of her, worn out and tired. "Thank God for that. You'd cost more than you're worth."

"Not worth anything since you lot took all my stuff." I started staring at the cane. Face might have gone red from the effort too.

"Taking '*stuff*' is school policy. I'll let you in on a secret, what you say?"

"Sure." Face went maroon.

"Our goal is to form community among the students, so we try to give you nothing but each other. See how it works?"

"I don't like other people."

"You've gone purple, dear, do stop." A flick of a finger and what was left of the water in her glass splashed into my face like it shot from a hose.

117

Which I think may be considered flinging bodily fluids. "I'm tired feeling your *efforts*."

"You can do that?"

"You'll learn . . . you seem dedicated enough. Or at least committed. And the right kind of committed too. We get both kinds."

"Who are you anyway, old lady? Don't you have to go play shuffleboard or take your pills or something?"

She laughed again. This time it neared cackling. "And you're fearless, which can be such a good quality if you're also a survivor. If not, at least you'll have a death worth writing about."

You're noticing the habit that Asylum types have of talking over students' heads, I hope. Annoyed the hell out of fourteen-year-old-me. Ceinwyn Dale and the Lady were the worst, but hardly the only ones. My math teacher, now there's a woman who loved to pretend she's talking to herself.

I came back with, "I'm not a toy, you know. You people seem to be forgetting it."

Lint got picked off her sweater. Tiny balls of string discarded from the whole. "We don't belittle you . . . you'll understand soon. With Elementalism there is so much to see we often don't look at the right clue, or don't have time to coddle you with so many wonders and terrors happening around us."

"Yeah, *whatever*—still looking for a name, lady."

"She's Maudette Lynch," Ceinwyn Dale said as she finally walked into the kitchen dressed for the day. "And even if you don't respect me, you should respect her, King Henry. She's the Dean of the Institution of Elements and Head Chair of the Elemental Learning Council."

Like I knew what that meant. I'm still working on *communal* here. "That some kind of teacher?"

"Lovely quality in the United States school system these years," the Lady muttered to herself.

"She's our Charles Xavier," Ceinwyn Dale simplified for my comic book prone mind.

118

THE FANGED LADY

"Oh . . . like a principal."

"Yes, you have it."

"My last principal liked wearing glow-in-the-dark latex. So as long as she's not into that, we're cool."

Ceinwyn Dale actually took it in stride. "There's a condition I haven't heard before."

"Sounds uncomfortable," the Lady muttered some more. I call her that, though fourteen-year-old-me didn't know it yet, because Maudette Lynch's nickname is '*The Lady of the Lake*' and that's all she's ever called.

The way the story goes is that the Asylum was founded in 1920 and the year it was founded, the first Dean came upon three-year-old Maudette walking on the waters of Lake Tahoe. She was adopted after the news came out about a boating accident which had killed her parents. She's seen every year the Asylum has existed. A hydromancer, a Riftwalker like our good lord Jesus Christ. Well, that's another rumor at least. Don't worry, fundies, they're probably both full of shit.

The Lady kept on grossing me out, "Awfully lot of work to get into, I'd assume."

"Surprisingly not," Ceinwyn Dale said, winking at her.

"Oh . . . just wrong . . ." I whispered, "Shove some air or water in my ears, man."

They ignored me. Of course they ignored me. They were grown women. What's new about that? "I'm going to have to cancel. King Henry still needs tested and Russell will be whining through the whole process. Best if we start it early."

"School first as always, Ceinwyn," the Lady agreed, picking up her cane like it was a sword. "Place him before he breaks something expensive."

"I'll find time for lunch."

"Yes, yes, that will be lovely." The Lady turned to me. "Thank you for the eggs, King Henry Price, and welcome to the Institution of Elements, Learning Academy and Nature Camp. I wish you best of luck in your testing."

"You owe me breakfast."

She laughed again as she walked out the door, metal prongs limping before her. "We'll call it even for you trying to break my cane, young man."

Session 108

THE PLACE WE ROLLED INTO looked more like an insane asylum than the Asylum ever did. It was walled. Big, thick, prison walls meant to keep in and keep out, that said *'this is my space, asshole'* better than those lying beware-of-dog signs ever do.

The walls were made of white stone, topped with preening angels and carved along the top with Latin script, which is outside the edge of even my overindulgent education to translate. The gate our car—we'd stolen another after the last flip job—went through was just as thick, crisscrossing metal that hummed as it moved. Metal resonating . . . music to my ears.

"You people don't like visitors, do you?" I asked Annie B.

"God, it's hot," was her only answer, flapping the neckline of her shirt to get cool air against her skin. It's a miracle the woman wasn't constantly getting arrested for public indecency.

My first trip to San Francisco and I can't say I thought much of the place. Sure, there's ocean, but I'm not a water kind of guy. The water didn't help. There's just too much of it: too many bridges, too many wharves, too much water trying to trap you in on three sides. The earth actually under my feet . . . half of it was worse than dog-shit—it was *human-shit*.

Trash, waste, broken buildings. It wasn't really soil or bedrock, it was fake, man-made. It made me feel sick, like I'd ordered bacon and got that tofu-turkey imitation stuff. No wonder the city kept trying to kill the people living in it.

Humans don't belong to the ocean—we come from dust. Vamps though . . . they belonged in the water still, made them right at home. Aphrofucking-dite rising up from the seafoam. Sirens giving a call. Yeah . . . myth fits sometimes.

The roads of San Francisco were even more crowded than Fresno, created by the same problem: too many people. California's problem as a whole. Too many people. People getting in each other's faces, people getting pissed and resorting to violence, people fighting over jobs, people fighting over supplies, people fighting over road space. All the time, fighting, and not the fun kind of fighting, just the pissy kind. *Learn to drive that tank, bitch. Fuck off, asshole, buy a real car next time.* Music to my ears more than the metal gate.

Guess overpopulation is good for the vampires too. If your business is eating people, then business is booming. If your business is selling condoms, doesn't look like you're doing your job, douchebags.

Before I met Annie B, I sized the people I saw based on their threat level to me. First off, are they a mancer? Second, are they physically dangerous? Third, are they female and hot? If yes, four, do they look crazy? Now though . . . I saw a little differently. Instead, I saw veal-shank over here and lobster-tail over there. Food, so much food. Vampires and mosquitoes and ticks and leeches and bed-bugs, blood brothers all. Each more disgusting than the last.

"You're basically naked and it's not even sixty, how are you hot?" I rose to the bait. I was still in my brown geomancer coat and my jeans, both of which looked like they'd been through a tough day of blue-collar work. Pair of fights will do that to you. I also had a circle of dried blood wrapping around my throat, where I'd been strangled, and the Band-Aid on my hand were Annie B had fed on me. Not my best look, I admit, but at least I actually could have passed for a normal guy on a winter day, not on some tropical island as part of the chief's harem of dancing girls.

Annie B parked the car outside the asylum-looking building. I don't know architecture, but it looked old. Same white stone as the walls, it could have been a church once upon a time. Now, it was the San Francisco Vampire Embassy.

Just about any town north of one-hundred-thousand people has one, but this was the oldest in California. Vampire presence in California predated the state *and* the United States, so the Embassy, if not the building, was the oldest west of the Mississippi. Vampires follow human migration about as well as the Indians used to follow the buffalo. The gold rush brought more than prospectors in gold, it brought prospectors in blood. Plenty of time for it to build its fair share of secrets . . .

No one was outside to greet us. Just trees and grass, a hint of fog with a hint of sun.

Annie B got out of our car and glanced up at the bright orb, her eyes glaring disgust. "Not only hadn't I fed for days before you provided such a wonderful breakfast, I haven't slept for days during the course of this investigation. We don't need sleep like humans, and can go without it for extended periods if required, but the longer we go, the more difficult it becomes to stay cool. To put it simply: you're not seeing me at my best."

I exited the car, watching her as she shaded her face with an arm. The same arm I'd seen buried under our last car. "What do you do when it's really hot and you have an *investigation?*" I asked, curiosity getting the best of me.

She looked away from the sun, back my way. I couldn't help but think it would be so much easier to hate this creature if she wasn't so appealing to my hormones. Every part of her and you wanted to stare. Not all Vamps are like that, some are the last you'd expect, but Annie B . . . a walking problem. I had to keep reminding myself this was just the shell. It helped .. . but only a little . . .

"I eat well, sleep through the day, wear as few clothes as possible, and take a great many freezing showers," she said.

"Guess that means you don't cuddle," I teased.

"No . . ." she whispered to herself, "no cuddling with humans. You're too warm . . . walking furnaces heating up at all the wrong times . . ."

That got a laugh from me. "Shit . . . it's really too bad you want to eat me, you know? You might just be the perfect woman. Can kick ass, don't wear clothes, perfect body, into freaky sex, and no cuddling. Damned shame . . ."

Her eyes caught mine. "But I'm not a woman."

I shrugged; *maybe* she's not so horrible after all. "There's always a damn string on the deal, haven't I learned."

As she walked past, Annie B elbowed me in the stomach hard enough that I forgot how to breathe. Yeah, and *maybe* I called it too early.

[CLICK]

I almost walked back outside. Whoever ran the Embassy loved AC more than I did, which is saying something, since I've been known to freeze out many an old lady shopping for teapots. Again, not the best for sales, but it gives me some peace and quiet.

"Santa's hairy tits," I mouthed since I couldn't speak on account of my vocal cords freezing shut. Didn't help the weirdness vibe when Annie B let go a little moan the moment the cold air hit her. My only reaction was my balls working their way up my prostate. I'd never expected to get frostbite on this gig, but it had just become a possibility. Cold, very cold, cold as Hope Hunting's twat cold.

Annie B walked over to a closet right by the door, pulled out a pair of gloves and handed them to me. There were fur sweaters and thick jackets inside too, but I guess she didn't like me enough. Pair of gloves, that's what I'm worth. "For our human guests. We understand our differences concerning . . . bodily needs."

"Yeah . . . bodily needs," I mumbled as I put on the gloves that didn't do a damn thing for the majority of my needs. "I don't think I'm ever going to pop a stiffy again after this."

A small smile cut her face as she led the way down the hall. "I find that hard to believe given your reputation."

Fog dripped from my mouth, frosting the air around me. Couldn't even escape the gray indoors. "Even I can't overcome biology."

THE FANGED LADY

"I can."

Our steps were loud in the empty hall. Had to be other people here, right? And how big was this place? It's San Francisco, realty was insane . . . but this place wasted this much space. It was a sign, I guess. Along with the walls and the cold, no one greeting you: *get out and stay away*. Annie B headed for a pair of closed doors, but you'd expected a waiter or something, like the little Igor asshole from the movies, scuttling around like a cracked-out midget.

She can, I thought. "I'm not rising to the bait."

She still answered. I would have dreams and nightmares over the answer for months. The kind of crazy shit where it mixes and you ain't sure which it is, one moment it's all good, then you're getting stabbed or ate . . . or a girl is telling you she's pregnant. Horrible stuff. "When I'm *inside* a human, I can manipulate their blood flow just as I manipulate my own. How strong it is . . . where it goes . . ." She gave me a look, tongue tip finding her lip, "How long it stays there."

"So . . ."

"Hours upon hours . . . no relief . . ."

Stay away from the pretty string, King Henry.

We found our reception committee on the other side of the doors. Finally it looked like a modern building and not a medieval crypt. Desks and chairs, a television on the wall, even a food setup that seemed to be sporting vamp enjoyable food and drinks of iced tea and fruit slices chilled over a tray of ice, even some kind of mushy looking ice cream the last color I wanted to see at that moment—red. The room had dark wood, not stone like the outside of the place or the hallway, and could have passed for a doctor's waiting room or a businessman's office. Four vampires sat behind their desks.

[CLICK]

A break again for me to give you a little explanation on Vampire society that isn't in moron-being-led-around-by-a-vampire voice. I'll keep it simple.

This is all the basic info you get from your *History of Elementalism* class first year at the Asylum, but I suppose we all need a refresher from time to time.

Vampires, you need to know about vampires . . .

The vast majority of vampires live in a nomadic hierarchy where rank is dictated by ability level, which in itself is often dictated by maturity. Real vampires—not the sparkly ones who hate garlic—ain't immortal; they simply live so long that they might as well be. This means where you and I take twelve or so years to hit puberty, vampires take a much longer time and even then they have more than one change they go through. Certain abilities are required for certain jobs, so you won't see a certain rank that isn't tall enough to ride the rollercoaster as it were. This means age matters a great deal, just like in the legends. Some trees live thousands of years, vampires can live longer.

The nomadic part of their society stems from chasing the temperature they need in a habitat to operate at efficiency. Anything over seventy which doesn't have industrial AC is out. You're not going to see vampires in Africa, South America, or Australia, at least not more than one here or there who has been ordered to be there. Mostly it's North America, Europe, and Asia, the northern part during the summer, drifting down during the winter. Only the Vampire Embassies are stationary, manned by a small staff all year long.

As far as the hierarchy goes, the first rank is *servantman* or *servantwoman*, sometimes just shortened to servant. That's the bottom floor, the just born vampire: new body, confused, getting used to their new world. A new vampire is never born into a Joe-Anybody. That doesn't happen. They live a long time, they're harder to kill than cockroaches, but they don't spawn at a high rate. We're talking a century between splits and centuries more before a vampire can reach the ability to procreate. When a vampire knows they're reaching that time, they pick out a target that's needed for vampire politics or something of the sort. Hence the servant—they keep living their normal life pretending to be human while actually helping out their new species.

THE FANGED LADY

The next rank is *gentleman* or *gentlewoman*, which is where most vampires stay at, the most common rank, usually those that are fifty to one-thousand years old. A gentle is a vampire that has done its time, entered society wholly and steps away from its human life without anyone watching their every move.

Then come the job titles. *Baron, marquess, count,* and *duke,* and of course for the ladies, *baroness, marchioness, countess,* and *duchess.* A baron is a kind of U.S. Marshall or Texas Ranger job, they go around finding vampires out of line or people messing with vampires and then they deal with them, usually with the harshest punishments. A marquess is in charge of money matters, checking up on embassies, and navigating estates for vampires keeping wealth in the modern world where a person must '*die*' every eighty or so years. A count is in charge of military matters when he is called upon by a duke to protect an embassy against outside threats: most likely being a Were Nation out of control or a certain mancer who is causing problems . . . *ehm.* A duke runs an embassy, he's in charge of the staff, visiting vampires, and with keeping his area quiet, he also communicates with other local dukes to know which vampires are coming his way.

There are also higher ranks . . . but I didn't know of them back when I first met Anne, so it's not fair to mention them, I suppose. We'll stick with what I've said. Back to the moron out of his league.

[CLICK]

I started a slow pooling of anima the moment I stepped into the room. I wasn't exactly expecting trouble, but it's best to be prepared for anything, especially when you're surrounded by creatures that want to eat you—it's a mancer rule too, not just a pussy-devoided Boy Scout one.

Four vampires sat behind their desks. Two were men and two were women. Unlike Annie B, they were dressed like normal people, not pornstars out for a night on the town. My gaze judged each in turn, looking for vulnerabilities and weighing whether they were going to give me shit. Judging intentions had always been a gift.

The woman closest to us stood the moment we stepped into the room. She was a short little thing, blond and blue-eyed with a strong, straight nose splitting her face, just attractive enough to be a problem, but not so beautiful she scared guys away, which means she's constantly asked out every time she comes in contact with single men. She had a very emotive face that hinged upon what her mouth was doing and now it was in a full grown frown, the whole of her face and forehead going along with it. **Lady-in-charge who's sick of men asking her out, ability to give me shit:** *lots.*

The second woman sat farthest away from the door and didn't bother to move, only continued to type at her computer screen, refusing to pretend we existed as long as she had work to do. Some kind of latina, not sure which country, but she had dark hair cut short, big black eyes and skin a color that battled over the border of bronze and full out gold. **Secretary, ability to give me shit:** *only if I need someone to get me a drink.*

The two guys were each bigger than the last. One looked like a linebacker that loved him some grilled food; red hair, green eyes, had a kind of ZZ Top beard going on that hadn't been in style since the Civil War, and a gut of fat hanging *just so* against his shirt where you barely noticed it. You got to be careful with fat people in a fight. Sure, they might tire, but on the other side, a fat gut can take some serious punches without feeling a thing. It can also hide muscles on their arms and legs and they might *not* tire out. **Muscle/thug, ability to give me shit:** *a sure thing unless I distract him with a milkshake.*

The second guy was a perfect mound of muscle, brown hair and brown eyes, another beard belonging in the Civil War, one of those on-the-sides-but-not-the-face kind of flaring sideburn jobs. The way he held himself, he thought he was something special and everyone else in the room should be bowing down before him in awe of his superiority, the kind who doesn't like it when you don't bow, especially if you are smaller than he is. **Second-in-charge, ability to give me shit:** *hit the bastard in the balls the moment he looks your way.*

THE FANGED LADY

The first woman, the little blond thing, addressed us—well . . . addressed Annie B. "Baroness, such a surprise . . . we were not expecting you again so soon," she apologized for the lack of greeting at the front doors.

Annie B's expression conveyed that if anyone gave her shit she'd shit right back on them, and she'd be using a sewage truck. "I told you this wasn't finished yet."

"But—"

"Did you disturb the crime scene?" Annie B asked, pausing only long enough to be answered. I was right on her heels, figuring it's the safest place. Not the time for my mouth to start up. Despite popular opinion—I can control it.

"Of course not, Baroness . . . but we agreed that—"

"No we didn't," Annie B snapped. So, she *was* a baroness, guess I should have figured it. Made sense given how tough-no-nonsense she'd been and given that she seemed to be dealing with a theft of some sort. Funny thing about that rank, it's the first step into the extended hierarchy of vampires, but it's the only one that gets to tear down the whole system if it has a bug up its bunghole. "You assumed this was finished, Gentlewoman Moore, I knew it *wasn't*."

"But we agreed our geomancer could not track the item in question and that it is pointless to continue exhausting him," Gentlewoman Moore tried another route to get where she wanted to go. Her frown only made her cuter, which is hard to pull off. It wasn't the frown of a stupid person, just the frown of a smart person at work.

"Yes," Annie B agreed, "Your geomancer is worthless and barely graduated from their school *and* is addicted to three different narcotics. Even if he *could* manage it, I wouldn't want to use him. There are, however, other methods and *other* mancers in this world."

Three Vamps looked my way, the secretary the only one too busy with her work. The mound of muscle with the freaky sideburns asked, "That what the little human is? A mancer?"

The other guy, the fat linebacker, grinned down at me. "Looks like he's just your dinner from the night before—look at him, low on blood. Don't suppose you brought him back to share?"

Gentlewoman Moore glanced at my neck, her face going tight. They could really tell just from looking? Could have been worse . . . they could have seen my *Carebears* Band-Aid. "We would have provided you with a donor, Baroness," she murmured. "It's our duty despite your belief in our failure."

Annie B said nothing and Sideburns filled the void, "Look at the pissed off look he's giving us, like he thinks we can't rip him in half and eat one side for breakfast and the other for lunch."

Linebacker agreed, slowly inching towards me. "Wouldn't make much a meal though, so maybe he should know his place as a human and turn his eyes like a good little treat."

Annie B studied my reaction as intensely as Ceinwyn Dale ever had. Me? I just shrugged and kept on staring at the pair of them, but I spoke to Annie B, "You know the problem with beating so much ass in a row? You just get tired of doing it. Then, when a couple of morons come along looking to measure dicks . . . it just bores you out of your mind."

"Regretfully, Gentlewoman," Annie B said across our standoff, "Events kept me from returning for a donor. I was unpredictably pushed beyond any limit I'd expected to near."

"What she means to say," I translated for the two men, "Is that we beat the crap out of each other. How about you boys back off?"

Annie B rolled her eyes. So did Gentlewoman Moore. Vamps or not, they were still using female shells. "What Artificer Price *means to say* is that he took extra convincing to agree to help us with our problem, but since he *has* agreed, he's under my protection and I'll be the only one feeding off of him."

"Yeah . . . I'm still not cool with that arrangement . . ." Thinking any feeding at all was bad.

"*Artificer* Price?" Gentlewoman Moore's whole face looked shocked, eyebrows going wide. Could she just have one uncute expression? It wasn't fair . . .

"Yes," Annie B showed teeth to everyone in the room, "He might not look it, but he's going to solve the problems you've created for me. Whether he solves your problems, gentles, depends on if you were involved with this theft. Why don't you stuff the threats towards him before I start to feel hungry again and start looking for other sources of nourishment?"

Her tongue darted across her lips for a spare second. Not a one of them could meet her eyes. Couldn't blame them . . . they looked crazy.

Just how much of a badass is Annie B?

[CLICK]

The place went down into the earth, or at least the human-shit passing for earth in San Francisco. The five of us descended—with me and Annie B leading the way and Gentlewoman Moore fretting behind us, her goons Sideburns and Linebacker relegated to the kiddy table at the very back.

It's this classical winding staircase of the same white stone as the outside, wide enough for five or so people to walk side-by-side without any bumping. What surprised me more than the secret underground passage—classic vampire bullshit right?—was that the place got colder the farther we went. It started freeze-your-balls-off and ended up freeze-your-fingers-off. By the time we hit the bottom of the stairs even the Vamps looked uncomfortable. They liked it cold, not freezing, and those rooms were freezing.

Only Annie B seemed unfazed, running hot like she was. The rest of us breathed fumes of fog. I was left to breathe into my gloves and rub my chest and shoulders to keep warm.

"You hiring cryomancers too? I think my teeth are going to crack."

Annie B glanced back over her shoulder. "No whining."

"It's a security measure against humans," Gentlewoman Moore explained, having caught up with me. She smiled, but even it couldn't beat down the worry in the rest of her expressive face. Made me want to hug her. Which ain't my usual instinct. "We don't like it this level of cold, but we can suffer it. For humans . . . it slows you down. It makes you less intelligent than usual, your brain too concentrated on the cold."

"A problem if you got a little brain to begin with," I growled back at her, thinking the concept sounded a whole lot like my Cold Cuffs.

"Are you trying to play dumb, Artificer Price?"

"Who's playing?" I asked.

Her face told me she didn't buy it.

The stairway ended, turning into a vaulted hallway of metal and tile. Suddenly we'd jumped from the Dark Ages into the 21st century, all steel and LED lighting, computerized locks on doors flanking the hallway, readouts and palm-scanners, plus some kind of hole that at first I thought was for a key.

Not for a key.

"Ain't there a duke or something running this place?" I asked as the hallway kept going, doors trailing behind us. The city government probably would have crapped itself if it knew there's a secret underground vampire complex running beneath the neighboring area of the embassy. I guess it's one way to beat unfair property taxes.

Annie B answered me, "The Duchess Antonia keeps a traditional schedule and is sleeping. Which is why we must deal with her trio of sun-fucking goons."

Judging by the look on Sideburn's and Linebacker's faces, 'sun-fucker' is a phrase that's going to fit right into my foul vocabulary. "Couldn't wake her up?" I asked my new buddy Moore. "The Law coming to town . . . kind of thing bosses like to be woken up for."

All I earned was, "We need our sleep," and a nod at Annie B's outfit and perhaps her attitude.

Yeah, beginning to see that one. So vampires needed blood and rest and cold temperatures. If not, they got erratic, started rubbing against cars to cool down, wearing almost no clothes and going full-out slut, drawing attention to themselves. As disadvantages went it wasn't exactly silver and garlic, but at least it was something to know they actually had disadvantages.

I'd made Cold Cuffs and those were a bust against the Vamps, but maybe something else would do the job. Hot cuffs? Couldn't use pyro-anima, too volatile, throw them on someone and the person's likely to spontaneously combust. Spectro-anima? Might work . . . might work . . . take a lot of it though . . . spectro-anima converted at the lowest rate, right beside scio-anima . . . but—might work.

"They're also hoping I'll be gone by the time the duchess is awake," Annie B pulled me back from formulas, "so they can pretend I was never here. Creating a myth that every part of the San Francisco Embassy is in perfect working order and that an item entrusted to them over one-hundred years ago wasn't stolen away right under their noses."

The gentlewoman glared as if her eyes could wipe Annie B off the face of the Earth. Finally something not cute . . . started to get worried. "We did everything we could under our own power."

Annie B only snickered back, still walking down the hallway-that-never-ends. "Your own power is surprisingly weak."

"And how are we supposed to track a vampire leaving no prints or DNA? Who somehow hacked a blood scanner?" Gentlewoman Moore asked heatedly, while behind me the goons nodded agreement. "We have no evidence *at all* and your attempt at using a geomancer to follow the item blew up in your face!"

Annie B gave a good shot of that deep gaze of hers, pulling you in, eating you up. "I have more faith in Artificer Price's abilities to notice anima than your coked-out blood-whore."

Blood-whore . . . look at me learning new words today.

"Where you find the little shit anyway?" Linebacker asked. "And what did you pay the Guild of Artificers for his services? You indebted yourself and your superiors won't like *that*, Baroness."

Annie B's gaze drifted to me. It's a miracle the woman hadn't walked into a wall the way she looked backwards. "Artificer Price isn't a part of the Guild."

Damn right he ain't. "He is getting paid, however, despite him being kidnapped and all," I added as a reminder.

"Hope he's worth the trouble," Linebacker muttered, cracking knuckles in a message so obvious it was almost rude. "Humans aren't supposed to know about this, even mancers. Especially his kind—it was part of the agreement for our holding the item in the first place. You might not have been here when it first arrived in town, but I remember the day well. Humans didn't just die that day, so did vampires. What happens if you find it and he uses it?"

So, an artifact for geomancers. That's interesting. For all our Artificing, it's rare to use geo-anima. We get so caught up in playing with other mancers' areas we forget about where we came from.

"He'll be a good boy," was all Annie B said.

What is this thing?

[CLICK]

That question flew yet again as we finally stepped into the room which had been holding the artifact. It was like some kind of anima bomb had gone off.

Humans and nature both produce their own anima in opposite ways, maybe even some animals theoretically can, but an *artifact?* It's not alive and it's not big enough to hold reserves, so . . . how? I mean, storage, yeah, we can do that. It's mainly what we *do* do. Can even make artifacts that recharge themselves at miniscule levels, take my Cold Cuffs. *But there are limits.*

As a simple explanation: think of ice cubes. If you put water in a tray, then freeze it, you can break out the cubes and put them in a drink to cool it. But eventually the tray is empty and you need more water—or anima. The other way, you get a closed container and fill it with water, freeze it, then put

134

the container on what you want to cool. Eventually the ice goes back to water and you have to wait for the water to freeze again. For anima this is called open-recharging and closed-recharging. But . . . the water level stays the same. Nowhere does ice make more ice or water make more water just on its own.

This . . .

With this thing . . . anima was everywhere. To produce this kind of result . . . and it had been in San Francisco for one-hundred *years*? Making anima the whole time? For some reason, it also had been made without a limit to what it could hold, or at least a limit that was mind-boggling, something like thousands of hours of pooling if not more. No wonder it dripped all over the place, if not used it had nowhere to hold it all, like some kind of cup that had a water stream which just wouldn't stop, eventually what you got was a full cup and a puddle of water.

And what would that much anima be used for?

"Jesus Christ fucked a goat . . ." I whispered, trying to use blasphemy to snap me out of staring at all the anima like a boy who had just seen his first tit.

"Did not," Annie B said, standing next to me.

Moore and her goons remained at the door. Maybe they were thinking of making a break for it. That or they didn't want to be around if something happened with all the anima.

"Take it you knew him?"

She gave a bitter smile. "Before my time. Met one of the apostles though. Care to guess which one?"

I grunted. "Don't suppose you know what happened to Elvis?"

Annie B stepped into the room and I was forced for follow. Once more our conversation happened with her shoulder between us. "He died."

"Bummer."

"His corpse sold for a considerable amount to a very rich duke, however."

Yeah . . . maybe conversation was a worse idea than just being in awe of the room.

I shut up as I studied the area. It was larger than I'd ever imagined a vault should be. Some real Indiana Jones, there-might-be-rolling-boulders type crap, only modern, so the boulders would probably have infrared tracking and a computer chip or something. Still, it was a circle with a podium raised in the middle, steps leading up to it and where *something* should have been, there was nothing. Around the *something*, I felt the geo-anima that had splashed down the steps, on and on as it had built up into streams that sunk to the sides of the room. I'd felt mountains with less.

"What is it?" I asked, growling just a bit of demand at the back of my throat. "We ain't going further with this until you tell me more. Payment or not. This ain't *natural*. It shouldn't be possible. It's some dangerous shit, got it?"

Annie B licked her lips even as Moore, Sideburns, and Linebacker flinched. "Can you see the anima?"

"Sight's the wrong word," I said. "But yeah . . . I could pool for a year straight and not do this. It's everywhere and it's saturated to a point where it's thick. I can't decide if I'm more confused over the *why* someone would build it or the *how* someone would build it . . . What is it, Annie B? No more games."

"Later," she said, turning back around to the other Vamps. "Come inside."

They did, reluctantly, but I wasn't getting passed over for politics. "I'm not joking, *Baroness*, tell me now or I don't give you another word, no matter what you pay me."

Her hand shot out to clasp around my throat. *Shit.* She pulled me close to her face and there was nothing I could do about it. Not *this* again. Doesn't matter if it's a beautiful face, I didn't like being so close to it.

"Cut your tougher-than-everybody act and trust that I'll tell you once we're away from here, *got it?*" she returned.

"Nervous?" I asked. "We can take them easy . . ."

THE FANGED LADY

Her eyes got older than I'd seen them. "Fighting only multiplies one's problems. One day you'll realize this." She shook her head. "One day I will too."

I would realize it, she's right, but it was a great many fights down the road. Even the Asylum didn't fix that part of my personality. It was hard to pull back and not throw down with her. I wanted my answer. Only the geo-anima and the possibility of it going off by itself if I conjured kept me from trying something.

"Fine," I told her. "Make your play, but I better get some answers soon."

Annie B released my throat, her hand patting my shoulder in the way you'd pet a dog. Yup, that's me. Faithful companion. Until I shit on the carpet at least. It was Moore that Annie B spoke to, "As I told you, your geomancer is a coked-out screw-up."

"We have only his word," Moore said, pointing at me. Like always, I looked like I was guilty of a crime that didn't exist yet, but would one day. "He's hardly a reliable authority and you said yourself: he isn't even Guild. What Artificer *isn't* Guild?"

"This Artificer," Annie B answered. "Which is why I trust him. A good friend endorsed his work, which makes me trust him even more." Annie B walked back and forth in front of the dais looking podium thing. There was a stand made of wood, not metal—which was probably wise given all the loose anima hanging around—it had a base and some kind of display with prongs close together, like it was made to hold a weapon a couple feet long. A short sword or a club maybe. Annie B paced from it, to the three San Francisco vampires, then back, repeating the patrol over and over, studying them all.

Linebacker spoke up after a bit of unnerving silence, "So our geomancer barely noticed the anima and couldn't track it, so what? Just because the little shit can see it or sense it or whatever he does, it doesn't mean he can track wherever the item went any more than our guy could."

"You're wasting our time," Sideburns agreed, backing up his boy. "Just let it go. It had to be a vampire who took it if they defeated the blood scanner, which means they can't use it. Let them have it and deal with the consequences instead of San Francisco. Good riddance."

Annie B was more like some tiger as she walked back and forth, not human. If she'd had fur it would have been standing on end. Even her dark hair seemed bristled. "Are they right, King Henry? Can you track it?"

I looked over the room again. The thing about the anima surrounding me is that it made me feel funny. If you're going to compare it to another sense, it didn't smell like the anima I was used to. Like someone had taken normal anima and distilled it and what I got was a smell of the strong vapors cast off. That beat of movement under my feet felt different than my own anima or the anima in nature. It *was* unique. *Somewhere in between them*, I thought. But that didn't mean I could follow it.

"No. I'd know it if I felt it again though. Maybe even if I got close to it. It's . . . *different*."

Moore and her goons seemed to relax. For being probably hundreds of years old, they were surprisingly bad at hiding their guilt. You could read them like a bad novel, all gushy and open, telling you what's going on.

They didn't steal it for themselves, that much was obvious. But they'd wanted the thing *gone*. Feeling all the strange anima, I couldn't help but see their point of view. Whatever did that . . . I'm an Artificer and I didn't even want to be in a room with it. No matter what it could do. *Make the Earth crack in two maybe . . .*

"Are you sure?" Annie B asked.

"It's not like I'm a damned dog and the smell sticks around. Anima doesn't work that way. Fuck, anima ain't supposed to work *this way*. But it's not like there's some line to follow. I can tell you it's been in this room. I can tell you if I walked into a room with it. I can tell you if I sat in a car carrying it. I can . . ." I stopped, frowning.

Shit.

So much for not fighting.

"What?" Annie B asked again, gaze gone old again.

138

THE FANGED LADY

"I can tell you Sideburns held the thing, it's all over his hands," I said, with a dreadful certainty I had killed the guy, but with not even a clue as to how horrible it was going to be. I mean, I didn't like the guy, he was a douchebag really . . . and he did steal it from the room and get it out of San Francisco probably, which wasn't very loyal to his Embassy, but he didn't deserve the hand he got dealt. No one deserves that hand . . .

Annie B sprung at Sideburns with a speed I'd never seen from her, even in our fights. Sideburns reacted with fists, trying to smash her flat, but she dodged. He was twice her size at least, shoulder muscles bigger than my head. But she's older by centuries, with years added on years to make her shell into a more perfect home.

Not a fair fight.

Her fists cracked out, stunning him with three punches before I could even react enough to keep an eye on Linebacker and Moore. Neither threatened us, luckily enough. They only backed away from the fight, glad it wasn't them and horrified of where it headed. They knew what I didn't yet. If I had, I might have kept my mouth shut.

Sideburns managed to grab onto Annie B's quick form even as she rammed a knee into his balls. I've already mentioned vampires can turn off pain receptors, but they have to be smart enough to turn them off. Sideburns took the knee before he seemed to remember he could do it. In that whole second, his body bent over and he completely screwed himself. A whole second—could have been *forever.*

He had no chance.

Grabbing his face, Annie B did the last thing I expected—I was expecting her to snap his neck—instead she kissed him. A deep, I'm-going-to-suck-out-your-organs kind of kiss—locked on like she never planned to let go. Only it wasn't tongue she gave him.

It was *her.*

In that instant of realization of what she was doing, sliding a piece of herself into his body to fight him vampire to vampire instead of shell to shell, I had a sick feeling of flashback to the rope of blood wrapped around my neck, of the wound on my hand I had thankfully been too knocked out to remember.

Fuck me.

Human, vampire, everyone in the vault screamed or gasped or grunted at what Annie B did as she grabbed at Sideburn's body, feet knocking him to the floor even as she kept their mouths locked together. "Tell me," she mumbled, barely understandable from the corners of her lips as she pressed them against his.

Sideburn screamed a sound that was nothing human. It came from deep inside him. Not his lungs pushing air through his throat, but the real him deep in his body, likely in his heart—screaming vibrations—and the sound carried out to the air surrounding us.

Fuck me.

"Tell me," Annie B said again, wrapping legs around his chest as he stopped struggling, in too much pain to order his shell to fight back. "Where?" He only screamed again. It took me the second scream to realize she was eating him alive. *"Who took it?* I'll make it quick if you tell me where?" she asked like her tongue talked around a rope.

Big bad tough Linebacker threw up. Gentlewoman Moore ran out of the room, eyes streaming tears. Yeah, if I was smart I probably would have too. But I'm not smart. Only I stood there watching every bit of the drama as Annie B kept asking the question, punctuated by a scream for each bite she took of him. Imagine every National Geographic show you've ever seen and then times the wildebeest going down to a lion by a hundred, then maybe you've got the same feeling, except it was happening right in front of you and not through several layers of camera.

"Where is it?" she asked again.

He finally answered. With the last word I ever wanted to hear. "Fresno!"

"Who? The duke?"

"Don't know . . ."

There was a final long scream before Sideburns gave up on even shaking, going all corpse on us much quicker than a human would. Annie B grasped at it for a moment, legs and arms tight around him like a snake, before they relaxed. She gave a little content sigh, the same all-filled-up-on-food sigh that's universal across cultures and apparently species too.

Finished with her meal, the man's huge body dropped down to the floor in front of her as she let go. Annie B turned around to smile at me. Her face around her lips was red with what I hoped was just blood, but knew probably wasn't.

"I don't suppose your teachers taught you we're cannibals?" A quiver of enjoyment hung heavy in her voice. "Only we taste better to each other than humans . . . it's a perk of my job." Something red, thin, and flexible poked from her mouth to wipe the last of the blood away from her lips and it wasn't her tongue.

"Nope, hadn't heard about that one."

RICHARD RALEY

Session 5

I GUESS YOU COULD CALL it my first school field trip. Not really. We didn't leave the grounds, and there were lots and lots of grounds—they weren't even fenced. Shocking, I know. You think they'd at least do it to protect the public from us. My first field trip actually happened about a month later, if thirty teenagers running around in the wild—alone—without adult supervision, trying not to be eaten by a mountain lion or kill one another with an accidental anima discharge—technical term—counts as a field trip.

The grounds of the Asylum are big. Plenty of room to get lost in or to find a nice quiet place to be alone, even with the three or four-thousand people that live there. It's like a small town. With lots of crazy people in it.

Looking down at it like a flying bird—or a floating Winddancer—you'd see a horseshoe shaped road, big enough for two lanes of cars, one way in and out. The four sections of the Asylum are all named as they relate to the horseshoe on the foundation map. West, East, Center, Top. Why Top and not North? I always wondered too.

West Section was where I started the day.

The teacher houses are pretty much all of what makes up West and there's quite a lot of them in a suburban grid, like they've been transplanted straight from my hometown of Visalia. Exiting Ceinwyn Dale's house and taking it in was a huge disappointment . . . trust me.

RICHARD RALEY

Well into the day, some of my teachers were already up and about doing normal neighbor things. There were even children out too. They played in the streets. I often think how strange it must be to grow up like that, knowing what the Mancy is from the start, living not so far from all the students. Even worse on those who didn't have the Mancy. Wives, husbands, even kids. They're essentially useless for the purpose of the place. Yet they stayed around. They even had normal school for the kids. Kindergarten at the Asylum. Kick me in the balls if they weren't tailor made to turn out psychopaths.

The Gullick house was particularly busy that day as Ceinwyn Dale and I walked by. It had a sign. *House Gullick.* There were flowers painted on it. Pretty pink ones.

Ceinwyn Dale waved at a man mowing the lawn. *Mowing the fucking lawn.* He waved back and yelled, "New one?"

She nodded, not glancing my way. Woman with a purpose. Might be she was trying to save me from my big mouth by walking quick.

There were kids my age playing basketball in the driveway. *Playing basketball in the fucking driveway.* Unlike Ceinwyn Dale, a few of them looked my way then. Mancers the lot.

One of the girls yelled out, "How strong is he?"

"Not tested, Naomi, and that question is rude," Ceinwyn Dale told her. "You know better."

"*Come on,* Miss Dale! He's already wearing the colors, I'm just curious," Naomi Gullick pouted as we walked by. Naomi was always a bit self-important over the years. Like she knew more than all the others since she grew up at the place.

Looking at that pout, knowing a few spoiled teachers kids in my fourteen years, I had myself an accidental anima discharge. Could they have thought of a dirtier sounding technical term? My dirty term broke the pole of the basketball court right in half. *Crack.* Damn thing clanged down with a thud.

Fatality.

King Henry wins.

THE FANGED LADY

"That strong, honey, maybe you get a taste sometime," I yelled back. Maybe if I'd known her father would be my *Elementalism* teacher for four years, I wouldn't have. Say what you will about King Henry Price, he knows how to make a good first impression.

Once we turned down another street, Ceinwyn Dale finally asked me, "Did you do that on purpose?"

"Still mad about the wall art?"

"You need to stop breaking things."

"It was an accident." I added a bit of probably the most insight I'd had in a while, "I don't like people talking about me like I'm a measuring stick or something."

Ceinwyn Dale smiled for the first time that trip. "You're going to be such a nice change of pace, King Henry. This place needs it. The last few classes have gotten too complacent."

"You're doing it to me, you know . . ."

"Yes, but you like it when *I* do it."

"You mean I put up with it because you can kick my ass."

"Either works."

We eventually crossed over a busy road filled with unmarked windowless buses. The setup is that parents dropped the kids off at a designated station in Tahoe and then the drivers ferried them in. Kept the Asylum free of sobbing parents and equally sobbing students. It also kept the exact location of the Asylum a bit of a mystery. So Ceinwyn Dale wasn't lying about drugging me with a giant needle.

Center Section is the corrupted heart of the place. It's always busy, beating away, even the day before class starts. Once class is actually in session, it would be packed for twelve hours a day, six days a week for the next eleven months. It had the Employee Dorms, plus the Single and Bi Dorms—one building according to the fact that freshmen of all kinds have to get the worst treatment, even magical freshmen—but the main workhorses are the classroom buildings. One for normal school classes any kids are going to get and another for anima classes, which only the unlucky have to put up with. Like me.

I'd grow to hate those rooms. Especially room M108—my math room for four years of arithmetic, algebra, and geometry. In case you're wondering about my feelings on those subjects . . . fuck algebra and double fuck geometry. Arithmetic I can live with . . . I need it for anima conversion formulas. But in case you didn't hear me correctly the first time: *double fuck geometry.*

There is also the Cafeteria, which ended up one of my favorite buildings during my stay. Good ass food for three meals a day. No running in to steal breakfast before heading to school or packing my raggedy backpack with enough snacks to get me through my weekends away from my drunk parents. No more square school pizza. That's some vile junk. Square school pizza disproves socialism more than any political argument ever did.

Those are the buildings, but Center Section also holds the Park, which is pretty much a park in the middle of the school. Trees, bushes, ponds, more bushes, and nooks for some privacy that led to plenty of awkward situations—nothing like being found making out with a cute floromancer girl by your *Languages* teacher. Jethro Smith. Thinks he's a rock star. Bastard started to give me advice.

It was always a danger. Teachers and students both like to walk around the place on off hours. Just like any high school, you have certain kids that hang at certain places. Parkies are seen as the suck-ups, always under the teachers' eyes, or in some cases protection. Guess what? I wasn't a fucking Parkie.

Nice place though. Thought so walking through it the first time with Ceinwyn Dale. Didn't like that a lot of the adults were waving at her as we passed by even then. Students were already there too. Mostly four-year Intras goofing off with friends they hadn't seen for a month. Ultras have better things to do than walk the Park. Only time you see an Ultra in the Park is when they're searching for a teacher or walking to get somewhere else.

146

THE FANGED LADY

Most of the other student hangouts are in East Section.

The Pools are literally these huge Olympic-size swimming pools, complete with diving boards and slides and other lawyer nightmares that no normal school would ever let you near without a bible-sized stack of papers to sign. I'd been swimming before, but wasn't good at it, still ain't, and don't particularly like it. Geomancer and all—floating ain't my thing. Unless my *P.E.* or *Survival* teacher made me get in, I tried to stay out of them.

Do admit to hanging around to check out the girls in their swimsuits though. Asa Kayode is a pain in the ass, but damn if that girl in a bikini with her fine brown skin and taunt long body couldn't make Prince Henry speak up every time I walked by her. That's the Pools for you, guys catching a look and hydromancers and cryomancers fighting for water space. The kids at the Pools are called Water Pissers. Or just Pissers.

Near the road in, to the west of the Pools, you have the Hall, which has games inside. Pool—the other kind, skeet-ball, table-hockey, bowling alley or two, even a few arcade games from the 80s and 90s. Sundays they'd set up big speakers and play music for everyone to dance to or just chill out. Hall kids are called Kids, some in-joke from before my time I think. I admit to spending time at the Hall. Not as much as you'd think though.

The Hall's full of a lot of Intra slackers who don't give a crap about learning the Mancy best they can or what rank they have in their class or year. All us Ultras cared—even me—so free time wasn't something to waste on a thirty-year-old *Pacman* machine. You get over that, and even then . . . Ultra walking into the Hall is going to get some dirty looks from jealous Intras. Can't blame them. If I'd been Intra, I'd have been beating some Ultra brains in for being smug assholes. It ended up the other way around and instead it was me walking into the Hall and taking those dirty looks, daring a brave bully to step up.

Above the Pools you got the Gym. Call them Rats. Obvious enough on that one? I liked the Gym in my time. Has two stories actually, and a basement. That count as a story? Anyway, first story is basketball courts or volleyball depending on the need. Basketball ain't my game. Guess why? Fucking short. *So* funny.

Second story is gymnastic junk: racquetball, handball, stuff like that. Basement is weights and weight machines. Spent time there alright. Started at a scrappy hundred pounds and by four-year graduation passed by one-sixty. And you wonder why a charmer like me gets the girls? Only annoying part about the Gym is that the corpusmancers treated the place like a church. About every seventh mancer is a corpusmancer . . . that's a lot of religion to have to deal with.

Above the Gym you have the Field. Which is a field. Fucking deep. Kids there don't even have a special name; collectively they were 'the Rest.' The Field is neutral ground. The Belgium of the Asylum. Oh, just like Belgium it got invaded sometimes too. Start a world war by Asylum standards. But mostly everyone just chose their huddle and sat on the grass. Intras at least.

Above the Field is the Mound. The Mound is a mound. Again, fucking deep. Hills, rocks, trees. The Mound is Ultra territory. Unless you're an Ultra or your boyfriend is an Ultra, best stay off the Mound.

Even then, bringing an Intra up there is bad form. Doesn't mean it ain't done though. I did it. Easy way to get yourself a shallow girlfriend. Even had a name for it. *Intra Poaching.* Bringing in the pretty Intras in exchange for trips to hang on the Mound. If the Asylum had itself a forest ranger or an ye oldie sheriff, my ass would have been on the Most Wanted list. Me and Robin Hood. He shot arrows. I break child safety locks.

Every school's got itself the top spot on campus to hang. Most, it was jocks and cheerleaders and rich kids or just plain kids that had a cool vibe to them. At the Asylum, it's all combined up in the Mancy. Chance again. For some reason, the Ultra Vires were '*beyond the powers*' as the name suggests. That made Ultras the cool kids—the ones who got the special attention from the faculty and got the Mound to hang out on. Rising above the rest of the place, looking down on the Parkers, Water Pissers, Kids, Rats, the Stuffers—

that's Cafeteria kids, forgot to mention that first time around—and the Rest on the Field.

Fourteen-year-old-me wasn't thinking about all that as he and Ceinwyn Dale exited from the Park. He didn't even know the Mound existed. To him, the Park was kind of nice. Trees, birds, squirrels, fish ponds. My old school didn't have fish ponds. I'd hoped the fish ponds were proof the place wouldn't remain boringly normal.

I *was* thinking about Ultras though. Special powers beyond normal mancers. That's what Ceinwyn Dale said. Hell yeah, I wanted it. Even with the extra three years it would cost me. Sign me up. Send me spam. Totally worth it. Exiting the Park, fourteen-year-old-me endeavored to kick ass on the test they were throwing his way.

The Park is separated from Top by the horseshoe road, at the time packed with people.

"If you try anything, I'll find you," Ceinwyn Dale told me with a certain don't-try-it look in her eyes.

"What I do? I'm being good. I didn't even try to break that bridge back there. Could have, *but I didn't.*"

She gave me an eye-see-you hand gesture.

Okay, confession time. I'd been trying to break that bridge. Trying to break things with my feeble Mancy efforts became about the only thing that kept my mind away from nicotine. All through the Park my fingers shook, my head flashed little screws of pain. Around and around the rising edge we go. Wonderful thing detoxing, you should try it sometime.

Buses were dropping kids off about one every fifteen minutes. Staring out on the students mingling, on the teachers and employees trying to exert some control, I commented, "That's a lot of people."

Ceinwyn Dale nodded. "The majority held off until the last day, but some have already checked in early, and others will be like you and stay through the break."

"Of course."

"Pents through Heps get their own rooms and keep them for three years, while four-year students move into their new dorms with a randomized class near thirty. We try to break them up year to year so they meet new people." In the thick of it now, some of the boredom had faded from the explanations.

"And Ultra assholes?"

The smile twitched. "Same class for seven years."

"Way to ruin the new car smell, Miss Dale."

"Are you so sure you'll be an Ultra, King Henry?"

"I can pass any test you got."

"It doesn't work that way. Like most of life . . . you either *are* or you are *not.*"

"You *are.*"

"Yes."

"And you think I *are.*"

"I've been wrong before . . ."

"Do I got to break a bus axle to prove it to you?"

"And on we go."

As soon as they spotted Ceinwyn Dale, with me trailing behind, we had about two-hundred eyes locked on us. Lucky I don't give a crap or I might have burst into flame from the attention. Lucky Valentine Ward wasn't there or I might have burst into flame anyway.

One plus about being with Ceinwyn Dale is people make space for you. If there was ever any doubt in fourteen-year-old-me's mind that she was a high up badass, one-hundred teenagers being elsewhere killed it. It's not like she didn't get waves or nods, but an undercurrent of respect ran through the air quicker than any anima manipulation I've ever seen.

Me? I got who-the-bleep-is-the-ten-year-old? faces. Didn't help that I was one of the few in uniform like a good little fellow or that wearing a uniform unbuttoned and hanging out is considered disrespectful to your Mancy discipline. Think I cared even when I found out? Think I tucked that bitch in? You already know me so well . . .

150

THE FANGED LADY

We made it into Top.

If Center is the rotting heart of the Asylum then Top is the decaying brain. It's got the Administration building in the middle, then behind it is the parking garage for all the cars and buses and stuff the students ain't allowed to see, the very back of the school proper, though the actual grounds extend for acres, if not miles. To the right of Admin, you got the Ultra dorms. That's right—little shits get their own hill and their own building too. And you thought jocks and cheerleaders were bad?

Normal dorms for the Intras are made utilitarian—that evil education again making me with the big words—since they got to pump a lot more bodies inside them. Ultra dorms are four stories. First story has four dorms, communal to fit up to thirty, I'll save them for a bit later when fourteen-year-old-me gets to them.

Top three floors are for the Pents to Heps. They get their own rooms. Figure an even hundred of them. The rooms ain't big, but being able to study on your own without Robin White singing gospel songs ten feet away from you? *Fucking heaven.* Having your own bathroom and kitchen? *Fucking whatever's better than heaven.*

Left of the Admin is the Library. Big building, lots of books. I know you're thinking, '*oh he never saw that place*' but I did as far as anima studies went. Valentine Ward was always in there, so was her best friend Miranda Daniels and a friend of mine, Raj Malik. Raj had a thing for Miranda. Had a thing . . . look at me with the past tense. He still has a thing for her.

Love . . . like I understand it. Kids in the Library get called the usual—bookworms or Worms. Save for Valentine Ward, who was named Boomworm by yours truly, and the name just stuck. Amazing chick, the best one I've ever met.

Next to the Library are the graduate Ultra classrooms. I don't think I ever stepped inside the Artificer classroom but the one time, first day of my Pent year. See, I was the only Artificer the whole time I was at the Asylum. One just before me, two just after me. But me . . . all alone. Me and my mentor Plutarch got us some one-on-one, Yoda and Luke Skywalker shit going.

Don't think Luke ever called Yoda a fucktard, but the little green bastard probably deserved it.

And that's it . . . that's the Asylum. Welcome for the stay.

Damn, I'm glad I'm done describing all that stuff. Buy a map if you still can't figure it out. Let's get on to my testing. Think I have enough time tonight to finish this . . . Ceinwyn wasting my time with this . . . Plutarch coming up with the idea . . . You better be grateful, you little assholes.

[CLICK]

Testing . . . what a disappointment it turned out to be. I expect you're sensing a pattern here.

Is there such a thing as perfectly insane? If there is, the Asylum bottles the stuff. I've heard psychopathic serial killers are often the last ones you expect—this knowledge came from television, which means it has to be true. The nice, quiet one. That's the Asylum. The whole place. The nice, quiet, perfectly insane one that tried far too hard.

The Admin building is like a giant principal's office. Secretaries typing at computers, kids going up to the Scheduling Room to pick up their dorm number—a teacher here, a janitor there. Eventually I'd find out the place also had offices, meeting rooms, and a chamber where the Elemental Learning Council met to deal with business, both Asylum business and greater Mancy business. School and Government all in one. No problems popping up out of that one. Commie bullshit.

The Testing Room is also there. Since most Singles didn't know any more about the Asylum than I did, they were hounded to the place by the Ultra grads who drew the short end of the stick. This means there was a line of about fifty kids when Ceinwyn Dale and I pulled up.

Another great thing about being with Ceinwyn Dale: she doesn't believe in lines. Or maybe she does in a general they-must-exist kind of way, but she doesn't think they have anything to do with her.

It felt good.

THE FANGED LADY

Petty, I know, but think about it: skipping a long line like that only happens a few times in most people's life, and every time it does, how do you feel? Right . . . completely awesome. You could make a religion based out of nothing but line skipping. We'll call the religion Hollywood. So back up off fourteen-year-old-me.

My Bi year *Theory of Anima* teacher, Audrey Foster, guarded the door. An aeromancer like Ceinwyn Dale, but not an Ultra, she believed in lines. In class, to teach us about anima currents and flows, she'd set up these big glass tubes that connected to each other with these breakers, then she would pump in air or water or sand to make whatever point she was looking to drill into our heads. She was in her mid-twenties back then. Long black hair, tight brown eyes. Had a thing for whimsical airy dresses. In the summer, when the classrooms would get hot . . .

You know what? For once, I'm going to keep my mouth shut.

So yeah, she's pretty. Bit of a hard case with some jealousy issues that she's not an Ultra though. Chance ruining more lives than just mine. She gave Ceinwyn Dale a do-not-cross-go glare. Ceinwyn Dale smiled back. The smile was way scarier. It said, '*I-eat-my-young.*'

"Miss Foster, so good to see you taking an active interest in recruiting for once," the smile said aloud.

"And so nice to see you returned and actually staying at the school for more than a single day, Miss Dale, and with another student—very productive," the glare returned.

For most mancers it's another discipline that grates on you. Pyromancers and hydromancers as the classic example. But for aeromancers, they get on with everyone but other aeromancers. Must have made Ultra class uncomfortable for them. You could probably blame the stick up Miranda Daniels' ass from Pent through Hep on that, if you didn't know she had the stick implanted in an exhausting surgical procedure when she turned twelve.

"If you'll move to the side and out of the way, I'm in a bit of a hurry."

Miss Foster gritted out a smile. It wasn't so much scary as pressured—the smile of a person caught between holding up a mountain and holding up the sky. "There's a line and I'd like to be fair to *everyone*."

Another kid got let through. A girl, red hair. No idea who she was beyond that. My school politics were not her school politics I guess and our path never crossed again. An invisible face in my story. Or maybe the paths did cross and I don't remember. Lots of Intra faces are fuzzy, Intra names even worse. Yet the redhead girl—if I could find her—would probably know exactly who I am. That's always bugged me, especially as I've gotten to be an adult and away from the place, but I guess all schools are like that.

"Audrey, would you please grow up?"

Miss Foster wasn't quite ready for it though. "He's already in his colors, Ceinwyn—it doesn't seem pressing. Perhaps you can leave him in line. No need to spoil him."

"Yeah, no reason to spoil me, Ceinwyn," I didn't help. Helping has never been my best quality.

"You'll call her '*Miss Dale*,' young man." Audrey Foster probably wouldn't have been one of my favorite teachers if it wasn't for those dresses and . . . um . . . oh, nevermind.

"Come on, Miss Frosty, trying to teach manners when you're all butthurt over letting another teacher do what they need to do?" There's me and my first impressions again.

"He has a point, Audrey," Ceinwyn Dale said. "Besides, if I left him with you, then you would have to listen to him."

"*Fucking right.*"

Miss Foster looked at me with pure disgust. Can't say she's the last woman to look at me that way either. "Fine. But only this once. Next time it's by the rules, Ceinwyn. We have to be examples for the children."

Yeah, think of the children.

I got ushered into the Testing Room, getting myself a glare from one aeromancer and a smile from the other. Like bitches in heat I tell ya. That phrase work in this situation? Whatever. Probably doesn't help that there's no such thing as a male aeromancer. I know . . . it's weird. Just one of those odd tics of the Mancy.

The inside of the Testing Room wasn't what I expected. No needles. No kids sitting at desks with number two pencils. No kids staring at targets neither. No kids at all. Just me, Ceinwyn Dale, and the Head of Testing, standing in a cluttered room with a door marked EXIT on the other side of me. *Come, escape while you still can.*

The Head of Testing is a nerd. Glasses, brown hair, shirt with an anime character on it that was probably a guy, but didn't look like it. Nothing professional about him. Nerd. Pure nerd. He checked out a checklist, filling in some info as we walked up. "And what's your name?"

I looked at Ceinwyn Dale, she nodded. "King Henry Price."

Which made the Head of Testing flip on through his papers. Back and forth. "I don't have a Price . . ."

"He's cheap," Ceinwyn Dale joked.

"Oh . . ." Testing guy finally glanced up. "C.D."

"Yes."

"Our late recruit?"

"Yes, Russell."

"Why's he in colors? Doing half my job for me?" Russell Quilt, early twenties, barely graduated a few years before I showed up. As Head of Testing he also doubled as a kind of counselor for the Ultras, though he's not one himself. Unlike Miss Frosty, it was never a sore point.

"He's broken enough for me to be sure." Ceinwyn Dale made herself at home, even flipping through Quilt's filing work. "No surprises?"

"Just the one yesterday I told you about." Quilt studied me for a bit. "Your gnome here passes and that'll make thirty. You're getting too good at this, C.D."

"Not good enough." I got what she meant. Still mancers getting missed, still people like Mom she didn't find in time.

"You got a *High Five*," Quilt shrugged, fiddling a machine with a fan of some kind on it. "First one in twelve years, give yourself a break." The fan stopped. "If he passes."

"I'll pass."

"Uhuh."

"And I ain't a gnome."

"An ewok then."

"Give me the test before I break your glasses."

Quilt laughed, pulling out another machine. "They're plastic, good luck."

Fourteen-year-old-me snorted. "Not talking about that way, man."

An eye-roll to Ceinwyn. "He always this aggressive?"

"Well, he's not calling you a '*fucking bitch*' so there's actually been some improvement."

An ink marked finger went up. "We don't use *fuck* in this room."

"Frakking bitch," Ceinwyn Dale relented with a sigh.

"Thank you."

Like I said: Russell Quilt, huge nerd.

Here's the vaunted test of the Asylum. The nightmare in the mind of potentials across the country, the threat of mancer parents far and wide—'*study hard or you'll fail your testing,*' '*eat your veggies or you'll fail your testing,*' '*don't talk back or I'll rig things, boy!*' The vaunted test of the Asylum is a circle of wood about three feet wide with thirteen glass globes attached to it at the edge. Don't get me wrong, it's a nice piece of wood—it's engraved, got Latin on it, even got a kick stand. But it's a *piece of wood . . .*

Fourteen-year-old-me was further displeased. "You're pulling my dick . . ."

"No, luckily not," Quilt mumbled as he started up paperwork to add me to his lists. "Very simple, no pain at all."

"Do I try to make the snow-globes blow up?"

"Of course not!" A flutter of paper and panic. "You couldn't even do that . . ." then after a moment's thought, "He can't do that, can he? Glass is technically earth . . ."

156

"Russell, stop giving him ideas." Ceinwyn Dale gave me the papercut-incoming face.

"If I don't blow it up, then what do I do to it?" I asked while making sure to remember to try to crack a window once Ceinwyn Dale wasn't around. "I got a cig headache, man, quit making this stuff drawn out."

"Touch the globe in front . . . right there," Quilt told me, pointing at one with a pen.

I did as told. Nadda.

"Next one, on the right."

Still nadda. "You fucking with me?"

"When we get the right one it will react to you. And no *fucking* in here, remember?"

"Only blow up dolls, got it."

"Next one."

We finally got our reaction on number twelve. The globe flashed alight for a whole three seconds then went out.

"Ah, there we are." Quilt smiled to himself. "You're a geomancer."

He said it like it's the most amazing thing in the world. I guess for kids who didn't have a clue what was going on, that's something. But not for me. To me, it was . . . phony. He used that voice on every kid. It made the whole thing shit. "We already knew that!"

"But now we're sure . . ."

"Why didn't you try the geomancer one first then?"

"That is a good point actually . . ."

"Miss Dale . . ."

"Be good, King Henry."

"But—"

"Next test, Russell," rolled me over before I could break anything.

"Right . . . the big one . . . big one . . . where are you, big one?" He rummaged through his testing devices, lost in the piles of machinery. "Sorry, haven't had another geomancer today. There we are!"

He pulled out a box, lined in some soft fabric—silk? Velvet? I'm not a fabric guy. Inside the box was a pair of magnets, iron. Old iron. Ancient iron. Not a fabric guy, but I know more about metals than anyone in the 21st century ever should have to.

The magnets were big enough to grip with your hands. Fourteen-year-old-me was littler than most, but I had muscles to lift them up and look from one to the other without struggling under the weight. "And?"

Ceinwyn Dale studied me like I might turn into either gold or dogshit . . . maybe even golden dogshit given our relationship. "If you're an Ultra, you'll be able to push those together . . . if not, you'd have better luck moving the building."

I studied the pieces, hefting them at my sides. "Can I control magnetism?" Probably thinking about becoming a super villain at this point.

"They aren't actual magnets," Quilt explained, pushing up his glasses with one hand and waving the other in the air. "They project an anima field. What makes Artificers special is they can store, draw out, and coerce anima not their own type by repelling them. You can't use them . . . but you can sidestep the rules to make something that can."

"Sidestepping rules . . ."

Ceinwyn Dale smiled my way. "Figured you'd like that."

I thought there was going to be some resistance or something, so I almost broke a finger clanging the things together. Russell Quilt gasped when I did. I only frowned. *Couldn't be it.* I banged them together again for good measure. "You sure these work?"

"Very . . ." Quilt whispered. "Very sure."

"Seems easy." Few more clangs. "Don't feel nothing."

"He's an *Artificer.*"

"I told you he was, Russell," Ceinwyn Dale said. "They do exist despite our dry spell."

"You're my first," Quilt told me in a way that can only be called creepy.

"Eww, man."

THE FANGED LADY

"No! Just! Of course not that . . . I've had . . . there was a very nice . . . I .
. . I didn't mean . . ."

"Russell," Ceinwyn Dale said, "Quit hyperventilating."

"He's the first Artificer in seven years!" Quilt did not stop
hyperventilating, he even got screechy when he became excited, "Russia and
Britain and France got one each last year, you know . . . and China has gotten
four in a row! DaVinci! Michelangelo! Colt! Browning! Some of the
biggest names in history!"

"I know, Russell. Try to compose yourself though. King Henry's got a
big enough head already, even if it looks small."

I put down the magnets or whatever they were. "What's this mean?
Seven years?"

Ceinwyn Dale studied me for awhile. I looked back. We both knew I
meant Mom. "Yes, King Henry. I'm sorry."

"It's okay . . . not your fault, Miss Dale . . ."

"First time it ever worked," Quilt muttered to himself as he put away the
magnets in one of his unorganized piles. "Means we got the *High Five*, C.D."

"I suppose we did." The Head of Recruiting didn't seem as happy as the
Head of Testing. Guess it's the difference between those that study and
those that go out and find. The optimism of cataloging what you've got
versus the pessimism of knowing what you missed.

Fourteen-year-old-me had similar if less philosophical thoughts. "Thanks
for finding me, Miss Dale."

She smiled at me again. Not the oh-you're-interesting smile or the
amused smile or the cutting smile. Her thankful one. The smile that every
time I see the damn thing it makes me feel like I've done something worth
mattering. "You're welcome, King Henry."

"My first Artificer. And a *High Five*." Russell Quilt—one track mind.

"What's that shit, a *High Five*?" That was me. Notice the *shit*.

Quilt happily expounded. "It has to do with the Ratio of Anima
Dispersion, with regards to human population specifically." The math again.
"Did you, um . . . study percentages at the school you came from?"

"I'm sure one of my teachers mentioned it."

Quilt glanced to Ceinwyn Dale for help.

She didn't help him. "I have a lunch date with the Lady, Russell, why don't you entertain King Henry until I return?"

He turned back towards me with a horrified expression. "I'm busy today, C.D.!"

"It will be informative for the both of you."

"I've got kids to test!"

"He won't get in the way."

"I was going to ask Audrey out for coffee . . ."

"You can do better."

Foster and Quilt were married during my Pent year.

"Don't break anything, King Henry. See you in a bit." Ceinwyn Dale waved at us, gave a last eye-see-you sign, then left.

"Shit."

That was Quilt this time.

[CLICK]

Quilt never actually told me about a *High Five* that day. Or the Ratio of Anima Dispersion. But hey, I was a teacher for two years during my graduate work as an Artificer. Poor kids. They learned some good words though. So why can't I be a bit of a teacher to a recorder?

The Ratio of Anima Dispersion works two ways that we know of. One way within human populations and the exact opposite way in the natural world. There's a theoretical third, but we won't get into it. Think of it as fractions. 2/3/5. 5/3/2. There are three tiers. In the natural world, the First Tier is the most concentrated. Among humans, the First Tier is the least concentrated. Necromancy, geomancy, aeromancy, pyromancy, hydromancy. That's your First Tier. In the natural world these appear as anima concentrations or flows or any type of that stuff. Remember fairies from an earlier session? Same stuff. Mancers can't use them or their anima, so I never gave a shit. In human population the phenomena *are* mancers.

THE FANGED LADY

This is all didactic as fuck, but it helps explain the *High Five*. One in ten-thousand people are mancers. One in twenty-five mancers are Ultras. Two in ten mancers are First Tier. Calculate the odds against population totals and the knowledge that the formulas don't recognize modern national cartography and it's amazing to think the five of us were pushed together, not to mention that Ceinwyn Dale found us or cajoled us to come to the Asylum.

Heinrich Welf, Valentine Ward, Asa Kayode, Miranda Daniels, King Henry Price. Did we cause problems . . .

[CLICK]

I stayed with Russell Quilt for probably four more hours. Enough to see the fiftyish other kids come through. No more Ultras, which ain't all that rare. We make more noise and the Asylum is actively looking for us. Ceinwyn's told me they figure on about twenty-five Ultras a year. My class had thirty. Another rarity. You'd think someone would have sacrificed a dove or something and known what was coming.

About a third of the Ultras are from overseas, with probably dozens left unfound in shithole countries. China's gotten pretty good; India's got an extra dosage of crazy people they didn't get in time. As far as Intras though, the Asylum only has so much room. Once population reached a higher limit than they can handle . . . well, kids have started to get abandoned to whatever fate they find. Mancers with no one to teach them. Going to go crazy just like my mom. Chance again, screwing over the poor and weak. More than fifty a year and getting worse. Why should normal schools be the only ones to do a shitty job? Sorry . . . it's a sore spot. It will be a sore spot when I'm a broken old man . . . if I ever make it to being a broken old man.

So four hours of testing. I was actually really good for fourteen-year-old-me. I think Ceinwyn Dale was already trying to plant the seeds to turn me into a Recruiter even back then. Or maybe it was the budding Artificer in me. All the tools Quilt used were made by my fellows.

That's the Artificer's gift. Items of repeat usage.

Seeing Quilt rummage through his stacks to find the tool he'd need—then seeing him lose the tool and have to look for it again ten minutes later—is interesting stuff. Electromancers have to spin a wheel then stop the spin—something to do with current control. Sciomancers put on a glowing cloak and are told to stand a foot from a dark corner—hell if I know why. I even saw another geomancer who failed what I'd passed. He couldn't move the magnets to within six inches of each other.

I was really good except for one teeny tiny detail. Detox sucks. Quilt told me the same thing Ceinwyn Dale did. No smoking on campus. Easy for him to say. I had a headache that could split rocks . . . and without the Mancy to help it out. Even an energy drink and a bag of chips he finally gave me to keep me from passing out didn't help. By the time the last kid went out the door, I was thinking about smashing whole walls to bits. Forget windows. *Walls!*

"Please don't," Russell told me while finishing up his lists.

"Huh?"

"Please don't break anything."

"Wha . . . I . . . you . . ."

He gave me a little smirk. Quilt's little smirk is about as mean as a Chihuahua. We used to have one at home—so I know about the little *putas*. Yippie shits. It was my middle sister's—Jordan Josephine Price, or JoJo—but she took it with her when she ran away from home about a year before my entry into the Asylum. She was fifteen at the time. Wonder if she still has the thing? Suppose she could, but it'd be ancient by now. Mean little thing. His name was Coñando. But back to Quilt.

"I'm a mentimancer, K.H."

"Like what? *Mind* guy?"

"Yes. I wish we'd call ourselves neuromancers, I wrote a paper on embracing modern styling actually," said the guy with a pen and a paper list. "But the Asylum loves tradition . . . even if it tries to hide it."

First time I heard the term, so I did what you'd expect. "What's the Asylum? Without math please."

"Oh . . . yeah. Um . . ." He scratched his brow. Simple answers are hard for Quilt. "Don't tell the staff I said it, but that's what the kids call the place. I liked it.

"So, mind guy."

"Yes, K.H."

"Can you make me do things?"

Didn't like the thought of that.

"No . . . at least, I'm only an Intra, K.H. Only reading and sending thoughts for me. Still valuable though."

"I'll say." Apparently, he was still listening in—or my motives were obvious—because Quilt blushed. "What about the Ultra ones like you?" Amazing how quick kids pick up ideas. Of course, by that point my expectations had been beaten down where I accepted anything. Probably helped that my mind's the type looking for any advantage it can find with new info.

"They're called Mindmasters . . . the strongest can suggest from what I understand, but mostly their gift is reading and sending long term memories. Also valuable."

Really didn't like that.

"Any in my class?"

Quilt checked his list. He knew already by heart, but Russell Quilt is a guy who double checks and always gives the right answer. "An exchange student from Dubai, Athir Al-Qasimi. Very wealthy family, excellent grades, very polite."

"Oh bull-fucking-shit!"

Quilt frowned. "Don't be like that."

"You're teaching some Arab kid to read minds? He tries to screw with me I'll choke him with his . . . um, are they the ones with turbans?"

Quilt's face had him at a step from calling the PC police. "Listen . . . K.H, we teach every Ultra we can get. A good number of your classmates are foreign. There's a girl from Nigeria, a boy from Mexico, another from Brazil.

You need to get along with them or you'll be in trouble. More than even you're used to."

I thought about that for a long while.

[CLICK]

Speaking of *long*, this went longer than I thought it would. Excuse me as I get dinner. Suppose I don't have to tell this to an invisible listener, but this stuff is still new to me. So . . . fuck off, recorder.

[CLICK]

Ah . . . the joys of the poor bachelor and late night fast-food runs. Oh, don't blame me—a man can't cook all the time. Probably hasn't helped that I got so used to someone at the Asylum making my meals for me.

Case in point, Ceinwyn Dale walked into the Testing Room while Quilt was attempting to distract my questions by making me play some kind of card game with elves and swords and crap. In her slim-fingered hands, she held a styrofoam meal holding thingy. Take-out box. That what they called? We didn't do take-out at Shithole Price.

"Your dinner," she told me, sitting it on the cards and sending poor Quilt into another convulsive fit.

Opening it up, I found it a plate of Chinese food. Also not a Shithole Price delicacy. Dad never got a hang of it. Sweet and sour pork, eggrolls, and a heap of fried rice. Told you the Cafeteria made good food. If Ceinwyn Dale is actually using this tape for recruits, then make sure you try the fish tacos on your first Friday and every Friday after that. I have no idea what's in the sauce, but it tastes like a whole tree's worth of lime has been squeezed into it and distilled and then stuffed with whole peppercorns.

"And where's mine?" Quilt complained.

"In the Cafeteria, Russell," Ceinwyn Dale shot back, "You aren't a child."

"Neither am I," got mumbled around a mouthful of pork. "Want the extra eggroll, man?"

THE FANGED LADY

Quilt was going to turn me down. I saw it in his eyes. Growing up like I did, you know how to read the eyes. You learn how to know when the slap's coming or learn to see if Mom's at home in that body of hers. Quilt was going to turn me down, but then he got a nod from Ceinwyn Dale, so he took the food from me. Guess she thought sharing's a good sign.

The rest of the food went down quick, then a goodbye to Quilt and out onto the school grounds with Ceinwyn Dale again.

It was summer, so it wasn't dark, but getting long in the day. The grounds had kids and teachers still, *but* they weren't all huddling around the Admin building. Brave Singles were checking out the school, returnees were hanging in the Park or Field or wherever. Clothes were being changed from street-wear to uniformed colors, where the street-wear would remain locked in closets for eleven months.

For me, I didn't see jeans except for two exceptions in seven years. As far as uniforms went, necromancers were walking around in their blacks like smarmy ninjas or assassins or something equally trying-to-be-cool, while the poor corpusmancers in red and white looked like a bunch of Santas after a stay at the fat farm. Every discipline of the Mancy has their uniform colors, I was happy mine didn't make me look like a douchebag. Brown it was.

"I'm an Ultra then."

"Yes, King Henry."

"What's that mean? I get the special powers and the seven years thing, but school wise? You wanted the interest right? Here I am. Give me the spiel."

Ceinwyn Dale glanced down at me. Given our height differential, I suppose the *down at* is redundant. "It means you'll be given a special place, just like I told you before. You'll be entering a world of which only twenty-thousand people on Earth are a part of."

"That's it?"

"I'm estimating. But, yes. We could all sit in a large arena at least. The normal mancers . . . the Intras as we call them . . . both the students and the teachers will be either in awe of what you can accomplish with your powers or jealous of it." She stopped me with a hand as a class of Tri's went past us, led by their student-advisor. Standing with Ceinwyn Dale, I already got funny expressions—proving her point, I guess. "Whether it's awe or jealousy will be up to how you act, how hard you study, the choices you make."

"That's some serious crap to throw on a fourteen-year-old kid, you know that?"

"We don't expect you to be the chosen one . . . just good at what your gifts are." She smiled at me with the grateful smile. Down again. Damn tall women. My whole life . . . full of tall women.

Reaching out with the same slim-fingered hands—that I swear I don't got a thing for—she pinned an emblem on my coat, next to my geomancer patch. The ring of thirteen stars. The sign of an Ultra. Then she kissed my forehead . . .

I didn't tear up and if Ceinwyn Dale tells you differently she's a liar. Okay. Maybe like . . . moist eyes. Could have been from dust though.

She asked me if I'd like to see the dorms and I think I nodded. I don't remember saying nothing back to her. I was going to live for the next seven years in the building, so it's a pretty big moment. What happens to big moments at the Asylum, class? Yup, disappointment.

Once we were in the common room there was a little bit of joy, however. "*Awesome*, a TV."

"It's controlled at the Administration building, so don't expect to pick up Pay-Per-View on it. You get one preapproved movie a night."

"Weak . . . Let me guess, seven years of Harry Potter movies?"

"Sorry, King Henry. There's not much time for entertainment at the Institution of Elements, and the time we do give you we feel would be better spent on more educated forms."

"Books?"

"With no pictures."

"Weak . . . where the hell is everyone anyway?"

Ceinwyn Dale and I were alone, inside what would be my living space or jail-cell—depending on your point of view—for the next four years of fourteen-year-old-me's life. Don't know if I really have an opinion on it. It was a place to sleep. Never really felt like home, not like my own graduate room would, or even Plutarch's house where I would spend many a night waking up every hour to watch over some anima experiment, but I suppose the Ultra dorm ranks ahead of my childhood shithole.

There was AC. Can't beat AC. The two couches curving around the front of the television were comfy—the kind you could slowly sink into and almost disappear—the television itself was new and modern, and the floor was polished wood, spotted with thirteen carpets in the discipline colors to match our uniforms. Behind the television there were four huge tables—the Study Tables as they were known, though they supported more than a few games of Texas Hold 'Em in my day—then against the wall was a row of stalls, computers with Internet access, though limited Internet access that came in but didn't go out. No escape, even the pixelated kind.

"Your class is having dinner," Ceinwyn Dale told me while she watched with those smiling eyes of hers.

"Huh . . ." I said with my amazing vocabulary.

"Want to see the restrooms?"

"I guess . . . never saw one before you know."

"Smart ass."

See . . . smart again.

Seen one restroom seen them all. There were showers each for boys and girls, restrooms the same. All divided into stalls for a fake sense of privacy. Psychologically, they wanted you clean quickly, not messing around and playing grab-ass. Or even playing kick-ass. So they made the experience about as uncomfortably naked in a room with other naked people as possible.

Ceinwyn Dale followed around behind me as I walked back into the common room. My hand reached out to slide over a table's top, feeling the pits and pencil marks. "These things look a million years old."

"As old as the building," was the answer I got.

How old is the building? About ninety years at that point. Too much explaining during this session however; so shut the fuck up and go look up the history of the Asylum on your own time. It will be under '*I*' in the Asylum library.

Case in point to the explaining: we eventually ended up in the bedroom. Singular. This giant bedroom with thirty beds set up and ready to go. They were nice beds . . . just the part that they were all together that threw me for one. Images of not even having the safety of gender specific showers pushed back and forth. Being naked in front of giggling girls and blushing girls being naked in front of me fought over my brain.

Embarrassment won over lust for once. "No privacy?"

Ceinwyn Dale went ahead and demonstrated the curtain system, like a hospital I guess—a really comfortable hospital with really thick curtains. "It blocks eyes and sounds that aren't too loud. Mostly, we prefer them to only be used sparingly, since the goal of this sleeping arrangement is camaraderie."

Camaraderie. The class of '09 didn't do camaraderie well. "What if we want to . . . you know . . . *get it on?*"

"You're so much more open than the other students, King Henry . . ."

"Maybe I know what I want?"

"As long as it's consensual and doesn't cause lasting physical harm, the staff doesn't care one way or the other what you do with your bodies."

"But . . . just curtains?"

"*Shy*, King Henry?"

"I'd rather not be getting tips while I'm trying to concentrate."

"Yes . . . I imagine if you got unfocused you would end up falling off."

"That a height joke?"

Ceinwyn Dale kept going. "You also have a cupboard next to your bed, with a supply of clothes. Colors only. While the bedside desk holds your school materials."

She eventually walked to my bed, desk, and cupboard to show me how they opened. I was distracted. "The staff really doesn't care if we fuck?"

"As long as it's consensual."

THE FANGED LADY

"Um . . ."

"As long as you both are into it," Ceinwyn Dale corrected for the 'C' I got in English.

"Oh, yeah. Of course." I thought some more while I checked out the brown colored backpack the Asylum had given me for classes. It was the first backpack I'd had which wasn't hand-me-down. Or stolen . . . "And . . . uh . . . what if girls get pregnant?" Unprotected sex for a year and *now* I'm thinking things through.

"They don't."

"What like . . . birth control?"

"Something like that."

She walked back into the common room without looking my way, so I followed. "The Mancy can do that?"

"No comment."

"*Win* . . . this place might not suck after all."

With a '*ha!*,' she sat down on one of the couches before giving me that Ceinwyn Dale which-way-will-you-jump gaze. "As long as it's consensual."

"You keep saying that like I'm going to be bashing girls over the head with a stick."

"This isn't Visalia."

"Kind of noticed. Not as hot out for one."

"Not to disparage your girlfriend back there, but these girls *here* are not white-trash-with-a-daddy-in-prison walking Freudian clichés. Yes, I checked up on her."

"Big words . . ."

"These girls you'll be attempting to romance will be just as impressive as I am. They won't take your crap anymore than I do either."

"Don't sell yourself short, Miss Dale," was the platitude I mumbled while facing the possibility of sleeping in a room full of teenage Ceinwyn Dales. Either a fantasy or a nightmare. Still not sure if I know which.

"They haven't grown into themselves yet, but they will. If you want to be with them, you'll have to give more of yourself than you have before. You'll have to work harder, make yourself something they'd want."

"Okay, now stop selling me short."

"I figured your size is obvious . . ."

"Guess I walked into that one . . ."

"Valentine Ward's father is a software engineer with his own company, Asa Kayode's father is a financial minister of Nigeria, Miranda Daniels comes from a family worth two-point-one billion dollars, and Hope Hunting's mother is a congresswoman. You already met Naomi Gullick. A teacher's daughter maybe . . . but do you think she'll put up with you?"

"Is this the make-me-feel-like-an-asshole portion of the tour?"

"Just be *careful*, King Henry. You're going to have to earn your place here. It's worth doing . . ." She gave me a pep-you-up smile. "I believe in you." Ceinwyn Dale getting sentimental—that shocked fourteen-year-old-me more than anything. I probably should have realized it was a warning signal for what was to come, but I didn't. 'Cuz I was stupid back then . . . still have my moments today. Back then it was all one moment pushed together.

Inside the big common room, so lonely in its size, I asked, "Will you stay until they get back?"

"Of course."

Half an hour, I guess.

Waiting.

In a way, I was the *new kid*, at least the *day late kid*. I'd never been the new kid before. When they finally walked into our common room, there were twenty-nine teenage pairs of eyes studying me, then Ceinwyn Dale, then back to me again. They knew her. Maybe liked her. Maybe didn't. But they *knew* her. Me . . . I was unknown and what did I tell you about the unknown earlier on these tapes?

There was also an Ultra graduate student, our advisor, or helper, or prefect, or whatever they want to be called—each four-year class gets one. I was one eventually. I had my kids call me 'Your Majesty.' Funny at the time.

THE FANGED LADY

Our advisor for Single was named Patrick Hanks. Seventh year, a Hep— always. Faunamancer, Ultra of course to be a Hep. What a white guy. Total dweeb. He made Russell Quilt seem cool. "Miss Dale . . . good to see you."

"Any troublemakers, Patrick?"

"Too unsure to cause much yet, but I'm sure we'll get there." He saw me. "Late arrival?"

Ceinwyn Dale stood, so I did too. She was still taller. There were a couple snickers from the crowd. I made a notation of who did it. "This is King Henry Price. He's an Artificer."

"Sup," I said. Elegant bastard.

I guess a few that knew what Artificer meant were impressed by that. I mean, we were all Ultras, but the First Tier is so much more rare, it made us stand out. Like I had anything to do with being one or the other. Like any of us did. But none of that matters. Might as well complain about being good at math instead of being good at singing.

One of them wasn't impressed at all. "He looks too small to be an Ultra," a boy with a hint of Europe in his voice said. "Are you sure he's old enough?"

Yup. Great start to another legendary relationship.

They were all there. If you think I've explained too much already this session, I can go on for weeks about this group. Months. Some would be very important, others would be in the background, but I'd know them all. Eat, sleep, study, fight with and against. Cliques and counter-cliques.

If I ranked them for having the most effect on me then Pocket, Jesus, and Raj would be up there, my best friends . . . first friends too. *Real friends.* I'd have romances, both successful ones and failed ones, with Valentine Ward and Eva Reti. Eva's short and dark, with gray eyes—so very calm and centered, but hiding emotional depth beneath the surface in her precious shadows where one had to look so hard to see it.

Valentine Ward . . . Valentine Ward. Boomworm. Just *Val.* Every man has the one that got away. Even then I noticed her right at the start. Already tall, but coltish and skinny. Light-reflecting blond hair that was frayed and short, but would grow long and full once she started paying attention to it. A face dotted with pimples, but a face with cheekbones that wouldn't quit. Her eyes that are black as pitch. Dark as anything I've ever seen. Smoldering embers, watching you. I got burnt and kept reaching for the flame. I still want to reach for it.

But the person that most affected me . . . probably Heinrich Welf. My rival. Necromancer. Bonegrinder. His family is old, noble when noble meant something . . . fought for the Germans in World War One before the Kaiser fell and the Welfs were taken as part-refugee, part-spoil for the good ol' U.S.A. Heinrich *von* Welf, he always corrected. Which always made calling him just '*Welf*' so fun.

Heinrich Welf—the boy who made fun of me in front of the entire class before I could even learn all these names I'm telling you. He was already tall then . . . fucker is six and a half feet now. Blond too, blue eyes, good looking if I have to admit it. Girls liked him. Nazi fucker.

Ceinwyn Dale had to sense the warnings in my posture. But Ceinwyn Dale is Ceinwyn Dale. She watched, small little smile on her face. The street rat meets the aristocrat. What's King Henry going to do?

I did what that stupid ass scar-headed Harry Potter should have done the first time that Malfoy bitch gave him trouble. King Henry Price asked himself some questions.

Q: He close enough to punch?

A: No.

Q: Get closer. Nod dumbly while you do. Done?

A: Yes.

Q: He close enough to punch?

A: Yes.

Q: He tall?

A: Very.

Q: Feel like punching him in the gut?

A: That wouldn't hurt him enough.

Q: Are there weapons nearby?

THE FANGED LADY

A: Sadly no.

Q: Can you jump?

A: I think so.

Q: There a stool nearby?

A: Couch work?

I jumped back onto the couch, then I flung one of the hardest punches I've ever thrown at Heinrich Welf's face.

I was up in the air when it hit. The Mancy snapped inside me, bones going all hard in my fist. Just like I loved. No time for reactions. I caught the fucker right on the button. His neck turned with a jerk from the impact, feet going out, uncontrollable pieces of noodle. His so tall, pretty faced body crumbled down to the floor like a corpse gone to dust.

"*Now who's old enough?*" I yelled down at him.

He didn't answer . . . but he kind of blinked eventually.

Patrick Hanks and the twenty-eight other kids gaped at me, finally turning to Ceinwyn Dale for a reaction on what to do.

Ceinwyn Dale is Ceinwyn Dale. She decided to keep watching how it all played out. Instead of papercutting fourteen-year-old-me, she just walked past with an interesting-choice expression and stepped over Welf. The class parted for her. "School starts tomorrow. Everyone have a good year . . . I'll try to stop by when I can." One smile back my way before she left. "King Henry, that's your freebie. Try to make friends, why don't you?"

"No promises."

Say what you will about King Henry Price, he knows how to make a first impression.

"Which one of you lit the dog on fire?"

RICHARD RALEY

Session 109

THE RETURN FLIGHT HOME TO Fresno was made all the more ominous by Annie B's snug winter clothing, which showed barely any skin at all. Her hunger issues were apparently under control enough for the pornstar look to disappear—there's a pity. But on the plus side: she wouldn't be eating anyone in front of me for awhile.

It was the first time I'd ever been in a plane. I'm guessing most people's first time don't go a lot like a private charter flight purchased by the San Francisco Vampire Embassy to get a murderous baroness as far away as they can, as quickly as they can. More likely it was packed in seats, stale peanuts, a five dollar in-flight coke, with the fatties getting thrown off as safety threats unless they paid double.

The plane was a small jet: posh, personal stewardess, wood-panel interior, comfy seats, even had a small pull-out bed hidden behind the bathroom. Annie B asked if I was interested in trying it out, but I turned her down. Before Sideburns, I'd been going back and forth on the whole *disgusted versus horny* thing, there's even a certain dirtiness to the whole idea of her hot-as-hell body being a shell and something that psychologically did it for me when she kicked my ass—guess I like strong women—but the cannibalism had thrown me on the '*no*' side as far as I could go. Even Prince Henry at his most lonely needs something to work with.

Instead of having wild-vampire-sex, the two of us sat in our seats, sipping drinks and studying each other, waiting for the plane to do its thing and rise up into the air. I drank my fav' rum and coke. She was having some kind of fruity martini that only women or vampires-pretending-to-be-women get to drink.

"How did you like San Francisco?" Annie B asked me, face deceivingly innocent. She knew she'd freaked me out past the point of no return, still didn't mean she planned to give up her game. Some people get a thrill out of just stepping on the field, winning ends up secondary to smacking around the other players to such a point they don't want to play any longer.

I watched her a bit, keeping my emotions close as I'd learned to do over my time at the Asylum. Gone was the little shit that'd stand up in the middle of class and cuss out a teacher. He stayed under a layer of dirt and sand and stone, covered in a layer of glass armor. If I'd learned anything dealing with the teachers at the Asylum, it was to only give away what you want. Sometimes—during a fight, maybe—that's harder to control. But business . . . I could do business.

It was odd how normal Annie B had gotten. Could have passed for human easily. Jeans, blue sweater, even a jacket. A young businesswoman dressed casual, late twenties, the kind who's modest until you get a few drinks into her and then who knows what's going to come out of the box.

Wonder how many men she'd ate on by using the same act? I'd seen in the box, seen her fight, seen her struggle with her hunger until hunger won. I didn't exactly feel guilty about it, but if I hadn't pushed her so hard in those fights . . . I had to wonder how the night would have gone differently.

She wouldn't have fed on me. I wouldn't be wearing my *Carebears* Band-Aid. Sideburns wouldn't have died . . . well, maybe he would have, but he might not have gotten ate in the process. I would have had some crazy-vampire-sex on the bed in the back of the plane, if not before then. That's the thing . . . I'd seen Annie B at her worst, at her own point of no return where she had no choice but to feed, her body blazing hot and who knows what kind of changes happening inside her.

It seemed to embarrass her.

THE FANGED LADY

That she'd broken the game between us. Like what happens when you accidentally see another person naked or drunk or catch them singing along to Lady Gaga. She might have beaten me twice in our fights, but by pushing her to such lengths I'd won the war. *Roma Victor*, Hannibal you stupid fuck.

When I looked at the twenty-something business woman façade, I still saw the woman she showed me, but I saw the beast inside she wanted locked away too.

I saw the real Annie B.

Vampire.

What to know something shocking?

I kind of liked her.

Liked her more than the fake her at least.

Sure, she kicked my ass, but it's *my ass*. Not easy to kick *my ass*. Got to respect that. Trying to seduce me? Okay, point against her, but she expected a normal guy. Funny thing about me is I've never gone big for women who come at me. I like to chase, I like to win the war, not the other way around. Turned down Isabel Soto, turned down a shitload of Intra girls that chased after me, turned down Sally after I came back from the Asylum.

Not Annie B's fault she expected something else. What seducing she did do, the careful dance between revulsion of her being a vamp but tempting me with that beautiful shell of hers, nicely played. The way she set up matters so we hit San Francisco the moment the duchess was asleep and out of the way?

Yeah, I noticed. Smooth move on her part.

Plus . . . Ceinwyn put her in my path . . . points in Annie B's favor. Ceinwyn was using me on Annie B and using Annie B on me. She wanted us to get something out of the relationship. Guess that means I needed to get over watching her eat a guy . . .

"Not very much," I finally said. "Too much water."

"Which keeps the temperature normalized," Annie B said, reaching into her travel bag. "We like coasts."

My eyes couldn't help but find the window nearest to me, filled with afternoon getting along with itself, not more than a couple hours of daylight left. By the time we got back to Fresno, the Fog would be forming itself to coat the whole city. "I've never been fond of water. Swimming ain't my thing. Only do it when I'm made to. I'm more of a sit-and-watch kind of guy around the pool."

She found what she was looking for, pulling out a cigarette and lighting it.

I stared. Been years since my last and I still remembered the feeling.

She took a draw, stray smoke lingering around her face. "You aren't going to throw up on me when we take off, are you?"

I watched the end of the cigarette, the burning gray and orange. "It don't make you too hot?"

"Not when I'm full," she said, glancing at it. "Want one?"

"Quit at the Asylum."

"*Poor baby.* They take the fun out of life, don't they?"

Outside my window, the plane started moving. Taxiing for the runway, I think they call it. "I've never had a problem with air or heights. Don't like too much water or douchebag necromancers though."

The stewardess came back, refilled our drinks, offered us some snacks in the form of little sandwich things. I ate, Annie B didn't. The stewardess was smart enough not to say anything about the cigarette, which got smoked down to nothing and replaced with another in minutes.

Annie B motioned with the new one, "Do you like aeromancers?"

"Generally, yeah. Have some problems with a classmate, but it's more because she's an ex's best-friend than the Mancy." I took another sandwich thing and bit into it. Hadn't realized how hungry I was. My gut didn't start hurting until the food hit my mouth. Hunger . . . makes us all stupid and greedy, human or vampire. "Plus, there's Ceinwyn."

"Yes," Annie B murmured, "There's always Ceinwyn."

Curiosity got me again. "How'd you meet her?"

THE FANGED LADY

Annie B's own eyes flickered out of a window near her, her face turning profile towards me, that long neck of hers leaning back. She took a long time answering.

"I've know the Dales for three centuries."

It made me smirk. "So you've known her since she was a kid? Almost impossible to imagine. Tell me she wore pink dresses, that'd make my day."

"She was a beautiful child," Annie B said. "Sad . . . driven. Responsible for her name and what it means to the Mancy. The more pain she's endured, the more she's sunk into her act."

"What act?"

There was a third cigarette. Not like she's going to get cancer, I guess. One of the perks of being a disgusting blood creature. "Pretending she's studying humans instead of being one."

"Guess you're the master, you'd know."

Her velvet eyes came back from the window to find mine, dirty brown all full of skepticism. "How many times do I have to prove to you I'm not human?"

I finished the last sandwich. "I know you ain't, Annie B. But if a human goes off into the wild and lives with some gorillas or some bears or some other wild animal, they ain't exactly like the rest of us when they get back, right? Same thing for you. Years of knowing our names, watching us, living among us—more than most Vamps I'd bet, on account of you being a baroness and all. You ain't as vamp as you like to believe, which is why it ashamed you so much when I watched you take care of Sideburns. Chomp chomp. Yummy yummy. Then that look . . . *what did I do?* Then you tried to make me hate you."

Her pale face got dark, the cigarette quivered in her hands. "I've done worse. *Much* worse."

"Not with me watching you."

"You don't matter as much as you think, Artificer," she hissed at me, looking just like many a woman I've pissed off before. "I'm paying you for a job, using your skills; this isn't some long lasting relationship between us. I don't care what you think."

"Now who's pretending?" I asked, with another smirk that positively pissed her off even more.

The plane took off.

[CLICK]

Sure enough, I didn't hate flying. It's not all that different from a good looking woman studying her ass or tits or whatever she likes most about herself in the mirror. High up, I got to see the earth in a new way. All those mountains and cities and coasts made small. Got to look at it from far away. Got to enjoy what I loved from a whole different perspective.

It was nice.

"Your face looks like a ten-year-old's," Annie B commented.

"Can't help it, I'm not a billion years old—I still experience new stuff," I said back.

"What else haven't you done?"

I thought about it for a bit, watching one of the most beautiful sunsets I'd ever seen. "Haven't been out of the country . . . never seen the Atlantic Ocean . . . still catching up on all the movies and television and music to come out the last eight years . . ." Each bit brought more thought into her expression. "Never voted . . . never broke a car axle . . ."

"Never killed a man?"

It stopped my list. "Not yet."

"Planning on it, King Henry?"

"Not really . . . but I've come close a few times just by accident. Bound to happen eventually once I put some purpose into it, don't you think?"

"Very flippant about death." Annie B frowned. "Most humans are much more reverent about it."

"When am I reverent about anything?" I took one last glance at the ground far below as the airplane drifted out over the ocean. *Be back on you in an hour, old friend.* "Enough bullshit conversation. Answer time."

THE FANGED LADY

"Why should I bother? You've served your purpose."

I was carefully noncommittal. "Going to bluff me, Annie B? Sure it's the way to go, after all we've been through? I've been patient up till now, but I'm done with the going along for the ride-on rails-magical-vampire-adventure. Time to break into some employee sections of the theme park."

"Let's see: you can't follow the item . . . I already know who took it . . . you're not *that* good in a fight . . . why should I bother putting up with your crass mouth any longer?" she threw back at me.

"Wrong. I can't follow it. But I'll know it the moment I get near it. Which means, whatever you're planning, you'll need me to confirm to you *it* is actually *it* and not a fake or a trick."

"And what's to keep me from getting what I think is *it* and then bringing *it* to you at a later time for confirmation, instead of hauling you along like the annoying little pebble you are?" she asked.

"Mostly me."

"Oh really?"

"Yeah, I'm done with this unless we do it my way. You can take your paycheck and shove it up your perfect ass."

"Compliments . . ."

We stared at each other. Neither flinched. It's a really bad spot to be having a stare down—thousands of feet in the air. If I broke apart any part of the plane to defend myself then things could get bad quick. I don't know if Vamps go squish, but I know I do.

She blinked first. Or maybe it was in her plans all along for me to tag after her. Never know with Annie B. "Fine."

I tried not to look too smug. She sneered at me, so I probably failed at it. "What's the plan? Break into the Fresno Embassy and steal it back?"

She called the stewardess for another drink and didn't say another word until she got it. I waved off another rum and coke, wanting to keep a clear head.

"It's Plan A," she finally said after a sip of blue liquid that smelled like apple. Blue alcohol—damned abomination. "Plan B is if we get caught, I engage in a duel with their duke in the very small chance it will distract them long enough for you to escape with the artifact and return it to San Francisco."

I frowned. "You said that like you don't expect to win the duel."

"He's a duke," is all she said to explain.

"That's it? Age wins?" I asked, affronted by the thought you couldn't break the rules somehow to win the fight.

"That's it, King Henry." Annie B finished her drink and motioned for yet another. Guess you couldn't blame her on account of her talking about dying. At what blood level does a vampire get drunk, anyway? "We fight, he beats me and begins to do to me what I did to Gentleman Shoals and I am left with a choice of dying to cannibalism or escaping my own shell and attempting to survive the night air . . . which is not very likely." She laughed with a particularly morbid note. "Even if I did, I'd lose the only home I've ever had. The one I've worn since my birth. I'd have to find another . . ." Her eyes flickered to me. "The closest on hand."

"Yeah . . . thinking you best get ate then."

"I wouldn't necessarily need to kill you." Annie B, back to licking her lips. Winter clothes or not, the hungry look returned when she talked of me as a shell. "You'd just . . . hold me for a while until I could find a suitable replacement. It's not painful . . . it can even be enjoyable. Like an invisible friend."

My stare was no-nonsense. "You don't pay me enough."

"You'd let me die?"

"I'd step on your gooey ass."

"And here I thought we were becoming partners."

I changed the subject. "What is *it*?"

"Is this another of your requirements?" she joked.

"Yeah . . . it is. That anima is out of this world. Whatever *it* is, *it* is some scary shit I don't want to grab without knowing what *it's* going to do. Fiddling with unknown artifacts is how Artificers get dead." I showed her a scar on my hand that ran down the length of my middle finger. "Touched what I thought was a yoyo in Plutarch's office; only it's actually a weapon which spins out blades on impact, some old Chinese thing. Only takes getting anima burned once. Or in my case: close to losing my favorite finger once."

She downed another drink. Guys trying to get her drunk must have a hell of a time. Then all the effort and cash and she eats them. Just cruel, Annie B, just cruel. "*It* is classified."

"By who?"

"They're classified too."

"Got Kings and Queens too, Baroness B?"

"Not quite, but something similar."

"I'm not helping unless you tell me," I said, putting my foot down.

"Really? All the curiosity as an Artificer, wanting to touch it and feel its power and you'd just give up and go home?"

I picked my foot back up. "Come on . . . don't make me beg."

She studied me. My shoulders, my arms, even my face with the scar on one cheek and the other scar on an eyebrow and the broken nose. Not an ugly guy, but not a pretty boy either. Wasn't one before all the damage, sure as hell not one after it. But Annie B still seemed to like something in it. "Maybe I should make you prove your reputation as a lover to buy the information from me. Tit for tat, as it were . . ."

"You know . . . I just don't get why you want to fuck me so bad. I ain't that interesting. Ain't good looking. You can have any guy on this planet, why try so hard for me?"

She gave me one of her looks that could make a metal table pop wood. "Don't sell yourself short."

"It can't be to get power over me no more," I thought aloud, wondering about it—it just seemed wrong, "You know me enough to know it won't work. Know I don't like being chased too, but you're still doing it . . ."

Her face turned sour as she tried to pump up Team King Henry. "You're smart in your way, you have nice muscle build, you're violent enough to hopefully fuck me like you fight, and you're young enough to have the stamina to keep up with me. Why wouldn't I want you? You humans and your emotional connections . . . It's not a damned big deal. It's something to pass the time besides cigarettes and drinks."

Each plus in my favor only made me smirk more. "I got it," I said to myself.

"Finally . . . take off your coat then . . ."

"No, not that. I know why you want to." My smirk could cut metal. "Got a bet with Ceinwyn on it, eh?"

Her face went extra sour. "Damn the both of you for knowing each other so well."

[CLICK]

After I finished laughing, Annie B finally gave me my explanation by pointing at a lone, abandoned seat near the pilot's compartment. "Get in my bag, there's a manila folder on *it*. Try to take anything else and I'll break your hands."

My Cold Cuffs were in there, right on top, but she was watching. No way to get them out without starting some more fighting between us. I'd finally got her to the point where she's spilling out info, so I didn't want to revert back to threats and bullshitting each other. It's fun stuff playing with another person like that—I learned the skill from some of the best at the Asylum, but too much of it became a bore . . . just like everything else in this world. Keep the peace, King Henry, at the cost of the first artifact you ever made.

My fingers ran over them, the polished metal still smooth, the glowing strip of white back to full force. They'd recharged their pool. I thought back to my workshop, to Annie B shuddering, in the kind of passion that only comes from chemicals or machine-grade sex toys. Then to that rope of blood not long after. There were some possibilities there . . .

I let my fingers slide off the cuffs, used them to shuffle through the rest of her bag. Guess it's her way of saying she trusts me. A person's suitcase or travel bag is personal after all, lots of private stuff in them. I'm not above snooping.

Annie B had her other sets of clothes in it. The ones that were dirty, smashed by the car, and gone through some fighting and then the skimpy set she'd used to keep cool. They weren't kept folded and neat, only thrown in wherever they would go, in a hurry. I pushed through them . . . *fuck me*. There was a set of knives, not cooking knives, the cutting into flesh kind. A semi-auto pistol too. Not a gun guy, so I don't know the model or manufacturer, but I'm enough of a businessman to know a top-of-the-line product when I see it. There was also a cell-phone, a swipe of my finger told me it was coded to use. No hairspray or deodorant or lipstick or makeup or any product you'd expect a normal woman to have. Annie B is all business.

Underneath it all was the file. "This one?" I asked when I pulled it out and showed it to her.

"That's it," she said, leaning back in her seat so far her eyes were on the ceiling of the plane. Her feet stretched out from her body like a pair of loose snakes, at ease, resting. Talk about bored. "We call it the Earthquake Baton."

I sneered. I didn't deal with *batons*. The name was going to have to change.

I flipped open the file. Inside I found a pair of pictures of the thing. No info at all. That sucked. I was hoping for Artificer notes. Something concrete. Vampires wouldn't care about them though. Not like they could use the *baton*. To them it's just another treasure. And it was a stick, a green stick somewhere between a foot and two feet. It had markings—mountains—chiseled up and down it.

That's got to be jade, I thought.

It also had lettering on it, Asian stuff that gives every American a headache. "Chinese?"

"Japanese."

"Huh."

She somehow rolled her eyes despite her recline. "I'm so lucky working with such a genius."

"Not much to say when I don't know anything about it. Jade, words I can't read, you call it the Earthquake Baton, and I know the anima it produces. But not much else."

"It's ancient," she mumbled.

"How ancient?"

"Older than me."

My eyebrows went up. That's old. "Not like artifacts break, but to still have pool power and be so old—it's some straight impossible stuff. Plutarch had a vase designed for hydromancers that dated back to the Roman Empire, but it was so old it actually not only lost its recharge, it was reworked enough times it had lost the *ability* to recharge and now it's just like any other vase." I thought about it. Be nice to have something you make last so long. Time . . . humanity's biggest enemy. Way worse than vampires. "We still use the same design today though . . . only its metal vases. Cheaper and quicker than learning how to bake clay."

"You can't pre-buy it?" she asked, curious.

"Not if you want the anima to hold."

She thought about it for a bit, then gave me what I guess you would call a briefing. "The baton is originally from Japan, at least 16th century, maybe before that, made by an obviously very talented Artificer. That Artificer eventually died and his family fell into hard times, his belongings sold and sold again, eventually ending up in the hands of the Emperor himself, passed on, prized as a great weapon of the Mancy. It was stolen back from the Emperor's treasure vault after the turn of the 20th century by one of the creator's descendants, who happened to be a geomancer and wanted his family's property back, if not for honor then for his own personal use. This man escaped to San Francisco hiding as a poor immigrant in 1906 and decided he'd use the baton the morning he arrived."

THE FANGED LADY

I put two and two together. Four's not very good. I studied the pictures of the thing. "Looks like a Shaky Stick to me. Better name, don't you think?"

Her eyes found mine. Rather a miracle given she sat almost horizontal and had a very perky pair of tits to try to look around. "I just told you it caused the 1906 Earthquake and that's all you have to say?"

"Doesn't it look like a Shaky Stick though?" I asked, shifting the picture back and forth like it was going to change. "Earthquake Baton takes itself too seriously."

"Neither is the real name, which was lost in history . . . like many other facts about a person's life and death and what they left behind . . ."

"Obviously. And yeah, causing an earthquake . . . that's something. Gives me a big ol' geomancer stiffy." Folding the picture, I slid it into my coat pocket. I was going to need it later. A plan formed in my larcenous little brain. Making an earthquake . . . not even the most amazing part about it. The way it used anima was. I downplayed my reaction. No reason for Annie B to guess my interest in this artifact. "Not very useful thought. You say weapon, and yeah, it could destroy a city's infrastructure, but something personal would be much more useful."

Her eyes went back to the ceiling of the plane. "Since this was before the Institution's foundation, a group of local geomancers who felt the artifact in action took it upon themselves to find it and when they did they hung the Japanese ancestor for his crimes against the city, taking the Earthquake Baton for themselves. They fell into infighting over where they would keep it until they decided no single geomancer could be trusted and fostered the item off to the San Francisco Vampire Embassy, where it remained housed for over one-hundred years, causing no harm except when a clumsy marquess auditing the embassy's possessions accidentally bumped it off its podium in 1989."

She gave me another look. I shrugged to keep off suspicion. Two earthquakes. And this thing is in Fresno. I don't know if it was pride in my home, after all—an earthquake or two might actually improve Fresno—but my shop's there and I didn't like the idea of someone else having such a nice toy in town that I had no ability to control. Either I needed to make it *mine* or I had to get rid of it. "This wasn't a simple theft, was it?"

"No," Annie B agreed, "this has been negotiated for a very long time. The Duchess Antonia has removed a very dangerous item she doesn't want in her territory and is either paying the Fresno vampires to hold it or got someone else to pay them. All sides are pretending it's a theft and will keep on pretending it's a theft, since it is a crime for embassies to work together in this way. And despite the fact that we all know this . . . I have to pretend like it is a theft as well and go after the stolen merchandise."

The view outside the window changed. My first flight or not, I'm pretty sure we were getting closer to the ground. "You're going to die for a lie."

Annie B's hand reached up on its own accord to touch the **B** at her throat. Through every change of clothing and jewelry it was the only piece that remained. "Wouldn't be my first time," she said in a whisper, her eyes looking at nothing, glazed over, her pale face covered in a frown. "At least this time they won't cut my head off . . ."

That time I almost believed her . . .

Outside of the window, the Fog formed below us. Just waiting to engulf our plane, to lock us in inescapable gray.

Session 6

IT'S BEEN TWO WEEKS SINCE my last session. I guess I could make some bullshit excuse, like saying I'm busy with getting my shop ready.

Truth that. Boxes are everywhere.

I keep asking myself: why did I agree on an antique store for a front, out of all the possibilities I could have chosen? An old lady already came by and asked if I'm planning on having any teapots. What the fuck do I know about teapots? And if I keep this going long enough does that mean *I'll eventually know about teapots?*

This shit could turn out worse for me than an STD. Breaking down what makes King Henry Price from the inside out, one teapot at a time. Badass Artificer turned teapot expert. The crap old ladies collect, you wouldn't believe it. Teapots. Plates. Glass chicken eggs . . . fucking shot glasses. Shot glasses are good for one thing and it ain't collecting.

Not the shop. Not the shop at all. It'd be the best excuse, but it'd still be a bitch-out.

Problem is . . . I've been asking myself what the point is. Ceinwyn wanted this tape as a part of our deal. She wanted me to give you some kind of real-crime version of my time at the Asylum. *'So the kids learn the lessons you did without all the blood and tears, King Henry,'* that's what she told me.

I've been struggling. Been thinking. Been wondering what this should be about. Then, once I got myself an answer to that question and realized what it *should* be about . . . I didn't know if I could do it.

I went into this whole thing thinking, *maybe I'll just give them a little bit of what life is like going into the Asylum, then a little bit of school time, that will get Ceinwyn off my ass.* Here I am now after hours of this stuff and I don't think that's the way to go. Don't think that's the story.

Two weeks and I've been playing the first five sessions over and over like some kid with a new song they've fallen in love with. Listening to myself talk. Each time I played them my plan went more to shit. I figured on giving you the first day of class next. Get into Pocket Landry and Heinrich Welf, tell you about some of the teachers I dealt with. About how weird the Mancy can make a man. But that's all gone to shit.

Epiphany. Artificers run on epiphanies. At least this one does. Can't do it the old way, got to do it better. Only way to make money. Only way to stay free of more strings than I already got. Maybe that's some insight. King Henry Price don't want to give the expected next. Doesn't like to be boxed in by the constraint of narration. Instead . . . epiphany. Listening to those five sessions, this shit's not about the last one I did. Not about the buildings, or my testing, or any of the technical explanations I wasted time on like the Ratio of Anima Dispersion. That's me ignoring the real tale as I got closer to the point where I would have to tell it.

Me stopping at smacking down Welf, not telling about the deep shit. Not telling about how I cried myself to sleep thinking about Mom and Dad. About how I couldn't take it anymore and got up at 3AM to write Mom the letter I promised I'd write. Not about the buildings. Not about my first day. Not about my classmates. About *me*. About the dagger in my heart that still pusses and bleeds to this day. About me and Ceinwyn Dale. About me and Mom. About me and Dad. The rest . . . it's gone to shit.

Here we fucking go.

[CLICK]

It's not like I didn't see Ceinwyn throughout my first two years at the Asylum. Usually it was a day here or there. And always weird times. I'd be at lunch and she'd stop by my table and tease me. Or she'd pull me out of a class and spend an hour grilling me about what I'd been up to—if I'd made friends, or girlfriends, that kind of stuff. We had a relationship somewhere near aunt and nephew if I had to guess at it. Not that I have any aunts I've ever known. Dad had a brother, but he died in a war . . . some misadventure in the 90s before war got serious again. Mom was an only child. So with Ceinwyn, it was a new relationship for fourteen-year-old-me . . . then fifteen-year-old-me . . . then sixteen-year-old-me.

Third year.

By then, I'd finally gotten over all my problems and was cool with the place. First year had been about rebellion, second year had been about finding my place, third year was supposed to be clear sailing. Supposed to be easy. *Theory of Elemental Prophecy. Elementalism as a Weapon. Advanced Elementalism.* I was pumped for those classes. We all were. By then, my little circle had formed. Me, Pocket, and Raj, with Jesus on the way. Welf had his too—Hope and Quinn and Jessica as the mean girls, with Jason as the muscle. His circle's better looking. Mine's funnier. All going good . . .

Then a grad student found me, first day of the year. First class of the year. I wasn't even completely awake yet. *Languages.* Jethro Smith handed out our first book assignment. *Hamlet.* He always started us out with Shakespeare. I'd just touched my hands on the book for the first time, flipping through the yellowed pages of a copy older than I was, when I heard my name. No biggie. Been called out of class for things before. Bit surprised though, since it was the first time in a while I hadn't actually done *something*.

Jethro Smith gave me the devil-rocker-sign when I looked his way. Dude wore a leather jacket too. Douchebag necromancers. My next glance went to Welf—expecting an expression of glee on his face over some game gone right, but instead I only saw puzzlement and trepidation, like he wondered if *I* wasn't making a game myself. About the last thing I expected was to be told to go to my dorm room and that someone was waiting for me there.

I was even more shocked when it was Ceinwyn.

She sat on our couch, looking the same as she always looks. Good. Beautiful. Clean. Out of the league of every man on the planet. There were clothes in her lap, cradled like a teddy bear. A t-shirt . . . new. Jeans. Shoes. Seeing Ceinwyn Dale stopped me at the door. Focusing in on the clothes . . . I thought, *what the fuck? A trip?* Or something like that. Then I saw she didn't have a smile on her face . . . and the world dropped out.

"What happened?"

She still didn't smile. "I'm sorry, King Henry."

"What the fuck happened?!? Just tell me! Don't give me fucking '*sorry*' and make it worse!"

She motioned to the couch, calm as always. "Sit down."

I didn't move. *"Fucking tell me."*

She didn't. She stood up and put the clothes aside. T-shirt. Jeans. Shoes. She walked over to me. Then, while I stared up at her, too frightened to move, she hugged me. *Oh, shit.*

"One of them dead?" I asked.

"Yes."

"Mom?" Certain I already knew.

"Yes."

I blinked. "But . . . she finally sent me a letter . . ."

"She's dead, King Henry."

"But . . ."

"She's had cancer . . . it came on very quick and nothing could stop it. The doctors gave her six months . . . but she didn't even make that."

And I lost it.

I cried; I grabbed on to Ceinwyn Dale like she was the only thing holding me up. I cried some more. She didn't shush me. She knew me too well. Knew I needed to get it out. She just held on. And I cried and cried and cried like only a sixteen-year-old boy feeling a new pain can. Every wall or trap or protection I'd built up over the years were just . . . *gone.*

"Momma . . ." I whined between gritted teeth. "Why didn't she wait for me?"

THE FANGED LADY

"It's not your fault, King Henry," Ceinwyn whispered as I shuddered.

"I could've helped her . . ."

"You aren't ready for that yet. You know you aren't."

"But . . . why? Why fucking *now*?" I finally pushed away from her hold. "Why? Fucking *why*?" I started pacing the common room—repeating "why?" over and over.

I'd been writing Mom for two years. Telling her all sorts of things I technically shouldn't have been. About the Mancy, about how I could help her one day. About my teachers. About girls. Stuff she always wanted to know but I'd never bothered with before, because face to face is too difficult.

I only got two letters back. One was from Dad saying that Mom got them and she read them but it was hard for her to write back, every time she tried things slipped away from her and it was a week straight of 'Bad Days.' The second letter, the one I'd just gotten during August break was finally from Mom. The letter I'd always hoped for: that she's proud of me, and read everything I wrote, and couldn't wait to talk to me about it all once we saw each other again.

Now she's dead.

"Fucking bullshit!" I screamed, glaring back at Ceinwyn Dale, flashing my teeth, snarling like some rabid animal.

She finally smiled at me. "It is. Death is . . . *fucking bullshit*."

Everything went out of me. The bubbling anger and mistrust of the universe as a whole fell apart upon itself, crashing away into a deep pit somewhere in the back of my mind where it could stew for as long as it needed to. It was a snap, something metal breaking, as cleanly as I could with the Mancy, but inside my head.

"I wanted to fix her . . ." I told Ceinwyn.

"I know, King Henry. She knew too. It was just too much to fight against."

I sat back down on the couch, feet shaking. "People die like this every year . . . crazy from the Mancy."

"Yes."

"That's why you are . . . what you are."

"Yes. I save as many of you as I can. As many as they'll let me . . ."

A whole bunch of silence built up.

"It shouldn't be this way," I finally said.

"You got smart since we last had one of these emotional discussions."

My lips turned up reflexively. "Oh, you know, grew up a bit."

"It had to happen eventually."

"If I laugh, will it stop hurting?"

"No."

I looked at my shaking feet and cried some more. "Thought so . . ."

[CLICK]

The clothes were for me. Surprise, King Henry! Mommy's dead and you get to go right to the funeral just as you find out! *Special Dispensation for Family Function*, signed by the Lady herself. Two days to grieve before I had to get back to school.

Lucky little bastard.

The jeans and t-shirt felt alien to me. Go two years without something and then go back to it, hard situation to adapt to. I might as well have never known it in the first place. '*Like riding a bike*' they say. Stupid phrase. You get yourself some forty-year-old people that haven't been on a bike in twenty-five years and tell them to start racing. Know the results? You'll get a lot of dead fat people.

Odd feeling, wearing those jeans and t-shirt. The uniform I'd grown accustomed to had the same fabric all over. Same feel on your arms and your legs, tailored to just my size. But jeans and t-shirts are opposites. Jeans: coarse, heavy, and restrictive. T-shirt: light, airy, baggy. Both felt weird in a different way. Yin . . . Yang. Mozart . . . Metallica. Wind . . . Earth. Least it's something to think about other than Mom being dead.

The car was waiting and Ceinwyn Dale drove us off without any fanfare or fare-thee-wells from either teachers or students. They were all locked up where they're supposed to be locked up. Only I escaped. Back to Visalia, along a route not so different from the one Ceinwyn took years earlier.

Car was a different color, different make, still new though. I was taller, I don't know, probably five-foot-six by then. Still short as fuck, but the days of being mistaken for a twelve-year-old were gone. Could have grown some real-non-fuzzy-facial hair by then too, if I'd wanted it. I'd grown, but there I was. Same shit. Going to the unknown. Quiet and brooding and pissed off at the world.

Miles and miles of driving, a stop for lunch, and then more miles, but this time only one conversation took place, not so far from the Asylum.

"Did you know?" I asked her.

"Know what, King Henry?"

"*Did you fucking know?*" She glanced at me. Felt the anima build up in my body probably. A strong breeze at her neck. "If you fucking knew, or the Lady or Russell, or any of you knew that Mom was dying . . ."

Her smiling eyes went back to the road. "I didn't know, King Henry."

And I believed her. "No one knew?"

"Your mother passed a few days ago. Apparently, your father has been in grief over the cancer and then this . . . he forgot about you or much of anything but her being dead."

Cut that bleeding heart again. Drip . . . drip . . . drip. "Oh . . ."

"Your grandmother was the one who thought of you. She found the number of the Institution on the Internet and had a conversation with the Lady. This happened yesterday."

"Oh . . ."

After a time of silence, Ceinwyn Dale had to have her curiosity satisfied. "What would you have done?"

"If you'd known?" I asked.

"Yes."

I found my eyes on the child-lock. "We would have had ourselves an experiment."

"Whether you can break an axle?"

"I know I can break an axle."

She smiled her *interesting* smile. "Then what?"

"I'd have broken the axle . . . then we'd have seen if you can actually fly."

That made her smile more. Which goes to show you why I love Ceinwyn Dale like the aunt I never had.

[CLICK]

Emotionally, I was completely fucked up by the time we reached the church where they were having the funeral service. Emotionally more fucked up than usual.

"Do you want me to come in with you or to stay here?" Ceinwyn asked me, showing some real concern for once. Guess I looked that bad.

How's a sixteen-year-old boy with a dead mother supposed to look? Can't say I knew back then. Shit like that gets blacklisted by we-want-happy-endings-Hollywood and how else am I supposed to see it? I was still at the age where death seemed like something that happened to other people in a world of black and white. You heard reports of death. You didn't see it. You especially didn't *feel* it.

I felt it, so I looked a little different than usual. A little quieter, little more contained with my foul-mouthed vocabulary, holding back against an eruption of anima of Old Testament proportions and ready to ruin people. I'd learned enough to control anima and the Mancy by then, but still, part of control is being able to let something loose. Damned if a piece of me didn't want to uncork it all and have an accidental anima discharge to rival all accidental anima discharges. Can a geomancer break the world in half? No . . . we can't. But we can scar the world's face if we put some effort into it.

My face ashen, I told Ceinwyn Dale, "I got to do this one alone."

"No, King Henry," she corrected me, "You don't."

"Getting all touchy-feely on me, Miss Dale?"

"I know the signs of someone hurting and, more importantly: I've felt what you're feeling many more times than you."

THE FANGED LADY

I couldn't bear keeping those smiling eyes in my sight. "You feel bad she's dead?"

"I feel bad when any mancer dies of madness, but I've also lost my father as a young girl and my mother as a teenager." She might have smiled, I didn't risk a peek. "I know it sends the world crashing down and a more dangerous one rises in its place."

The car door opened before me as a flick of anima unbolted a latch, bleeding off the energy on what seemed inconsequential . . . before I got into that church and sent the building crumbling down, creating a new round of martyrs and saints out of the petitioners. "Tell you what, I'm going to go bury the old world right now, when I come back . . . you can tell me all you want to about the new one. How 'bout that?"

She didn't reach out for me. That's not a Ceinwyn Dale kind of thing to do, instead a Ceinwyn Dale kind of thing to do is to accept the choice I made and see what I made with the next one coming on up. "I'll be waiting, King Henry, don't try to run away."

I stood up outside the car. T-shirt. Jeans. Shoes. Ashen face. Not looking very much a mancer but feeling like one on the inside more than ever. That's earth for you. Holding it all in, keeping everyone protected, but then—bang. Mountains crash, buildings fall, rivers are dammed and civilizations end. "Where would I run to?" I asked.

"I didn't say run to," Ceinwyn Dale corrected me again, "I said run *away*."

"Right . . . but I gotta face this one."

"I'll be waiting," she repeated.

My feet went forward.

[CLICK]

That's the first and only time I've ever set foot in a church. Can't say it's a good event to be first experiencing God's hallowed ground, but Shithole Price was never big on drinking the Jesus Juice. By the time Sunday rolled around, Dad was exhausted from working hard the other six days of the week. So he did like God and rested, usually in front of the couch with football on our television and too much liquor stored in one of those cheap styrofoam ice-boxes at his feet. The older I got, the worse Mom got, and the worse the Sunday drinking got.

Friends would talk about church to me, and Sally even tried to get me to come to hers a few times, but I never took the jump. That's too close for my tastes. Too close to something permanent once you began doing activities together. Given how she ended up a stripper, her preacher couldn't have been much worth listening to anyway.

Darkness held onto the church, cradling corners and draping from the rafters. I always thought of light on the rare occasions I thought of God, but suddenly I was in his house and my eyes were left to adjust to the dimmed haze. Maybe for funerals they turned the lights down. Seemed practical. Harder to see the body's rotting face that way. That thought stuck and stopped my feet.

I hung near the doors like a coward, trapped between running away, despite my brave words to Ceinwyn, and going forward. There were probably an even hundred people in the pews, no one noticing me. Old friends of Mom, or work buddies of Dad showing support. All of them were staring forward, heads drooping just a bit or looking off to the side. Not many eyes meet at a funeral. People don't want to see the question in another's gaze: *what if it was me?* Instead they find the ground or even close their eyes.

A preacher spoke. Quoting verses I'd never heard before. Jethro Smith had us read *Genesis* and *Exodus* for *Languages* the year before and that's the entirety of my biblical knowledge outside of movies and TV shows. It was good stuff, I guess. Good enough to keep me lurking near the doors, unable to go forward, my ears running my body as I listened. My eyes . . . they found the casket. That opened piece of polished wood, Mom's body being shown to those who claimed they loved her, but not a one had tried to help her. I put myself in the same category.

We all tried to understand at first, but eventually we all stopped caring, we abandoned her to misery. Dad tried the hardest to keep her alive. That's love, I guess. He didn't do a good job, couldn't stop what happened for nothing, but he stayed firm with her and that's more than anyone else did.

He sat in the front row, crying into his shirt. My grandma sat next to him, pretending she couldn't hear him. Mom's mom. Dad's mom died of breast cancer when I was three. Grandpa Price a couple years afterwards. I barely remember them.

I remember Mom's mom though. She didn't have a last name attached, she was just Grandma, the only one by the time I got old enough to say it. *What a bitch.* Surprise, surprise—another shit role-model in King Henry's life. See . . . Grandma had exacting standards to which my father didn't fit, which meant Mom had married down below her station. Grandma always saw Mom marrying a doctor or lawyer I think, not marrying some high school football star turned warehouse worker. But he loved her, adored her even, and that was enough for Mom. Maybe she did it just to piss off Grandma . . . wouldn't surprise me. I have to get the attitude from somewhere and it doesn't seem to come from Dad.

Grandma still came over for the holidays well into my lifetime, but the minute Mom started getting sick, having her mood swings, I never saw Grandma around but rarely. By the time things got really bad and the 'Bad Days' grew . . . never at all. Her own daughter and she was forgotten. A mistake, a failed creation, something to rot and die unseen, left to its misery.

And there's Grandma. Sitting in the pew. Right beside Dad. Not crying a tear. Glad it's finally all over and she can remember what she wanted out of her daughter's life, not what it had *become.*

As always . . . anger got me moving. There's something special about striding down the center of pews with people watching you. That's probably the secret of weddings. Sure, the dress, the ring, the lifelong commitment, but we all know the vast majority of humanity is shallow enough to want to alter their lives just for a chance to show off in front of their friends and family. I've known people who would give up more for less.

About halfway to the casket, realization dawned on those that knew me. King Henry had made it to his Mom's funeral from wherever he disappeared to for the last years. Heck, maybe his parents had even been telling the truth about the *special school* and he hadn't run off like the other two before him. Yeah, assholes, what do you know about my life? What gives you the right to ask yourself questions about it? What gives you the right to think about it at all? Wallow in your own shit, I know you got plenty, I can smell the stink.

The preacher started to wane in his eulogy, distracted, the room quieting to a hush that opened up a void for my footfalls to echo again and again, a *tap-tap* approaching on the carpet-covered wood floors. I could have found an empty seat. I could have had Dad and Grandma make room. I could have done some very private type stuff, but I didn't.

I stopped in front of the casket. Dad gave a gasp behind me and knowing Grandma she glared at the back of my head . . . I wasn't being *mindful*. Be mindful of others. Be mindful of your elders. Be mindful of your parents.

"Before you even start," I said to the room, my voice croaky from lack of moisture, "Shut up and give me a minute here."

Mom looked beautiful. Her dark hair was still lush, her lips were still pouting—like death refused to touch her. It would eventually. But not yet. Corpusmancer, Ceinwyn Dale had guessed, and here was the proof of it. Mancers sense what normal people can't and now that Mom was gone and her natural protections were down I could feel it all. Mom's body was filled to the brim with strange anima, enough it unknowingly kept her young all these years, even as it drove her insane. Enough of it that even if I'd taught her what I knew it would have been too late . . . but that thought gave me no relief.

I still felt guilty. All the 'Bad Days,' all the 'Good Days,' all the times I'd blamed her and cursed her and wished her dead and here was that wish come true after I'd finally hoped for something better. Too fucking late, kiddo. Too late before you were born. Some Recruiter for the Asylum screwed up and missed her back in the 80s and that's it. Your Mom got fated to end up here. Dead and still so beautiful.

My hand reached out, hovered over her, doing as I'd been taught—what she'd been denied—and feeling the anima saturation inside her. It was so damn much anima . . . twenty-odd years of a mancer's resting rate of anima building, minus the few accident discharges she probably hadn't even realized had taken place. Eventually it would turn into necro-anima. Life to death. The decaying side of the world as the rest of her turned to something moldy. Even anima can only keep time at bay for so long. We all rot in the end. Nothing is eternal.

There was a void in the pool, near her lungs. "Oh, Mom . . ." I croaked aloud.

Her first use of anima and it had been used to kill her. To end her pain. She gave herself cancer to end it, I realized with a sob. That hole of anima burned into my mind.

"I'm sorry they didn't find you . . ." I whispered, "So sorry I couldn't do anything to help you . . ."

Over my shoulder, Dad kept crying. Big tough guy reduced to tears, his eyes puffy, his face worse than mine. Mom had been his world. He'd stuck by her through everything. I only hoped that one day I could love a woman like that. Knowing my childhood, fuck if I will. No chance. But I'd settle for a fourth of it. That's a big ass fourth . . .

"She was like me, Dad," I told him. "It's not her fault."

"Like you?" Dad asked, voice muffled in shock.

"The school . . . they never found her . . . so this is what happens," I explained. "I was hoping I could help her when I got home, but I guess . . . well, I was too late." Quite a few people, including the preacher and Grandma eyed me like I was the crazy one and maybe that's what I'd inherited. "There's nothing either of us could have done. Save maybe understand it, at least . . . so I guess you did right by her. More right than I did."

Dad's face crushed up in grief. "Sit down, boy. We'll talk after the funeral and you can come home for awhile. Forget that place, okay? If they did this . . . just forget them forever."

I guess I didn't expect him to understand it all, so when he didn't get it . . . well . . . oh well. Maybe one day it would click for him. "I can't, Dad. I learn or I end up like Mom. After that . . . I got to do something to make this right. I gotta go. Sorry."

Dad looked at the casket again. "She wanted you to go, but I didn't."

"I know, Dad."

"Best do what your mom wanted then. She always knew best."

My feet moved. I walked from the casket, away from Mom's dead body to the sound of my dad's new chorus of tears.

"See you in five years, Dad," I said mostly to myself.

I walked past all of them, the journey of heading back up the center of the pews not nearly as fun as it is the other way. I recognized faces, Dad's boss and co-workers. Sally was there with her mom. I didn't even give her a second glance. I'd moved so far beyond that by then. This life fit worse than my brand new jeans and t-shirt. It all felt wrong. Too free and too confined at the same time.

[CLICK]

On the way out of the church, in my haste to get through the doors and to Ceinwyn Dale's car, I ran into a woman who was hanging outside, like she couldn't decide if she wanted to break the barrier. We both staggered from the impact. She yelped out, stepping back, while my hand lost its hold on the church door, sending it to close on me, a thud of wood on my shoulder.

Around the wood, I saw black hair and a beautiful face and for just a moment some part of my mind not in touch with reality took over and my lips betrayed me to utter, "Mom?"

The woman's head snapped up, hair falling farther away to reveal a face much younger than I'd ever seen my mother's, back before she got sick, back to a time I only knew from picture frames and an old high school yearbook that occasionally got dug out of a closet. Only this woman had my dad's nose, much sharper than Mom's. She frowned at me and I realized my mistake.

A gasp escaped from her pouty lips. *"King Henry?"* she asked in surprise.

THE FANGED LADY

"Susan . . ." I said back, staring at her. I stepped around the door to finally let it close, but my mouth stayed shut for once.

My eldest sister smiled down at me. She'd gotten Dad's height too. She had to be twenty-two by then, I'm pretty sure. I hadn't seen or heard from her in four years.

"You grew up," she told me as a greeting.

I could have asked so many questions. But I settled on the present. "What are you doing here?"

Instead of answering right off, she motioned for me to hug her, so I did. One of my lost sisters appearing just like that . . . and the one I liked. Susanna Belle Price. It made my mind turn off more than Mom's death had. I just kind of . . . became a part of the moment.

"I heard about Mom, but . . . it's hard to work up the nerve, Lil' Bro. Here I've been, sitting outside on my butt, not able to go see Dad or you or JoJo."

I frowned. "JoJo left," I told her. "Year after you did. No one's seen her since."

There we were, two siblings talking about the missing one on the sunny summer day, outside of our mother's funeral. Susan's expression went pretty shocked at my news. "She left? What do you mean *she left?*"

"Her and Dad got into a fight like always and it was one too many," I explained, "So JoJo bailed on us."

"It's just you and Mom and Dad?"

I grimaced. "Not quite. The parents got me hooked up with this special boarding school a couple years ago, so I've been gone too."

"You left them *alone?*" she accused, face disapproving.

"And who do you think you are giving me shit for this one?" I yelled back. "You *left* first, Susan! JoJo *bailed!* What I did was fucking *escape!*"

"Right . . . you're right . . . I just . . . I never thought it would get this bad," she admitted to soothe my anger.

"This bad alright," I agreed, my whole body tight, anima bubbling, "and no way to fix it."

She studied me, up and down again, a frown on her face, probably still thinking how much I'd grown. I'd been twelve and not even five-foot last she saw of me. "So where are you going to, not staying?"

"I said goodbye, that's all I needed. What about you?"

"I can't, Lil' Bro . . . it's too weird. Especially with JoJo gone. They'll blame me for that too."

"Dad could probably use a visit later if you have the time," I tried to find some middle ground for her, "Wait until Grandma's not around."

"Yeah, I guess." She hugged me again . . . hard, like she didn't expect to do it again. It reminded me of the hug I got before she left home. "You're just going back to school?"

"Yup."

"I never took you for the type."

"It's a bit different than normal school." We started walking towards the parking lot, getting away from the church. "I was tenth in the class last year."

"Out of ten?" she joked.

"Out of thirty."

"Lil' Bro doing well at school . . . things sure have changed." Susan stopped us in front of a SUV newer than Ceinwyn's car. "This is mine."

Nicer than Ceinwyn's car too. "You're doing well for yourself then?"

She nodded with a smile, a little nervous, maybe a little ashamed too. "I settled in Washington, up north, not DC . . . and worked my way through community college, got a secretary position, have a boyfriend . . . it's pretty nice and normal. I like it . . ."

I was just tall enough to see into the SUV's interior; plush leather, premium electronics. My eyes caught the child-lock. I had a dreadful thought. *The Mancy finds itself.* "Anything ever break around you?" I asked, serious.

She seemed confused. "What's that mean?"

"Start any fires, walk on water, hear voices in your head?"

"King Henry . . . you're not sick like Mom, are you?"

204

I gave her a hard look. "No, I'm fine. Are you?"

"Of course not," she said, giving me an expression back that said I might be a *little* sick. "What are they teaching you at that school? New Age Religion?"

"Something like that."

Susan opened a door and stepped inside to the driver's seat. "I thought about taking you with me when I left the first time, but you were so young and so much trouble and it probably would have been considered kidnapping if they caught me with you . . . so I talked myself out of it."

"It's okay, Susan," I told her, giving her conscience an ease. "It worked out for me. You go have your normal life, Big Sis. One of us should."

She couldn't meet my eyes when she offered, but she did ask, "You sure you don't want to come with me this time?"

It meant a lot. To have another out. But by then . . . there's no way I was actually getting out. After Mom, after Ceinwyn, after the Asylum . . . I was a mancer through and through—and I had to protect my own. "No, Susan. I'm going back to school. It's the only way."

She gave me a last smile. "If you ever change your mind, then come find me. Seattle, remember that."

"Seattle, sure. Rainy ass Seattle. If you're not mad yet, you will be," I told her, backing up to let her close the door.

With a final wave, she pulled out and drove away, gone as quickly as she appeared.

I haven't seen or heard of her since . . . and I've looked . . . she's disappeared . . .

[CLICK]

Ceinwyn waited for me like she promised. "So soon?" she asked with a questioning smile as I stepped into the car and sat down.

"I don't like funerals apparently."

"No one does," she told me. "Not even necromancers."

"Wouldn't put it past them," I mumbled, staring out the window.

"Who was the familiar looking young lady you talked to?" she finally asked after the prescribed time she figured I needed for her to wait.

"My sister."

"Interesting."

"I asked her if mysterious things were happening around her."

"Were they?"

"She said no."

"That's good."

"Yeah, it is," I agreed.

"We have an extra day off, you know, if you want to go somewhere else to relax." Coming from Ceinwyn Dale, the idea of taking a day off is a miracle. She barely saw her house—relaxing . . . vacations . . . those were things for other people. "Have you ever been to the Pacific Ocean?"

"Back to the Asylum," I told her. "I might not beat Val or Welf or Miranda this year, but I think I have a shot at top five with the classes we're taking. Be nice to see the look on Asa's face when I pass her."

The car started with a purr of its hybrid engine. "You've not only grown up, King Henry, you've become a good student. What a world . . ."

"Mom would want me to," I said, as if that explained it. Maybe it did. Maybe in the end, King Henry Price just needed someone to save. Mom was gone, but others like her still remained.

Session 110

"HOME SWEET HOME," I MUMBLED as I unlocked the front door to my shop with a small burst of anima. One of the perks about being a geomancer is not needing keys. Which comes in handy during those situations where you've been kidnapped by a vamp who don't care if you ever find your way back. I guess I should have been glad she even bothered to lock the door.

The vampire in question followed behind me, taking a second glance around my shop. Unlike the first time, she was armed with the pair of knives that had been stashed away in her traveling bag. Also unlike the first time, my shop wasn't immaculately cleaned. Instead, it looked like some kind of derby had taken place, which I suppose ain't so bad of a metaphor for the fight Annie B and I had. Glass, ceramic, and my shelves took most of the pain. The comic rack was fine, so was my little LED 3D television I'd bought to watch my make up television. Least we'd broken the stuff I hated.

"Is that your motorcycle?" Annie B asked, closing the door. Back at the curb, a year-old modern-looking bike sat forlorn, the only transportation in the parking lot during that hour. Sorry to ruin my image, but it's not a chopper.

I pulled out a broom from under my checkout counter. It was a collapsible model. When I bought it, I'd been thinking about the occasional accident, not a whole store of them. "Yeah."

"Why?"

"Why a bike?" I asked, dumping my first load of glass in my trashcan. Five-hundred dollars down the drain.

"Why an electric?"

I let out a sigh; put the broom against a display. Guess the mess could wait until after I survived the night. If I *did* survive. I had other shit to do, lots of shit, Artificer shit, mancer shit, Annie B's questions weren't even near the most important and cleaning ranked below *them*.

"Will you believe it's for the planet?"

She laughed. Annie B had a nice laugh, vampire or not. It was dark and deep, kind of dirty. Just like the rest of her, it tempted you . . . to keep talking, keep making her laugh. "Will you believe not a single part of me wants to eat you, King Henry?"

I studied her face, still saw the beast lurking, waiting. "Nope, see it in your eyes. You won't . . . but you want to."

Her tongue touched her lip like it continually had when she'd been really hungry. "Then how about you tell me the real reason for the electric?"

"It's embarrassing . . ."

She squinted at me. "I'm not sure how car choice relates to embarrassment unless it has something to do with sexual compensation and very big trucks."

"Goes like this," I reluctantly explained, "I had a girlfriend at the Asylum who was on again and off again. Liked the shit out of her. Humped the shit out of her too. For awhile at least. One moment she'd be all over me, the next moment she was standoffish. Confused me pretty bad. Scared me pretty bad too when she'd get that look like she was going to smash me across the room."

Annie B kept up the squint, it was kind of cute. That's different . . . Annie B did sexy extremely well, but cute . . . cute's new. Didn't think she had it in her. "And this relates . . ."

Yup, about as embarrassing to speak about as I'd expected. "She's a Firestarter. So I don't trust flammable vehicles."

THE FANGED LADY

Now that got her to laugh again. Women are all on the same side as long as they don't actually know one another. They get to know one another . . . then it gets even worse.

[CLICK]

What does an Artificer do?

Let's go back to one of my very first sessions. It might have been the very first one actually, I can't remember, but I do remember using the example.

So it's thousands of years ago and there are these two groups of Irish or British warriors, I think I called them fucktards the first time around, and these warriors are waving their asses and peckers at each other, which is more cruel than terrifying. Like a guy wants to see another guy's dick hanging between his ass cheeks just before he's about to die in a gruesome battle and have that be his last mental image. That's just rude. Why not bring out the tribe's most beautiful woman and get her naked and show her off against the other tribe's naked woman?

Look at me, King Henry the Diplomat.

Only one guy ain't in on pecker waving, he's standing silent, concentrating so hard he might be constipated and then, after five minutes, a bolt of lightning flies down from the heavens and smashes into the other side, killing a couple guys and running the rest of them off. We'll call the guy Merlin. As a normal mancer with preparation and a proper use of theatrics and bluffing about having a second bolt of lightning, he keeps his soldiers alive.

Or maybe it was just the pecker waving.

But let's change the situation, maybe in this situation Merlin shoots down his lightning and misses and while a couple guys get so scared they crap themselves, all the peckerwavers still man it up and charge each other and what you got is a lot of dead people, while Merlin is standing around for five more minutes pooling anima for another lightning bolt.

Surviving this, Merlin goes to his cute friend Nimue who happens to be an Artificer and Nimue whips Merlin up a nice staff with a snazzy crystal on top that can shoot a preloaded set of lightning bolts. Next time, Merlin's got his staff and by thinking even further ahead he's got more than one lightning bolt right off the bat.

This is the easiest example of artificing. The control and storage of anima for specific pre-set tasks. The bigger the task, the more tasks, the more types of anima, the more complicated it all gets. Trust me, it can get complicated in a hurry.

The Shaky Stick?

Up to that point in my life and a long time beyond it . . . I'd never imagined something as complicated as controlling earthquakes. I'd pooled an hour to flip a car. Okay, maybe it had been overkill and I let most of my anima run loose, but an earthquake . . . what kind of power and complication and mastery of anima manipulation did it take to make something so big? And the special anima it had . . . *how's it doing it?*

I was a long time from finding out.

[CLICK]

I left Annie B in the storeroom, watching a set of old *Walking Dead* Blu's while I got down to work. I had to be fast. She wouldn't just sit around playing with her knives forever. Sooner or later, done or not, she'd drag me out of my shop. I *had* to be done if I wanted the night to go my way, not just her way.

My way had both of us living, the Shaky Stick under control, and Annie B leaving Fresno after handing me a big check. If I didn't finish these bits of artificing . . .

Without one: Annie B died. Without the other: The Shaky Stick stayed under the wrong management.

Got to finish fast, King Henry.

A snap of anima I'd pooled returned my worktable back to level, the pieces I'd manipulated to trap Annie B slowly sliding downward like some metal mudslide looking to wipe out Malibu. I walked by it, ran my hand over it, felt the cold metal. There was a single seam in one spot that had held her left thigh . . . but the rest . . .

"Good enough," I said aloud.

Underneath the table I pulled out a drawer, took out a piece of paper and a pencil. Setting them on the table for later scrap-work of anima conversion formulas, I went over to my wall of vials. There were thirteen rows of holes. Most were empty. Pulling my electro-anima vial out of my coat pocket, I slid it in its row . . . all lonesome.

My eyes went down the line, type by type.

"Just enough."

I pulled out a pair of cryo-vials and a pair of geo-vials.

Yeah, I'm not going to be telling you how I ever *exactly* make something, like twenty-two-year-old me would say, the cocksuckers at the Guild of Artificers might be listening in to these things. Better to be careful with my designs, even the very oldest ones. Just know it was a lot more work than you'd guess.

I'll let you in on one modification I made and that's to my static ring: I changed the trigger from an anima pulse to a pressure switch. I had a feeling it was going to be another night for big anima pools.

The others? They are just going to have to be surprises.

But it was going to work.

It had to work.

[CLICK]

Apparently, vampires have a thing for big walls. Unlike the one in San Francisco, this one's in Fresno, so it's made out of those ugly gray concrete bricks construction companies use for tract-homes because they're cheap and easy to make, which means more money for developers and more depression for the homeowner. Only Annie B and I weren't in a tract-home area of town, which is surprising, about 99% of Fresno has been nasty live-in-your-box tract-homes since the housing boom-then-bust a decade back. Miles and miles of tract-homes, painted the same three different shades of tan, with the same doors and the same roofs and a whole five different models over and over, all engulfed by the Fog.

How could anyone hate the place?

Annie B stopped the car, which she'd rented at the airport. The first one being flipped over in Los Banos but still rented out in her name, the rental guy had been just a little bit befuddled over why she needed another one, but money moved him towards enlightenment with the speed of most televangelists. Annie B not having a psycho pyromancer ex-girlfriend, it had a normal gas engine.

"Okay, game plan time," she told me, giving me a significant glare that said shut-up-and-listen.

My usual self, I ignored it and gave her trouble. "Yeah, I know. Sneak in, tell you what I feel, we find it, get out, or you die and I get ate, you've told me enough times already. I get it. I planned some backup plans. It's all good." My hand motioned outside the car. "Sun's coming up and the Fog don't have forever—let's get this over with."

Annie B listened calmly through the whole thing. She even nodded along. But when I finished, she right up punched me in my chest with a jab hard enough to slam me into the door. "Shut up and listen," she ordered.

"Are we never going to stop with the beating on each other?" I asked, rubbing my chest and wincing with every motion. She'd hit me right where the muscle was smallest over the bone and damn did it hurt. "I gave in and gave you I'm-going-to-die sex, you can't keep punching me after that."

Yup, we did. I fucked the evil blood creature. Ain't I a softie. More on this later.

She only glared. "Sex isn't enough, maybe after we fall in love and get married and have a family and all is right with the world I'll stop hitting you though."

"That means never, right?"

She punched the other side.

"Damn it, lady," I groaned.

212

THE FANGED LADY

"*Quit talking,*" she hissed with a dangerous glint in her eyes, velvet gone predator. When I'd been silent for more than ten seconds—besides my chest rubbing and wincing—she continued, "We can't be caught. You understand, yes? And when I ask you a question over the next five minutes, might I remind you that I'm only looking for a nod, not your usual crap."

I nodded. The things I put up with to get my hands on thousand-year-old artifacts. Taking beatings, working two artifacts even though I'm exhausted, having sex with gone-loopy vampires. Awful I tell you, completely awful.

"Vampires have very good hearing, good enough that they can hear a heartbeat from down a hallway. Understand?"

I nodded carefully.

"Once we get over that wall, you aren't going to be able to talk or they'll know a stranger is in the area immediately, understand?" she asked, with one of those mother-nodding-at-child-to-get-a-similar-reaction nods. She had such a beautifully long neck that it took her a much longer time between movements than it did my short stumpy ass. Her neck choker flashed at me in the gray.

B.

B.

B.

I never had asked her what it stood for after we got over the Anne Boleyn bullshit she peddled. Getting her real name before the sex probably would have been a good idea.

I nodded again.

She gave me a smile along with an expression somewhere between her *I-want-to-wear-you* face and her *so-you-aren't-a-moron* face. "You'll be limited to hand signals. Pointing will work best and try to keep your middle fingers under control. But, most of all: I want you to know that while we're somewhat cooperative at the moment, if it's your foul mouth that happens to get us caught among the many likely possible accidents and mistakes that can get us caught, I will try to kill you before they manage to take me down."

I believed her. Not going to do what she wanted, but I did believe her.

I raised my hand more warily than I ever had at the Asylum with my teachers. "So . . . this," I motioned at the gated community for wealthy, stuck up, white people that our car sat across the street from, "is really the Fresno Vampire Embassy?"

Annie B glanced farther down the street, her eyes trying to pierce the gray fog and make out the huge gate that announced the name of the community. "Not quite. The Fresno Embassy is inside the place, but the houses are rented out to vampires staying in town. Fresno is a very popular hunting spot during the winter, it gets a lot of traffic and it was decided years ago that we should go this route instead of buying a hotel or apartment complex out. We require a certain amount of privacy . . . as I'm sure you understand . . ."

I got conflicted between a pair of absurdities. In the end, I let my comment about someone actually finding Fresno popular or worth traveling to stay inside my head and went with, "Wait . . . you're telling me there's *actually* a whole vampire gated community in the middle of the suburbs? Wasn't that a shitty TV show a few years back?"

"I wouldn't know, I'm a busy person—but you're the one who made me watch stupid zombies for three hours while you played with your toys, so I suppose you'd be the expert, wouldn't you?"

She got out of the car before I could get a rebuttal in, especially a rebuttal with a question mark at the end. Guess it's time to get stuff done.

Up and over the wall proved easy. I could have even burned my pool of anima and made us a ladder of stone if I'd wanted, but I needed the anima for later. I'd been pooling for the customary five minutes by the time my shoes hit the manicured lawn on the other side of the wall and I didn't plan to stop there.

Pooling on the run is harder than pooling while locked in a car's trunk, but I figured I could managed something bigger than normal and still do whatever I needed to do. Besides my pool, I had my static ring fully charged, my fists and feet just like the old days, and my pair of surprise artifacts. Both of which were completely useless to me unless things stopped going the way Annie B planned and started going the way I planned them.

THE FANGED LADY

She wasn't going to like that.

Sneaking all the way in, getting the item, sneaking out. I'd stolen things before and there's a thrill in it. Lots of little stuff as a kid before my time at the Asylum, then some bigger stuff when I finally reached the Asylum. Get in under the morning fog, steal the Shaky Stick, get out under the morning fog, and take off. But then what? I'd been thinking about it since the San Francisco vault, letting events percolate in my devious little mind.

Standing in that vault, I wanted to study *it*. The only artifacts I'd ever seen were the stuff at the Asylum Russell and Plutarch played with. The Guild of Artificers *might* have had something equal that could make the amount of anima saturation, but I doubt it . . . sitting in my workshop, running the anima conversion formulas on what it would take, even over a hundred years being locked up, accounting for the accident in 1989 . . . if I built something like it today, it would have cost tens of millions in anima, maybe more. Either some artificer had access to an army of geomancers once upon a time, or . . . Shaky Stick made its own anima somehow.

I had to study it.

It could change everything.

But if events proceeded like they were meant to, like Annie B planned . . . if we snuck in, stole it, snuck out, if I didn't get to use my pair of surprises I'd designed just for the occasion . . . Well, maybe I'd only known her for two days, but I'd fought her, seen her operate, *had sex with her*, I knew Annie B wasn't going to let me get more than a glance of her *Earthquake Baton* before she drove it back to San Francisco.

Mission Accomplished. Cash is on the bedside table, King Henry, thanks for the quick tickle when I thought I might actually die.

This outcome is unacceptable.

Which meant the moment I touched down on the other side of the wall it became time for King Henry's plan to start. Annie B would just have to survive it. I'd already given her what she wanted—it was time for what *I* wanted.

"Are we in someone's backyard?" I asked in a voice fit for a library but not fit for a theft in progress. "Is that a fucking swing set?"

Annie B turned to look at me with a dangerous slowness in her stance, this kind of predator-like stillness, her whole body locked tight but pivoting on her feet.

"You little son-of-a-bitch," she hissed at me, eyes not quite sure if she should glare or let them go wide with fear.

[CLICK]

We'd left San Francisco at dusk, got to Fresno an hour later. It was winter, so we waited for sunrise at my shop, me working, her pacing, checking her knives, generally in a sour mood. She'd stepped into my workroom six times total, fretting, asking questions about my work that I'd answered with lies.

"Fog thickening artifact," I'd mumbled over and over. Number three or four, I can't remember which, she came in with a determined expression, sitting down in a spare chair I had leaning against a wall for when T-Bone designed with me.

She waited until I looked at her and gave her some type of what-are-you-doing? motion with my hands . . . then her clothes started coming off one by one, staring at me more boldly than any human woman I've ever seen.

I worked through it, piece by piece, small smirk on my face. By the time she finished there wasn't a bit of fabric left, nothing but that glinting **B** and a body that could get a stiffy out of a dead man. She leaned back in the chair, ankles crossed, all her good parts—and she has a great many good parts—visible.

"Last chance," she told me with that flick of her tongue to her top lip.

"You really bet Ceinwyn some serious cash, didn't you?" I asked with my smirk still prominent. Damn . . . that's a view, let me tell you . . . the kind of body a woman would make for herself . . . since really, that's what it is. Vamps don't have to bother with plastic surgeons or silicone or Botox, they just get to improve their shell the way they like it naturally, and Annie B liked it mighty fine.

"Do I disgust you so much, King Henry?" she asked, a sudden flashback to the quick expression on the airplane, the expression of a monster who doesn't want to be a monster.

"Nope, you're gorgeous. Tell you the truth . . . I'm even kind of over the whole strangled with a rope of blood thing." I kept working, no time to waste, even for horny vampires. "And for that body I might be convinced to forget about the whole cannibalism incident."

"Then *what?*" Annie B growled, putting her clothes back on since she realized it wasn't going anywhere *yet again.*

"You try too hard."

"I don't have time for soft . . . never have had time for soft in my life," she murmured, snapping on her bra, much to my pupils' regret. "Now it's worse . . . I could be dead tomorrow. Can't you give me a parting gift? One last tumble? Think of the ego boost." Still without her sweater or jeans, she got up to lean over my worktable, sliding in next to me, whispering in my ear with enough seduction that my formula paper got fuzzy as my eyes went cross, "I'll let you trap me in the table again if that's the way you'd like it. You can be in control . . . I'd just be stuck, helpless . . ."

I turned toward her and of course, being her, she didn't back up. She had trouble with submissive. We were inches apart and there would be no retreat. "I don't have time for this right now, Annie B."

We were the same height when she wore heels. Which means I got the full on force of her pleading with me. "Please . . ."

I put down my pencil and paper. Her eyes, damn weren't they big and brown and the most emotive things I'd seen in months. Her body pressed against me, pleading as well. Her knee along my thigh, her other foot pressed against my heel, her breasts so close they disappeared inside the excess of my unbuttoned coat. She was really using the Dead Soldier Ploy. *I might die in the war tomorrow, those nasty Japs and Nazis.*

The fucking Dead Soldier Ploy.

Guess I'm a bitch. Cuz I fell for it, for just one second, but once you taste an apple so sweet it's the only thing on your mind until you've finished it. It was enough to doom me all the way.

I kissed her, a little peck on the lips. She followed me as I pulled back, hungry, but I raised my hand to her cheek, holding her back. "No vampire shit," I whispered.

"Fine . . ."

"No eating me, Annie," I told her, catching her eye and dropping the B to give the name some intimacy between us instead of the teasing connotation it had held before.

"Fine," she whispered back, lips closing on my mouth for something more prolonged than the first one. Lasting about ten seconds, with a playing swap of tongues, it's the scariest kiss of my life. Scarier than my first kiss with Sally when I didn't know if I did it right. More unknown about what could happen than even virgin sex.

In that moment, I realized supermodel body or not I'd never get over the cannibalism and I'd never forget the strangled by blood thing either. I would never be able to trick myself into thinking she's actually as human as she looks.

"I . . . can't do this . . . bad idea . . ."

"Please," she begged again, throwing her lips at my neck, hands running up inside of my coat, pulling it down, her leg wrapping all the way around my thigh, almost up to my waist as she grabbed onto me. "It's not about the bet," she whispered as she dropped my coat to the floor, hands finding my shirt next. "I'm really going to die."

"You're not," I told her, but not doing a thing to stop my shirt coming off either. "I wouldn't let 'em."

She laughed at me. "Men . . . humans . . . sure I am. We'll get caught and the duke will deny he has the Baton and then I'll duel him and I'll die because if I *don't* duel him Inanina will do something worse to me as punishment— probably take my shell away . . . make me live in a glass prison for failing.

THE FANGED LADY

"You can't imagine the agony of it, hard and unforgiving and unmoving and then they offer to let guests light fires under it, heating it up like they're some cruel child with one of your hamster mazes. No eyes to see your innocent faces, no ears to hear your hopeful voices, no skin to feel," she ran her hands over my chest to exclaim her point better than any little excited period ever did. "Please give me this." Her face pressed against my wide shoulders, teeth nipping. "I won't tell anyone. I'll lie to Ceinwyn, lose the bet, even if I *do* live. Please, King Henry . . . give me one good memory of this last day . . . so I can have the strength to choose death and not what's worse . . ."

Dead Soldier Ploy.

You try saying '*no*' to it some time.

It's impossible.

Why you think we had a Baby Boom anyway?

I gave in to her. Maybe I couldn't trick myself into thinking she's human. She's a vamp. She used us as shells. She ate us. But if she could fear and want to hold onto something and feel completely vulnerable before death then maybe Vamps weren't completely worthless . . . just mostly. "My back office has a bed."

She didn't smile, she cried. "Thank you," she said, probably the most honest as I've ever seen her.

And while I describe a lot of stuff I probably shouldn't during these tapes, you ain't getting what happened next. No one would confuse me with a gentleman, but I still ain't telling.

[CLICK]

Inside the gated community, she wasn't happy. The reason we'd waited, the reason I had time to make a pair of artifacts and also had time to give Annie B something to remember me by—which, okay, I was going to remember for a very long time too—was 'cuz we'd been waiting for sunrise. Sunrise is when the vast majority of vampires go to sleep, even in a Fresno winter.

Except . . . sleeping Vamps are still Vamps. *Let dragons lie* as it's said. They're going to hear someone making fun of their swing set even if they're asleep. Which is why the bedroom light turned on, along with the sound of unpracticed but vigorous cursing. Great . . . my plan was working and Annie B's got fucked over a chair with a twist.

Annie B grabbing me by the throat and hauling me through the backyard hadn't been in my plan, but it happened anyway. So did her switching me into a fireman's carry despite my not so quiet protests and her launching the pair of us over a backyard gate in a single sure leap, booted feet smashing down against concrete on the opposite side.

Annie B didn't stop. I hung on for my life as she sprinted away from the house, down a driveway and out onto the road. There was a man-made—or vamp-made I suppose—lake in the middle of the place, with the homes built all around it in an oval, so every home had a lakefront view, nothing on the other side distracting them. Seemed like a waste of space, but that's rich people for you.

Annie B knew where she was heading even if I didn't. To me it all looked the same, what I could see of it with the Fog still holding on. For morning, even for morning in the winter with gray all around, the place looked deserted. A normal neighborhood you'd expect kids walking to school, cars packing up for work—sure, it wouldn't be a busy summer afternoon, but there would be little specks of life inside the gray.

Here, in the gated vamp community, there was nothing. 8AM and they were all in bed, or at least all inside. It was only Annie B hauling me at thirty miles-per-hour, no suspension, no seat, my ribs banging into her shoulders, my hands grabbing onto her arms and chest in a purely I-don't-want-to-smash-into-the-pavement kind of way that's not sexy at all. Behind us, the one lone beacon of light faded away.

No one followed.

Well . . . *crap*.

I got dropped to the ground without much love. Guess I'm-going-to-die sex doesn't buy you as much as it used too.

"Pretty impressive, what's your forty time?" I groaned another question.

Her whole body quivered. Her velvet eyes went especially dark in the gray. All around her, vapor twisted. "*Why?*"

"Huh?" I asked, rolling to my stomach and pushing up.

"Why *after I told you to shut up* are you still *fucking talking*, you *asshole?*" she screeched at me, louder than I'd ever been.

"What?"

"Do I have to rip your tongue out?" she asked like it might be a serious possibility.

"Pretty sure I'd scream if you did."

A pair of house lights near us came on. Annie B paused to watch them. "Did you really not understand the part about how if we get caught I'm going to die?"

I winked. "I won't let you."

I had the warning of her face scrunching up only a moment before she punched me in the chest, just like in the car. I managed to turn my shoulder in time and didn't collapse to the pavement yet again, instead I only *felt* like I should collapse to the pavement.

"You can't stop it!" she growled at me, eyes flashing.

Another light turned on.

"We need to get to the Fresno Embassy," I told her.

She blinked at me, unable to believe the words coming out of my mouth. "Through the entire community?"

"Sneaking is a bad idea, sorry, but this is better."

Her hands found my coat, pulling me right up close to her face. "Then why didn't you point it out *before* we set off, if you had so many concerns?" she hissed.

"Well . . . you never would have changed the plan to do it my way."

Another light turned on.

"Trust me," I continued. "I got this totally under control."

She pushed me back hard enough that I fell on my ass. Which is not of the plump and well-cushioned variety. "If I'm forced from my body, King

Henry, I'm taking yours. For your sake, I hope you do have it under control."

Yup, I'm-going-to-die sex definitely doesn't have much shelf life nowadays.

"What's going on here?" came from the nearest driveway.

A skinny guy in a pair of boxers and nothing else stood with his arms crossed, typical pissed-off neighbor expression on his face, just a touch below a glare. For all the world normal, but vampire given his lack of clothing.

Weird.

"I'm all for some morning funny, but keep it down, you hear? Some of us don't have the constitution for the day-humping."

Day-humping . . . I liked that one better than *blood-whore*, but not as good as *sun-fucker*.

"I can't believe this shit actually exists," came out of my mouth.

The vampire guy's expression changed as he actually stopped being pissed and moved towards seeing us for who we were. We'd cleaned up after the hump-that-shall-not-be-talked-about, gone was my *Carebears* Band-Aid, the ring of blood around my neck, and all the obvious stuff. But we weren't dressed for . . . *morning funny.*

I had on a new pair of jeans, a fresh shirt, and a spare geomancer coat of deep brown—$49.95 at the Asylum Administration building—a sign that said mancer to anyone that knew we existed, and my static ring glinted on my finger, the initials of KHP shining, might as well have flashed *'artifact'* over and over like a neon sign.

Annie B had dressed to kill, her darkest clothing, her jacket, a pistol at her hip and a pair of knives hanging from the other side. Then there's her choker and that great big **B** at her throat and the fact that—*she looked like what she looked like.* Even among vampires she's downright, stop-your-breath stunning. For wanting to be sneaking, the woman sure did stand out.

The vamp guy's eyes went wide. "Baroness?" he asked.

That well known? Hadn't guessed that . . .

THE FANGED LADY

Annie B moved across the rest of the street and into his space before either he or I could react. A knife sprung in each hand, a slice and dice job on the way.

Odds were the guy's a gentleman, so give him a hundred years, maybe more, maybe less, but nothing extra special. Just like the average mancer doesn't get in a life or death fight and find their extra tricks, it had to be the same for vampires. This guy probably ate off donors, his death count a handful out-of-necessity types. But Annie B . . . she knew what to do to him.

Trust me . . . the woman has tricks.

She sliced out his throat first, a backhand slash that went right across his vocal cords; biting deep, but not deep enough to hit his spine. Her other hand stabbed, three quick gut wounds, painful as hell. Then she stopped, apparently finished. It wouldn't kill him. I figured that right off the bat. She'd shut him up and put him down. Guess killing random vampires ain't in her protocols, just those connected to the theft.

At her feet, vampire guy bled a pool of red goo.

"How long we got?" I asked as she trotted back to me and grabbed my shoulder to get me jogging with her.

"Not long."

"Like a minute not long or five minutes not long?"

More house lights were going online.

"More like a minute." She glanced over her shoulder. "Not from him. One of those houses will phone the embassy about a vampire sneaking around with a human. They'll send out what will look like your usual rent-a-cop patrol car, but are really gentles trained for combat to protect the embassy."

"Sounds like fun."

"Fuck you, King Henry."

"Love you too, Annie."

I was more out of breath than Annie B as we hurried down the street. In fact, she wasn't out of breath at all. Douchebag showoff vampires.

"Why did you do this?"

"It will work out," I gasped, shouldn't have made her pick up drive-through before we came, the indigestion was brutal. "Trust me. I got this."

"*Tell me now,*" she growled.

"We get into the embassy, we get caught, you kill the duke, I take care of the Shaky Stick. Simple."

"Only I *can't* kill the duke."

"I got it covered."

"How?" she asked, starting to look just a tad hopeful.

"Later."

"King Henry!"

"There's the rent-a-cops!" I pointed.

Annie B pulled her gun. And I thought the knives were sexy. She headshotted both of the poor bastards from fifty yards before they could even stop the car. They didn't have a chance. The car kept going until it ran into a minivan parked along the sidewalk.

"Well . . . that was *noisy,*" I muttered.

"Shut up!"

"Now what?"

She checked out the rent-a-car as we ran past, apparently fine with the way one of the gentles got wounded but put another bullet in the second one's shoulder just to be safe. "Now they'll get together the embassy guards and start searching for us."

"Good, that's what I thought."

"Good?"

"Yeah, good."

Her expression reminded me of a pissed off Miranda Daniels thinking about shoving air up my dick-hole. "If I didn't need you to run hard, I'd kneecap you."

"Lucky for me, you do."

"I can't believe I slept with you . . ."

"You were desperate."

THE FANGED LADY

She pointed at what was apparently the community recreation hall. "That's the Fresno Embassy."

I couldn't help it. "This just keeps getting weirder."

RICHARD RALEY

Session 7

"LISTEN, DUDE, I DON'T CARE what this is if it means we don't have to take Dingle's final for a whole extra day. It can be the most boring experience in my life, it can be sex with Soto-crazy, I'm still going to suckle the thing at the teat and enjoy the crap out of it, ya feel me? Besides, we've been hearing about this for four years. It's *our turn*, dude, so quit whining and stand up like a man—you're going with us."

That's my best friend in the whole world. Preston Landry, *Pocket* to his friends. Pocket grew up in the part of California that mattered, the part where they still used '*dude*' as a word, on the coast. Floromancer, Ultra of course, he started out a better student and ended up a worse one by the time we graduated. Not his fault so much as mine. Pocket's a middle-of-the-road kind of guy, but he'll stand up for you, even when you're the one that's blasting yourself.

"Why did you even try to go with her again, *El Rey*? Last time you said '*never again, Jesus, she's plain crazy.*' I remember because you said my name like a white boy back then, yet you did it *again*. And now look at you. She dumped you *again*, she called you scum, and you went and got pissed drunk. But, more importantly: where are you getting the booze and why haven't you told me about the connections?"

Jesus Valencia, on account of being named Jesus didn't need a nickname, though sometimes I called him '*Lord and Savior*' when I felt particularly blasphemous. He came to the Asylum speaking not one word of English, born and bred an orphan of Mexico, which means he's a bad motherfucker when he wants to be. He's also a certifiable genius and if it wasn't for the fact he played catch up from so far behind, he'd have lapped everyone else. Faunamancer, Ultra, has an affinity for dogs, especially strays. By the first week of Single year, he already picked up the important words, like '*fucker*' and '*bathroom*'; by the time this conversation is taking place, he spoke better English and had a bigger vocabulary than I did when he actually wanted to use it. Jesus has a thing for playing weak and playing dumb, kept him alive for many years he's told me.

"Who are we to stand in the way of love? Valentine and King Henry are meant to struggle through life together, fighting and breaking apart and coming together again, creation and destruction, it's when they are most miserable that they are happy. Look at him, a broken man hugging his pillow and he's enjoying every moment of the angst."

Raj Malik. Cryomancer, Ultra. Second-generation Indian-American, second-generation mancer. He was born in Oregon of all places and his father owns quite a few businesses up that way, mostly franchise stuff. He's never had an enemy in his life and hate has never entered his heart. Guy's a walking Hindu stereotype, but then who am I to talk with *white-trash* stamped on my forehead?

Pocket poked me with a finger. "You have to get up, dude. It's the *Jobs Fair*. We've been talking about it all year. Been dreaming about it since Single. The moment has come, dude. Ball up. Bros before hoes!"

I was face down on my bed in the Ultra dorms, enjoying the misery of being dumped by Valentine Ward for the second time in my life, for trying to do something with her we'd done plenty of times before, though not in a while leading up to the moment, sadly.

"She said she'd never speak with me again," I mumbled into my pillow.

My three friends huddled around me. Raj in white with blue trim colors that always matched with his turban, and Jesus and Pocket looking like the least identical twins in existence, Jesus dark-skinned and as short as I was, Pocket tall—not a rival for Welf, but still over six feet—and the archetypical white guy of brown hair and green eyes. It was only made worse by their colors, one brown with green trim and the other green with brown trim. Like I told you earlier, commie shit those uniforms.

Raj kept as optimistic as always. "She'll speak with you again, she lights up when you are with her. You can't beat that."

"Unless you're good looking and wealthy," Jesus didn't help.

"Like Welf," Pocket helped as well.

I screamed into my pillow—but like a guy scream . . . roar even. Not girly at all. "How do I keep screwing this up? One month she's sneaking into my bed and the next she's acting like one little hand down her skirt while we're making out is the end of the world!"

They talked over me. "But Welf already has Hope and they would never break up," Raj pointed out.

"Well, yeah, but he might drop her for a chance at Boomworm," Pocket decided. "And what better chance does he have than rebound sex?"

Jesus didn't agree. "I don't think anyone's making a move after she lit *El Rey's* ass on fire . . . is that the *'light up'* you were talking about, Raj?"

"Leave . . . me . . . alone," I growled. "Go to the Jobs Fair without me, it's not like I can do anything but become an Artificer for the Guild anyway."

"Come, guys," Raj took the lead, "Leave the man alone. He'll be back to normal and creating havoc in a few days."

"Only if he tells me who got him the booze," Jesus said, punching me in the shoulder.

"Jethro Smith," I told him, mouth moving into pillow, face starting to get hot from the CO_2 build up.

"You shitting me, *El Rey?*"

"I was walking through the Park trying to find a place to chill when he came across me and asked if I wanted to go drown my sorrows," I explained in a muffled tone. "No hidden stash for graduation, sorry."

"Why were you in the Park?" Pocket asked.

"I didn't want to run into Val."

"Good thing he didn't or the Park would have burned down," Raj joked.

"Not funny, dude," Pocket, the floromancer as always protecting his trees and flowers.

"Well then, I'm content with my gleaned wisdom from *El Rey*: go to Smith for booze. Let's take off," Jesus decided. "Fair's supposed to have real-world food from outside the Asylum."

After three butts getting off my bed and a round of three goodbyes, I was alone to the sorrow only a man who screwed up with a woman he probably loved could feel. My final chance with Valentine Ward . . . *over*. One little hand under her skirt after we'd humped and grunted on and off for almost three years . . . you'd think I'm an asshole.

[CLICK]

I'd lied to Jesus, which I guess puts me in the company of that pussy St. Peter. Four gospels had been a Tri *Languages* assignment . . .

I'd nicked a bottle of rum from Jethro Smith's liquor drawer in his teacher's desk, not that he'd ever miss it among so much booze, really makes you wonder about the standards the Asylum has for teachers. The bottle was about a third full after the night before, so I rummaged through my closet stash of goodies and filled it to the top by mixing in three cans of coke. Sitting on the edge of my bed in that big dorm room all alone, I took my first sip and smacked my lips in appreciation.

Oh, no, drinking!

Shut the fuck up, it happens all the time in this world. I was eighteen by then, in Europe that's legal, and in that moment, Europe was good enough.

I suppose I could have shared it with my friends . . . would have been a bonding experience. But we'd bonded plenty by then and when I get really hurt I'm not the kind to turn to people, I'm the kind that wants to be alone. It probably stems from not having anyone as a kid and it's stuck with me to this day. Makes it hard to trust, even Pocket, Jesus, or Raj. There's really only one person I did trust . . . *still* trust, to this day.

Ceinwyn Dale.

THE FANGED LADY

She's not the type to go to about girl trouble, but then it's not girl trouble that really had me bummed out and pissed off. Sure, Val giving my head a nice mindfuck ain't enjoyable. I'd have killed for that girl and she just kept making me feel like a retard. Like we were in two different worlds with two different memories of what had happened between us. I still have feelings for her to this day . . . but . . . well . . . not like she'll let me do anything about it. She might have talked to me again after our brief time together in Quad, might have even been friends, but never much more than that. King Henry's love life—good and messed up as usual.

What really bummed me out and pissed me off was the Jobs Fair. My friends didn't get it. Jesus as a Beasttalker could be a vet or work in animal testing or ride as a cowboy for all I know. Raj, Winterwardens get to do icebreaking on ships, create ice sculptures, save the planet from Global Warming, tons of stuff. Pocket, Forestplanter, what the fuck *couldn't* Pocket do? Everyone wanted Forestplanters: farms, lumber companies, zoos, gardens, carpenters. Plus all the other options open: working as a teacher at the Asylum, as a Recruiter, as part of the Learning Council's police force, or just being a normal person with a normal job.

But me? Artificer? You work for the Guild and that's that. If you didn't . . . shit-storm, epic shit-storm. *Surprise*—but I'm not the kind of guy that likes to be boxed in, paying my dues, designing by the Guild's laws, not experimenting for myself. I hadn't even been trained beyond normal geomancer by then and I already dreaded my fate. Any machine that tried to make me a cog was going to be stripped and flaming.

A bottle of rum and coke. Good enough for Mom, good enough for me. The bottle was about half-empty again by the time I decided to man up and see the Jobs Fair for myself. Great idea, King Henry, great idea.

I took the bottle with me.

Better fucking idea.

[CLICK]

RICHARD RALEY

There were four-hundred and one students set to graduate as mancers in two weeks time, so there were four-hundred and one, seventeen and eighteen-year-olds pushed in among the stalls that had been mounted over the Field. Asylum bylaws state that the maximum capacity per class year is no more than four-hundred. The one left over ain't me actually. It's a corpusmancer girl I've never met, but was set to be kicked from the rolls the moment I arrived the last day before class to replace her. Ultras are more valuable than Intras. Everything is more valuable than an Intra corpusmancer, especially an Artificer.

I'm told the Lady called it a '*regretful situation*' and that it was only after Ceinwyn threatened to resign when the girl was allowed to stay on instead of facing an early death to insanity. A one-time deal for one very lucky girl.

I don't know her name, I don't know what she looks like, or what she did with her life, but I'm glad I didn't force another mancer into 'Good Days' and 'Bad Days.' I don't know if I could have lived with that, especially it being a corpusmancer like Mom . . . which is probably why Ceinwyn insisted . . . she's good at looking out for me, even when I don't realize it.

So the Jobs Fair was crowded. An easy place to disappear, even for King Henry Price, the living fucking legend. I wore my colors like a good boy that day, tucked in, just one of many geomancers. My emblem designating me an Ultra stayed off, safe in my pocket. Just a normal geomancer, looking for a job at some earthquake relief center or something equally boring that had nothing to do with the Guild of Cocksucking Artificers.

I was drunk.

Not totally out of it, not even walking in a zig-zag, but I definitely had a buzz going. That bottle might have been mostly coke, but the proof on that bitch was pretty good. Good enough to make me forget about Val. My lovely Boomworm. Those cheeks that could cut. Those dark eyes that were a void without iris. That long blond hair I'd grab onto as I wrapped my other arm around her waist and . . . well . . . let's say I miss her now. But back then . . . forget about her. Rum and coke, that's my lover of choice.

THE FANGED LADY

I couldn't forget about the Guild though. They had one of the biggest booths. As big as the Asylum did. It's a serious operation: clerks, assistants, mancers willing to supply anima, accountants, sellers, and of course: the Artificers themselves. I was the only geomancer in Quad who walked far around the thing the first time by. The rest of them would have given anything to be an Artificer. Even Robin White, Sandra Kemp, Tamiko Lewis, and Naomi Gullick were inside, playing with the anima toys the Artificers had provided to entice applicants.

Later, I told myself, and walked a circuit around the stalls. Just another geomancer . . .

[CLICK]

One horrible fact about this world is that there is only so much booze in any bottle.

I'd walked two circuits through the maze of stalls and tents by the time I ran out. Not one teacher noticed me, or at least bothered to say something about it. None of my classmates either. Though I did get a rude glare from a pair of floromancer girls when I threw the bottle away in the trashcan instead of the specially marked recycling bin. Take that, environmentalist hippie-commies, one glass bottle at a time. I'd have clubbed a polar bear to death with it if one had been on hand too!

I saw stalls for everything. Fire Department Consulting, Algae Regulating Assistance for the green power push the United States government is working on as our way to escape shithole status, Psychotherapists looking for mentimancers as understudies for mental wards—already in one, bitches—even the US Marines and the other armed forces hitting up corpusmancers. Super soldier alright, Cap.

Anything you could think of to do with the Mancy—there was a stall for it. But for me . . . only the one. I hit up the Guild tent with my feet finally starting to feel the effects of the booze. I staggered inside . . .

And there were Boomworm and Welf, standing together, laughing with one of the Guild of Artificers bozos. Val never got why I hated Welf, she never saw the mean side to him, that cruel superiority. He wanted her, so he lavished her, treated her like a goddess, better than he even tried for Hope Hunting, his long time girlfriend the whole time we were at the Asylum together. Not that Val ever *liked* Welf. Poor sap got into the friend zone and never got out no matter how hard he tried. Not that I'm saying I did much better in the end . . . still, least I loved and lost as some British guy once wrote.

None of the three saw me. I'd come up behind them, but they were unmistakable. Welf's height, Val's hair, and the Artificer in Guild robes of brown not unlike mine, with the Guild skullcap sitting on his head looking like a spectacular cocksucker. Welf had his hand at Val's elbow, lightly touching it, trying to make it casual, but I saw how his eyes raced to the spot of contact. I knew the look.

Yeah . . . *fuck this shit.*

I staggered right back out, catching sight of Hope near the exit, playing with some kind of Artificer created game of bars and puzzles manipulated by anima control—little five second bursts that wouldn't have done anything in the real world. I tapped her on the shoulder and got a pissed off look in return.

Hope is as light as Welf, blond towards the platinum side, eyes toward gray, and skin right at home on the ice shelf. No figure to her though, tall and thin, but that muscled and hard kind of tall and thin that some guys can get into. Given her attitude, her twat might have also been frozen shut, but I got no proof on that one.

She turned, a piece of the game getting messed up in the process. I got a glare down at me—again with the tall women—and a, "What could *you* possibly want?"

"Little tumble back behind the tent would be nice." I leered at her, hazy and feeling more reckless than usual.

"*Are you drunk?*" she asked, face frowning at me and petite nose sniffing for liquor.

"A little . . . just like the rest of me. Well . . . save for one part . . ." I leered again.

"Leave me alone." She turned back to the game.

"Sure . . . sure thing, Hope, just . . . pay attention to your man, will ya?"

There was a turn and a glare eventually, when she saw what I'd seen. I left the Artificer tent to yelling and screaming. Shouldn't have touched Val's arm, Welf.

[CLICK]

There was only one other place I could go. I still had three years to decide and the Guild would protest and the Lady would have to rule on it, maybe even forcing me to join them instead, but . . . it might be my only shot.

I headed to the Recruiters tent. A familiar face manned the place, but not Ceinwyn Dale. "Quilt, what up!"

He still hadn't married Audrey Foster by then and worked the geek like a champion, despite the fact he neared in on the top side of the 20s. Cords, t-shirt with either a power ranger or a gay ninja on it, and his always present glasses.

"K.H," he greeted me. "My favorite Artificer."

"Your only Artificer," I corrected, sitting down next to him behind the counter, in what I took to be the worker area. Only way I got my butt down in the chair was to lean on the table for support, else it would have been right down to the ground.

He gave me a roll of his eyes. For some reason, we were the only ones there. Though from the small stacks of brochures and '*Recruit Yourself*' guides, many had already come and gone. "Where's your Ultra sigil?"

"Incognito," I explained with a wave of my hand at my tucked in shirt. "Like Tsar Peter in England, right? I seem to remember that from a history exam . . . I'm told it's a kingly thing to do and I'm a kingly guy."

"Eventually they found Peter out," Quilt reminded me.

"I'm shorter than him . . ." I mumbled, leaning back in my chair, eyes going to the ceiling of the tent. It was blue. That's all I remember about it. "Odds are, right? I'm shorter than everyone else."

Quilt finally took a good study of me. "K.H, are you *drunk?*"

"Reading my mind?"

"Just your breath, actually . . ."

"Okay . . . a little."

Always an advisor more than our student-advisors ever were to us Ultras, he pushed his glasses up and gave me his full attention. "You break up with a girl again?"

"Not just *a* girl . . . *the* girl . . . *my* girl . . ."

"Valentine again?"

"Yup, dumped me off cold at third base. You're out, King Henry Price. Next attempt . . . three innings."

"Perhaps you should get another girlfriend that's more interested in what *you're* often interested." Quilt could sure be tactful when he wanted.

"I will . . ." I leaned down to put my face on the tabletop. "This is nice and cool."

"Where are your friends, by the way?"

My forehead on the table, I said into the wood, "I left them for a day. Needed alone time."

"I'm always here when you need to talk," Quilt reminded me like we weren't already doing just that.

"I know . . . Miss Dale ain't here though? That's who I'm hoping to see . . . you see . . . I see . . . we all see . . ."

Quilt blinked. "No, C.D's in Jamaica last I heard. Geomancer we think, maybe even an Artificer like you."

"Slave like me, you mean. Can't do what we want; only what the Learning Council orders us to do."

Quilt probably had a facial reaction resembling enlightenment, but I was too busy staring at my reflection in the table to check. "*Ah* . . . that's what this is about."

236

"Yeah. I don't get to have fun deciding and thinking over my options at the Jobs Fair, do I?" A fist pounded on the table. "Nope, I have to be a Guild Artificer. Making the same boring shit that's been approved for fifty years."

"There's reasons for the rules."

"There's reasons for prisons too."

"Right . . . have you even been to their tent?"

"For like a minute. They look like cocksuckers with those hats."

"You can't *not* see them, K.H," Quilt pointed out, "they'll just set up a private meeting for tomorrow. Which, you'll now have to go through with a hangover."

"I figure I can avoid them for at least another week," I said to my reflection, which didn't look too hot.

Quilt tried a different route. "Fine, what else would you want to be then? You're always talking about how you already get Artificer principles and could go ahead, yet now you're complaining? You can't have it both ways."

I sighed. He had me there.

Some time went by.

"Oh . . ." said a voice. "Sorry . . ."

I raised my eyes just in time to see Val's sunshine-like hair as she twisted around quick-like and exited without saying anything more. Quilt was nice enough to not make a comment.

He gave me more time to sit there and think, maybe sober up a little, forget about the Guild and Val both. "I love the Mancy. It's the best part of my life. I'd do anything to become an Artificer . . . but one thing, and that's become a slave to someone else's rules. I don't work that way. It'd end bad for both of us."

"But is there a way out of it?"

Scooping up a bit of dirt from the tent's floor, I sprinkled the gravel out on the tabletop. A burst of anima I'd been saving up magnetized the dirt, pulling it together until it formed a hand, with a single finger pointing at the stack of papers. "So tell me about recruiting, Quilt. Give me the pitch."

Quilt studied me through the rims of his glasses, alternating between my face and the hand on the tabletop. "You've got wonderful control of anima, you know that?"

"That's what Mr. Gullick tells me. Maybe I should try to date Naomi . . . she's got a nice pair of tits . . . I used to be into tits . . . tits and air conditioning . . . if only Miranda could stand the sight of me, eh?"

"Sometimes, when you're showing off what a genius you can be with the Mancy . . . I forget how crude you are . . ."

"Yup, that's me . . . little foul mouth fucker . . . Guild of Artificers Member No. 62523. I even get a lunchbox."

Quilt ignored my sulking. "You really think you're Recruiter material? You have to know how to read people."

"I do that really well actually . . . other than Val at least . . . impossible crazy woman . . ."

"You think the Lady will allow it?"

The dirt hand kept on pointing. "I know Miss Dale will fight for me . . . whatever I decide to do."

Quilt gave me a pat on the back with the force of a coked-out Chihuahua behind it. "I will too, K.H."

"If only your opinion counted for anything, Quilt . . ." I muttered.

"Recruiters," Quilt continued in a deeper voice to let me know he had ignored my opinions about his opinion, "are our frontline against all forms of supernatural troubles . . ."

Session 111

"BARONESS BOLEYN," A VOICE CALLED from the door, "As stupid as always, I see."

The Shaky Stick sat in the middle of the room. The room itself had to be some kind of dance floor most of the time, or at least what was pretending to be a dance floor—though what do I know about Vamps? Maybe they like to get down with their bad selves?

On the dance floor stood a foldout table and on the table sat the Shaky Stick, lying on its side among that pop-wrap stuff kid's love to play with during Christmas.

The moment Annie B and I stepped inside we'd met each other's eyes. It might as well have had a sign that read '*touch and a cage will fall on top of you.*'

It's a trap, but why is it a trap? We both asked ourselves that. I could see the crinkle across Annie B's forehead. She was thinking, just like me.

San Francisco wants to get rid of the Shaky Stick because it ain't safe . . . so they pay the Fresno Embassy to take it. Sure, in this scenario, we are jumped in the room as the Fresno vampires realized what we're there for. That's in my plan. That's the way I wanted it. But this . . . this was long term.

This trap had been set up in advance.

We'd made a mistake.

We'd assumed the obvious of why Fresno would take the Shaky Stick from San Francisco, but Sideburns hadn't been all that knowledgeable about it. It was guesswork—and it was *wrong* guesswork. If we'd played it Annie B's way and snuck in we *still* would have walked into it.

Having crossed the dance floor, standing an arm's length from the Shaky Stick and hearing the mocking voice shatter its way right into my worries . . . Sideburns had definitely been full of shit. About twenty vampires full of shit—that's how many burst from the doors into the room to join us and not a one of them pretended to be gated community rent-a-cops. The reason is because all of them were nuns . . . twenty vampire nuns, ready to kill us.

Okay . . . I'm full of shit too.

Not nuns.

But trust me, after you hear what really went down in that room, you'll be thinking twenty vampire nuns would be a lot less weird.

What actually happened?

I ran into someone more holy than a nun.

"We're in trouble," Annie B whispered.

The vampires didn't seem to have guns. That's good. "The duke here?"

"Worse."

"Worse than if you have to duel the duke?"

A strange expression came over Annie B's face. "For me? Better trained opponent, but not as old as the duke. For you? You aren't exiting this room alive if I die."

I scanned them all, weighing their threat levels just like I did every person I came in contact with. Normal clothes, mix of races and ethnicities, all of them young, none older than thirty. Men and women both, different heights and body types, but, whatever the type, it was a perfected version of it—plenty of fit muscle, little flab. And of course, they were vampires, which means the only way to kill them is to destroy their hearts.

And me fresh out of wooden stakes.

My eyes stopped at a woman being bracketed by a pair of particular buff guys. Tall, red headed with her hair pulled back behind her so it **v**-ed down around her eyes. She had a dress on, simple and white, not modern, old-fashioned. Not decorative, like something a peasant would wear without any cut, but immaculately clean and pressed. Virginal.

At her hip hung a longsword.

What the burninating-the-village fuck?

"I don't plan on letting you die, remember?" I told Annie B while not taking my eyes from the lady with the sword. She was pretty, could have been beautiful, but wasn't bothered in trying. She quirked her lips when I spoke. Guess that meant no secrets. Vamp hearing, it's all out in the open.

Annie B had no expression at all. Her hands were on her knives. "Countess d'Arc, as sanctimonious as always, I see."

The vampires formed a circle. They were all smirking, smug, some even laughed. They had us outnumbered ten-to-one, if those were my odds I'd have been smirking too. But I'm on the other side.

My thoughts were flashing with some good curse words. Whole sentences of them. My eyes danced around the room. Down at the floor. At the ceiling. At the walls. At the vampires' clothing. Metal beams in the ceiling. Not a whole lot else to use the Mancy on.

The Countess . . . d'Arc . . . wait a sec, I just got that . . . *holy fuck*! That's way better than vampire nuns! "You've got to be kidding me with these names."

D'Arc bowed to me. "We are very long lived." She gave Annie B a grimace. "Sadly."

"So she's saying she's *the* Joan of Arc and you actually are *the* Anne Boleyn?" I growled out. "What the fuck, Annie B? Thomas Jefferson going to pop out next? Maybe Genghis Khan? What is this? A shitty *Bill and Ted* movie?"

"Shut up, King Henry." Annie B didn't have the senses available to deal with me; her eyes, ears, and everything else focused on d'Arc. "This was you from the beginning."

"Yes," d'Arc said, her hand resting on her sword's pommel. "I promised you would pay, Boleyn. You had no right to interfere."

"Where's Duke Cassius?" Annie B asked, her arms tensing like she might fling her knives into d'Arc's body at any moment. "If you've killed him, you won't long survive me."

"I'm not stupid like you . . . I do not murder innocents without the merest hint of evidence, I do not punish the innocent!" d'Arc screamed back.

"Then what?"

"I have restrained him." A humorless smile. "In glass."

There were gasps from some of the vampires in the circle. Apparently not all of them had been keyed to the Discord channel.

Annie B seized on it. "I hope you all know that you'll suffer together. Whatever the Countess d'Arc has done, you'll be guilty of as well."

D'Arc waved the accusation away. "They are all loyal to me; you need not bother trying to rend them away. Every single one shall watch as I kill you."

"Timeout on that, if you don't mind," I interrupted. "Why does there even need to be killing here? You went to a lot of work for this, lady: stole something that you shouldn't have, paid off the guards, gathered a hit squad. What did Annie B do to you that could be *that bad*? Let me guess . . . stole an old boyfriend?"

Anger crossed that pure face, leaving it blotchy. "She killed my servant."

"Your European history can't be good enough that you would care," Annie B decided for me. "But he was a noble loyal to Louis XIV, a king who caused far too many troubles against the Papacy's enemies; I was ordered to remove him as my first mission as a baroness. You see, King Henry, Joan has often been rebellious against our masters, while I have done whatever was ordered of me. Yet . . . *I'm the bad girl.*"

"You had no right to destroy him *with* the body!" Joan drew her longsword . . . it was long.

"It was an accident! It was my first mission!" Annie B screamed back, pulling her knives, one in each hand. "I've offered time and again to pay you reparations for the mistake, haven't I?"

"Money is the Devil's tool! It will never bring him back!"

"I can't time travel, Joan, so that's all you get!"

"Wrong, Boleyn, *very wrong.*" D'Arc did some flashy salute with the sword that looked dangerous. "I get to return the favor back unto you."

"Timeout, damn it!" I interrupted. "Did I not say timeout?"

I grabbed Annie B by the elbow and hauled her a few steps away from d'Arc, into the very center of the circle. "*Chill out*, alright?" I told her, my hand sliding my first surprise artifact into her jacket pocket. She felt it there; I could see her flinch as she felt it against her side. "Just like in my shop, no need to get bent out of shape," I hinted.

Understanding flashed in her eyes. "You smart bastard."

"Told you I wouldn't let you die," I said with a grin.

D'Arc laughed, her sword's tip buried in the dance floor, the hilt crossed to the ground. "The two of us want this. We have built to this moment for hundreds of years. You think you can stop it, little human?"

Short joke . . . gotta love 'em. "Are you two telling me that you Vamps are still fighting over the Reformation in the 21st century? That your whole culture is two-sided between Papacy and Protestant after all us humans stopped giving a shit centuries ago?"

"No," Annie B corrected, "Vampires have long grudges, but even we've given up on that. What I'm telling you is that Joan is a pious cunt who can't let things be."

"*Pious cunt?* You fucking dare, you little slut?" D'Arc yelled.

"Whoa now, even I don't use that word," I said to buy more time. "I mean '*twat*,' yeah, I'll give you '*twat*.' '*Twat*' is funny. It sounds like a giggle. But '*cunt*'? Nothing funny about '*cunt*.' It's like '*faggot*' or the n-bomb, even HBO thinks twice before they use those words. You can't use '*cunt*,' Annie B. You got to call her a pious twat." The circle of vampires were open-mouthed and wide-eyed. "See! A few of them even want to laugh."

D'Arc shook and not with laughter. Her hands were white, bloodless, which for a vampire running with such a heavy pulse is saying something. "Who are you to get in the way of my justice, you foul mouthed creature?

"Coat gives it away, don't it?"

"A geomancer, milady," one of d'Arc's biggest goons put in when the countess looked for a loss. Apparently, in all the planning for revenge she hadn't been keeping up with Asylum fashion choices.

Hearing what I was, d'Arc dismissed me as a threat. I saw it in her eyes.

Big mistake, honey, *big mistake.*

"Of course . . . she hired you to help find the item we stole; only our trap has caught a scavenger along with our prey. Let me guess, she paid by letting you bed her?"

"Nah, that got tacked on extra as a tip, I don't come cheap."

D'Arc's face twisted in disgust. I got the feeling she'd kept up the whole virgin warrior of God thing over the years. "You never change, Boleyn, always thinking with your . . . *twat.*"

Annie B smirked back. "At least I know what mine's used for, *maiden.*"

Could these two have been more opposite?

Loyal whore, disloyal saint.

"Really? Hundreds of years and *really?*" I asked, completely horrified by that much lack of sex. "Eventually you'd just think the thing would go off by accident in a hot bath or something."

"Enough!" D'Arc yelled, back to being blotchy. "The geomancer is as inconsequential as the artifact. This is between her and I. Any vampire in this room could kill you, little human, shut your mouth or I will order them to do so."

She thinks I'm a normal geomancer. Pretty easy assumption to make. Artificers are rare enough and an Artificer willing to hire out to a vampire and who didn't belong to the Guild? The woman didn't know what the coat meant; you just know she's out of the loop when it came to my somewhat-fame in Mancy circles.

Big fucking mistake on her part.

Annie B and I were surrounded by twenty vampires, one of them a countess trained in war when they knew what *war* really meant. My European history ain't great, I'm American, even at the Asylum they'll only teach you so much about other countries. But if Annie B *was* Anne

THE FANGED LADY

Boleyn—which I still think is bullshit—then Anne Boleyn was around when they were just figuring out muskets. Joan of Arc was a purely sword and horses kind of gal. That meant like a hundred, maybe two-hundred year advantage to Joan.

But I'd been figuring on an even bigger disadvantage in age when Annie B had been fighting the Duke . . . Cassius was the name apparently. Really hoping it's not *the* Cassius, 'cuz . . . that would be too much. Okay, d'Arc probably knew how to fight. But a general ain't a champion. To use one of Jethro Smith's favorite stories, Agamemnon needed Achilles for a reason.

Annie B could take her.

Which left me and nineteen vampires I figured for gentles. Surrounded. In the middle of the room. No chance in hell normally.

But it's not normally.

Genius Joannie D had placed an Artificer within five feet of the Shaky Stick and thought she had him trapped.

Why not just give Arnold Schwarzenegger a Minigun while you're at it?

If the Shaky Stick was indeed a Minigun, a weapon and tool, and not in fact something like a thousand-year-old jade dildo.

That would suck.

There are lots of ways I don't want to die, but dying while holding a dildo is Top Five.

"You sure?" I asked d'Arc. "Really sure any of these underlings could take me? I mean, I'm a fight fan, you know? And you never have the main event without one undercard bout. Seems like we should have ourselves one now."

D'Arc looked at me like I'd mutated into something worse than a foul mouthed creature. "If you just shut up, then I promise I will not kill you."

"Nah, can't do that. Guess I got to kill one of your thugs, prove myself, ya know?"

"I will never understand why they are loyal to you," d'Arc whispered to Annie B. "What is it about you? There is not a good quality to you. You betray them, use them, your soul is as dark as midnight, but they always protect you."

Annie B and I caught eyes again, velvet and dirt. Why indeed? Why save someone that ate her own kind? That beat me up way too often for my tastes. Because I wanted the Shaky Stick? Because we'd had great sex? Because I wanted paid? Maybe . . . just maybe . . . because I liked her?

"It's cuz she's so purdy," I teased.

A smile split Annie B's face, her tongue flicking out to tap her top lip. "Don't die," she told me.

"I got this."

Muscle number left stepped up to the plate. "Make it quick," d'Arc said tiredly, "It's getting late."

Lefty had half a foot on me and at least one-hundred pounds. He looked like he belonged on some of the t-shirts I used to wear as a kid. He probably did this kind of thing a lot. A tough for a high-ranking vamp. Probably found d'Arc her food, took care of donors, protected her from anyone that gave her crap.

He was dressed in a suit without a jacket, but not a modern suit design, something older, turn of the century maybe. He had some years on him, but not enough to do what Annie B did. I'd beaten her . . . that means I could beat him.

Right?

Only I couldn't use the Mancy.

I'd been pooling like crazy. I had a little less than half of what I'd had in the car trunk. Which meant I could have smashed Lefty like a bug. If I had to. I didn't want to. I had to save that anima, had to keep it for the Shaky Stick. Means the Mancy's out. I had to *actually* beat the vampire straight up, keep my pool, use it later. I'm not fighting the guy for any loyalty towards Annie B. I liked her enough to give her I'm-going-to-die sex, but not to actually die for her in some white-knighting futility. I fought Lefty for *time*. I needed to find out how big of a pool I could manage.

THE FANGED LADY

It's the only chance I had to use the Shaky Stick and not crack a piece of California into the Pacific. In this case, bigger is better.

So time . . . so beating a vampire without the Mancy.

This is exactly why I'd rigged my static ring to fire off on impact.

Lefty took a couple practice swings, big looping punches that would have crushed my head into goo if they'd connected. I stretched a bit, even did a jumping jack. It got some laughs. Lefty grinned at me. He knew a fighter when he saw one and I wasn't acting like a fighter. I was acting like a lot of the loud mouth douchebags that I had smashed into the ground over the years.

I took a stance, feet a foot too far apart, right hand too high, left hand too low. Lefty saw the opening, grinned even more.

He took a stance too, doing a little wiggling, got some laughs for himself. I faked a gulp, paused . . . readied myself . . . then I pleaded with Annie B with big brown what-did-I-get-myself-into eyes.

The punch I knew would come the moment I got distracted landed with a thud on my face. Annie B winched, then I lost sight of her and I staggered back, pretending I'd never felt a punch before.

The vampires hollered. D'Arc looked bored, but nonetheless said, "Do you think he will last two minutes, Boleyn?"

"Which one are you talking about?" Annie B asked with some nice bite.

Lefty hadn't thrown barely anything into the punch. It was all snap. Hadn't really hurt at all. Don't get me wrong—punch is a punch. Knuckles ain't pads. But this thing wasn't even an arm punch, it was a wrist punch. Would have been a point in amateur boxing . . . but this ain't boxing.

I righted myself, got back in my screwed up stance. I bounced on my feet a little, playing it up again. If I sucked at this stuff and had never done it before, what would I do this time? Throw a punch, I figure. So I threw a punch, wild, looping, even used the left arm instead of the right. Lefty's fist slammed into my stomach. I grunted.

Okay, that one had a little more on it.

I toppled over, landed on my knees. Tried to get up, fell back down. Yeah, just give me the Oscar already. Lefty pushed me over with his foot. I rolled convincingly. My pool of anima kept growing.

Getting to my feet again, taking my time, I rubbed at my stomach to the jeers from the watching vampires. "Going to eat you, little boy!"

"Going to wear you to your family's thanksgiving dinner and dinner's on them!"

Yeah, yeah, you sun-fuckers, I hear you.

Back to my stance. This time . . . leery. Lefty punched at me and I backed up. Punched again and I backed up again. He gave me a sneer. "Entertain me or I just kill you, mancer," he told me. His voice had such a low pitch it sounded like rocks grinding against each other.

The perfect time to get real.

I'd gotten five minutes or more of extra pooling. I backed up close to the table with the Shaky Stick. Lefty still didn't act serious; *he thinks I'm a pushover.* Best to surprise a guy when he least expects it.

That's why I threw a kick. Not some flailing thing at his head or some karate move that had me twisting around like a movie star—this is no nonsense kicking. Real kicking. A leg kick right at his knee. Lefty was so busy concentrating on my stance, on that huge hole in my guard he could have punched through at any time, his eyes were caught high. He didn't see it coming. It's always the one you don't see coming that hurts the most.

THUD.

Lefty's face crunched in on itself as my shin snapped right into his thigh muscle. His gaze reflexively shifted to see my foot pull back to the ground. Being a big bad vampire, Lefty did what you'd expect him to do when he gets hit: he punched back, right into the hole in the guard that I've had for minutes.

Only it's not there anymore.

When his eyes moved, so did my hands, right into the correct positions. But why risk it? I knew exactly where he would punch. I didn't need to take the punch on my arms. I could just dodge the whole thing.

THE FANGED LADY

I stepped to the side, bent my shoulders, and watched as a big bad vampire punch flew past my chest without hitting a single part of me. My whole life had been about assuming you're the smallest and finding a way to survive it, whichever way you could manage. I guess vampires run the opposite direction. They always assume they're the best, the smartest, the strongest, the toughest. Bullies the whole lot of them, even Annie B sometimes.

I can't stand bullies.

My first punch of the fight went to his wide open side, my left arm, a hook to his kidney, nasty painful punch. His arm that had missed flew back towards me, backhand trying to catch me with an elbow or forearm, but I ducked under it. Not hard to do that given how tall the fucker is. Throwing a backfist like that, Lefty's already getting into things, realizing I'd been playing him.

Time to end it.

It's not a situation to take chances in. I still had the Shaky Stick waiting. Didn't need to go into using it bruised and bleeding. I'd need all my concentration.

The thumb of my right hand found my static ring, turned it around so the KHP got centered and then my fist flew. I'm going to tell you the truth . . . I'd have loved to brand my initials right on his forehead, but it was way out of my reach.

I'd reworked my ring to take pressure as its trigger. Not as safe as anima, but it needed a nice sized bit of pressure, not just smacking someone on the ass either. I needed bone. Needed a place without lots of clothing like his chest, something that didn't move like his arms, and something that didn't give like a man's stomach or balls.

I aimed for his hip, right on the pelvis, and I punched downward into it as hard as I could.

Maybe all the running had built up an extra charge, I don't know, but the ring did a lot more than stun-gun. It sizzled Lefty in his boots, from his feet to his head. His teeth clamped up on themselves, his jaw bounced, and his whole body kind of shook before he collapsed, every muscle in his body out of it. Vamp or not, biology is a bitch. You use our bodies as shells then the shell works the same as our bodies. This guy didn't have the skills to leave his shell like Annie B did. He was stuck, like a car without a spark plug and a fifteen minute walk to get a new one.

Ever heard nineteen vampires gasping?

Sounds great.

"That was too much damn work," I mumbled to myself, using the excuse of the fight to sit on the table, right next to the Shaky Stick.

D'Arc studied Lefty like she wasn't sure if she was angry at him or at me. "Did you kill him?"

"Nah, he'll get up a little after Annie B kills you."

Blotchy came back. Looks like she decided who she's angry at. "You finding God's favor does not mean she will."

I shrugged, still acting all tired. "Not to be sacrilegious, but I think I'll probably be more help to her than God."

D'Arc raised her sword. "I have changed my mind again. After Boleyn dies, so do you."

"Right," I agreed. "Only be sure to get the name right on the tombstone. King Henry Price. And right after that put Artificer." I picked up the Shaky Stick. Earned me another round of gasps.

I had their attention. "Anyone interferes with this fight and I use this thing, got it? Then we see just why the San Francisco Embassy is scared of it."

Know what sounds better than nineteen vampires gasping? Nineteen vampires crapping their pants.

"Do as he says," D'Arc commanded in a tone not to be disobeyed. "I will deal with her myself. No trickery before the eyes of God."

Everyone but d'Arc and Annie B nodded. Even me. I also handled the Shaky Stick carefully, passing it from my right hand to my left and stuck it in my coat. While touching it, I could feel the vast power of it, anima downright bubbling, but I wouldn't begin to know what that power really

250

ranked until I threw my anima pool at it . . . I think . . . I mean . . . I don't actually know how it works.

But they think I do.

Assumptions just be screwing up people all over the place . . .

Reaching back into my pocket, I pretended I'd thought twice about its location and pulled out what looked exactly like the Shaky Stick back into my hands. I smiled. Hello, second surprise artifact.

Once a thief, always a thief . . . and this time my distraction proved to be a lot bigger than a falling shelf.

[CLICK]

Annie B didn't wait. No stretching here. No jumping jacks. No taunts. No faking about what they were and what they could do. Two trained killers who had been killing for hundreds of years were going to try their arts on each other. Two vampires who had hated each other for hundreds of years were finally going to kill each other. It was that simple.

And I got to watch.

Where's the beer and beef jerky? Cuz, baby, it's fight night and I didn't even have to use Pay-Per-View.

D'Arc had a sword over three feet long, a big thick heavy thing that had a good chance at cutting a limb or head straight off in one whack, especially with vampirized muscles behind it. Annie B had a knife in each hand, better to say a dagger really, a full foot of steel for each. I expected Annie B to be quick and feign and stab at the edges, for d'Arc to load up and swing hard.

Assumption gets me too sometimes.

Annie B launched herself at d'Arc like she couldn't see the three feet of steel that pivoted on d'Arc's wrists to point right towards her chest. I almost let loose my pool to flash a blast of anima and break the sword in half.

Which would have sent all the vampires at me. Which would have meant me trying to activate the Shaky Stick with no pool at all. Which would have been very bad. I would have done it to save Annie B, stupid male that I am, only it all happened too fast.

One second she rushed d'Arc like a crazy person and the next second she had shifted just enough so the sword stabbed her through her shoulder and not her heart. Annie B gritted a smile as she used her knives . . . daggers . . . whatever . . . sharp pointy steel stabby things. Before d'Arc could resist, Annie B's arms pumped, in and out, in and out, in and out and in again, each arm like a piston and each time it went forward the knife plunged into d'Arc's stomach.

Blood spluttered from the wound, then goo that wasn't blood came with it. The goo changed in a heartbeat, soft and dripping down skin but then twisting up into a sharp point.

D'Arc threw herself at Annie B, a point of blood leading the way. Was this how vampires fought? Older ones at least? They tried to get their real body into the other vampire's shell? Formed their blood into the weapons? Every little cut a potential death sentence?

Annie B didn't allow it. She shifted with the motion's force and went all Judo on d'Arc's ass, dropping down, rolling her shoulder, throwing the countess ten feet away and to her back.

Each woman got up to their feet, weapons still in their hands. Annie B's shoulder had been cut, but had little blood showing, dark sweater, dark jacket covering it.

D'Arc on the other hand was already a mess. Her white dress was stained red with blood all around her stomach, dripping and dropping all the way down the front of her skirt. If she'd been human, she'd have been dead. You could see her stomach where the knives had sliced away the cloth. I watched as goo slid back into the wounds and the wounds sealed themselves, leaving only muscle and white skin.

Nice stomach even if she's a religious freak.

"Next time, you will not get away," d'Arc hissed. "Then you will be mine . . ."

"King Henry?" Annie B asked.

"Yup?"

"How do I chill out?"

"Just . . . um . . . put it on."

"Later then . . ." Annie B's face went hard. "I'm not done bleeding her yet."

D'arc charged.

The longsword chopped sideways, from d'Arc's shoulder and away, like a baseball player flaring the bat in practice swings. It missed, too slow, but would have cut Annie B's head off . . . *again* . . .

Annie B ducked, sliced twice, moved. The longsword came back across, two'o'clock to eight'o'clock. Slide, slice an armpit and stab with a tip into the side. D'Arc's hand caught the end of her blade and then her shoulders pushed.

That's not good, I thought.

Her hilt, that nice thick piece of metal, smashed right into Annie B's beautiful face and cracked the cartilage in her nose, throwing her backwards.

"Fucking low blow, bitch!" Annie B growled. She had knives up in front of her, blood dripping down her chin.

D'Arc smiled, cold for all her heat. "This is my cross and every piece is a weapon with God at my shoulder."

"Guess I'll cut the shoulder off."

"Do try . . ."

That's when Annie B dropped a knife and fired the fifteen rounds she still had loaded in her semi-automatic pistol right into d'Arc's chest, before anyone could say anything against it. Guess it's true what they say about '*as fast as you can pull the trigger*' because that vampire finger pulled faster than a human one, a blur of white. Not a person in the room wasn't shocked.

I was shocked.

The vampires were shocked.

D'Arc was damned shocked.

Bullets lanced her from her stomach to her neck, Annie B firing as her handgun rose up in front of her. Quicker than you could see. A sound of explosion after explosion, *pop* on top of *pop*, then blossoms of blood on the other end. The action happened in next to no time. It was the aftermath which lingered.

The red flare on d'Arc's white dress, right up her body, each of the fifteen flares slowly widening. Then . . . spurts. Goo . . . vampire, sliding out of its shell, sliding down milky white skin.

D'Arc grunted.

Annie B glared as the countess tumbled forward, only her sword keeping her from falling to the floor. She leaned on it, staring at Annie B, unsure what had happened. First time d'Arc had been shot. I could tell. Eventually I'd come to hate that look of disbelief.

Annie B put her gun back, bent over to pick up her knife from the ground. "My cross has more stopping power," she told d'Arc.

Lefty's friend, we'll call him Righty, moved to protect d'Arc. Some of the other vampire's started walking towards Annie B too.

Oh crap, I thought, just before I took my pool of anima—better to call it a lake of anima, huge, if not as big as the one in the car trunk—and slammed the whole thing into the Shaky Stick to get it to activate. I could have gone bigger . . . I'd hoped to go bigger . . . but I didn't have time.

Now or never.

The anima torrent inundated inside of me, like rocks cracking in my body, an avalanche of anima, turning and whirling until it burst forth. I held to what I could, the vast majority of it, but not all of it, just like before. Even knowing what was coming, there was too much, too strong. It snapped and got loose and I threw it towards the Shaky Stick in my coat pocket.

Nothing.

Not.

One.

Thing.

Oh holy fuck.

It was the excess anima, the anima that had gotten loose from me, the anima that had escaped around me that saved my ass.

THE FANGED LADY

A pair of supports in the ceiling popped so loudly they could be heard. Pieces of metal: buttons, zippers, cell-phones, glasses, small insignificant pieces shattered to dust. In front of Annie B, her knives melted like mercury, rolling over her hands to dribble on the floor. D'Arc's longsword snapped in half, throwing her weight forward onto her knees. Blood splattered the dance floor in front of her.

Eyes swiveled towards me.

Oh holy fuck.

"Everyone remembers our deal, right? This is the warning," I said, my balls getting bigger by the word, "the next time we all fall down."

"She fucking shot Countess d'Arc!" Righty yelled at me.

"King Henry, you stupid shit!" Annie B yelled at the same time, holding up the useless hilts of her knives.

"Ah," I said. I put these two things together. "But now I've eliminated all the weapons, that's fair, right?"

"After she shot the countess twenty-fucking-times!" Righty yelled at me again, waving at d'Arc, who was working her way back up her chest and into her body.

"It was *only* fifteen."

"That's it, duel over!" Righty growled at everyone. "We're taking off."

"No!" D'arc gasped, eyes going crazy like you'd imagine from some girl that believes she communes directly with God. Here was the woman, a vampire, six-hundred years old, and she still believed. "It looks worse than it is, Pierre," she told him, standing up. "They went right through. It is hardly a scratch," she added, blood dripping from her mouth.

"It's just a flesh wound," I mumbled in the appropriate accent.

Annie B turned to me. "I'm still mad at you about the knives . . . but that's funny."

"Kick her in the balls so we can get out of here already," I told her.

Annie B glanced at the artifact in my hands, then up at my eyes. She knew I'd fucked up. It was all bluff from here on out.

"Behind you!" I yelled at her, but too late.

D'Arc didn't even care that she bled and oozed all over the place. The holes on the front of her body twisted up, blood hardening until there were fifteen spikes of blood in their place. No matter how many times I saw it, it still freaked me out.

She jumped forward, honor out the window once the pistol got brought into play, and chopped with the two feet of sword she still had left.

Annie B is quick. Smart too.

Somehow she must have tracked my eyes and figured out where d'Arc came from. Or heard it. I'm not sure, but when she sidestepped to get out of the way of the chop coming for the back of her head, she stepped the best way, not the wrong way. Instead of her head getting split or her shoulder getting gashed halfway into her chest, her arm took the blow. Just above the elbow, her forearm was lopped completely off. It cartwheeled from the impact, sliding onto the dance floor.

Annie B barely acted like she felt it. She turned into d'Arc, her other arm flying in a backfist that smashed across the countess' jaw. It threw her back just enough for Annie B to bring up a knee into d'Arc's stomach.

Fifteen spikes disappeared as d'Arc grunted. One single spike reappeared with a vengeance, spearing itself right through Annie B's ankle.

The baroness cried out, caught. A cheer went up from the vampires and I knew this was bad. D'Arc's arms grabbed at Annie B's shoulders, her sword forgotten as she dragged them both to the ground. Shells were suddenly unimportant. Here is the true fight of vampires. Real vampires. Of blood on blood. It took place inside Annie B's body.

Really bad.

Annie B's next scream was so primal it dragged my body off the table and dragged my thoughts back to the Shaky Stick.

I couldn't put anima into it, but what if I can take anima out of it? I thought to myself.

An Artificer can trap anima into a vial, we can take it from the vial into an artifact, we can make the artifact act as its own recharge or as a storage chamber, we can make the artifact do certain things once we figure flow and formulas and certain requirements. Most artifacts are keyed to be set off by either a small burst of anima or by a simple mechanical trigger. My original static ring is by a small burst, as an example, and my Cold Cuffs by the trigger of being shut.

But the Shaky Stick . . .

The Shaky Stick basically threw anima at everything that came near it. Hence all the discharge over the years. It wanted to give anima away.

Humans can only use the anima they pool inside of themselves . . . you can't take from nature, it's impossible. But what if some artificer a thousand years ago had figured out another way? What if he made an artifact that could take from nature and then refine it for a mancer's use . . .

I think I'm holding the most valuable item in the world in my hand, I thought. *Or. . . in my coat pocket with the thing pretending to be the most valuable item in the world in my hand . . .*

"Don't even think about interfering," Righty told me, pointing from across the other side of Annie B and Joan d'Arc struggling on the ground, bloody goo flowing from d'Arc's stomach and into Annie B's ankle. "I'll kill you even if you bring the whole building down on top of us."

I believed him.

On the ground, Annie B screamed again.

D'Arc laughed over it all. "You like that, you whore? Your own medicine! Exactly how you killed him, you disgusting cannibal!"

Another scream as Annie B tried to push her off, but d'Arc went nowhere.

"This is how you killed him, is it not? This is how you *ate* him? This is how you destroyed the man I *loved*? The man I was going to marry once his service as a human ended? He was a true saint, a man of God, and you *murdered* him! Scream, you bitch!"

Screams turned to laughs in Annie B's throat.

D'Arc looked *pissed.* "What is so humorous?"

"The . . . man . . . you . . . love," Annie B gasped between whatever happened inside her body as the two warred over veins and arteries. "Your .

. .true saint . . ." Another laugh. "It's funny because . . . he . . . fucked me like a jackrabbit . . . that's how I got close!"

"Liar!" D'Arc hammer-fisted Annie B across her broken nose, but the baroness only kept laughing.

"He wasn't even . . . good . . ."

"The words of a dead woman!"

"King Henry . . . the Artificer . . . right there . . . he's better . . ."

Hell yeah.

"Your betrothed . . . wanted me . . . to spank him . . . did you . . . spank him, Joan?"

D'Arc full on pimp-slapped Annie B. "Shut up! You will be dead in a few minutes, just shut up!"

Annie B turned her head so she could see me. "If this doesn't work . . . glad to know . . . you, King Henry."

"Same," I told her, motioning the fake artifact.

Annie B's right hand, the one still attached to her, came out of her pocket with the ring I'd given her on the tipping point of sliding down her finger. It worked the same as Cold Cuffs only it didn't impair movement, didn't even try to last for a long period of time, it just straight up slammed cold into a person. One really good jolt.

Might kill a human . . . a vampire . . .

"Joan . . ." Annie B said, "Sorry . . . you're a . . . self-righteous twat . . . that couldn't . . . give it up . . ."

"What is that?" d'Arc asked in puzzlement. Last words she ever spoke.

The ring slipped on.

Annie B met d'Arc's eyes and you could see the battle turn just by the way their faces shifted. Raising her other arm, the one that had been cut off, Annie B held it over the countess' heart. "You were never supposed to survive the fire," she whispered. "Heretic. Blasphemer. Godless."

D'arc's eyes went wide the exact moment a huge spear of vampire-manipulated blood shot through her chest. Some straight up *Terminator* shit. The spear shifted behind d'Arc, shrinking back into her body, until I could

THE FANGED LADY

see Annie B's wound was forming an arm and a hand made entirely of manipulated blood. Her teeth showed as she grasped within the countess and then d'Arc's heart tore from her chest. Shells are useless without a heart . . .

What a way to die.

All left to d'Arc was to see if she'd grown old enough to survive the atmosphere by herself, where she might do better than survive and be declared a duchess.

Die or flourish.

Goo slid from the body, onto Annie B, and then to the floor. It moved towards Righty, making no sound, but there was something in its movements that could only be called shrieking—a wiggle like a lightning bolt that said pain without words.

Halfway to him . . . the gooey mass stopped.

Righty gazed down at his countess' true form, then to her body, then to Annie B as she breathed heavily, then to me and the Shaky Stick, finally at the vampires still surrounding us. Looking for a way out of what had just happened. When he couldn't find that way out, he was happy with someone to crush.

I was already moving to stand over Annie B, to protect her.

Righty snarled, he stared at d'Arc's body and snarled again.

Annie B went ahead and put salt in the wound. Not just a little shifting salt shaker. She took a mound of fine white salt and slammed it down into the wound. Then she rubbed it in. "I claim her body by right of duel."

"Murderers!" Righty screamed.

That was my cue.

I *pulled* at the anima inside the Shaky Stick. Feeling what came out of it, I instantly realized my mistake and realized exactly why it got called the Earthquake Baton. It's not made to cause an earthquake, but it *could*. It's exactly like my hour long pools, only at such a size that it wasn't even a *lake*, but an *ocean* of anima.

259

The problem is that some idiot—like me—comes along and instead of picking at the scab they yank the whole thing off and take Annie B's arm right on with it.

All that anima and how could you control it?

I grabbed at an hour's worth and still missed enough to crack every metal object in the room. Plutarch told me once that I'm one of, if not *the* strongest geomancer he's ever met. A poor normal geomancer? Not an Ultra? He didn't have a chance.

Me?

I grabbed at every piece of anima I could and started slamming it into *things* . . . and I knew the second I started doing it, that it wasn't going to be enough. There was just too much . . . how long would it take to drain the Pacific if you had yourself a container for all the water and really tried? We'll even give you industrial pumps. Months? Years?

The earth shook under my feet, the earthquake building. My first piece of anima smashed into the ground at Righty's feet, the concrete foundation riding a wave of soil strong enough that it catapulted a block the size of a VW Bug up into the air, rolling right on top of Righty and killing him where he stood. Cars might be made to give, earth ain't.

More anima escaped.

There wasn't enough to do. Not enough targets. Not enough earth around me. Not enough time to think of ways to use it. I couldn't stop it, no matter how much I tried. One-hundred years worth of anima.

The building shook.

Outside, you could hear the car alarms start going off, even as metal on those cars shattered when unleashed anima found them. I grabbed more, trying to hold back the ocean. More concrete slabs flew, smashing vampires that wanted nothing to do with me now, that were all trying to escape, but I had to do something.

I broke those slabs into dust and then formed them back. I made the metal of Annie B's knives reform. I made art out of what remained of d'Arc's sword. I spewed soil from deeper than the foundations, sending it in waves all around the dance floor. I pumped anima into my own body, my old *iron fist*, but for every single bone.

Annie B got to her feet and kept her balance despite the shaking ground.

I could feel deep into the earth now . . . our shaking was localized, but not for long. The anima poured and stretched and wanted to be used.

In front of me, Annie B reattached her arm like nothing special. D'Arc's body stayed at her feet. "Can I do anything? Knock you out?"

"Won't work," I gritted out through my teeth. Around us, the soil formed into people and the concrete coated them like clothes and they danced around the room in a waltz as I controlled each of them in turn, even each grain in turn.

Below Fresno, deep in the ground, the anima found it's outlet among the deep faults running over California and the entire earth shifted. All around the city, home for half a million people coated in gray fog, the ground moved, their houses swayed . . . an earthquake, a huge earthquake up and down the fault and what could I do . . . there was still more . . .

"I need to burn it all," I gasped, "But it's too much."

Annie B watched the room of dancing soil people. "*This* isn't enough?"

"Not even close . . . can't you feel *it*? It's a big one!"

Across the room, where I'd earlier broken two pieces of steel reinforcement in the roof, the roof gave way, crashing down on a pair of earth dancers. The magnitude built . . . not one earthquake but consecutive ones as the anima streamed down into the fault, like water that had found its way through a single hole.

4.9.

5.3.

5.7.

5.9.

6.0.

6.1.

"Help me!" I screamed.

"Artificing," she shouted over the rattling building and the moving earth. "Make one."

"You need a design and formulas and more, it'd just go wrong and that'd be worse than this! I need something else!"

Annie B grabbed at me to keep me standing. One of my hands stayed in my coat, the other holding what looked like the Shaky Stick.

She didn't seem to notice as her eyes lit up with an answer to our problem. "Divination! You can do that, right? Do the biggest geomancy divination ever on all this soil!"

"Brilliant! That's brilliant!"

I threw almost all the remaining anima of the Shaky Stick into the soil around me, finally getting a handle on it. I flooded it all, so hard and thick the soil and concrete snapped like it was explosive. A pair of gigantic concrete hands gathered the divination soil into a huge ball of earth—soil, broken metal, ground-down rock, even glass, all the types I could control—it was almost ten feet wide. It hovered before us, concrete hands shattering themselves to nothing, anima alone keeping the ball of earth in the air through magnetism, waiting, anima saturating more and more, pushing it even more tightly together until . . .

It burst apart, littering the dance floor with cursive writing, a clock-like shape of twelve verses.

Holy shit . . .

This wasn't a divination . . .

This was a full on Anima Prophecy.

My eyes found the words.

And I think it was about me . . .

Daerht reh stcelloc ydal eht
For idle play not a king's heart is
Can break more than one madman's mind
Ruoy slavir stiaws, eht tsol stiaws uoy

THE FANGED LADY

Tnuocca ot dellac eb nac sgnik
When another possesses found never enough
But not yet has been shell-less
Ro ylerus htob lliw gnah

Yadot maercs senivid, yawa klaw daed eht
Stand again and meet anew
Relief comes among ring and steel
Evivrus ro ton, rof eurt s'neeuq noisiced

Netaeb eb tsum gnik trid eht
Go away easily pain will not
Stolen by he of gruesome renown
Eh gnilliw ot ecifircas llahs niw

Yawa sdaelp yad s'tnias fo ehs
Other's face the both hate
Mangy canines ravage at chest's latch
Dna ecaep tsum eb edam, trid gnik

Kcohs ni nopu decnahc buc tsol
Will be needed all the ladies
Out of past comes a Virgin Foe
Rof sebab era knil ni erom naht tsuj tneserp

Neeuq daed gnol dna gnik trid
And neither gives in King Dirt King faces Dog
No matter how big a chorus sing
Erom sedir no siht tset naht a elgnis doohilevil

Gink, lleb ruo seog gnir
In eternal battle mortal enemies lock

RICHARD RALEY

Yet both will face the same fate
Won resolc ot a gnik naht reve erofeb

Gnik trid, ecnirp daed
Have run ahead a pair and more
All your secrets will be given
Sdneirf sevil od gnah yb a s'llub nroh

Kcolc eht tuo dessim, dekcol era spil
Broken and gone what is thought
Armies are gathered
Ecaf niap yb gniwollof a s'lavir dnuoh

Ylowls sehcaorppa yad wen
Once been headless has Long Dead Queen
Red sweet must be had, Dirt King
Eht gnik tsum worth meht sih enob

Llah ot semoc dloc, llac eht seog wak
Love gone scorn to forget another
A king must hold back the powers
Tseildaed fo nek ot hserf sdnah og

A burst of anima wiped the words out. That didn't make sense . . . it was gibberish . . .

One last bit of anima . . . small . . . not even a second worth . . . went into the artifact in my hand, the very last to remain in the Shaky Stick.

The earth stopped shaking.

I could barely breathe. I could also barely stand.

"King Henry?" Annie B asked, worried.

It was over . . . I'd done it . . .

The artifact in my hand crumbled into jade dust right before I passed out.

THE FANGED LADY

The ground caught me softly, just like always.

RICHARD RALEY

Session 8

"I HEAR YOU'RE STILL A free agent, King Henry."

I was on my favorite bench, up near the top of the Mound. It was old as dirt, some floromancer construction of wood that refused to give into the elements, the rain and wind and snow, refused to rot. I liked that about it. Instead, it was hard and smooth, the lines of grain cracked open near the surface, but still holding together on the inside.

Guess you'd call that a metaphor. Beaten and used, still fighting despite the scars. I liked the bench. We had some shit in common.

The bench sat on the side of the Mound facing south towards the Field. Four-hundred-ish mancers, including twenty-eight Ultras, had graduated three days before, the entire Asylum and selected parents turned out to watch. I'd worked hard so my dad would be on the list, but he'd been unable to get the time off work, which is nothing new for me, I guess . . . at least I'd gotten a phone call out of him, even if it had ended in cursing . . .

Three days, but that's a lot of mess to clean up. The Field still remained covered in debris—discarded programs and tissues, even a graduation cap or few—the platform where the diplomas had been handed out was still erected, but it wouldn't last another day. The Asylum had moved on from Class 2009. I was the only one left. Still undecided. The last one . . . just like Day Number One.

"You hear right, Miss Dale."

She'd snuck up from behind, as sneaky as always. I'd never gotten her actual age from her, but she'd probably gotten to forty by then. Not that you could really tell. Few more wrinkles maybe, but she looked just as good as always, just as alive. Long blond hair with not a trace of gray, eyes still blue, and lips that still smiled with mystery and curiosity. Hands soft and thin and ready to push your buttons. Ceinwyn Dale and the bench have some things in common too.

I sat up and she sat down next to me, looking out over the same garbage-filled area I'd been since the day dawned. The sun was on the way down, if not falling into view. I'd been out there for a long time, but I had a lot to think about, and even more to decide. Nothing would sit right with me.

"Tell me what your thoughts are, King Henry, and maybe I can help."

"You want me to join the Recruitment team," I said, blunt as always, if a not as vulgar as always.

She shook her head. "No . . . I would take you if you offered, but . . . no, not that. You've graduated, you're twenty-one now . . . you've earned the right to do what you want without my pushing, don't you think?"

"Earned what? A piece of paper that ain't taking me anywhere?" I shook my head too. "What the fuck have I done with my life?"

That earned a 'ha!' at the least. "You were stealing, smoking, fighting, cursing, had emotional problems, were lucky to get a 'C' on most tests you took, were rebellious, racist and sexist, and look at you now. You've grown up, you're near the top of your year, you've done great things for your friends and enemies alike, and you're the most sought after mancer to graduate in probably twenty years . . ."

When she said it like that I had to downplay it. Twenty years, maybe, of course Ceinwyn Dale graduated about twenty years before I did. I met her eyes, wondered what it had been like for her. When I talked, it was still about myself, "That still fights and curses and has more emotional problems and to this day loves him some old-fashion rebellion, especially if there's whiskey involved."

Her smile twitched. "We'll work on those over the next seven years."

THE FANGED LADY

"And that's the point . . ."

"King Henry Price can only change so much?"

"More like, I'm not ready to change anymore yet." I gave my chest a pound with my fist. "I want to be this me for awhile. Not some other person's tool."

Leaning back over the bench, she pulled a bag from where I'd been unable to see it. Clipping it open, she removed a pair of sodas, handing me one—next came a pair of sub-sandwiches from the Cafeteria, which were split. Ham and Pastrami, no mayo or mustard, but onions and mushrooms, just the way I liked it—what didn't Ceinwyn Dale know about me? "You've been out here awhile," she explained.

I guess I had. Was used to waking up at 6AM, it had to be almost 5PM . . . so yeah, *awhile* was a word for it. "The Guild wants me."

"Yes."

I took a sip of coke. "You'd take me."

"If I have to . . ."

I took a bite of sandwich, reminding my stomach it existed and earning a rumble. I wouldn't miss much from the Asylum, but I'd miss the Cafeteria food. "Plutarch thinks I should become a teacher."

"I've heard."

"Well . . . those are the three choices I'd actually consider doing," I told her.

She let me hang myself up in silence as she had some of her own sandwich, some kind of duck or pheasant or other expensive organic avian meat in some Frenchy looking hole-filled bread that only the teachers got to choose from.

"What are the negatives of each job?" she asked. "Why are you unwilling to try for some more *change?*"

I put three fingers up, my favorite one and his best two buddies. "The Guild's a constrictive piece-of-shit filled with moldy, dust-filled cocksuckers who make this place seem like a New Age cult. Five *more* years of training to learn the Guild designs and then . . . what? Pumping out pre-designated item after item based on whatever the economic needs are, or based upon whichever containment vial of anima they send to me for the day? Forget that shit. That's cog in the machine work.

"And that's not even getting into their *rules*. *No* experimentation. *No* design upgrades. And of course, '*I hereby swear to never make an artifact that can harm another human being, especially a mancer, or change the elemental nature of the world.*' So no weapons, no defenses, no change at all with that one. Just the same old bullshit while the problem keeps getting worse."

She finished her sandwich, giving me some more quiet like she always knew how to manage.

Eventually, she asked, "Then why haven't you crossed them off?"

I looked at my three fingers, brought up right in front of my face. "I want to be an Artificer before a normal mancer. I love working over anima experimentation. When I finished my Cold Cuffs Hex and showed them to Plutarch, that's one of the best moments of my life. But . . ." One of my fingers dropped. "I can't stomach the rules . . ."

"Speaking of Plutarch . . ." she prodded.

"Me teaching . . ." I couldn't help but laugh at the absurdity of it all. "Haven't we learned this lesson? I can't believe the Lady would even accept it."

"I doubt she'd have you teach *Languages* again given the vocabulary your class exited the year with," Ceinwyn Dale agreed, "but Plutarch is getting old. We've known it was coming for some time and we'll need a replacement in the next ten years. Better to have someone training up to the spot, maybe as an *Elementalism* teacher. Keith Gullick spoke highly of you before he caught you making out with Naomi during Pent."

"Not my finest moment," I commented. "I seem to remember tequila from Jethro Smith's liquor cabinet being involved."

She ignored me. "Or perhaps *Theory of Anima*, you couldn't possibly do worse than Audrey Quilt."

"You really need to get over the whole aeromancy thing, Miss Dale. You ladies all know it's the Mancy making you do it and you still can't let it go."

THE FANGED LADY

She gave me a cold look. Frigid gale cold. Cold enough to shrivel my balls up to nothing and it was summer. "Mind your business with another's rivalry, King Henry, unless you want me to bring up Heinrich and your idiotic feud that has cost this school so much."

I grunted. She had a point. "Consider me chastised, I guess."

"Indeed . . ."

"Getting away from the Asylum, that's why. I don't want to be locked up here. And if I take over for Plutarch . . . my experiments would have to be approved by the Lady . . . then her replacement whenever the old bag finally keels over. I have good memories . . . but . . ." The other friend went down, leaving only the flipping bird, saluting the entire of the Asylum down below us.

"And what is so horrible about becoming a Recruiter?" she asked.

My final finger dropped down to make a fist. "It's not artificing. You've become family, Miss Dale . . . I'd love to be out there helping you . . . but . . . it's not artificing. So what's the point?"

Her smile went wane and sideways. "Call me Ceinwyn, King Henry. You're too old for *miss* any longer."

"I could call you C.D. like Quilt . . ."

"Please don't . . . one person doing it is enough."

"Right."

We watched over the Asylum, the August sun beginning to get lazy, sinking slowly. Ceinwyn put our trash back into her bag. I felt the buildup of anima from her, a soft rumble at my feet, then, with a flick of her hand a soft breeze blew across us. "You've spoken quite a bit about what you '*don't want*.' What do you really *want*, King Henry?" she asked. "If you could just do what you wanted, with no other considerations . . . what would you want?"

I didn't even have to think about it, I'd already been thinking about it for days. Years even. Stewing in the back of my head, since that Jobs Fair, since before then even. Back to Mom dying, back to finding out she was sick, back to the first day I'd met Ceinwyn Dale. It had all built to me saying these words, something much stronger than a simple breeze.

It led to: "I want to stop it."

My voice hung in the air. A stone trying to fly.

Ceinwyn didn't need to be told what I wanted to stop. She wanted it too. She fought a battle every year and it was getting worse and no one was stepping up to end it. Year after year, the kids left to the Mancy grew, population spiraling out of control, the Mancy swelling all over the planet. It dragged on and on and one day, one of those we missed was going to be powerful enough to not only be insane . . . but powerful enough to hurt a great many people. Butterflies don't start hurricanes, but mancers do. We do volcanoes, and tsunamis, and earthquakes pretty good too. Years of anima saturation bursting out . . . it's a nightmare.

"I want to stop it," I repeated. "I don't want to save the ones I can, out on the frontlines with you. I don't want to teach the lucky few and I don't want to follow the party line. I want to be an Artificer, *my way*. I want to experiment. I want to move this world forward. I want to cure them. Artificers can teach any normal mancer to give to a vial, why not something better, something that can fix Anima Madness? That can pull the saturation out of their bodies so they stop going crazy. That's what I want. I want to *'change the elemental nature of the world.' That's what I fucking want!'* I ended on a yell that carried up and down the length of the Mound, my chest tight, my voice hoarse.

Consider it the Manifesto of King Henry Price. I want to stop it. That's why I do what I do. That's why I'm putting up with the fucking teapots. That's the goal. A brand new day. Where no one ends up like Mom. Where no kid grows up with a crazy parent like me. Where we can actually fix the problem fate made for us after a mancer gets missed by a Recruiter. Second chances . . . where would this world be without them?

I don't know what I expected out of Ceinwyn. Not what I got, I know that. Maybe a hiccup or a tear or surprise, but I got none of that. Instead I got her smile . . . maybe a bit bigger than usual. I got the Ceinwyn Dale look.

THE FANGED LADY

How Interesting. That's her Manifesto. "Would it surprise you to know that the Lady, Plutarch, Guild Master Massey, and I have been meeting all day about what we've been calling the *'King Henry Problem'*?"

It took the wind right out of my sails and she didn't use a single bit of anima. "Oh . . ."

"Yes. Guild Master Massey thinks we should just hand you over to him and be done with it."

"Maybe I should punch Guild Master Massey in the face . . ."

"Perhaps that would work . . . however, the Lady and Plutarch were more open to compromise and this allowed Massey to eventually find the light himself." Her still slim-fingered hand reached up to sit on my shoulder. Maybe she was looking for strings. "I've been ordered to come up here and offer you a job."

My eyes found the dirt floor. "Recruitment then . . ."

"No," she said, "not recruitment."

I frowned. Not recruiting . . . then . . . "Ceinwyn . . . how long a game have you been playing?"

Her smile flickered. "Aeromancers read reactions well. We have to be quick to catch air, after all. When I first met you, I hoped . . . hoped that you would be one to spurn the Guild. There was another before you actually— Obadiah Paine, a classmate of mine who discussed the problem with me— but he disappeared, went too far away from everyone. And there have been Artificers who have worked for various countries over the Guild or those who didn't particularly like Artificer work. But you, King Henry, you've always felt *just right*—just rebellious enough, but seeking to do something good. I hoped all these years and watched you grow and I've been so proud of you.

"I'm the last of the Dales, one of the greatest mancer families in history . . . we make the Welfs look like newcomers, did you know that?" She didn't wait for me to answer. "But for all the family trees I can draw, there's no one else. Just friends and colleagues and you . . . King Henry. I live in a house provided for me by the Institution, I'm paid a wage I never spend and

I already had family money to begin with. I've had plenty of it, just sitting there, no one to offer it to. I tried to get the Guild to take it in exchange for some experimentation on what you have in mind, but they wouldn't hear of it . . . before you came along, I had no hope . . .''

I looked away from her before she could meet my eyes, hers were already tearing up and I didn't want mine to go along with them. "Ceinwyn, if you make me cry in front of you, I'll never forgive you."

She sniffled. Badass Ceinwyn Dale . . . emotional. "I'd like to loan you the money, King Henry, to start your own Artificer shop."

Oh . . .

What could be more perfect?

"How would it work?" I asked, curious but unsure of strings. I wasn't going to let emotion entangle me. Not again.

"There would be conditions . . ."

"Always with you, apparently."

"I'd pay you a wage, provide you enough containment vials to get started, secure property for you to work in and, of course, we would have to fund the front of the shop as well, but eventually you would have to pay me back. This is the Lady's first condition," Ceinwyn explained, back in control. "She doesn't want me '*blowing my fortune on a fool's errand.*'"

"What are the others?" On one hand they were strings, big huge strings. But on the other . . . being an Artificer . . . dear Mancy, I felt like whooping out in joy and planting a big kiss on Ceinwyn.

She finally caught my eyes. Blue and brown, air and earth. One wearing the other down, the other standing in the way of the clouds. "You would be on call to the needs of the Institution and the Council, should something drastic come up."

"Like ESLED? Like Pak and Ramirez signed up for?"

"Not quite that."

"Then what? That sounds like shit that's going to fly back up my ass at the first chance it gets."

"Do you think anyone really wants you investigating a *crime*, King Henry?"

THE FANGED LADY

"One minute you're telling me I'm your long lost nephew and here you are slapping me around . . ."

"She wants to have the string, King Henry, give it to her."

I've found that the problem with strings is that once you get a few, you figure one more ain't a big deal. Then you count and you realize you can't move on your own. I counted to make sure I had room for one more.

"Fine," I decided after awhile.

"The shop would also have to be within a day's travel of the Institution," Ceinwyn went on.

"I ain't going back to Visalia."

"We'll decide on it later. Reno maybe? Or Sacramento? The Guild also has three considerations before they sign off on it."

"Fuck the Guild and their racecar hogging monopoly."

"That's what they worry about; you'll be direct competition, so they want guarantees of their own."

I crossed my arms and sighed. "Let's hear the bullshit then."

"They expect you to experiment; however, they don't want you creating destructive weapons for the use of anyone but yourself and even then have asked you to experiment with defense in mind, not hurting anyone."

"Fine . . . it's not like I'm going to make a lightsaber or something . . ."

"Number two: they also require that you can be brought before them in trial should you do anything worth explaining."

"Does '*suck my dick*' count as explaining?"

"And number three: they want the designs of anything you create."

My whole body went still. "They're joking, right?"

Ceinwyn shrugged. "I told Massey it would never go over, but he made me ask just in case you agreed."

"Massey doesn't know me as well as you do."

"Apparently not."

The sun dipped down some more in another bout of silence.

"A shop."

"Yes."

"Like what? Comic store?"

"I don't think that would be a good idea, you would never get any work done. What about stationary?"

"Yuck."

"Or a bakery."

"The FBI will think I'm a drug dealer."

More silence.

"It's a lot of strings, Ceinwyn," I finally said.

"I know," she answered. "Please say yes anyway."

So many strings. Strings to the Asylum. Strings to the Guild. Strings to Ceinwyn. Strings to my hopes and dreams. But like I found out when I first said yes to the Mancy seven years before, sometimes you just have to grab on or else you'll fall on your face. It's not even as bad as back then . . . now I know who held onto me. I knew how to rip that son-of-a-bitch away from them if they tugged too hard.

And I could rip plenty hard.

"I'll do it.

"Let's stop it . . ."

Ceinwyn Dale gave me another smile, not interested or scary or humorous at all. One she really meant that time. Her best kind. "Thank you."

"Says the woman who's going to own me."

We got up from my bench.

"I promise solid rates."

"Do you have any idea how much anima vials cost?"

We started walking down the Mound, toward the buildings below.

"Do you have any idea how much artifacts sell for?"

"Only after I invent them. The Guild will lowball me on the designs they've already got."

"But time is on your side. You'll pay me off eventually. Twenty years give or take."

"Is that all?"

We reached the Field, cutting around it to the Administration building.

THE FANGED LADY

"You know, you never told me what Plutarch wanted," I said, thinking back.

Her smile got interested. "Instead of teaching, I got him to agree to a series of tapes about your time at the Asylum, so that recruits could learn from your mistakes. I promised him I would make you do it as part of the loan."

"That sounds fucking retarded. Who wants to listen to me for hours?"

To which I ask you: really motherfuckers, you don't have something better to do?

But if you really have to listen, with Ceinwyn Dale smashing the headphones on your ears probably, trying to get you to come to the Asylum at all costs . . . that's the why of it. The why I am what I am.

I want to help them.

I want to help you.

That's my why.

That's why you accept strings.

That's why you do a tape like this.

Now . . . I just have to actually do it . . . fix the world.

One teapot at a time.

RICHARD RALEY

Session 112

A KISS DRAGGED ME SOFTLY from the darkness. *Guess that makes me Sleeping Beauty . . . who'd thunk it?*

I opened my eyes. I was in the backseat of the car; Annie B was outside, leaning in over me through the open door. The sun was finally out, having pushed back the gray for the few hours it could manage. It only poked through slots in the clouds, but more than I usually got to see in the winter.

It was nice.

So was the kiss.

So was the expression of gratitude on Annie B's face.

Right up until the moment she smashed her closed fist into my stomach so hard I stopped breathing for a good ten seconds.

"If you ever try to pull something like that to me again!" she yelled. "If you ever don't tell me what you're doing beforehand! If you ever let me think I'm going to die without telling me you have an ace up your sleeve! If you ever—"

"If I ever," I sputtered, "I got it. No *evering*."

"If you ever . . . I'll kill you next time . . ."

"I hear you, Annie, I hear you."

Her hands grabbed my coat at my shoulders.

Shit, I thought a moment before she yanked me out of the car and let gravity do its thing to smash me down onto the pavement ass first. My poor ass . . . I'm telling ya, it's not plump enough for this abuse.

279

"There's no reason for theatrics. Theatrics get you dead, King Henry. I thought you were levelheaded, Ceinwyn said you were levelheaded!"

"Ceinwyn . . ." I mumbled, "is a pants-on-fire liar. Just like *you*."

I was too tired, too worn out to stand back up right away. I'd taken a beating from Lefty. I'd saved Annie B. I'd used the Shaky Stick and barely survived it. I caused an earthquake, but stopped it before it got too big . . . I think I deserved a quick rest, even if it was on the ground. That's where I'm most at home, after all.

Annie B glared down at me. "What's that mean?" she growled.

She looked like shit. Worse than I did. Guess fighting a vampire countess bent on your death to the point where they're making elaborate plans will do that to you. Joan of Arc . . . vampire . . . still can't believe it. Anymore than I could believe Annie B. Her clothes were torn and cut and bloody . . . or gooey I guess. Especially on her hands. So red they were scarlet. But her stance . . . it was damned sure of itself. Annie B. **B**. Shit me. Couldn't believe it's real.

"You know what I'm talking about, Baroness *Boleyn*."

She crossed her arms under her breasts, face framed in a 'V' of forearm from where I looked up at her. Her neck choker just barely peeked over the edge. "You're the one who thought I'm some crazy woman screwing with you based on *your* name."

"I saw your picture once, you don't look like it," I decided.

"That portrait was made five-hundred years ago," she pointed out. "We didn't have digital cameras back then."

"Still . . ."

"Fine . . ." she agreed. "I've changed a bit to keep up with the beauty of the times. It's my shell, I'm allowed."

I studied her harder than I ever had before. More than the first time I judged her in my shop, more than the times I'd judged her since, more than even when we were in that bed, grinding against each other.

Face was a bit different, but not as much as I thought. Eyes were the same. Skin color's the same. Whatever time period, she's beautiful. A woman to bring down a kingdom. My namesake didn't have a chance.

"I did ask you directly one time, you told me you weren't."

She thought about it for a bit. I didn't mind. I was comfortable on the ground.

We were outside my shop, I noticed. Far away from the crazy ass vampire gated community. Vampire duels in the community recreation center, what's wrong with those people?

KING HENRY'S HIDDEN TREASURES.

My sign. Hidden treasures all right. The cold ring worked like a charm. So did my second little helper. I solved my problems the Artificer way.

"Anne Boleyn was a silly little girl," Annie B said finally. "I'm not her."

Guess that's true. "But when did you take over in the story I know . . . that's the question, ain't it?"

"The vampire . . . *leaders* . . . had been looking at a way to pay back the Papacy and the Catholic Church since the Inquisition caught and killed so many of my kind," she explained coldly, without emotion, like she hadn't lived it or played a part in it all. "Luther's Reformation had already sprung up on its own, but it was decided that it could use a push. All across Europe, what reformers there were weren't fairing well. Small pockets, hidden meetings, even more hidden books on the subject. They needed a beacon and England . . . an island backwater, important but not *too* important, but with possibilities, not a large army, but also well defended by geography and the ocean, as the Spanish would eventually learn . . ."

"Got to love them natural disasters," I snapped with a smile.

She smiled too, but ruefully. "I can't believe you destroyed the Earthquake Baton."

"Maybe I didn't."

"You did."

"How you know until you strip me naked to check for it?" I asked, very curious. I hadn't expected to pass out. If I'd been awake, I never would have let her touch me . . . but passed out . . .

Her expression seemed insulted. "I did search you, not naked . . . but I touched more pieces than I want to ever again. I don't trust you *that much*."

Now that's interesting. Cuz here's the game if you haven't figured it out yet. Shaky Stick's still around. It was hanging out of my coat pocket. If you opened my coat, you couldn't miss it. The thing I destroyed in front of the Vamps was a replica made for exactly that purpose. Fine bit of artificing on my part. Even more fine bit of acting on my part.

I'd hoped Annie B would buy it too. But she hadn't. She'd checked. *And she hadn't seen it.*

What is this thing?

"So Vamps hate the Pope," I distracted the conversation, "How do you come in?"

"A . . . *leader* . . . was personally dispatched to oversee the ploy and searched for a suitable human girl to split inside and spawn a new vampire," Annie B said. "Anne was chosen . . . I was born and ordered to seduce the king away from the queen. You know the rest of the story."

I frowned. "What about Elizabeth?"

She didn't like those memories. I could see it in her face. "Our shells can do everything humans can, King Henry. Even children. Even lose children . . ."

"Your *whatever-the-fuck* made you manipulate your body into still-birthing?" I thought aloud, figuring how the plots were weaving.

"An heir was forbidden. She wanted England at war with itself like the country was a testing ground for further conflicts into the next century," she explained. "Only . . . my husband grew tired of me despite all my skills and wiles . . . at politics and in bed—"

"Very nice wiles, I got to say."

"—And I grew tired with hiding what I was and got careless, slept with other men from Anne's past as a way to try to remember what it was like to be human even though those are just memories I'd stolen. He even caught me feeding once, though he thought it to be witchcraft."

"Explains that one."

She nodded. "I was arrested and ordered to be executed. My mistress grew furious with me."

"And you got your head cut off," I remember from school.

Annie B nodded again, dropping herself down onto the pavement with me. Her hand moved up to her choker and undid the latch. I was shocked to see a smooth scar around the length of her neck. She enjoyed my reaction. "My one mercy was a very talented executioner. One stroke to the neck."

"Which doesn't kill a vampire . . ."

"No. They put me in a coffin and buried me. I burrowed my head back to my body and then attached it just as you saw with my arm. Even as a servant, I've always been very skilled with my true body's manipulation."

"Then why the scar?" I asked.

Her velvet eyes glinted. "To remember I'm not human."

There was that . . . "Guess not. Kind of still like you though, especially when you ain't punching me."

Which earned me a hammer-fist to my forehead.

Ceinwyn always said my big mouth was going to get me into trouble.

"I like you too, King Henry," Annie B smiled down at me.

I rubbed my forehead. "Especially when . . ."

"Especially when you let yourself care," she decided.

"Yup, that's me. Caring all the time. Used to have the Band-Aid to prove it."

She got herself up and helped me up too. We brushed off, then we just stared at each other for a bit.

People were out in the shopping center, walking by us, but giving us wide berths on account of the bruises, scrapes, cuts, and blood. After all that fun, it was over.

"That's it, I guess," I finally said. "Unless you want to have I'm-glad-I'm-still-alive sex."

"I can't believe you destroyed it," she accused.

"I didn't mean to."

"Yes, you did."

"Yeah . . . I did." At least the fake one. "Can't let anyone have that thing in my town."

"But you saved my life."

"Yeah . . . I did."

She tossed me the cold ring I'd given her. "Thanks for the loan."

I held it in my palm. *Nice piece of work, King Henry.* "What about the cuffs?" I asked.

"No idea what you're talking about." She poked her head back into the car and came out with an envelope, which she handed over. "Your payment."

"Money ain't gonna distract me," I pointed out, crossing my own arms.

"A list of your services is included." Annie B gave me a wink as she went over to the other side of the car. "Don't spend it all on one anima vial."

I sighed. I didn't feel like getting into another fight over the cuffs after everything I'd been through. Plus . . . I'd stolen something from her too. Guess it's fair. Hopefully she'd think of me when she used them.

"Tell your friends about the *things you don't have that really belong to me.* I'll make them a pair if they pay."

"Will do." She opened the car door. "You enjoy it?" she asked, meaning the whole experience.

I shrugged. "Pretty straightforward. Could have been more complicated, don't you think? I mean, go to San Francisco, look around, come back, kill the Vamps responsible. Where's the twists and turns, ya know?"

She grinned at me. "Maybe next time, Artificer Price."

I grinned back. "Stay away from me, Baroness Boleyn."

That's the last time I saw Annie B . . .

. . . for a whole year.

284

THE FANGED LADY

[CLICK]

My shop was as messed up as it had been the night before, but I didn't have the strength left to bother cleaning it up yet. Another disaster for another day. Actually, it was worse than the night before. I paused only briefly, but long enough to check out apparent earthquake damage.

"Motherfucker," I said aloud, feeling particularly foul. I hefted the thick envelope in my hand. How much had she paid me?

"It can wait," I told myself.

I walked away from the disaster zone, eyeing a two foot crack in one of my walls with disgust. I had other answers I wanted first, way before what was in the envelope. Only one person could give them. And I'm going to give something back to her. Like a whole bunch of grief.

My phone in my office was on the floor. The receiver barely hung onto my desk. *I feel you, buddy.*

Bending over, I picked up the phone, wincing. Office didn't look too bad. My bed was trashed, but it hadn't been the earthquake that caused that. I smiled, a thin line forming over my lips. I had sex with a vampire. Killed another vampire. Caused an earthquake. Saw San Francisco. Flew in a plane. Stole the most powerful artifact I'd ever heard of and better yet . . . no one knew I had it.

Hell of a couple days.

I pulled the Shaky Stick from my pocket now that I was alone.

Anima already built inside of it, but the pool seemed small compared to what it had been before the quake. "How did you hide from Annie B?" I asked it.

No answer.

Go figure.

Jade alright, pure pale jade, the whole thing carved like it was wood not precious stone. Mountains, rocks, and Japanese lettering. I was going to have to buy a translation book. And a safe . . . a hidden safe. With lots of padding . . .

I set it carefully on the desk, changed my attention to my phone. I dialed.

"*Bonjour*," Ceinwyn greeted me.

"You're in Paris?"

"Belgium."

"Don't they have a school? Academy of something?"

"The Continental Academy of Elementalism, founded 1950. I'm not recruiting. The Lady sent me as an Institution representative."

"Sounds fun."

"Any reason you're calling, King Henry?" she asked, just barely keeping the smile out of her tone, but I knew her well enough to know it blossomed the minute she saw my name on her caller ID. "I usually have to call you every hour on the hour to get a hold of you."

"Yeah."

"So?"

"I hate you."

"Oh dear."

"What possibly possessed you to mention my name to a vampire?"

"Did Anne bruise your pride?"

"Ceinwyn . . . I could have died."

"With her around? I doubt it. It's good experience for you. It got you out of your workshop. How was San Francisco?"

"Too much water."

"Always a nice breeze though."

"Ceinwyn," I tried again. "You realize Annie B and I got into a huge fight right off the bat and you caused it, right?"

"Who won?" she asked, eyes going all *interesting* I'm sure.

"Kind of a draw."

"That means you lost?"

"That means I got choked unconscious with a rope of blood and then the second time I dropped a car on her."

Silence, then, "And how did you manage that with a small little insignificant five-minute-pool, King Henry?"

THE FANGED LADY

I nodded. *Knew it.* "That's what you wanted."

"Welcome to the one in a million world, King Henry. Not even every Ultra gets this far. About one in four we think."

"Yeah . . ."

"Don't experiment too much to begin with; you have time to figure all the limits out. No need to rush."

"Yeah . . ."

"Call if you need advice."

"Ceinwyn . . ."

"Yes?"

"Thanks."

"You're welcome, King Henry."

"One more thing."

"Yes?"

"You think it was just an easy job where I went to San Francisco and looked around for her, don't you?"

Her voice got sharp real quick. "What happened?"

"Ask Annie B."

I clicked off the phone. Yeah, that was cruel. About as cruel as Ceinwyn had been pitting us against each other. I couldn't help but laugh thinking about the conversation those two would have. "Almost makes it worth it."

I sighed, picking up the Shaky Stick again. "Got you and anima pool limits and static rings and maybe if Cold Cuffs go vampire sex toy, those to churn out too. Busy, busy, busy, Shaky Stick, how we going to find the time? Or the money for that matter?"

I finally opened the envelope.

Fifty-five hundreds.

I whistled to myself. Not bad for two days work. The receipt listed five-thousand as the payout for consultation, but Annie B had scrawled a note in flowing cursive handwriting at the bottom of it. *"Four-fifty is for the blood, you can figure out the rest, I hope.* Fifty bucks . . . damn insulting, Shaky Stick, damn insulting. See if I have I'm-going-to-die sex with her ever again."

The phone rang. I put down the cash to answer it.

"Yeah?"

"Boy?"

I almost dropped the Shaky Stick. Which I think we can all agree would have been bad. "Dad?"

We hadn't talked in probably six months. He called me for my birthday in June. Longer than six months. Hadn't even talked to him for Christmas, kept telling myself I'm too busy. It really wasn't that. It was just hard with all the Mom stuff between us. Plus . . . I'd never really wanted to tell him about the Mancy, especially not artificing. It just . . . got in the way . . . made us think of her. Better to pretend it didn't exist. Better to pretend you were too busy.

"Who else would call you '*boy*'?" he asked.

"You got me there, Dad."

Silence.

"I was just checking on you. Saw the quake on the news, everyone's talking about it. 6.2, big one. Warehouse is always shaking anyway, we didn't realize it had happened until one of the office gals came in and told us. Visalia is pretty far from Fresno, but people still felt it here."

"Yeah . . . it was something alright." *6.2, not bad . . .*

"You okay though?"

"Yeah, I'm fine." I walked out of my office, through my workshop, and out on the store floor. "Broke some of my merchandise, so I'm closed for the day." *Almost died . . .* I thought, but didn't say it.

"Good to hear, boy. You doing okay besides that?"

I thought about the question. Five-thousand dollars or not, I was still broke. The Fresno Vampire Embassy knew who I was. The San Francisco Embassy too for that matter. But it could have been worse.

I had the Mancy. Had Ceinwyn. Annie B too. T-Bone. The Shaky Stick. *I can kick a vampire's ass*, I thought. *I can pool for an hour straight. I can make an artifact in under five hours.* And I got Dad when it comes down to it.

"Working, ya know," I said.

"I hear you, boy."

"You okay?"

"Me? Yeah. Well . . . actually . . . there's something I wanted to tell you."

"You trying to give me a heart attack?"

"Nothing like that. I'm fine."

"Then what?"

"I been dating a woman, boy."

Oh. "That's one of us."

"Don't get mouthy now."

"It's okay, Dad. Mom would get it. I get it too."

"I'd like you to meet her."

This ain't the way I expected the day to end. But, okay. It's the Asylum way. Expectations smacking you in the face. Go with it. "Sure, why don't you guys come up to Fresno next weekend? I'll show you the shop finally. Take you out to dinner."

He seemed on the edge of turning me down, but made the jump with me. "Sounds good, boy. Sounds good."

"See you, Dad."

"See you too, King."

The phone clicked off. I let out a sigh. In my hand, the Shaky Stick pulsed with anima. I held it in my grip, looking down its length, studying how it set against my fingers. I couldn't believe it . . . "And now I have a magic wand."

RICHARD RALEY

JOJO
SLO-MO
REPLAY

About the Author

Richard Raley was born and raised in Fresno, California and even still lives there on account of the city being an evil vortex you can't escape. He grew up on *Star Wars*, *Transformers*, *Legos*, and *Everquest*—he never escaped them either. *The Foul Mouth and the Fanged Lady* is the first novel in *The King Henry Tapes*; it will not be the last. Keep an eye out for *King Henry Tapes* updates at:

http://richardraley.blogspot.com
www.twitter.com/richardraley
richardraley@gmail.com

Made in the USA
Monee, IL
04 April 2022